How Can a Man Die Better

Books by Roy V. Gaston

How Can a Man Die Better

PETE HORSE SERIES
Beyond the Goodnight Trail

Coming Soon!
PETE HORSE SERIES
Book 2: The Estelusti Trail

How Can a Man Die Better

Roy V. Gaston

SPEAKING VOLUMES, LLC
NAPLES, FLORIDA
2022

How Can a Man Die Better

ISBN 978-1-64540-832-1

For my sister Debra Gaston Brigman,
thank you for standing by me, for always believing in me, and for
the hundreds of hours of unpaid and often thankless time you put in.

Acknowledgments

I'd like to express my deep gratitude to Michael Bugeja, my writing professor at Ohio University. Your guidance, excellent and honest criticisms and true understanding of your students has stayed with me for thirty-five years. It took a while, but I hope you like the book. Thank you, Michael.

Chapter One

Limehouse Slums
Victorian London, 1837

Lyman Dunnock sprinted past the gospel grinders gathered around a coin-pot under a dying gaslight, their bells tinkling eerily in the pre-dawn London fog. On the opposite street corner, a cluster of wretched three-penny uprights cackled and cursed the missionaries, bitter that the Salvation-Sallies had run any late-night business away. He huffed around a dim corner and flattened a gaggle of charity workers like they were frumpy bowling pins, righted himself, and hurdled down a black alley over an obstacle course of slumbering tosspots. With a last burst of speed, he popped out the opposite end through a troop of slumming mandrakes posed on a stairwell as they spouted witty verse in their parrot-colored neck scarves and billowy French sleeves.

Two blocks later, he entered the first filthy whorls of the rookery, the dark alleys that looped like guts to nowhere, a putrefying maze of narrow backstreets that the sun never reached. To Lyman, the dangerous streets were like garden paths through the blackened tenements, and policemen and interlopers pursuing the young street toughs gave up in frustration when they arrived at this realm.

He stopped, sides heaving, catching his breath as he strained to hear the shout of any pursuing bobbies, or the lecherous pantings of the old silversmith himself, Boggins. He heard nothing beyond the usual sounds of the Limehouse slum, his home until he had been apprenticed to Boggins four years ago, at age nine, and away from his flashhouse family. He'd missed Duncan and Cedric, Petunia, Georgie, the others, even Frankie a wee bit. Boggins had allowed him rare visits home, but now he was back, at least for a while.

No one lifted the soot-covered rag curtains to peer out the iron-barred windows as he ducked under the banners of drying, yellow clothes on the lines that stretched from building to building, carefully avoiding the prismatic sludge puddles and cinder-heaps. Hearing no pursuers, he walked casually and listened to the night-music coming through the windows. Slurred shouts and smashing bottles, heavy blows landing. Snoring and rutting. Screaming children and sobbing wives. Safe now, Lyman waved at the look-outs for Castle Blackheart, adjusted the heavy sack slung over his shoulder, and entered the flashhouse.

"Well, Halloo! Look who's here! What a wonderful surprise. What brings you home?" shouted Duncan, Lyman's closest friend since beyond remembering. The cavernous room was filled with his family, the orphaned and abandoned crib cracksmen, snakesmen, dippers, fanners, and any other child who had nowhere to go.

"I think I killed old Boggins," said Lyman.

"Wot? Wot? You killed him? You murdered him, you mean?" shouted Duncan.

"Almost certain," said Lyman. "He weren't breathin' that I could tell when I made my exit."

"And there was those that doubted the size of my chuckaboo's chestnuts," said Duncan. "Ol' Boggins learning the hard way, apparently."

"Where is he?" asked Cedric the Fierce, older, stronger and with a love of violence the others didn't share.

"In the shop. I was pinching a bob, just adding an odd coin to my savings, as I do from time to time, preparing to take my leave in just a few weeks," said Lyman. "I knocked over a tray of silver and the old bastard was out of bed and on me before I could run."

"It ain't 'cause of all them 'orrid, unnatural liberties he took with ya?" asked Frankie, always nosy about everything, especially liberties of any sort.

"That was coming soon enough," Lyman said. "But I overheard him telling the peelers I was the one pushing fake silver, and claiming it were completely unbeknownst to himself, wot's really doing it. That old bastard's been passing poor silver for years. They all know that, but they make a fine penny looking the other way."

"He was setting you up?" snapped Duncan. "It's lucky for him if you already killed him, or I'd slay the old pederast myself."

"I weren't about to do a Newgate swing in Boggins' place, as has been the fate of some snidesmen of late," said Lyman. "The Queen don't approve of no silver forgers but her own."

"What's in the bag?" Cedric asked. "It jingles like treasure."

"And treasure it is," said Lyman, upending the burlap bag and clattering a dozen silver goblets, teapots, and candelabrums across the floor. "I grabbed this much on the way out, and, if Boggins is dead, they'll be plenty more. I'll split it, but I'll need a good share, and you'll need to keep me hid until I could get away clean to Addiscombe."

"Now, that's my lad. Look at all that silver," whistled Duncan. "Never a finer gent have I seen, providing for us in this way."

"Ya think the mighty East India Company will hire a common murderer and robber?" said Frankie.

"The Company is the common murderers and thieves," said Duncan. "They make the worst of the warm organ reapers look like harp-strumming angels."

Duncan shouted and clapped his hands. The circle of grimy children, ages ten to six, ended their dice games, collected the pots, passed the brandy and waited for instructions. Lyman sat down and showed the nippers how to properly use the jeweler's files. Most already knew how, and the soot-covered urchins were quickly at work christening jack, removing any link to Boggins.

"How certain are you he's dead?" asked Frankie.

"Very nearly. I hit him good, but he wouldn't stay down, not until I bashed him with a bun warmer," said Lyman. "I should have given him a few taps with the ball-peen to settle the issue. The bun warmer was sturdy, but perhaps not sturdy enough for the task at hand."

"We need to go back, tonight," said Duncan, the strategist of the house. "Before someone else notices. Or if he's alive, and sends the peelers after my chum. As Lyman stated, there's piles of silver in that shop, more than just wot he has brung us now. Not to mention, if we get to him before he goes foul, the docs at St. Bart's will pay a handsome finder's fee."

"Them ghouls and their body snatchers is gruesome," said Frankie. "Resurrection men, indeed. You'd never catch me doing such a thing."

"Duncan's a hunnert percent right. Some depraved, low-life thief might sneak in there and take wot is rightfully ours," said Cedric the Fierce, settling the issue.

"We'll bang on the doors until the skulls of Enon Chapel roll down the hill," said Duncan. "If he answers the door, he ain't dead, clearly. If he don't, likely he's passed on."

"Wot if he answers and 'e's half dead?'' said Frankie, always challenging, because he could not quite be the muscle, nor the brains, of the gang.

"I wouldn't ever expect my chum to leave a job half done, and don't expect to find it in such manner," said Duncan. "But, we'd be poor mates if we didn't finish a job if he'd somehow neglected a detail."

"And if he's merely surly?" asked Frankie.

"'At would be an orful state for him to be in when he meets his maker," said Cedric. "Let's pray it ain't so."

They hurried to the silver shop, and when there was no response to the pounding at the front door, Lyman led the others in the back.

"E's dead, all right," said Duncan. "But you've left a clue."

Lyman looked down at the dead man. A Coat of Arms was stamped deep into the fat skin of Boggins' bald forehead. The tell-tale bun warmer.

"Will they look at him and say this is the diabolical work of our favorite lad, Lyman?" asked Duncan. "We've no choice but to dispose of the body now."

"Oh, do be quiet, Duncan, you idiot," said Lyman. "I pray they never question you about my activities."

"Now, Lyman, you know I'd turn states evidence against me own dear mum before I'd point the crushers towards my best chum."

"You sent your own dear mum to the gallows for the murder of your lordsman, which you yourself had committed," said Lyman.

"It wasn't like that at all, and you know it," said Duncan. "We both done it, the same, equal. My coming forward wouldn't have kept the rope from around her neck. I never enjoyed it, and am bothered by it to this very day."

"Nobody faults you," said Cedric. "But it was only last Yule season."

"Exactly. Leave the tykes a poor Christmas?" said Duncan. "Who woulda took such good care of me siblings as I?"

"Send some nippers to the hospital to see Sawhappy and Fondergin," said Cedric, as the crew gathered the silver. "Let them know we have a new admission."

"Why even bother?" said Lyman. "You'll have all that silver."

"Two quid is two quid, is why," said Frankie. "For those wot's too good to remember the rough life."

"Besides which, we're helping all mankind and such persons," said Duncan. "Someday, one of them stiffs we take them doctors will provide the answer to some 'orrid disease.''

"Them two ain't ever sober enough to spell 'orrid disease," said Cedric as they dumped the fat silversmith's body into a loose-wheeled, manure-caked cart. "I hate to think about it, them two showing no respect for the dead that way."

They filled their burlap sacks until they bulged, and made their way through the fog.

Addiscombe Military Seminary

Lyman marched boldly down a long polished hallway, every step sounding as sharp as a gunshot. The last twenty paces had been into the hard squint of a burly officer in a smart, red tunic whose desk sat below a gilt sign that read, "Office of the Lieutenant-Governor, Addiscombe Military Seminary, Surrey." The officer's stare never wavered, but neither did Lyman's as he gave the man a false name and a thick envelope of forged documents filled with lies about his age, home, heritage, education and every other statement on them.

"Well, your papers certainly all look in order, and you have your tuition deposit here, Master Dinwiddie," said Captain Hollingberry. "From Piccadilly, is it? Where's your quite-well-off parents at the moment? And quite well off they must be, to pay so easily for your tuition. Can you bring them down?"

"They're sailing, General. To America!"

"Ho-Ho, I'll bet they are," said the Captain. "And a long voyage it must be, too, for them to have allowed their otherwise well-dressed son to present himself with fingernails crammed with Thames River sludge and smelling like a mudlark."

"I apologize for my appearance, sir," said Lyman. "Our servants have been ill, and I've been helping in the stables. I'm no better than anyone else, and I won't put on airs about it."

"That's mighty noble of you," said the officer. "And when do you expect your parents back?"

"I wouldn't know, sir. They gave me no date of return."

"Aye, and you just left here to fend for yourself, not even seeing their dear son off to military service," said the Captain. "Perhaps they've been lost at sea and shan't ever return."

"Well, sir, now that you mention it, it's entirely possible they've been lost, sir, entirely possible," said Lyman. "Reports of 'orfully rough seas, and some questionable dealings with the shipping line, I've read just recently.''

"Well, I'll give you this, you've got cheek enough," said Captain Hollingberry after getting Lyman to reveal his true name. "For the moment, just call me Holly. Should you be admitted, there'll be none of that, though. Is that clear? You've proven yourself, young Master Dunnock, to be fearless, to come here with such a tale. And all your documents, well, they're fine, other than being the fantasy of an outstanding screever. I don't know where you came up with the money to pay one, though I'd venture you've not been spending it on bath soap and violet water."

"Yes, sir, I apologize for all that, I meant no disrespect."

"Is there a court case against you?"

"None that I'm aware of."

"Oh, My!" Holly laughed. "A fresh one, with them hot on your trail. Ho-Ho my boy, I like you more every minute."

Lyman nodded his headed ever so slightly.

"Not to worry. Unless you killed the Queen," said Holly, "It's the magistrates are happiest to be rid of you young felons anyway. You seem bright enough. Have a seat. How old are you really? 15? Tell the truth, boy."

"Almost 14."

"Good lad. You're a big one. I was that young myself when I came," he said. "It was more common back then, not so much now, but in exceptional cases, we never want to push away great potential."

"Am I exceptional?"

"Well, I'll admit I like the cut off your jib. I see boundless potential in ya, I do. You remind me a bit of myself at that age," said the Captain. "Here's a couple coins. We'll just call it an advance on your Queen's shilling. Go to the abbey down the road, say I sent you. Get yourself cleaned up, clean clothes, and come back tomorrow. Get those finger-nails clean. Little Cockney slum rats like you and me only get one chance to get out. This is yours."

"Thank you, sir," said Lyman. "I won't let you down."

"And go back to your screever. In a few days, if no fuss is raised, we'll put your name back on, with the other documents. Should he want to quibble over price, tell him I'll be to see him. If there's a fuss, you'll remain Percy Dinwiddie for the duration of your service, and no one will know but us."

Lyman looked at the man closely, looking for ulterior motive, wondering what price he'd have to pay.

"In case you're wondering, and if you're not, you should be, I'm not one of them pervy gents," said Holly. "I've a lovely, creamy skinned, fat little freckled bride here in London. I have a dark-skinned beauty in India, and the tiniest little thing, with the longest black hair you ever seen, in China. When the East India Company decides to start selling their own ice back to the Eskimos, I'll have a fine little blubber eating lass, too. I'm one of them fellows what likes a gal around, you might say."

Lyman let out a relieved sigh. When a week passed, and no fuss was raised, Holly escorted Lyman for his Attestation before a Magistrate. He took the Oath of Fidelity and the Oath of Allegiance, swore he had no hidden illness, did not already belong to the Crown's service, and that he wasn't an apprentice. No claim was made of any crime against Boggins, and Lyman became one of 75 first-term cadets.

The sudden academic military life was a shock, but with Captain Hollingberry's help, Lyman prospered. At a very early age, he had stolen candles to read by, and, at a later age, stolen books. Don Quixote. Defoe. Scott. The Adventures of Roderick Random. Finally, a couple of bookshop owners, happy to see a child from the slums reading, had stacks of battered, free books waiting for him. He had favorites, but read them all. It was the only luxury the silversmith had permitted him. He'd also taught himself some basic figuring at the shop, and was not completely overwhelmed with the mathematics, natural philosophy, and chemistry at Addiscombe. True to his word, Captain Hollingberry was no pervy gent. He arranged scholarships for Lyman, and tutors as well, but was an unyielding taskmaster. After time, the lessons of Hindustani, Latin, and French became easier, and Lyman was a natural in the engineering and military sciences.

Chapter Two

Louisiana Bayou Country
June, 1831

"Don't call me that no more," Francois Devol cried. "Why do you do that? Why do you hate me so?"

"You're useless, you're a stupid cripple. You make me sick," his father slurred, reeling drunkenly across the wagon ruts toward the dilapidated cabin. Devol wiped his tears and ran his finger along the broken bone-handled knife he kept hidden inside his shirt. At fourteen, he was the youngest of eleven children with his father and a series of wives ruined by madness, alcoholism, and stupid brutality. His siblings had fled as soon as possible and never looked back.

Today, on the last day of her life, his stepmother had slapped him before the sun was even up, and spat screams in his face because his father was in the parish jail. Again. Like it was his fault. Two hours later, Etienne, the filthy, scab covered degenerate bootlegger, rode in on his sway-backed mule as he usually did when Devol's father was in custody. He wore a leering grin, and a heavy liquor jug dangled from his saddle horn.

Devol's stepmother was profoundly grateful. The blue horrors of delirium had seized her wretchedly for two days, with waves of snakes slithering out of the woods and coiling around her knees. In her best greasy, yellowed dress, she beckoned Etienne from the doorway, gripping it with the strength of Hercules for fear she would spin clean off the earth. Etienne waved the jug and followed her into the cabin, locking the door as they always did. When they emerged a few noisy hours later, it was clear his mother had knocked the bottom out of the moonshine jug and Etienne had knocked the bottom out of her. But, as soon as Etienne disappeared down the road, she started in again, slurring, crying, and Bible versing like that would wash away her sins.

Devol couldn't understand much she said except "Don't walk away from me!" And, he didn't, except to go to the shed and bring back a bundle of filthy rags. He slid out his stolen pistol and held it to her face, the tip of the barrel resting between her bleary, lopsided eyes. He made sure she understood what he was about to do before he pulled the trigger, then buried her deep in the woods. When his father got out of jail ten days later, there wasn't a trace of her to be found.

Devol's father was brought home in the back of a wagon by another drunken neighbor. He was unconscious and slobbering from a just-got-out-of-jail, three-day bender, pants half down and wet with piss and vomit. The neighbor started to drag his father into the house but Devol stopped him, saying he would clean the man up before taking him inside. They stretched him out in the yard, and Devol sat beside him, shooing away flying insects, chickens, pigs, and their sharp-ribbed-hungry red hounds. Hours later the man began to stir. Soggy-eyed, he demanded to know where his wife and his liquor were. Devol nudged him back down, eyeing his father's ragged brogans as he did so.

"Gimme them shoes," he said, and pulled them off. He poured a quart of Etienne's finest moonshine on his sputtering father's face, dropped the match and jumped back when the flame whoomped and singed his eyebrows. His father screamed and ran circles through the yard, his flaming head as big as a bushel basket. When he stumbled toward Devol with a melting face and flailing arms, Devol stepped aside, stuck his foot out, and doubled over laughing when his father tripped and left a trail of flame as he rolled across the ground. Too soon, the screams stopped. Devol scraped out a shallow ditch under the cabin next to the first couple women his father had bludgeoned to death over the years, threw fifty pounds of lye and a thin layer of dirt on the body, and never gave it another thought. No one missed the man. No one came looking: not the sheriff, not the neighbors, not his stumblebum drunken friends, nor the pastor of the church his father crawled to when the hangovers and hallucinations were the worst. Not until weeks later did Etienne return.

"I ain't seen your pa around for a while," Etienne said, sneaking glances around the property. "Your new-ma neither."

"If you come out here looking to get fucked, you come for nothing," said Devol. "They're gone. Both of 'em. Be gone for a spell, I figure."

"Where'd they go?"

"Just to get some peace and quiet. I can show you," said Devol. "I imagine you could join them in no time if you hurried. It's not far."

"No, no, that's all right," said the man. "Just whenever he gets back, tell him to stop around. I always got a jug for him. The best."

"He quit drinkin'."

"Your pa? When rain ain't wet. He never said nothin' to me."

"It come on him of a sudden," said Devol.

Devol's left foot was clubbed, and the other children ran from him, shunned him like it was catching, and teased him like he was stupid. They called him Quasimodo and sometimes pelted him with stones or apples or corncobs or anything handy. They shrieked and ran and laughed when he chased them, dragging his foot, because it only made him look more grotesque. When he'd collapse in the dirt road with their laughter in his ear, and his tears in the dust, he swore he would avenge this torture. For years, he'd begged his father for shoes, but he could not even get that. It had been that way his whole life, hated and beaten by his father and scorned by everyone else.

"What do you need shoes for boy?" his father would growl. "They ain't one to fit that tree knot you got. What am I supposed to do? Sell one shoe? A horseshoe maybe."

Before quitting school the year before, Devol had often walked down the endless red clay road to the schoolhouse wearing ragged, handed down clothes which an ignorant field buck would have been embarrassed of. He'd pass the Asbury estate where blue eyed, golden haired Betsy, and her high yella house-girl Annie, led attacks against him with a cruelty usually reserved for condemned men and sodomites. Asbury treated his slaves like they were attending an ice cream social, carefree and saucy, speaking to white people in such a way they'd have been whipped bloody anywhere else. The story which the Asburys passed was that after Annie saved Betsy from a vicious dog years ago, the family had essentially given her white person status. Devol didn't believe the dog story. No one did. Mrs. Asbury was the only person in the parish to feign ignorance of the fact that speckle faced Annie was the half-sister of Betsy, daughter of Mr. Asbury and the slave Catherine.

To escape his father, Devol had often slipped away into the woods, to a quiet spot beside a secluded pond. He'd sit on a soft bed of pine needles in the shade, listening to Betsy's voice telling him how strong and smart and handsome he was. She was not laughing at him, but with him, in their happy, secret world. She'd never really said it, and never would. He knew that, but it filled his thoughts anyway, and the dream of it was one of the only joys in his life. Other times, in heated fantasies, he shared an intimate ecstasy with Betsy, eyeball to eyeball, mouth pressed into hers, feeling the energy charge between them, his body in the forest as hard and hot as a furnace. He had thoughts of Annie, too. Bloody, violent, pain filled, arousing thoughts. And, just as with Betsy, his body was as hot and hard as a furnace as they were eyeball-to-eyeball in her last seconds, the watery pleading in her eyes drying up, the sexual energy in her mouth going limp as his twisting blade drained her life away.

13

The Asbury property fronted on the road for more than a mile. When the others weren't around, Betsy was sweet to him, and such a moment lasted him a month. Devol understood that because of her station, sometimes she had to put on a show for Annie and the others when she tormented him, but he didn't mind if he could just see her. And he always wanted badly to see her, but today Betsy was nowhere to be seen. Instead, as he rounded the bend in the road, he saw Annie standing behind the white picket fence.

" Ahoy, Mr. Blackbeard, I see ye have yor peg leg," growled Annie, in her best pirate imitation and pointing at his club foot. "Have ye lost ye ship? And ye mateys?"

"You better stop plaguing me. Where's your blonde missy?" asked Devol, proudly atop Etienne's old mule. He'd claimed it after the bootlegger's sudden disappearance, shortly after that of his parents. It was ugly, half-blind, and nearly dead, but it didn't limp.

"It's rare to see a pirate in these parts," said Annie.

"I ain't no goddamn pirate," Devol said.

"Arrrrr, I'm not sure I care for the set of your sail," Annie said, giving it her saltiest old swashbuckler.

"You sure like to let people know you read a damn book. You think you're the only nigger in Louisiana ever read a book?" said Devol. "You think that's gonna get you free? You're ignorant, is what you is."

"Scupper that! Missy went in to New Orleans for a few days. I was invited but declined. What you want to know fo? She ain't want nothing to do with yo shiftless self. This ain't no charity farm," said Annie, stroking an imaginary long black beard. "I don't know how many times Massa gots to run a shot across your bow, but you keep prowling these waters, and it will be a short drop and a quick stop for a scurvy bilge-rat like you."

14

"You'll pay for that one day," said Devol. "I'll buy you same as I'd buy a hog. That's how damned ugly and smelly you is. I'd throw you in the bayou, but I ain't trying to poison the gators and fish."

"Arrrrr, you ain't nothing but white trash, boy. It don't take no one-eyed pirate to see that," said Annie, skipping away toward the big house. "Now, don't lets me hold you up, Mr. Tycoon. Best get your sails in the wind, and start amassing yo vast wealth."

Bliss

Devol watched from the shadows as Dr. Makepeace Bliss carried his tattered carpetbag from whorehouse to whorehouse and through the seediest and most violent saloons in the New Orleans underworld. After the doctor's license had been revoked, the man had built a furtive, but profitable, practice removing bullets, stitching knife wounds, providing poison, distributing opium in times of drought, and performing abortions.

Devol had worked anywhere, and stolen anything, and saved his money. He'd even made a little money off the sale of the farm, although not much. Buyers for fallow farms being sold by a 14-year-old without the deed holder, and without at least the grave of the deed holder, were difficult to find. But, it was New Orleans and there was little that couldn't be negotiated. Finally, the time came. Devol had more than enough money. Dr. Bliss didn't appear to be a souse, and was rarely in jail, two common failings for the physicians in the French Quarter. Devol knew appearances could be deceiving, but Bliss's legal restrictions seemed more to do with gambling, greed, and lack of ethics than incompetence. Whatever Bliss might be, it no longer mattered. Several licensed doctors had refused to do the surgery, saying it would be pointless.

"I don't know that I can fix it," said Bliss, squeezing Devol's foot. "Most likely I can't. It should have been done when you were very young, but I won't know until I cut you open. Just depends on what's in there. It could just make things worse."

"I have plenty of money," said Francois Devol. "I've never heard of you refusing money."

After a few days of haggling, Bliss agreed to perform the surgery. They went into the back of the boarding house where Dr. Bliss kept an office, passing through an odious tavern full of cutthroats and lechers that looked like they belonged in a carnival freak show. In the room was a relatively clean bed, and a table with a stack of rags the color of old urine. The cluttered, dingy room smelled slightly of chloroform, and the array of knives, saws, pincers and hooks sent a flutter of nausea through Devol and Bliss quickly administered the expensive and hard to get chloroform.

After being confined to the bed for several weeks with his foot heavily wrapped in bandages and plaster, and his head wrapped in laudanum, Devol nearly cried with joy when the bandages came off at the unveiling. His foot was bruised halfway to the knee in ugly shades of blue, green and yellow. The pain was nearly unbearable when he moved his toes, but the foot was straight, perfectly straight. Bliss ordered him back to bed for another month, but when he was finally allowed to take a few tentative steps he felt like he'd never walked before. In appreciation, Devol volunteered his brawn to Bliss's brain and their relationship blossomed.

The Partnership Begins

"Can't you hurry up some?" whispered Bliss, his breath a cloud in the icy sepulcher. "I don't want to be out here all night."

"Are you scared?" asked Devol, tapping the chisel with a padded hammer. "There's no such a thing as zombies coming out of their graves. That's just some voodoo nonsense."

"Hurry," said Bliss. "Please, just hurry."

Devol finally cracked the mortar sealing the tomb and withdrew Reynaud Deschamp's casket. Lighting a small candle, they lifted the lid and admired the considerable bounty inside, just as Bliss had promised. Deschamp's funeral had been one of several Bliss had attended last week wearing his finest clerical collar. The efforts were being rewarded. Mingling with the mourners, he had made several turns past the casket, noting the deceased wore two massive rings of sapphires, rubies and diamonds. A gem-studded crucifix was looped around the deceased man's neck with thick gold braid. As always, no one questioned Bliss in his garb, not in a church full of devout Louisiana Catholics. Chilled in the cool, damp air of the graveyard, Devol worked fast and they left the Deschamp mausoleum an hour before dawn. They had plundered three vaults in the St. Louis cemetery, and Bliss's huge hollowed-out Bible jingled with stolen gold and jewels as they strolled down the street.

Favreau

"I'm not sure I understand, Mme. Favreau," said Dr. Bliss, sipping rich chicory coffee in the luxurious Favreau parlor. "You want me to sell your husband's mistress? A free woman of color?"

"Dead husband, but, yes, that's exactly what I want," she said. "Immediately."

"I wouldn't know where to begin."

"Which is why I just said to do what I tell you. It won't be hard. You have the morphine. You have the chloroform. Take that big strong boy with you. You put the woman in the wagon and keep her dosed up," said the silver-haired woman. "And then you drive the wagon to Georgia. It's quite a long trip, but your job is simple. I have some associates meeting you there. They'll take her and create some records for her, and sell her to a nice rice plantation, or to the Tsar of Russia for all I care. The further away the better."

"There's significant risk in what you propose," Bliss said.

"There's significant reward as well," said Mme. Favreau.

"Kidnapping a prosperous Quadroon would be a hanging offense."

"Yes, Dr. Bliss, but exhausting the patience of a prosperous white woman could have equally dire results," Mme. Favreau said, exasperated. "Especially one that has knowledge of the tragic demise of several young girls who died horrible deaths during one of your procedures. Are you in or out?"

"I'm in," he sighed.

"Good, I'm thrilled. I knew you would be," she said. "And make sure to get that little half-breed brat, too. My dear, dead husband's brat."

For a week, they watched Mme. Passibone enter and leave her boutique. She was a vital woman, beautiful, petite and always dressed expensively but tastefully. Her jewelry would be a bonus Bliss had not discussed with Mme. Favreau. She walked briskly, with her shoulders square and confident, passing those she met with a smile and a quick greeting. The aspiring kidnappers learned her routine. She opened her boutique at nine sharp and stayed until one, when two young women of color arrived. She had lunch at a Creole cafe on Charles St., with one or two other well-dressed ladies, then walked home. She stayed inside until the evening cooled the city and she strolled with her baby along the flowered streets of the French Quarter.

When the day came, Devol followed the woman while Bliss drove the carriage. When Mme. Passibone turned the corner with Devol a half block behind her, Bliss adjusted his costume and pulled the carriage to the curb. As Mme. Passibone grew near, he stepped away from the carriage, tripped, and spilled his box of Bibles at her feet.

"Excuse me, Madame, could you help me for just a second?" Bliss said. "I can't believe I was so clumsy.'

"I hope nothing was damaged," said Mme. Passibone. "Or yourself. Certainly, I'll help."

"Oh, thank you so much," said Bliss. "I think I have wrenched my back. If you could carry the box to the carriage I would be forever grateful."

As she lifted the heavy box into the barouche, Devol grabbed her from behind, pinned her arms to her side, and clamped a chloroform soaked rag over her face. While the box of Bibles spilled on the sidewalk again, Devol shoved the unconscious woman inside. Bliss looked down the street for meddlesome bystanders and when there were none, they calmly rode away.

Mme. Favreau was elated when the person once known as Mme. Passibone disappeared and the wench Laudie Mae, Bessie Bell, or Daffy Dill was born a thousand miles away, and with the most preposterous story. No one would believe her, no white person anyway. It was too delicious for words. But it wasn't perfect.

"But you didn't get the child?" screamed Mrs. Favreau.

"We couldn't get near her," said Bliss. "For two days we watched the house. Sometimes there were fifty people there, and always at least twenty. Half had guns. They were waiting for us."

"You idiot!" screamed Mme. Favreau. "I was specific. Damn you!"

"Excuse me, ma'am," said Devol, when she paused. "But, forget the child for a moment. Think about all them jewels and gold inside. Don't you think this thief would have found a way in, if it was humanly possible?"

She stopped and considered.

"Why are you worried about that brat?" asked Devol. "She ain't entitled to anything of yours. There won't be no evidence of her dear mother's final travels. No papers. Nothing. And there never will be. She can't even prove her mother's dead, let alone make a claim to the estate. I'll make sure of it. She'll never show up again."

Mme. Favreau smiled at the youngster with mild surprise. She had known Dr. Bliss for years, in various capacities. Several times she had referred him to friends whose daughters had been careless and needed to immediately, and discreetly, take care of the problem. She had, however, always told them to lock up their cash, jewelry and silver when he was around. He was clever, and capable of small jobs, but often made greedy, impulsive decisions when he saw sparkly trinkets. He was too panic prone for stressful situations, and there was little evidence to suggest he could handle the slightest danger. He would never be more than an underworld medicine man and a fairly imaginative grifter, but she saw potential in the other one, young and big and strong, and much smarter than most people noticed. Bliss might be the one calling the shots now, but not for long, not with Devol's ambition and her grooming. She thought of the Favreau family businesses, specifically her inherited slave auction house on Esplanade and the stock that passed through it. With her softheaded husband dead, and his plans to sell the auction house dead with him, she would need a new overseer soon. One not shy to lay the whip on the Africans.

Mme. Favreau began sending Devol to the auction house with her aging foreman to learn the business, and hired an accountant to keep him from getting cheated. He was eager, but needed some polish and training before he could thrash it out with the black hearted swindlers who called themselves honorable slave merchants. Although very bright, Devol could barely read or write. She had a solution to that as well. Within a few days her good friend Delphine LaLaurie was tutoring the boy at the opulent mansion on Royal Street, and in exchange, he would administer the physical discipline to the slaves that she and her husband were too weak, or disinclined, to do.

The arrangement thrilled Devol immediately. On his days of instruction, he dressed in his new, fine clothes purchased by the two women and imagined himself a lord. He was soon reading Sir Walter Scott, De Sade and The Sorrows of Young Werther as he soaked in the mansion's wealth, the rich, lustrous wood, the silver and gold, the sculptures and paintings and gilded ceilings. Still, even in the trappings of aristocracy, Devol recognized a little insanity in Mme. LaLaurie. A little evil. A coldness in the eye. A smile at pain. He knew it because he'd long recognized it in himself. He often pledged to her he would have even more than this one day. When he said that, she always told him, "Well, if you want it, you have to be ruthless. Can you be ruthless?" The queer woman was generous with gifts, and promised there would be more to come. One day she called him into the parlor, and greeted him with a wide grin.

"You have done well, very well. I have a present for you. I believe you're ready for it. Have fun now, Francois, I have my own enjoyments to attend to," she said. "You certainly have a lot of promise, and every good boy deserves a treat every now and then. Come, I'll introduce you to Lia."

She took him to the catacombs beneath the mansion, and pushed a young slave girl at him, one he'd never seen before. He smiled, but when the frightened girl smiled back, all he saw was Annie laughing at him. A savage lust and red-hot rage blasted through him, and soon the girl was torn, bloodied and laughing no more. That evening, he climbed the curling, mahogany-railed staircase to the cupola on the LaLaurie mansion's roof. He looked down at the spot where Lia's broken body had landed, then gazed down upon the stately homes of the French Quarter.

He savored the bouquet of jasmine blossoms coming from the Vieux Carré, and watched the ships on the Mississippi. One day soon, it would all be his.

Fire
April 10, 1834

Devol whistled La danse de Mardi Gras as he strolled through the French Quarter on his way to the LaLaurie Mansion. He rattled his walking stick lightly on the iron grate fences along the way, thumbing the ridges of the black onyx Baphomet handle, lingering at the fiery red garnet eyes. He'd been with Mme. LaLaurie and Mme. Favreau for three years, and everything he'd ever wanted was within his grasp. At seventeen, he already had a healthy percentage of the Favreau family business, which was expanding rapidly. He had so much money he could buy that bitch Annie ten times over. There was no way Squire Asbury could turn it down, not when the details of the deal would be shown to Asbury's wife. Including the detail of her paternity, if the man resisted. Or, he mused, he could simply slice the man's throat and leave him in the sugar fields. Either way, Annie would soon be on display in Dr. LaLaurie's menagerie of half-dead freaks where he conducted his "experiments" on his slaves. Just like Bliss had straightened his foot, the mad Dr. LaLaurie assured him he could shrivel Annie's hands and feet up like a monkey's claw, and could even attach more perverse limbs to her body, leaving her to scurry through these caverns like a blind spider.

"Nooooo," Devol cried, his happy grin disappearing when he turned onto Royal Street. Smoke billowed out of the roof of the towering LaLaurie mansion. A mob on the sidewalk was screaming "slaves," and "murder," and "torture." Everything in his life was about to be gone. Everything, he despaired, as he rushed toward the house.

He dodged the crowd and slipped through the small, ivy covered side gate hidden behind the coach house and raced toward the slave pen buried in the cavern beneath the house. Once below ground, he grabbed a torch and ran down the icy tunnel, past the chains and shackles along the wall and into Dr. LaLaurie's operating room and laboratory. From their cages, those miserable experiments with eyes stared back at him, and those with mouths screamed and frothed. Those without arms howled. One moaning slave was still strapped to an operating table among the clutter of festering pails, soiled rags and bones.

"There are people dying in there," the crowd roared from the street. "Murderers!"

Above ground, metal smashed against metal, and the barred and blacked out windows shook. He crept through the dark tunnel until he heard Mme. LaLaurie's voice, shrill and indignant, shrieking orders at her slaves. Around the turn, two black women in rags cowered as Mme. Lalaurie lashed them with a horse quirt. The broad shouldered and trusted house-slave Bastien stood behind the unsuspecting Mme. La-Laurie, with a club in his raised hand. Devol sprang forward and crashed a coal poker into Bastien's skull, knocking the brawny slave witless to the ground with a deep, bloody rip in his head. Leaving the slaves to their fate, he raced past them and up the stairs three at a time. The kitchen was engulfed in flames, and the upper stories were filling with smoke. The crazy old nigger woman cook had chained herself to the cast iron stove and started the fire, prepared to endure death by fire before continuing life as a slave.

Out the back window, the outraged horde of white, black, French, Creole, mulatto, quadroon, free and slave, rocked the gate. They weren't climbing over the walls yet, but he knew they would be soon. He ran to the stable where the frantic carriage horses scuffed and bucked in their stalls. He hitched them quickly while watching the flames spreading in the mansion and the enraged crowd surrounding the estate. They were nearly through.

"Hurry. Hurry. Get these in my wagons. You'll all be free once the danger is over. I promise it. Get these bags in the carriage!" Mme. LaLaurie screamed at two women dragging heavy trunks from the house, brandishing the riding crop above her head. Eyes wide with fear, they flinched at the whip and snuck looks at the frenzied mob at the gate.

"They are in chains, this is murder," shouted the voices pounding at the heavy double doors Devol had braced with the coal poker. When weak, pathetic Dr. LaLaurie only whined at those slaves struggling with the luggage, Devol snatched the bags away in disgust and strapped them atop the coach. Madame LaLaurie reappeared in the black bombazine veils of a grieving widow, her features unrecognizable.

He heard the battering ram split the front door and the mob smash through. Through the window he saw the fire was spreading fast, following the trail of coal oil he'd left. Black smoke rolled out of the dungeon and the shackled slaves could be heard in their crypt, yanking at their chains and screaming like they were in the fiery pit itself. That should slow the good citizens down, Devol laughed as he leapt onto the carriage. With the LaLauries huddled inside, he pointed his pistol at a slave and ordered him to open the back gate. Devol lashed the blacksnake whip and the big black horses burst onto the cobblestone street, parting the angry horde rushing toward the burning house. It seemed everyone in New Orleans suddenly knew of Mme. LaLaurie's sins.

"Stop that coach!" the crowd bellowed, then: "She is running away!"

"Drag her out."

"Shoot her."

"Shoot the horses!"

He careened the carriage through traffic, running down anyone in the way, tilting dangerously at corners. He barely escaped a dozen collisions before the lathered-up, gasping horses reached the lock of a low riding schooner at Bayou St. John. Devol peered around for pursuit. There was none, but he knew this respite would be short lived. He threw some coins at a couple idle Negro dockhands, promising them a handsome reward if they could get the contents of the carriage onto the waiting sloop quickly.

"And now, you old witch," Devol smiled, as he helped Mme. La-Laurie out of the carriage. "Your gold, or I give you to the pitchforks and fire."

Chapter Three

Army of the Indus

Lyman had arrived in Afghanistan in August of 1839, at age 15, a 2nd lieutenant in the 20,000-man Army of the Indus, the British East India Company's expedition to Kabul, the ancient city which controlled all the great military roads of Central Asia. The invasion was the British response to Russia's maneuvering in the Great Game, the competition between the British empire and Russia for resources and territory on the Afghanistan/India frontier. Fearing Russian expansion through the Hindu-Kush mountain passes, the East India Company had forced Afghan Emir Dost Mohammed from the throne and returned the despised British puppet, Shah Shuja Durrani, to power. Shah Shuja had ruled Afghanistan from 1803 to 1809, when he had been overthrown in one more episode in an endless series of treacherous seizures of power by his brothers, half-brothers and cousins. He left power at gunpoint, just as he had taken power, and had been living in luxurious exile in British India since 1818, collecting an exorbitant pension from the East India Company, who had gambled that he would be useful one day.

Even in this ruthless part of the world, Shah Shuja was considered a diabolical sadist, notorious for removing ears, tongues, and testicles of anyone who displeased him. Slaves and peasants suffered the worst, but many of his closest advisors and courtiers were mutes and eunuchs and no one was spared Shuja's rage.

The Army of the Indus was under the command of General Sir William Elphinstone and Sir William Hay Macnaghten, the Viceroy's envoy and chief British Political Officer to Afghanistan. Sir Alexander Burnes, the second ranked envoy, was the most experienced British Political

Officer with the expedition, and had spent the last several years traveling throughout Persia and Central Asia as a diplomat and spy.

The column was swollen and slow, accompanied by 38,000 camp followers: craftsmen, servants, barbers, tailors, cameleers, animal handlers and the families of both Indian and British soldiers. They rode in on 8,000 horses, driving thousands of ox-carts, with 30,000 camels loaded down with the finest comforts from home. Most senior officers and government bureaucrats brought at least a dozen servants, and some brought more than fifty.

Burnes knew the people and customs of Afghanistan better than any other European, and he was well-acquainted with the rulers of the minor kingdoms and caliphates along the march. Many of them had grown rich on his bribes and favors during his earlier travels, and now, in addition to their current demands for tribute, they warned him ominously that the vengeful Afghans were outraged at the British meddling in their government.

Against Burnes' advice, the caravan forged on and entered Kabul expecting the warm welcome of liberators. Instead, the natives saw a massive army of occupation entering the city, and throngs of glowering Afghans watched silently as Shah Shuja led the military parade through the Shor Bazaar courtyard. A cantonment was built outside the city to house the enlisted men and their families, and the European merchants and officers moved into the Bala-Hissar, the immense hilltop fortress that towered over Kabul and had served the region's warlords for centuries.

With Shah Shuja back on the throne, The Army of the Indus had achieved its objective. Peerages were awarded, and Macnaghten was made a baronet. For the next two years, the British officers, in their finest uniforms, and ladies in the latest Paris fashions, treated themselves to grand dinner parties with never-ending liquor and English delicacies.

They held lavish theater productions, cricket matches, hunting parties, and hot-blooded Arabian horse races. The soirees were well-attended by local dignitaries and potentates and rivaled anything the Buckingham Palace staff could put together. For the common soldier, drinking, fornication, prostitution and all manner of debaucheries prohibited by Islam were always available.

Ambush

"Are you hit?" Lyman yelled, hidden behind a boulder on the narrow mountain trail.

"No, lad, just some sand in the eye," said Holly as bullets chipped the rock above his head. "Those bloody bastards are going to have to try better than that if they think they can dispose of Old Holly."

"Think we're finished?" Lyman asked. Hundreds of feet above him, the men and boys in the cliffs, those that Lyman knew as modest shepherds, now moved as quietly as mountain leopards and harassed them with sniper fire. Attacks on British patrols in the mountain passes had become a constant hazard. Oblivious to the threat of the resentful Afghans, the British East India Company had cut the subsidies to the mountain tribal chiefs by half and recalled several regiments of troops home to India. Making things much worse, Shah Shuja had become more grandiosely cruel, punishing minor offenses with torture. Beheadings performed for mandatory crowds in the courtyard of the Shor Bazaar were common.

"Not this time," said Holly, peering at the cliffs above them. "If they kill us all today, they'll have no amusements for the winter. They've killed plenty of the native boys this afternoon, so I imagine they'll be off to gather up their goats before too long and go scampering home."

Lyman checked himself for injuries. Two bullets had snipped away bits of his blouse, but hadn't broken skin. Others in the patrol weren't so lucky. Four dead sepoys were lying on the dusty trail, close enough to touch with a stick. In their bright red uniform tunics, they were excellent targets to the invisible Ghilzai warriors and Lyman had grown accustomed to losing these frustrating battles. The Afghans came after the British patrols like packs of wolves, traveling light, moving fast and easily staying out of reach of the frustrated, immobile British riflemen trapped in the narrow canyon trails. With their long-barreled, homemade jezail rifles, the Afghans picked off the sepoys from five hundred yards away, easily staying three hundred yards outside the range of the antiquated British Brown Bess muskets

"Ain't they ever sending help?" said Lyman, listening to the cries of the wounded.

"Not here, not now. Not until spring. These passes will freeze up and close for the winter soon. The outhouse is tipping, but the Baronet Macnaghten is about to become the next Governor of Bombay, so he sure don't want it to splash back on himself," said Holly. "Perhaps the Envoy's waiting for some divine intervention for the situation to right itself somehow, but it's unlikely anybody in Buckingham Palace even knows the dusky mussulmen are perturbed. He desperately hopes to keep it that way. If they think he can't control the natives here, it's likely they'll rescind that honor and he'll end up as one more subaltern in darkest Africa. However, if he can convince them he turned back the great Russian peril, who knows? They just might make him king."

Into this rode Akbar Khan, Afghan warrior-hero from the Battle of Jamrud, and the most favored of all the fifty-some sons of the Dost Muhammed, the emir who the East India Company had toppled and replaced with Shah Shuja. Akbar Khan had proven himself to be a fearless and savage fighter, and he had become a uniting champion for the Afghan people, gathering forces and making alliances ever since the British had removed his father from power two years previously. Now, the regional dynasties, provinces and caliphates had united behind his call for Jihad against the infidel European invaders, and Khan arrived in Kabul with 25,000 bitter Afghan warriors and a blood-feud to settle.

When word had reached him that Akbar Khan was closing in, Shah Shuja had ordered the British out of the Bala-Hissar fortress and promised his loyalty to the Khan and his growing horde. The Afghans overpowered the British magazines and removed tons of food, coal, ammunition, and medicine. A patrol of 300 sepoys was ambushed and massacred, and many of the bodies were dragged to within sight of the cantonment, beheaded, and disemboweled. The 4,000 soldiers and 12,000 civilians in the British cantonment were now under siege. Those who had been merely cold and hungry were now starving, freezing and under relentless sniper fire.

As a blizzard whipped across the prairie two days before Christmas, Macnaghten rode out of the fort to a meeting with Akbar Khan on a snow-drifted knoll half-way between the cantonment and the Ghilzai tents. Three junior political officers rode tightly on Macnaghten's heels, and fifty yards behind the diplomatic party rode six British soldiers, including Captain Hollingberry and Lyman. It had been made clear to Macnaghten that any more men, or any closer, would be seen as aggression.

When they crested the hill, Akbar Khan was mounted on a prancing white horse, his eyes twinkling brightly in the cold. Behind him, a dozen glaring Afghan warriors smoldered through the swirling snow. Lyman felt inside his heavy wool poshteens, squeezing the two pistols tucked inside, making sure they were still there.

"It is splendid you have come, Macnaghten, so we can clear up some misunderstandings," said Khan.

"Absolutely. I want us to have complete understanding," said Macnaghten.

"Excellent. Let's start with this item," Khan said as he reached into a goat skin pouch and withdrew a bloody, battered human head. "So, do you know him?"

Lyman choked and clung to his saddle with both hands as the Afghans smirked in amusement and he expected the next thing he'd feel would be warm urine running down his leg. Or a bullet in the chest.

"I know him."

"He works for you?"

"He did," said Macnaghten. "That man did not need to die."

"Perhaps not. But he certainly had a fascinating tale. As I dug out his eyeballs, he said you hired him to assassinate me. You, Macnaghten."

"Preposterous! Never! There is no need to frighten us. I would never do that. We're frightened already, but we must tend to the matters at hand," said Macnaghten. "The Crown is ready to appoint you Wazir of Afghanistan. You'll be the richest, most powerful man in the country. A hundred thousand rupees, five hundred thousand, a million, you can name your price. Pounds. Gold."

"Tell me, how is it a European functionary appoints anyone in my country, for anything? I already am Wazir, Macnaghten. And, unlike you Europeans, I have no price. It's my country, already, Macnaghten, not the Crown's, or your "John Company's," said Khan, smiling pleasantly. "It belongs to my people. I'm baffled by your inability to comprehend that. I don't want your rupees gained by tyranny or pounds that carry the scourge of decadence, whoremongering, blasphemy, and secularism. It is said every pound note in England has passed through your whorehouses at least three times."

"Be that as it may, we can come to something mutually beneficial."

"If it will be as mutually beneficial as it has been for the last two years, there will not be any of my countrymen left alive."

"Now, look Khan, you're not being reasonable."

"The man with his boot on the other's neck always considers himself reasonable," said Khan.

"We'll give you all the power. Protect you from treachery and carry you to the throne," Macnaghten gushed, searching for words. "And those thousands of British pounds. Gold."

"It's not yours to give. This is a new era, Macnaghten. Don't treat us as fools. I'll soon have every grain of gold, every rupee, and British pound in Kabul, all of Afghanistan. You British will return with more armies and more guns, not bearing gifts as you say," said Khan. "But the only thing you'll provide is the blood of a thousand ginger-haired dupes to enrich our soil."

"The East India Company will take wonderful care of you."

"Are you deaf, Macnaghten?" shouted Khan. "Allah and my blood-line give me all the power and authority I will ever need. You British have no power. Your vanity is ignorant and repulsive. It is I who have the power, the power of life and death over you. I only wish I had some of your filthy pigs. I would cut off your eyelids and force you to watch as I fed you to them, starting with your feet."

Akbar's hand sliced through the air and a howling Ghilzai on a black stallion lunged forward. With a guttural curse and a vicious swing of his sword, he severed Macnaghten's head which spouted blood plumes as it bounced across the snow. The head came to rest with eyes and mouth locked open, staring at the tommies from a spreading crimson pool. The screeching, hugely bearded warriors charged and the British soldiers whipped their horses around, emptying their pistols over the shoulder on the gallop. Lyman looked back as Macnaghten's headless body swayed in his saddle, held there by an Afghan sword. The Ghilzai warriors roared with laughter as they pulled the other agents from their horses and chopped them to pieces.

Christmas in Barracks in Kabul

Lyman followed Holly in a slipping and sliding sprint across the frozen cantonment and into the barracks of the 44th a Foot. It was Christmas Eve, with little joy except the alcohol, and the soldiers of the 44th were well into the brandy and gin and were singing as festively off-key as if they were in a warm country pub. The tommies had a nice fire of English coal, stolen by the Ghilzais, and sold back to the Brits by a clever and brazen thief. There were times the young soldiers didn't mind the Muslim bandits so much, since they never stole the liquor. Putting their plight out of their mind, the hungry men laughed and told happy tales of holidays past, describing, in minute detail, feasts of goose stuffed with oysters, sugar plums, and Christmas puddings packed with beef and raisins. Or candies and fruits and chocolates. Or the imagining of them for the ones from the slums such as Lyman, who had tasted few such treats in his youth.

"Listen up, men," shouted Holly, after the bottle passed a few times. "Akbar Khan has promised safe passage through the mountains if we leave within the week, through the Khyber pass. Elphinstone has agreed to it. We are to march to Jalalabad, taking all military and civilian personnel."

"Safe passage? The garrison at Jalalabad is 90 miles away," said a veteran. "It's below zero with a blizzard bearing down on us."

"Nobody goes through the Hindu Kush in winter," said another old sweat. "It's a death sentence. Its unthinkable."

"No argument there," said Holly. "Maybe one or two of us can shoot our way out, but nursing 12,000 store clerks and housewives won't make it easier."

"Let's fight them right here, right now," said a young tommy.

"Fighting them anywhere is futile," said Holly. "There are now 50,000 of them, and five thousand of us. Supplies are gone. Maybe someone will get through."

At dawn on the first day, the cavalry led the caravan of seven hundred British infantry, 4,000 Indian sepoys, and 12,000 civilians as they marched out of the cantonment. The lucky ones rode on starving horses, in decrepit carts, or stuffed into woven baskets slung over the backs of camels. Most trudged on with frozen feet, through the ten inches of freezing rain and snow that fell before they reached the first mountain.

"Five miles," said Holly, when they stopped at dusk, barely inside the mouth of the snow-bound Khoord-Cabul pass. "That's how far we have come. Five bleeding miles. The column itself is two miles long. Macnaghten, Elphinstone. Fools."

Lyman was exhausted and fell asleep under heavy robes. At dawn, the pass exploded with gunfire that ripped through the defenseless column. Above him, the snow-covered cliffs overflowed with Ghilzai warriors, and the narrow canyon rang with the all-too-familiar echoes of banging hammers as they loaded their long-barreled rifles.

"Keep your head down, lad. No need to make it easy for them," Holly screamed from up the slope as the Ghilzais bounded from one rock to another, scaling the cliffs as gracefully as the white mountain goats they hunted. On the trail, the Ghilzais grew more daring each day, rushing amidst the shattered column and snatching women or children before disappearing into the rocks. The attacks never relented, and an unbroken line of dead men, women, and children, buried under mounds of snow, stretched all the way back to the first British footstep into the Hindu Kush. The weak and wounded froze to death overnight, and camels and horses were shot down by the hundreds. Desperate people squeezed against the steaming dead animals for warmth, chopping away haunch meat before the animal froze, and sometimes even slicing open the steaming animal carcasses and crawling inside the bloody cavity. Toes and fingers and noses of the refugees blackened and fell off. Multitudes took their own lives. Weeping parents smothered their own children, and others clutched their babies as they leapt off the straight vertical cliffs. Hundreds of Bengal soldiers, less equipped, and suffering worse than the British in the elements, turned back, praying for Akbar's mercy.

"Captain, over here!" shouted a young soldier careening down the trail at dawn. "Gen. Elphinstone snuck off in the night. Gen. Shelton, too. Surrendered themselves and their wives to Akbar Khan."

"That damned old bitch! That bloody Judas!" stormed Holly. "If I make it back to England, people will know the name of that coward. I wouldn't be surprised if all this wasn't his plan to begin with. Maybe it's best. Maybe we have a chance of survival without that fool giving orders."

"I wouldn't know, Captain," said the tommy. "But someone has to give orders."

"What do you mean?"

"Elphy Bey named Brigadier Anquetil commander before he surrendered, not knowing Gen. Anquetil had gone out on a night raid. The lads carried him in at first light, after the monkeys put about 20 lead pills in him. I've seen no other officers. They've dropped like dominoes. It looks like you have been promoted to general."

"Bloody hell," said Holly, "The last thing I need when I'm preparing to die is worry about five thousand others."

Lyman joined the raging packs of British soldiers charging up the narrow side trails again and again, screaming old Saxon war-cries that had lain dormant in their blood for centuries. They crashed into the Ghilzai sniper nests and fought like madmen with death already a certainty. Chasing packs of startled Muslim warriors over boulders and snowbanks, Lyman emptied his revolvers until they burned red hot and thrust his bayonet until it flowed crimson. The tommies killed ten to their one, but the attacks never slowed. Finally, Holly gathered the surviving members of the 44th as they staggered into a narrow canyon at sunset, half frozen, ice-heavy beards and faces that glowed frostbite red. Of the 16,000 refugees that had fled the cantonment less than a week earlier, only sixty soldiers and a few hundred civilians still survived.

"Listen up," shouted Holly over the arctic blasts cutting through the sheer cliffs. "We have sixty men from the 44th effective. Forty rifles, and no more than 80 balls. A dozen pistols and fifty rounds. We've stripped the dead and that's it, entirely. As soon as it is dark, we're going to break out. We'll meet at Gandamak and make a stand."

"But what of the others?" several soldiers called out.

"They're all dead anyway, tonight, tomorrow. No more," said Holly. "Certainly not another fifty miles. Nothing we can do, but we need to try to get a messenger out, tell the truth about what happened here."

At midnight, the British soldiers waited silently, calming their saddled horses and praying, when shrieking Ghilzais leapt out of the dark and swarmed over the column. Gun shots, clattering swords, and ancient curses filled the night as desperate knife-and-club battles twisted and spun in the dark.

"Go!" bawled Holly at Lyman. They fought their way through their attackers, charging bloody and blindly toward Gandamak, side-by-side, slashing and clubbing and kicking until they reached the crumbling citadel.

"I have a mission for you," Holly said to Lyman after the 44th had assembled.

"What's going on, Captain?" asked Lyman.

"Walk back this way," said Holly, moving toward the rear of the fort. "A horse has been saddled for you."

"Me? Where am I going?"

"To Jalalabad. You've been there several times, I'm sure."

"Yes, of course, but not at night. In a blizzard, and on a horse ready to collapse, with fifty thousand bloodthirsty savages chasing me. We're not halfway there," said Lyman. "And it don't feel right leaving the others."

"Don't worry. Your chance of getting yourself killed is still as much as ours. Perhaps greater. But this is an order. Time to go. You must get out," Holly said. "Tell them what happened here. All of it. Avenge us."

"They won't be watching?"

"This trail is very rarely used, too unstable even for the ragheads. But tonight, they'll be everywhere. They tasted English blood and they like it. But, you have a little time in between lookouts," Holly said. "Keep your puggaree low. Your mount's hooves have been muffled. You must be silent."

"I'd rather stay here and kill these bastards until they kill me."

"True, enough," said Holly. "But wouldn't you rather come back with a bigger army and kill them all?"

"No way I can do both?"

"Unlikely, son," said Holly. "But I like the way you think."

"I'll miss you, sir," said Lyman.

"Think no more about me, lad," said Holly. "Pass my regards on to my wives, should you see them. Give 'em a lusty boinking if you can. Tell the lasses I sent it, as that was my last thought of them.''

When a murky figure appeared below, Holly snapped a wire garrote around his throat. The Afghan kicked a time or two before blood spurted from his throat and the wire sliced to his spine.

"Go, now!" whispered Holly, "Only seconds until another one shows up."

Lyman lashed his horse into the blackness. Eight days later, bleeding, failing and snow blind, he topped a hill and saw a city wall on the horizon. He urged his dying horse through the stone field and watched the wall through eyes scraped dry by sand and wind. His lips were split through and clotted with blood, and he had not felt his fingers or toes, nor slept, ate, or drank, since escaping Gandamak. His coat was sliced open, bloodstained from a dozen wounds, and his horse had deep slashes in both hindquarters. The wind sent ice spikes through him and he wanted to hurry, to gallop, to charge, but knew that would kill his horse, and himself with it. He drifted off and when he opened his eyes the wall was gone. Snow swirled around him, and tears froze on his cheeks. As he sank into hopelessness and confusion, he couldn't remember where he came from, and didn't know where he was going. He knew his eyes and ears were playing tricks on him, but he couldn't tell what was a trick, and what wasn't, no matter how hard he tried. He thought he heard horses coming, and a small detail of cavalry suddenly surrounded him.

"Where is the Column?" they asked.

"I am the Column," he mumbled. "Where am I?"

"You are in Jalalabad. Where are the others?"

"All Dead. Murdered. Tortured. Akbar Khan."

They slid him off his mortally wounded horse as it fell, and laid him in a cart. He slept for 72 hours.

Chapter Four

Ghat Mountains, India

The Prisoner, a Bangladeshi merchant, sat sprawled in the dirt and chained to a rotten log. Ashok's father sat on the log behind the man, and Ashok faced the prisoner, squinting, trying to read his thoughts. The beaten man looked at him, terror and pleading in his eyes, and when Ashok smiled, the prisoner spat something in Bangladeshi. Ashok didn't understand it, but his father did, and smashed the man in the temple with a tree limb. Blood oozed down the prisoner's face, and Ashok smiled again. His father, Thug Behram, the King of Thugs, was old, but still virile, as attested to by his collection of beautiful wives and a string of children younger than Ashok. He said it was because he took the spirit of his victims.

The old bandit motioned Ashok to kneel behind the wounded man, grabbed the man's hair and snapped his head back, cracking it on the log. The man shrieked, cursed them, and weakly lifted his head. Ashok sprang forward with the rumaal and looped it around the man's throat, yanked and twisted. The doomed merchant struggled, sputtered hoarsely and pissed his pants as his bound hands clawed the air. When the man slumped, Ashok released the garrote and the man slowly regained consciousness. His face was smeared with blood and tears, and he sobbed through crusted mucous. He pleaded and begged, promising money and gold. He offered his daughters. Thug smiled at his son, and Ashok smiled back, proud he had done well. The old bandit nodded, and Ashok slid the yellow scarf around the weeping man's throat. Several of his father's Thuggee bandits gathered around, offering encouragement and advice while sipping tea and eating sweet pastries.

A few weeks later, Ashok watched from behind a banyan tree, chewing mango and sugarcane and rubbing the smooth ridge of his well-worn emerald Kali figurine, his birthright, passed down from his grandfather's grandfather.

Five loud white hunters rode in howdahs atop the lead elephants, with a small company of miners, scientists, pioneers, merchants and bearers following behind them. The Europeans were all tired, careless and overconfident, the Thuggees' most desired traits. They were also clearly affluent, which was odd in these mountains, so close to the territory of the feared Thuggee. Most pilgrims looked as destitute as possible, hoping bandits would overlook them. There were hired guards on this trip, but they were slovenly, unimpressive, and likely to disappear into the forest at the first hint of danger. That was common with hired guards. Worse for the merchants, several of the guards were actually Thuggee.

With Thug Behram's men at the lead, the caravan had been twisting and winding through the treacherous Ghat Mountain jungle trails for 20 days and had reached the fork in the road. The Thuggee men were excellent at their roles of veteran guards and experienced guides who, after much excited bickering and gesturing, led the caravan down a canyon trail, just wide enough for a wagon to enter. Watching these performances, Ashok always giggled. So exaggerated was this ruse, he was surprised they were so rarely detected.

The Thuggee pilots - the mahout - guided the elephants expertly through the jungle and the pack train had stopped so they could tend to their animals. All mahout, Thuggee or not, valued their elephants more than their wives, and took great care of the animals. Twice a day the train would stop so the hunters and miners could have tea, and the mahouts could scrub the elephants with coconut halves. While everyone rested, trumpets from elephants in the pack train were answered by elephants in the wild and birds and monkeys chattered in the trees, all good signs that no one was watching them.

That night around the fires, the travelers were jovial, happy that the trek would be over in just two or three more days. There was no hint of fear or suspicion, no anxiety that he could detect, just the normal sounds of a caravan pushing through the tangled wilderness. A grinning, drunk trader walked into the forest to urinate, giving a small wave and Ashok smiled. They had passed earlier in the day and the man had stopped him, calling him a good lad. The nearly man-size Ashok was only eleven, which confused most people. Thuggee children his age ran from him, and few people talked to him. He already possessed more physical strength than the cult's most powerful men, and even in this closed society of mountain bandits and murderers, the others feared his brutality. After tonight, Ashok would no longer be a child, but he was filled with a boy's excitement. He tingled from head to toe, anticipation at its zenith, and in the cool, black air, he felt goosebumps on his skin. He was fighting the urge to urinate when his father crept over.

"Are you ready son?" asked Behram.

"Yes, father," he said, pointing to an old man sitting on a wagon gate. Thug whistled softly, and his two lieutenants materialized from the darkness, eyes shiny with anticipation. Thug whistled again, and the bandits sprang into action, garrotes in hand. Ashok leapt on his man and twisted the rumaal until his arms burned and the Kali figure crushed the flailing man's throat like a dry almond shell. Ashok dragged the body toward the fire, where his father's men had also dragged their victims before plundering the baggage. The stripped bodies were thrown into two light wagons, which Ashok and three teenage boys drove to the banks of the shallow, muddy Mahanadi River where the great herds of water buffalo and blackbuck antelope crossed and crocodiles lurked in the stagnant water, awaiting their next meal.

The boys dragged the bodies to a ledge, six feet above the water, shouting, joking, and clapping their hands as they pelted the crocs with rocks and sticks, daring each other to get closer. When the giant reptiles were alert and watching, the boys heaved the bodies in the water. With each, there was a violent splash as the croc slammed its jaws shut and spun its meal underwater to ripen.

Sleeman

Mouthwatering smells coming from clay ovens mingled with the overheated odor of elephants and buffalo in the remote, dusty village. Ashok sat at a table outside a thatch-roofed mud shack with his father and uncle who had come here to sell their latest loot. The men had been throwing dice across the wide table and drinking the fat barman's potent desi daru for several hours. Several mahouts had their elephants out, rubbing them down as Ashok snacked on baba ghanoush and chaat, watching a man in the elephant pen running his hands over one of the Thuggee's new elephants. The man Ashok watched was not a mahout. Instead, he shouted and waved his arms at a group of men walking toward him, pulling out one of the elephant's ears and pointing behind it.

"Look, my brother's mark. These are his elephants, these are his wagons," the man shouted.

"Hey, hey," another shouted, "Whose elephants are these? I know these elephants! They belong to Kaamil. Where is Kaamil?"

The man's companions hurried over and studied the markings of one elephant and then another. A hostile rumbling came from the men near the elephants, then outrage and threats. A tall man cried out and pointed at Thug Behram.

"No, he would not sell these animals!" the man raged. "Murderers! Thuggees!"

"Shut up you liar, you behnchoot," Thug Behram screamed, but the mob was already forming. Thug grabbed Ashok's hand and ran between a row of huts, but a dozen angry villagers leapt from behind a weather-beaten shed. Behram whirled and stabbed at the closest man with his kukri knife, moving the pursuers back, but not far. Rocks flew, and armed with clubs and machetes, the seething crowd surged toward the Thuggee. The bandits didn't know these people, didn't know the area, had never been in this village before, and had no place to run.

"Get the murderers!"

"Thuggee!" voices yelled behind them, and it became a chant. "Thuggee!'

A cast-iron bell clanged out the alarm, and faces contorted in fury, a hundred villagers charged into the parched streets. Clouds of dust billowed up from their running feet, and, suddenly, the camp was full of Governor-General Sleeman's red-coated British soldiers. The Queen had given Sleeman one job: "Kill the Thuggee!" and he had become proficient. The tiny mountain villages had become traps. The Red Coats swarmed through the village, using their rifles like clubs. Gunshots blasted, and trumpeting elephants broke free and trampled the huts in terror. Thuggees started down street after street, but marauding natives blocked their escape. They tried to resist but the British soldiers were too many, too disciplined, and as the circle closed in, the trapped Thuggee were shot down in the street.

"If I surrender, they will stop," said Behram, pushing Ashok toward his Uncle Ajit. "I must do it. It is the only chance we have. Run, run to Bengal, to Elizabeth Street, go with your uncle. He will get you to America. Be safe my son, I love you."

Texas, 1842

The two hooting owls were coming closer, and a horse nickered under the clouds drifting past the red Texas moon. Ashok couldn't relax, and had felt eyes on him all day. He had continually scanned the plains, but saw only the buzzards and hawks circling in the sun or perched in the cottonwood or willow trees beside the river. The scenery hadn't changed much since Uncle Ajit had bought his way onto this small wagon train in San Francisco, a modest collection of people, mostly European immigrants, traveling across the rolling prairie toward Dallas. Ajit had pronounced Dallas a thriving hub for bandits, pimps, whores, and murderers. He said he could easily find work.

Now in the blue grama, the wagons and carts had been pulled into a rough circle before dark, and anxious men carried muskets at the edge of camp. Ashok, with a kukri knife across his legs, wondered about those sounds in the dark as he rubbed the Kali figurine. Suddenly, the owls screeched from inside the camp as whooping Indians charged. Gun shots cracked in the dark, and screams of terror carried far out into the desert. Crouching with his uncle under the wagon, Ashok watched men drop to the ground, gushing blood. The cries of the dying mixed with drunken laughter when the Comanche warriors leapt into wagons and found the hidden whiskey. Horror-struck, wailing women were yanked from the wagons and dragged toward the fire by their hair as clubs, whips, and rough red fists punished them.

Standing mirrors, rocking chairs, steamer trunks and barrels of flour crashed on the ground. Barking dogs were crippled with stone clubs and thrown into the fire, and the air filled with howls and the stench of burning dog hair as braves danced by in bloody dresses torn from the women that lay raped and mutilated. Ajit screamed and fell on his face, a store-bought axe wedged deep in his skull. Scalped pioneers staggered about, blinded by torrents of blood and a naked Indian lurched through overturned boxes and twisted bodies chasing a small boy. He weaved with a whiskey bottle in one hand, and a drunken, dark grin crossed his face when the terrorized child collapsed, bare ribs heaving. The boy's father, sliced open in the back, stumbled around a wagon and threw himself between his son and the Indian but the brave crushed his tomahawk into the father's forehead without breaking stride.

A strong hand grabbed Ashok by his hair and jerked him from underneath the wagon. A deeply scarred barbaric face, painted in furious red and black stripes, peered at Ashok and twisted his hair, forcing him to his knees, pulling his head back. Long feathered earrings swung as the frowning warrior barked a harsh, guttural language. He pinched Ashok's cheeks and forced his mouth open, then stared, holding his hand to Ashok's face and ran rough fingers through the boy's hair.

Texas Plains, 1846

"Why aren't these Ethiopians singing?" Francois Devol demanded as they neared the Texas fort. He was ready to be free of his burden and back in New Orleans with a trunk full of cash and a belly full of whiskey. But, for now, under the scrutiny of a few dozen gun-heavy overseers and patty rollers, his coffle of 600 dust-covered slaves marched on, the new, wild-eyed ones clamped to long chains.

"I suppose they don't feel like singing, I'm fairly certain I wouldn't," said Makepeace Bliss.

"We could soon find out. Get 'em singing. Get 'em happy. I want 'em happy goddamnit, when we walk in that fort. No one wants a pouty nigger, not even Jesus. Tell 'em that."

"I'll remind them," said Bliss.

"That's better," said Devol, after he heard the blacksnake whips cracking and the slaves singing. "No need to be sullen."

Devol's coffle was the first to reach the fort. The big auction was two weeks away, with expectations of more than 1,500 slaves in addition to his own stock, and high prices. He would use the time to fatten them up, and conceal as many flaws as he could. Newspaper announcements for the auction had been left in every town along a twenty-mile-wide strip as they navigated up the Trinity River from Galveston. Heavy broadsheets were tacked up, and personal invitations from dealers and auctioneers had been delivered to all the big ranches and plantations in central Texas.

It wasn't his first venture into Texas, but it was hopefully his last. He knew on those deceptive rolling prairies, a raiding party of painted savages could suddenly appear out of the ground, like red ghosts, making less noise than a scorpion. He had a small army of experienced patty-rollers, but fighting a horde of blood-thirsty devils screaming for your scalp was something different. And if the slave-stealing redskins weren't bad enough, rattlesnakes, snarling wolf packs and the murderous heat had all been threatening his string since marching west from the river a week ago. Yet, it was a risk worth taking. With cotton in the new state of Texas setting at 10¢ per pound, the price for a good field hand had leapt to $1,000 - $1,200 and rising. The demand for slaves was growing so fast that when big cotton farmers went to the Galveston slave markets, they often found the pickings slim.

There was a fortune to be made. Bringing in brand new stock from Cuba or Brazil, through Galveston Bay in a black-birder, wasn't difficult and the profit was 500%. In the first months of new statehood, there was widespread confusion among the Mexicans, Texans, and Americans about who ran what. They could not agree on jurisdiction and responsibility around the borders, but all were quite united in their eagerness to accept Devol's gold. Since the notion that anybody in the tangled bureaucracies cared enough about a boatload of jungle aboriginals to turn down a bribe was not supported by facts, Devol had decided to bring the stock to the ranchers. He had purchased a nice selection of carpenters, millwrights, and even a couple trained mechanics for Eli Whitney's wonderful cotton gin. With saving the ranchers the cost of time, travel and frustration, he could easily get an extra $300 for the most ignorant field bucks and plow boys, and $500 for the tradesmen.

"Welcome to Ft. McCullough," said the Major as Devol entered the fort, which was just a cluster of adobe buildings and half-walls surrounding a large parade ground. Long barracks and stables lined the back, in the middle of nothing but open grassland as far as the eye could see. "Damn good to see a civilized white man after so long in this godforsaken frontier."

"Thank you, Major, we've had a good trip, very little trouble, no dead, no escapes," said Devol. "We were able to sail up a good bit of the river, so it wasn't at all bad. Easy trip, especially on the jigs, though you can't tell it by their sullen disposition."

"Some people just don't know how good they have it," said the Major.

"You jest, Major. But still, you'd think they'd enjoy such undeserved largesse," said Devol. "Instead I've got the biggest bunch of complainers ever."

"But where can you find all these slaves?" asked the Major. "Interesting accents I heard from some of your bondsmen just now. Are some of them still speaking in their African language?"

"It's hard to say what the jigaboos are saying. They may be saying "That Major in the blue-coat would look good in a soup pot with carrots and taters," said Devol. "This bunch here is from Mississippi, Louisiana, Georgia, Tennessee, even a few Kentucky purebloods."

Devol wondered briefly if the officer wasn't some do-gooder that would see the wild-eyed brutes had never set foot on American soil.

These Texas riverboat captains sure took his bribes without a fleet second of conscience. When the officer let it pass, Devol extended a 20-cent cigar and $200. The Major accepted both without a word, and walked away. Half of the coffle, the wild ones from Brazil, had been at his old friend Monroe Edwards Chenango plantation for three months, getting fat. Edwards was the man who had first opened his eyes to the profits to be made from illegally captured Caribbean slaves in the booming Texas market, and Devol would have liked to see him. However, the greedy forger was wasting away in the Sing Sing prison. They said he'd lost his mind.

The slaves were herded into several acres of cattle pens which spread out toward the creek. The ones in chains, the untamed ones with the raw whip stripes across their backs, stared at Devol's men, ready to fight. He hadn't broken their spirit yet, but that was fine with some of the ranchers. They preferred to do their own breaking. Devol watched as the wise, grizzled old hands spoke softly and tried to calm the spirited ones, the only value they still held. The bulk of his stock, the domesticated ones, arranged whatever meager belongings they had and gathered on stumps and homemade chairs. Fiddlers and harmonica men played sad tunes as the sun went down, while mothers held the young children close, singing lullabies and stirring kettles of pork bones and field peas.

"Not even a bathtub, or a bed that's more bed than bug," said Bliss, a few days later. "With a high probability of getting scalped. I can't stay here."

"Well, you don't have much choice, do you Bliss?" said Devol. "They'll hang you in Philadelphia, Boston, Cleveland and just about every city in Louisiana. Maybe you should hire yourself out to a sailing ship. Visit those islands you're always talking about. The weather might help your complexion."

"Oh, calm down. You're not losing any money. That should make you happy. They are amazingly healthy, for the most part. Even those pregnant wenches seem to have survived the trip all right," said Bliss. "Probably deliver within a week."

"Excellent," said Devol. "Birthing a wee niglet any day. Perhaps a patch full. What a blessed event. An economical long-term investment for some lucky Texian rancher."

"I guess its common practice to rut with your slaves, but what would happen if you got one of those women pregnant?" asked the Major, joining them. "Good Lord, I guess that's something I've never considered."

"Well, I'd shoot this quack, that's what I'd do, and then sell the creatures immediately. The new man will get a two for one deal. After that, it's not my concern. Pregnant wenches are not much good in the field. Nor one toting a brat."

"Why him?" asked the Major.

"He's the one that's supposed to be giving the Peruvian powders, so those problems don't arise," said Devol. "Further steps, as necessary. Although, frankly, I find abortionists despicable. No respect for human life."

"That means a lot, coming from you," Bliss said, as the Major paled.

By the end of the first week, ranchers and cotton farmers had trickled into the fort, but Devol was bored and surly. He was tired of walking buyers along the pens with the auction handbills as the patty rollers shouted orders to jump, dance, or strip naked. Even knowing this trip would make him a rich man, his unhappiness in this remote Texas outpost grew. He had told himself he wouldn't touch the merchandise, but finally pulled a young girl from the pen. She was delicate, black as coal but finely featured and without a blemish. An unmarked daughter of Nefertiti.

"Here ya go," said Devol, forcing a peppermint in her mouth when she was outside the fence. When she spat it in the dirt, he slapped her across the face and knocked her down. Fat tears streaked the girl's face as she scuttled backwards like one of Dr. Lalaurie's hideous experiments gone wrong, her thin, frantic black arms and legs flailing and her fingers digging trails in the dust.

"How old are you, sweetie?" asked Devol.

"Fo'teen," she whimpered.

"Nooo, now, I know when your massa sold you, he told you to say that, so he can get more money for your little juicy black ass," Devol cooed, giving her a big conspiratorial wink. "I figure you right about eleven, and that's just the perfect age for me, indeed it is."

Devol yanked the child to her feet, grabbing her hips and pressing her to his throbbing groin as he braced his walking stick tight across her back. Her mother clutched at the child from behind the fence, but the patty-rollers beat the howling woman to the ground. Devol looked at the girl and saw the young ones Madam LaLaurie had once given to him, or that bitch Annie, and he burned with fever. He had never found one like Annie, not one of the scared slave girls, nor one of the many pretentious debutantes that dared a tryst with a rogue of his reputation. Neither was this one, but she would do.

"Here, get this little slut scrubbed down and brought to my cabin," Devol said to Bliss, pointing toward the shacks at the far end of the compound.

"Massa, massa, she's too young," the child's mother sobbed.

"Too young? Hell, she's almost too old."

"She only 'leben!"

"Ha, as I suspected," Devol laughed delightedly. "All the better. You want to watch mammy?"

The woman slumped, weeping wretchedly.

"I expected not. Mind your own business or I'll whip the black outta you, and then I'll whip her, and I'll do it every goddamned day," he snarled. "Now, I paid $1,000 for the girl, so you don't need to worry much. I didn't spend that money just to throw it away. Wouldn't be prudent."

Comanche Village

The hunting party came into view at mid-morning, just specks across the prairie. Three whooping braves loped ahead, and a group of young boys and women dragged two buffalo carcasses behind their horses with rawhide ropes. The braves raced their horses through this small camp of fifteen tipis, their booming boasts carrying far across the plain as the tribe responded with cheers and laughter. The small Comanche band of Penateka, "Honey Eaters," ten braves and twenty or so squaws, children and old people, was camped in a strip of cottonwoods along the banks of a clear stream off the Brazos. A fast rider was sent back to the main band, and the big hunt would commence when the sun rose. Fires were started, and children fetched water. As Ashok walked through the camp, he heard nothing but joyous chatter about the buffalo just beyond the hills. They were not hungry, but the first buffalo of spring were here and all were always excited for fresh meat.

As the women worked, some boys played in the meadow with curved sticks and a large leather ball. Ashok started that way, but the game ended abruptly. Lately, they would not allow him to play, saying he was too big. He towered by a head over the tallest warrior in the tribe, and was as thick as a bull. He excelled in wrestling, challenging older braves and winning. He had fought viciously when he was captured from that Dallas-bound wagon train, and, for a year afterward, he had fought every day, sometimes all day, until not even the most ferocious warrior could beat him. They called him Angry Badger. He had been made the slave of Old Gar, an old man, once powerful. Gar had many seasons behind him, and nearly all his vision was gone. He was not unkind, but Ashok knew it was only because the old man would have been helpless and left in the desert without him. The Comanche were not a people given to kindness, but neither were the Thuggee, he supposed.

Choice cuts of fat hump meat roasted over blazing campfires, and feasting began at dark. Little Elk offered Ashok a raw liver dipped in gall. Ashok sliced off a thick piece, slimy and slippery, massaging the gall into it, smacking loudly as he bit down. Dogs snarled over scraps of the two skinned buffalo cows that lay stark and bloody near the fire. Suckling calves, still rooted to their dead mothers, were sliced open where they stood and before their slashed throats quit spurting, the calves' stomachs were removed and placed in a large rawhide bowl. Bow Legged Bear made two delicate incisions, and his friends Angry Badger and Turtle scooped the curdled milk from the stomach in a gourd, chewing happily and slapping the hungry dogs away. Gar played an antelope bone flute, Sky Bird played a drum, and the people danced happily around the fire, the bells and brass cones on the leggings jingling merrily.

In the hours just before dawn, the one they called Angry Badger sat cross legged in front of the rawhide tipi he shared with Old Gar. The old man sharpened his knives, especially the huge steel one he claimed he got from the American Jim Bowie, in trade for some Mexican scalps.

"I wish I was a young brave and could hunt just one more time. To race horses and count coup," Gar said.

"You couldn't race horses and count coup as a brave," said Ashok. Gar rasped a laugh. Outside the tipi, horses nickered and snorted misty clouds, and in the flickering light of the campfires warriors chanted and sang to their spirits, their upper bodies and black braids slick with bear grease.

"Angry Badger, I know you will hunt well today. Someday you will be become a great warrior," Gar said.

"I am already a great warrior, and the Comanche will always know my name," Ashok said, holding the big steel knife that Gar cherished.

"It is sad there are so few Mexicans left to kill here in Texas," Gar often said. Led by Ashok, the old blind man liked to walk around and wave the knife and talk loudly about killing Mexicans. Tonight, remembering past hunts and battles, Gar grew expansive and Ashok encouraged it. After some time, Angry Badger walked behind Gar as the old man sat on the thick pallet of buffalo robes. He drove the heavy knife through the ancient war chief's ear with a pop like puncturing a ripe melon. He tugged and twisted. Blood and tissue spurted out of the wound, and Gar's mouth yawned open and closed. Ashok stomped Gar's head and the knife came loose, then he nudged the old man over on his side with his foot.

Ashok's hair had grown long, uncut since he was taken by the Comanche. Meticulously, he brushed his hair with porcupine quills and painted his scalp. He tied feathers in his hair, and tattoos of animal spirits ran down his arms. He opened the jars of paint in Gar's parfleche, and smeared red and black streaks down his face and chest. The big knife hung in his breech clout, and his dagger was in a pouch. He picked up Old Gar's battle-scarred lance, and looped his hair-pipe breastplate around his neck.

Ashok peered out of the lodge as the sun appeared over the horizon. Yapping dogs broke the silence as older children brought heavy bags of water from the nearby stream and the younger ones hurried to gather dry buffalo dung for the sputtering fires. Blackened chunks of meat still hung above the fires, as did simmering pots of tripe.

All the braves were already gone on the hunt, along with several women to butcher and haul the meat. All except Ashok, who crouched in the rushes along the creek, watching Two Moons, wife of Blue Otter, as she removed her baby, born in the coldest of winter, from the rawhide cradleboard. Too Moons had shown kindness toward Ashok when he was first captured, three years ago. She first called him Angry Badger, and he had hoped one day to make her his wife. He had fought and worked his way into the tribe just for that purpose, but she had married Blue Otter.

Another woman helped Two Moons start a small fire, and he watched silently as they giggled and teased the baby, cleaning him with warm water and rubbing him with buffalo fat. As they wrapped soft moss around his bottom and pulled the warm animal skins around him they did not see Ashok coming up behind them. Afterward, Ashok walked down to the pony herd as they trotted in a circle, caught up in the excitement of the morning. Two boys, younger than ten, resentful that they could not hunt, rode at the edge of the herd and stared bitterly as he led his best horse away.

Grandmother Talking Bird was kneeling on a rug, singing to the hunting gods for good fortune when he looped the rumaal around her throat. A young boy walked behind the tipi and leapt on him, but Ashok killed him quickly with a stone club, then prowled through the camp until no one was left. Satisfied, he knocked the night's accumulation of ticks and scorpions out of the foul-smelling buffalo hair saddle, threw it on the pony and rode east.

The Patrol

"Hey, what's that?" said Devol, pointing toward the horizon. Out of boredom, Devol had joined the major on a patrol along the river. The afternoon sun was hot, and the only life had been the circling vultures in the sun. "Who's that coming? They're moving."

"Single rider, can't tell what or who."

The rider pushed the horse hard, leaning low and kicking up dust. The Major pulled out his spy glass and searched the prairie for pursuers but saw no one.

"Comanche of some sort," said the major.

"What do you mean, some sort?" asked Devol.

"Hair's right. Clothes right. Paint's right. Skins awful dark, and he's too damn big."

The yipping Comanche slid his lathered pinto to a stop twenty yards away, then pranced the horse in tight circles, holding a feathered lance high. The Major waved his arm for his men to lower their rifles. Coming closer, Ashok pulled a maroon and black slimy mess from a beaded leather pouch. He brushed sand away, then smashed it into his mouth, chewing loudly as plum jelly oozed through his fingers and dripped down his chin.

"What do you have there?" the major pointed, making an eating gesture.

"¿Quieres un poco delicioso hígado?" said the boy, extending his arm.

"He wants to know if we want some delicious liver," said the Major. Devol shook his head.

"Hígado es muy bueno. Hígado de un niño pequeño hace a uno fuerte."

"What?" said Devol. "Spanish?"

"Yes. Liver. Liver is very good. The liver of a young boy makes one strong," the Major said.

"Good lord. Whose is it?" Devol asked.

"Some days I really regret my sinful ways," said Bliss.

"Where are you from?" asked the Major in Spanish.

"Hindustan. India."

"What in the hell?" said Devol as the Major and the rider conversed a while longer.

"Says he came here on a boat, kidnapped by Comanche three years ago, been biding his time. He claims to have killed the whole bunch of them this morning," said the Major. "Says he wants to work for the army. Says he wants to kill many Comanche and fucking Mexicans.".

"I speak English," Ashok said, in a sing-song voice, grinning grotesquely as flies buzzed around his bloody face. He showed open palms and pointed to the bag. They told him to continue. A squirrel sized ball of tangled, bloody long black hair emerged. The boy knelt on the ground, separating the pieces until he had more than a dozen clotted strips. "Prime Comanche scalps."

"Are you sure those are Comanche scalps?" Devol asked.

"Not completely, they could be Mexican, although the hairs pretty long," said the Major. "Does it really matter to you?"

"No, I suppose not, as long as he's not lifting wooly ones and cutting into my profits."

The patrol followed Ashok toward the river, and there was an hour of daylight left when they rode hard into the Comanche camp with pistols drawn, scattering the buzzards and coyotes that had been feasting on the bodies. Wisps of smoke still rose from cooking fires and ragged dogs snarled and stalked resentfully between the tipis. The Major emptied his pistol into the pack when they ventured too close, killing two, and after the others slunk away, the men walked through the camp at the ready.

"Major," shouted a soldier galloping back from the creek. "There's two Comanche women down there, and half a dozen kids, all killed, all scalped."

The hulking Indian boy looked bored, absently chewing on a strip of jerky while the Major hurried his troopers to the stream where they found the hacked-up bodies with loops of intestine and blood smeared in the wildflower patch. Ashok giggled when a soldier slipped and fell in the mess, and several retched in the weeds.

"Son," Devol grinned, with a quick image of Annie's nappy scalp hanging from a lodge pole, and her roasting liver dripping juice into a crackling campfire. "I'll pay you a hell of a lot more than the army can."

Chapter Five

Veracruz, Mexico

The sun shined brilliantly above the clear waters of the Gulf of Mexico as Pete Caballo sat in a small surfboat, one of a fleet of forty small boats rocking in the gentle waves a few hundred yards offshore. Each of the flat boats carried forty U.S soldiers or Marines, waiting nervously since dawn to assault the Collado Beach. His eyes moved anxiously between the beach in front of him, and three miles up the coastline at the huge fortress of Veracruz.

Pete, a free Black Seminole and scout who'd spent the past years with Jack Hays' Texas Rangers, had been on land for weeks. He told the Mexican soldiers that he was an escaped slave seeking freedom in Mexico and hated the Americanos every bit as much as they did. Once he had convinced them of his story, he had been able to get a close look at the fort's defenses. For the past few nights, he had guided 1st Lt. PGT Beauregard and a squad of engineers and Army scouts over the terrain as they searched for a plan of attack. They had reported back to Colonel Totten, Chief of Engineers, and Captain Robert Lee, Totten's right-hand man, that a landing southeast of Veracruz, at Collado Beach, would be a relatively easy one, and wouldn't leave the ships vulnerable to the daunting shore artillery.

Veracruz was the mightiest fortress in North America, with a garrison of 3,500 Mexican Regulars in its three forts. Over two hundred cannons mounted along its walls faced the water, enough to sink every ship in the American Navy ten times over. That strategy would ordinarily have been right. However, they were completely unprepared for Gen. Winfield Scott and his Engineering Corps' audacious and revolutionary idea for a beach landing. The United States military had never attempted a large beach assault before, so the General had personally designed a fleet of flat-bottomed assault boats just for this attack.

Now, Captain Lee rode in the first boat, immaculately groomed, with his square jaw and sculpted beard tilted high like he was posing for a portrait. Behind him, the Gulf of Mexico was filled with full-rigged battleships belching smoke from their booming cannons as they feinted for the city, bombarding the forts and pinning the defenders down. Lee looked exactly like a general should, and everyone knew the bright young officer, Gen. Scott's undisputed pet, would be a general sooner than later.

Pete smiled. He knew somewhere in the armada of thirty gunships and transports in the Gulf, his old friend, the imposing, six-foot-five, white-maned, General Scott was enjoying the spectacle, standing bare-headed on the deck of the Massachusetts urging his brave men on amid the shouts and cheers of adulation from the excited soldiers eager for action. Pete knew better than to assume anything would be this easy, but when the assault fleet was within 90 yards of the beach, signal flags ran up the mainmast of Scott's ship. When the bugles blew, Pete jumped into the waist-high surf with the others, yelling and laughing and trip-ping through the waves. Three hundred yards behind them, the brass band on the deck of the Potomac played "Yankee Doodle" and "The Star-Spangled Banner" as 10,000 men landed without a loss.

Cerro Gordo, April 18th, 1847

After the unopposed landing above Veracruz, the American army had lain siege to the city for twenty days before the garrison surrendered. Afterwards, Scott's force had faced little resistance as they marched toward Mexico City, but they'd been blocked for two weeks at the Devil's Jaws, the heavily fortified twin peaks of Cerro Gordo Mountain.

Santa Anna waited on the crest with 12,000 troops, and his artillery was trained on the only possible route of the outnumbered American column.

"The left is almost completely unguarded," said Lt. Beauregard, with Pete standing at his side. They had just returned from a night out scouting the sheer canyon walls around Cerro Gordo, and were under the tent of Captain Lee as the sun came up. "Santa Ana is convinced those cliffs are impossible to get over. I'm not so sure."

"Intriguing," said Captain Lee. "You seem certain, Pierre."

"It can be done," PGT Beauregard said. Beauregard detested being called Pierre. Pete knew it, and he knew Lee knew it, as well. "Those mules aren't going to be able to get up it. The men will need to pull our cannon up by hand, and in some places, pull themselves up by ropes. But, it can be done."

"Excellent," said Lee. "How many men can we get over in the cover of darkness?"

"Most of them, if we can get some pulleys set up quick enough," said Beauregard. "It's straight up, and as jagged as a porcupine, but it's fairly wide."

At the crack of dawn, Pete was in the first wild charge over the crest, smashing into the Mexicans with such force and fury that most of them threw their muskets over the cliff and their hands in the air. He surged forward with the Illinois Infantry as they plunged after the panicked Mexican survivors fleeing down the road below, so hot on his heels that General Santa Anna abandoned his carriage and fled across country riding a harness mule. The Americans let him go and swarmed into the deserted camps where they discovered the many treasures left behind, including $20,000 in gold and silver coin in the same chest with Santa Ana's ornately carved wooden leg.

Chapter Six

Bliss

Philadelphia, 1855

"Good to see you, Dr. Bliss," Mrs. Cabot said, with a long, gusty sigh, recumbent on her thousand-dollar chesterfield sofa.

"And you as well, Mrs. Cabot. Your eyes are bright, and your voice is exceptionally strong this morning," said Dr. Makepeace Bliss, although neither of those were exactly true. Nor remotely true. It was true, however, that if he never saw another cow, cowboy, cactus, bow-legged rube, slave, or goddamn red heathen, it would be too soon.

Mrs. Cabot's decades-long love affair with hypochondria had bloomed when she had come under the care of Dr. Bliss, upon a recommendation from her good friend Mme. Favreau. That he had taken time away from his church ministry to be her personal physician touched her deep in her soul. Finally, a doctor that wasn't a quack, that didn't insist on the frivolous nonsense that leaving her divan once in a while might help her constitution, nor suggest that there might be a better diet than wine and chocolate. With a doctor like this, that held her hand for hours and fluffed her pillows, and had honestly guessed she was 35, and not 55, her faith in the medical community was restored. He had quickly and accurately diagnosed every illness she'd known she had for years, and a few more, which no previous doctor had diagnosed. Some were so rare that Dr. Bliss said they had never been diagnosed before, period. But recently, to his dismay, and hers, after more than a year of excellent health, her condition had been declining. She hadn't noticed it was declining much more rapidly since Dr. Bliss's discovery of many thousands of dollars in her safe. After months of conniving to get inside it, he had finally seen the treasure, if only a glimpse. She had no family to speak of, not here in Philadelphia anyway. Her two sons, flush with cash, pampered, and enormously stupid, had gone on safari in Africa and had not been heard from again.

Bliss painstakingly checked her temperature, and peered down her throat. He slid his stethoscope to a dozen different places. He tapped her knees for a reflex. He twirled a sofa pillow and fought not to suffocate her. Weak as she was, however, Bliss was not a stout man. He brewed some tea loaded with goatweed, valerian, enough laudanum to sedate a team of mules, a minuscule drop of arsenic, and generous milk and sugar. She was snoring within a minute, and Bliss made his way through the elegant old mansion, mentally inventorying candlesticks, silverware, and paintings as he did every visit. He went through drawers and cabinets looking at jewelry, and wondered how many pieces would be missed. As her spiritual minister and medical doctor, he was frustrated and irritated, and a little hurt, that she would not trust him to see to her affairs. But, as yet, she had not. Also troubling, a couple traveling cheats and con artists he knew from his days in the French Quarter said police had been around. They were asking about the latest girl that had died in the blood-soaked bed in a rooming house. She was not a street waif after all, but the daughter of a congressman.

Bliss spent the two hours after Mrs. Cabot awoke sitting with her, reading aloud from a dog-eared book on Pacific islands, dreaming of perfect beaches and palm trees. Perhaps Hawaii or Tahiti, certainly nowhere cold. Far away from sallow skinned dowagers, and, no more fat-bellied New Orleans whores. He could taste the ocean air and feel the breezes as beautiful, bare-breasted, grass skirted Polynesian girls danced around him, cooling him with palm leaves. Soon.

Bliss's Church

Bishop Bliss walked softly through his magnificent new church, thinking this would not be an unpleasant way to live. Certainly, the finest church he'd ever had. His upper crust parishioners often told him how fortuitous it was that he had become available, from his Canadian faith-healing ministry, exactly when their pastor had surfaced in the Delaware River, brutally and mysteriously murdered and robbed. That the publication of the open pulpiteer position had inadvertently never gone out to other ministries could only be seen as the hand of God.

The church's dimwitted deacon, Mr. Bosley, hummed "Rock of Ages" and busied himself tidying the pulpit as Bliss checked the time and hoped Fat Fanny Ginn and Jasper would get here soon, and that they would be reasonably sober. He couldn't use her in the same town often, but before Fanny had gone west with an evangelical revivalist, an organist, and a lively line of Venezuelan dancehall girls, she had tripled his tithes. On the other hand, at his last church, it didn't help much when paraplegic Fat Fanny fell out of her wheelchair dead drunk. Even less so, when she sprang to her feet and punched the startled blind man behind her who had been patiently expecting the touch of Jesus's healing grace instead.

Looking out the window, Bliss was chagrined to see Fanny and Jasper talking to five burly Philadelphia detectives half way down the block. They were bobbing their heads, pointing across the street at his church. Saving their own hides, he thought with a disappointed sigh. But, he understood, and he would have done the same. They all would. But it still stung. One of the policemen wrote in a small journal as they walked briskly up the street, and Bliss hurried down the aisle and up the wide oak staircase, shouting at the church's deacon.

"Bosley, there are men coming. I don't believe they are who they claim to be. They are Pilate's Romans. They are fornicators and whoremongers. And heretics and blasphemers most of all. They have ill will toward the church," Bliss prattled. "And God and baby Jesus himself. Don't allow them in just yet. Just tell them to stay right here. Make sure they stay right here."

He knew his large and completely devoted assistant would gain him a few minutes. Bliss sprinted up the stairs and pulled all his cash and jewelry from the safe, then stepped to the balcony rail. Bosley was arguing with the uniformed men through the crack in the door.

"Yes, gentlemen, be right down," he beamed warmly but the policemen muscled their way inside and slammed Bosley to the floor, compelling him to quote Psalm 23.4 as he pulled a tangle of them down with him.

"Rev. Bliss...or Dr. Bliss, is it? Bishop now?" shouted the lone policeman still standing, ignoring the demons wrestling at his feet.

"Yes, yes, I'm just out of the bathtub," Bliss shouted, ignoring Bosley grappling with four policemen, backing away, "Give me just a moment. Can you tell me what this is about?"

"We need to talk to you about a dead girl in a boarding house off Revere Street. And, as a matter of fact, your name has come up in a couple of mysterious passings, Mrs. Stansfield from Washington Street as well. In fact, we have quite a number of things we want to talk to you about."

They knew much more than he thought. He ran down the hallway pulling chimneys off all the lamps. He scattered newspapers and torn hymnals on the floor, splashing lamp oil over the carpet and curtains. He touched a match to the sopping curtains and a ball of flame roared down the hallway as the shouting policemen thudded up the stairs. The angry voices bellowed, and glass shattered as he ducked out the servants' entrance. Halfway down the alley with no one behind him, he thought wistfully about Mrs. Cabot's piles of money as he trotted to the docks.

Chapter Seven

Cawnpore, India

Captain Lyman Dunnock scanned the desert from behind thick walls of sandbags, watching for the big trouble that was coming for them from across the plain. In the fifteen years since the Kabul massacre, Lyman had grown into a huge man, 6'4" with skillet sized hands and shoulders wide as an ox yoke. His curly chestnut hair was streaked with silver, and his sharply creased, square jawed face was permanently and deeply bronzed. A life of hacking through steaming jungles, climbing hostile mountains, crossing deserts and surviving a hundred fist fights and gun battles had chiseled him.

June 1857 was hot, even for Cawnpore, and the sun broiled the British East India Company garrison, which sat in the plain of the mighty Ganges River. During the wet season, the river was a mile wide here, at the critical junction of the Grand Trunk Road and the Punjab, Sindh and Oudh roads. Now, as the sun blazed down day after day, with no relief, the river thickened with silt and was as sluggish as the wandering Brahmin cattle.

Nine hundred civilians, three hundred British soldiers and officers, and four regiments of native troops were housed in a cantonment outside the city. Rows of neat bungalows and well-tended flower gardens sprawled over six miles of parade grounds amongst the complex of barracks, houses, schools, and East India Company offices. Long lines of tents covered half the acreage, and there were many abundant, colorful orchards of peaches, mangoes, oranges and limes. At tranquil settings like this all across India, the Native Army was rebelling against their British masters. The Indian regiments of Cawnpore had not revolted, yet, but Lyman expected it any day.

Lt. Cox Drunk Arrested, June 2nd, 1857

"What in God's name?"

Lyman bolted up in his chair. A dozen fists hammered his front door, and urgent voices called his name. It was pitch black out his windows and his mouth tasted of dried plum brandy. His watch said 2 AM. The door swung open, and breathless tommies filled his room while his punka walla quietly lit the lamps and returned to pulling the cords of the ceiling fan over his bed.

"Lt. Cox, sir," said the nearest soldier. "He shot at a Yappy. Just missed, and then wanted to fight us that took him to jail."

"He's on the peg?" asked Lyman.

"He is. Yes, sir."

"Ferociously drunk, I'm assuming?"

"Can't see the holes in a ladder may be understating it."

"Good grief," said Lyman, rubbing a wet cloth over his face. "What of the natives?"

"Quite perturbed. The red ass would be accurate. It tends to reinforce the idea that some chicanery awaits them."

"I'm here to see Lt. Cox," Lyman said ten minutes later at the jail gate, but the two Indian guards took great pains to ignore him. After twenty minutes, he'd had enough, and finally snarled through the heavy barred gate. "You make me wait one second longer and I'll slice you balls to brain cells."

"No, no, sahib," said the smaller one, signaling someone to tug the cables. The yappy bent low and waved Lyman through the creaking gate with a slow sweep of his arm. "He take you down now. My apologies. Sahib Dunnock important busy man. This way please. Very much thank you."

The big mute shot Lyman a look of loathing before leading him down two flights of stone stairs. Howls and curses came from the pitch-black cells as Lyman walked toward Gen. Wheeler, who stood under a torch at the end of the corridor.

"Try to get some sleep, lad. We'll have you out of here before breakfast," Wheeler said to Lt. Cox who was barely visible in the dark cell.

"In the morning, sir?" Lyman said.

"Well, certainly, just as we would do for you. I've pulled your drunken ass out of jail more than once, don't forget," said the short, silver haired general. "This is merely an accident and horseplay. Everyone is a little tense at the moment, a bit jumpy. Cox is the son of a knighted general, after all."

"You do understand, don't you, there are revolts happening all over this country, because they think we have ill will toward them?"

"Pish posh, of course I know, Captain," said Wheeler. "You're honestly concerned?"

"I certainly am, when they are twenty times, many more than that, our number. And we trained them all."

"Don't be a goose. A few days of strutting around like generals and shooting their bang boom guns will pacify them. Then they will happily submit again, just like a good dog that got off the chain," said Wheeler. "Pack animals. They're lost without the nurturance of a master. We should have a parade once they wear themselves out. Some shiny gee gaws for their wives perhaps."

Lyman squeezed his forehead until his hand lost feeling.

"Just please, keep him a day or two. This will be held against us. One more insult for Nana Sahib to recruit with."

"Nana Sahib is an honorable man," said Wheeler.

"You're not listening to the right people, General," Lyman said. "Nana Sahib plans to murder us."

"Let him play out his little melodrama. He assured me his loyalty and cooperation."

June 3rd

"Dunnock Sahib," shouted an Indian boy of ten racing across the dusty grounds, "Captain Thomson say hurry come. Say, don't arse about."

"Is that right?" laughed Lyman. "The Captain's a good one to lecture on another's arsing about. But lead the way."

"G'morning, Mowbray," said Lyman, entering the headquarters building. "Something new?"

"Some traders came in this morning," said Thomson, his chest-length beard swaying like an autumn willow as he spoke. "Nana Sahib is only a day or two out. The mutineers are emptying treasuries and armories as they cross country. Thousands of these damned religious malcontents are joining daily. Because their feelings were hurt. Someone offended their cow, for the sake of Mary."

"I need no instruction on the Nana," said Lyman. "He's promising land and wealth to any that join him. At this rate, he'll soon have all of India. His cobra-like charisma is impressive, and it's not just the bleeding Hindus that he has mesmerized. Wheeler is so beguiled with the Nana they need to be chaperoned. Almost a father figure since the Nana was a tot, or so they say. Old Hugh's lost all reason. Like a mooning school boy in spring."

"We don't have much time if we're going to make a break," said Thomson. "Delhi, Agra and Lucknow have fallen. How many of the black hearted ingrates do you suppose there are across the way now?"

"Between five and ten thousand, much closer to ten I believe," said Lyman. "Do we even have three hundred, that can stand?"

"If we do, it's not much more than that," said Mowbray.

"Well, if I know my stout-hearted tommies, the cow worshippers will need more men," said Lyman.

Nana Sahib History

Nana Sahib, born Nana Govind Dhondu Pant, was enraged. He had stayed enraged for six years, ever since the British East India Company had abruptly cut off his generous flow of money. Nana's father, Baji Rao II, deceased Peshwa of the Maratha Confederacy, had controlled vast portions of India during Nana's youth. However, in 1818 the British East India Tea Company's powerful army vanquished Rao and outlawed the Peshwa system of self-government. They installed their own government, and paid Rao II a lavish yearly pension for life. The bribery to Baji Rao gave the Company complete freedom to loot and plunder, always with the heavy hand of the world's mightiest army and Britain's powerful navy hulking in the shadows. The bribes had made Rao II one of the country's richest men, and at his adopted father's death, Nana, his assumed heir, expected the same arrangement. An apt observer, he was not at all opposed to bribery, from any source, but he was shoved aside. In a glaring insult, the British claimed that since Nana had been adopted, and was not a blood heir, he would not get the stipend. And, it was more than just personal insult and personal theft. Across the continent, the British East India Company was claiming large portions of princely lands through The Doctrine of Lapse, a fraudulent annexation policy that annulled Indian sovereignty. Nana Sahib lobbied hard on his own behalf. He sent an envoy, Azimullah Khan, to London, to petition the Queen directly, but to no avail. Every day since this affront, Nana had seethed with visions of dead Englishmen. As always, the Europeans were boorish and impertinent, arrogant and blind. As they abused the natives and did as they pleased, Nana dreamed of ways the English would pay for these insults, these and many others, for a very long time.

A few months ago, the bumbling British themselves had given Nana the perfect cause to exploit. The East India Company Army had swollen to 311,000 native sepoys and sowars, commanded by 40,000 European soldiers and officers, and the army, almost entirely Hindu, thought their British handlers were trying to corrupt their souls. At every British garrison in India, the Indian soldiers had been issued new Enfield rifles, which came with an unfamiliar type of ammunition, the minie ball and gun powder enclosed in a greased paper cartridge. Loading the muzzle required the paper be ripped open with the shooter's teeth and the bullet rammed down the barrel. Rumors flamed through the Hindu units that the grease was made from beef tallow, the taste of which would make the soldiers live in low caste anguish for eternity. In Meerut, on May 9th, eighty-five Cavalry sowars refused to use the newly issued cartridges. They were charged with mutiny and arrested immediately. Court was immediately convened, and they were sentenced to life imprisonment on the spot. In response to the Native Indian soldiers being led away in shackles, hundreds of their enraged comrades stormed the town and freed them. When British officers tried to control the mob, they were shot down, along with fifty British men, women and children, and the city was torched.

Nana and other princes fed fuel to the rumor of damnation, and the sepoys fled their forts. The deserters were warmly welcomed, and promised a glorious victory over the British and an end to the century of enslavement. The East India Company had bullied India since their one-sided tea and spice trade beginnings in India in 1600, but it was their overwhelming victory over Sikh Nationalists at the Battle of Plassey on June 23rd, 1757, that had given the Company unchecked economic and military tyranny over the country. The One-Hundred-Year anniversary of the Battle loomed, and with it came the popular prophecy of a great Indian victory of their British tormentors. The time to strike had arrived.

June 4th

Lyman and Mowbray left the cantonment before dawn and crept to a hilltop overlooking the enemy's tent city, which teemed with thousands of jubilant deserters working themselves into a frenzy. In late afternoon, messengers galloped in from the desert, and soon banging drums, gunfire and blaring trumpets announced Nana's arrival. As his opulent palanquin was carried through the mass of cheering rebels, Nana Sahib reclined on satin pillows behind layers of gossamer veils and gauzy curtains glistening with a spray of gleaming rubies, green emeralds, and sunbursts of yellow topaz. Behind him, his trusted friends since child-hood, Azimullah Khan and Tatya Tope, rode on sleek, mane-tossing, Arabian stallions. The three notorious friends were rarely separated. Nana's war minister, Tatya Tope, was cruel, and his European educated Prime Minister Azimullah Khan was cunning and scheming.

"The Nana and his two boyhood chums," said Mowbray. "Lord help us."

"I'd trust a pit of vipers before I would trust those three," said Lyman. "But I sure wish John Company had paid the Nana his daddy's pension. It seems it would have been a bargain."

Nana tired of his exalting parade after an hour, and his bearers stopped before an immense tent and laid him down as gently as an egg. His painted fingernails curled around the shimmering veils of his chair as he emerged with an actor's nonchalance and a dozen umbrellas leapt forward to protect his perfectly shaved head from the sun. His lips were bright red, his eyebrows were plucked, a long thin moustache curled around his cheeks, and thick loops of pearl fell across his barrel chest.

"Those more men you said the Nana would need to whip our stout-hearted tommies?"

"Yeah?"

"It looks like they got 'em, our four regiments of them. My count now is 10,000 for them, and 300 for us."

"Well, as long as it's a fair fight," said Lyman.

June 5th

On June 5th, 1857, at 1:30am, Nana Sahib entered the British armory magazine with his contingent. The soldiers of the 53rd Native Infantry who were guarding the thousands of rifles and tons of ammunition assumed Nana Sahib, who had publicly declared his loyalty to the British, had come to guard the magazine. The guards were surprised and easily overwhelmed, and forced to watch helplessly as a train of elephants was required to carry away all the booty. After seizing the arsenal, a signal gun fired, and the Cawnpore rebellion exploded in the night. Amid the chaos, the rebels smashed into the provision go-downs and plundered them, then torched the barracks and most of British Cawnpore. Only a desperate stand by the Brits stopped a stampede of rioters at the entrenchment gates. The following morning, Wheeler called his exhausted officers into the briefing room.

"Quiet, quiet," Wheeler shouted. "There is no need for such alarm. Last night was a celebration that got a little out of hand, a bit too much to drink, getting out some pent-up frustration. Confusion and lack of communication. Nothing more, and it is to be treated as such. Inside the entrenchment, we need not fear any harm from Nana Sahib. He's still understandably upset about his stipend, but that had nothing to do with last night. I told him I would try to intervene on his behalf, on his financial situation, and that calmed any resentment he was feeling. He assured me once again of his fidelity."

"He stole most of our rifles and ammunition, and we're just supposed to sit here?" shouted a captain in the back.

"I have met with Nana, and he knows the danger such incidents can cause. Some of the natives were clearly out of control," said Wheeler. "So, he secured the weapons until things settle down. You'll see the wisdom in all this, when it's over peacefully in a very few days."

"On what evidence? You're gambling your intuition with all these people's lives, over an empty promise of Nana's stipend?" shouted Mowbray.

"I've known him since he was a child. His father and I were close friends," said Wheeler. "I've been in India for fifty years. I have some experience in this area. I think I would know if treachery was afoot."

"I rather doubt he would announce his plan to murder us over tea and a cookie," said Mowbray. "Though apparently, you'd ignore it if he did."

"Remember your rank, all of you. Nana Sahib has promised his loyalty, no more arguing," snapped Wheeler. "He will provide five thousand loyal men if the need should arise."

"Just a few days ago, his men were our men. The ones that deserted us are now his soldiers, but loyal to us? With our own rifles and powder and lead? Good God, have you gone completely round the bend?" shouted Lyman.

"This is no time to be insolent!" snapped Wheeler.

"On that we agree," said Lyman, staring into the eyes of a crazy man. "I should have been insolent long before now."

The Nana's Note

"Captain Dunnock, somebody coming!" shouted a sentry in the trenches later that afternoon.

"Who is it?"

"Don't know. Three riders carrying a white flag. Yappies, by the look."

Lyman took two men and rode out to meet the messengers. His salute was ignored, and one of the rebels handed him an envelope. All three smirked as Lyman read the contents.

"Very well, I'll inform the general," said Lyman, returning the letter to the envelope. The men stared silently for a few seconds, then galloped back to their camp.

"What does it say, Captain?"

"Nana Sahib, Peshwa of the Maratha Confederacy, expresses his condolences that he must attack his great friend Gen. Hugh Wheeler in the morning. He expects to arrive around ten. He sends the note as a courtesy, and hopes this will not prove to be an impediment to their long and rewarding friendship."

"You can't be serious," said the man beside him.

"Sadly, I am," said Lyman. "As they are, apparently."

"Thinks mighty highly of himself, don't he?"

"He says handing over our remaining weapons would keep this situation civilized, and any ugliness avoided."

"If nothing else," said an old sergeant, "We British have taught these pea-eatin' heathens civility and proper manners."

"That gives me solace," said Lyman. "I suppose I better let the general know his old and trusted friend will be coming by for tea tomorrow, and to put on a pot."

June 6th

By 10:00am, the temperature in the entrenchment had risen to over a hundred degrees for the seventh day in a row with not a drop of rain. Across the sand, the rebel sepoys, still in their British uniforms, swaggered like it was a dress parade as they moved into formation and started across the field. Whistles blew, and the Sowar cavalry broke into a trot toward the entrenchment and the waiting tommies.

"Fire!" Lyman screamed, when the rebels were almost upon them and the British rifles roared. Screams of men and beast came through the swirling gun smoke and dust cloud, but the gaping line of rebels was still

74

coming, stepping around mangled bodies and thrashing horses. The stubborn rebels thundered forward, but more British volleys tore through them until, leaderless and missing half their number, they turned and fled.

Every day after that, with little effect either way, the Indians made dispirited charges as hundreds of dead rebels swelled and ripened under the broiling sun. Sluggish, overheated breezes filled with the stench and settled on the trench and festered. Buzzards swarmed over the cadavers, gorging themselves until they waddled like ducks between the bodies, too heavy to leave the ground and too stupid to stop eating. There was no escaping any of it, anytime, not during the day and not in the moonlight, when packs of cackling hyenas and howling wolves slunk through the carnage. The sharp cracks of their powerful jaws crushing the bones of dead soldiers carried far across the flat prairie.

Prema in Trench, June 15th

"Well, old friend, if you ask me, it looks like it's time for the Queen's wedding night advice for nervous brides," said Mowbray. "I don't see much way out of this one."

"What would that advice be?" asked Lyman.

"If the fucking's inevitable," laughed Mowbray. "Close your eyes and think of England."

"Is that right?"

"For centuries, they say. I believe that is the standard instruction given to Royal brides," said Mowbray. "As the story goes, I suppose."

"Perhaps so," said Lyman.

"If you've seen Victoria up close, you might think that was advice for the groom," said a young woman's voice behind Mowbray, who spun around quickly at the tap on his shoulder.

"Oh, Mrs. Dunnock, excuse my language. I did not know you was behind me," he stammered, snapping to attention.

"Oh, my, Mowbray, is that a blush I see behind that bronze skin and red thistle-bush?" Prema said. "Not to worry, Captain Thomson, as an army wife I've heard the word a time or two. In all senses. And its advice is something I follow as a matter of practice, anyway. Those English Queens know their way around a boudoir."

"My agony and embarrassment amuses her," said Lyman, as Prema stretched up on her tip-toes and smooched him long and loud on his cheek, giggling all the while.

"Your agony and embarrassment amuses me," said Mowbray.

"I can see that," said Lyman.

Prema pulled the oilcloth off the light carbine Lyman had found for her. She had been beside them for every charge, and when it was over, sprinted back to the collapsed hospital and the latest wounded. There wasn't much to sprint back to. The barracks being used as a hospital had a partial roof and three teetering half-walls. Everything was blackened by cannonballs and fire, and the long, ashy floor was thick with splinters and dust. There was no medicine, no clean bandages, and little clean water. Sweat-soaked patients were crammed inches apart on the floor, wrapped in filthy, blood-crusted strips of cloth. The nurses inevitably fell, too, and sniper bullets dropped anybody that moved. Every day the bodies piled higher, and once it was dark, the tommies hauled the day's dead to a dry well, and dropped them in.

"I'd offer you some tea, but our cupboards are embarrassingly light at the moment," said Mowbray.

"Think nothing of it. I've heard an army travels on its stomach and I just happen to have a few pieces of delicious chupatti here," Prema said, of the flavorless flatbread. "I'll bet that's a treat you weren't expecting when you awoke this morning. Am I right?"

"I doubt I've had, nay, even heard of, a finer spread," said Mowbray. "Your husband and I were just speaking on that earlier, your culinary skill. This may be the best chupatti I've ever had. Tell me, what's in it?"

"Water. Flour," said Prema. "A good bit of sand, I would imagine."

"It puts spotted dick, sheep's trotters or a pickled whelk to shame," said Mowbray. "Jellied eels, even. Fine dining."

"I'm sure there's a compliment in there, somewhere," she smiled.

"Simple yet delicious. Just wonderful. It must be au de camel in the flour," said Mowbray, as Prema chuckled and rolled her eyes. "Should we get out of here alive, perhaps you'll open a cafe. In London, maybe."

"You're hopeless," she said.

"Well, after this glorious repast, the Bow Wow Mutton on tonight's blackboard will surely be a disappointment," said Mowbray.

"A feast awaits us. An old bull wandered inside the trench last night," said Lyman. "He's been tenderizing in the flesh-pots since. I'm sure that would disturb the natives, if they knew, but I get the sense they're not happy with us as things stand now."

Lyman sopped the sweat from his face with a foul rag, and his parched tongue rattled and caught on the scabby, bleeding splits in his mouth. In front of the trenches, wild dogs and hyenas growled and tugged at the rotting sepoys, scattering the carrion birds. Closer to him, scorpions and red ants and horrifying desert spiders waged war as lizards skittered across the golden sand.

The earth had baked to a crust, and sledgehammers and railroad spikes were the only tools that could crack it. Around him, young tommies labored to the point of collapse without complaint, digging their trenches wider and deeper. The water situation was even worse than the food shortage. There was one working well inside the cantonment, but the Bengal snipers had shot away the brickwork, tackle and a dozen men with buckets. Water could only be pulled up in the middle of the night, in buckets from seventy feet below, hand over hand, and even in the dark the men had to duck bullets.

"How are you holding up?" Lyman said, squatting next to an old sergeant.

"Fine, sir," said the man. "I can handle the rest, sir, but this godawful stench."

"This is a fine fix, wouldn't you say?" said Lyman. "I had the opportunity several times to get transferred to another post, one without cannibals, infidels, and dog eating celestials. People that don't burn a dead man's wife alive. I sure wish I'd taken it."

"I'm with you, sir," said the man, brewing meager tea over a small fire. "I'm bloody tired of these simple-minded heretics across the way, them and their black Jesus arts. But, heathens is heathens. Let 'em be heathens. They ain't hurting nobody but Christ, and he's not one to hold a grudge, from my understanding."

"The heathens really go to hell if they get that cow fat on their mouth?" said a young soldier.

"There's some that believes it," said the old-timer. "I figure they have it bad enough just being heathens. But be assured, I've no problem getting as many to their final bovine paradise as I can, in my own fashion. Much less piously, I'd expect."

Lyman heard footsteps coming fast, and he looked up just as Mowbray flopped into the trench.

"I bring good news," grinned Mowbray. "Would a section of cannon help you out?"

"A section of cannon? I'd kiss you on the mouth if I didn't find you so repugnant," Lyman laughed. "What the devil are you talking about?"

"There's an old warehouse back there that collapsed years ago, and no one has given it a thought since," said Thomson. "All this shelling shook some debris loose, so we decided to explore. Imagine my surprise!"

"Shabash, you debauched old goat, Shabash, indeed," sang Lyman. "Where the hell are they?"

"Still buried, or mostly so. I think it best to position them after dark. I want to see the surprise on the Hindus faces when they are six inches from the muzzle, thinking they're walking in the bleeding park."

"Brilliant," said Lyman. "Maybe we can hang on until help arrives after all."

"This should help anyway. There is a good stock of balls, and enough canister shot to last a month of hard fighting," said Mowbray. "The ammunition is three pounders, and the cannon are nine pounders. We won't have much range but if they charge us, that grape shot will clear the field. We'll blow them to holy cow heaven by the wagon load."

June 23rd Final Charge

The 2nd Bengal Cavalry, once the cream of the East India Company regiments, carried themselves with élan as they trotted proudly through the ranks and fluttering flags. Horns blared, drums rippled merrily, and the hum of nervous warriors preparing for battle reached the British trench. A thousand white shako hats jutted above the shimmering heat wave across the prairie as deep battle lines of red jacketed sepoys formed up for the attack.

"Poor lads," said Mowbray. "They have no idea we found these old guns."

"Personally, I like surprises," said Lyman. Beside him, young soldiers vomited from sunstroke, too weak to walk, unable to sweat because they had no water. But he knew they would stand and fight. "Let's hope this is a good one."

"Well, I'm going to enjoy it. I doubt those gents will, but I will, re-gardless," said Captain Thomson, as the rebel soldiers started across the field.

"Probably time to let them know then, wouldn't you think?" asked Lyman, watching the rebels approach.

"Another hundred yards," said Mowbray.

"At your will, Captain."

When the sepoys broke into a trot, Mowbray counted to three, then bellowed the order to fire. The five cannons blasted a thousand rusty nails, jagged scrap-iron, and red-hot musket balls through the rebels. A wall of cotton bales, three or four sepoys crouching behind each, lum-bered across the field. When the glowing-hot metal hit the bales, the cotton burst into walls of flame, blowing back into the rebels and setting them alight. The terror-stricken, burning men crashed into the men behind them, and the flames leapt from bale to bale and man to man. The entire field was covered in fire as a hundred flame-covered men ran and rolled in every direction, their cartridge boxes exploding and killing dozens more.

"Again! All of them!" Mowbray screamed. His cannoneers blasted another volley into the rebels, and a mass of them disappeared into bloody bits or caught fire. Crazed cavalry horses with manes and tails blazing galloped wildly through the tumult, dragging burning cavalry-men stuck in the stirrups. Another blast cleared the field of any strag-glers, sending the sepoys fleeing in terror.

"Shabash! That was stupendous," said Lyman, surveying the death and destruction.

"Like I said, Ala Kazaam. Poof. They all disappeared," said Mow-bray.

Satichaura Ghat
June 27th

Eventually, Wheeler had no choice but to surrender his starving force. Three days later, six hundred filthy, defeated and sick survivors left the cantonment under a white flag, bound for waiting boats at the Satichaura Ghat, a small Hindu Temple used for ritual burials on the bank of the Ganges.

"Nana has promised flour, and all the sheep and goats we'll need for the trip," said Mowbray, riding beside Lyman as the caravan staggered down the palm-tree lined road, through a gauntlet of cursing rebels that spat and threatened with bayonets.

"Ain't it just like him to think of romance at a time like this? A mighty fine gesture," said Lyman. "But I believe my dance card is full."

"Sahib, Dunnock, sahib, mem-sahib, you not so powerful now, are you fucker?" a rebel jeered from the trees. The sepoy, cowardly before the mutiny, rushed Lyman with his bayonet, jabbing first his leg and then his horse.

"If you think I won't kill you, try that again," Lyman said. "I've nothing to lose."

"Ah, the toothless tiger roars," he taunted as another sepoy charged Prema, but stopped short and only spat on her leg and glared.

"You frighten no one. No one cares. Clean my boots, toothless tiger, lick them clean," the man snarled until Lyman's boot caught him under the chin and he dropped like a sack of wet sand. The slumbering man's friends dragged him away when Lyman unholstered his pistol, but the road was still filled with gleeful tormentors throwing rocks and rotten fruit. A stone cracked Lyman in the side of the head, stunning him and he slumped forward.

"Are you all right?" asked Prema.

"I'm all right. Nice knot already. Just keep going."

"You're bleeding."

"I know, don't worry about it. We need to get in the boats before these savages tear us apart," he said, but doubted the outcome would be different. They rode on, ignoring the taunting rebels as best they could. A few feet from Lyman, Prema's father rode shriveled and slumped in a cart. He was nearly 80, barely 90 pounds, and mostly blind. He couldn't lift a soup spoon. He would be dead within days, one way or the other, but she refused to leave him.

"Jesus, Mary and Joseph, the river's near dry," said Lyman, as they passed the last cluster of trees. His heart sank. At the Ghat, the mighty Ganges no longer flowed freely over the bottom steps. The temple stood alone, cluttered and water worn. In the scorching Cawnpore summer, the river had shriveled a half-mile from its normal shore, and the lifeless, silt-filled brown water was hundreds of yards away. Even the air was dead. The ritual burials at Satichaura Ghat were so frequent that the incense of death and flowers and perfume never left. The mud and drooping weeds of the exposed river bottom was littered with rotting riverbed creatures and tatters of candles, bells, bangles, baubles and oil lamps from the skeletal funeral pyres that didn't float and fires that didn't burn. Everything was covered with fishbones. Scattered human rib cages, leg bones, arm bones, even muddy, weed shrouded corpses were within reach. Skulking pariah dogs watched nearby, yelping and running away when hit with a rock, but they never ran far, and their eyes never left the coming disaster.

A ragged fleet of fishing boats waited for them at the water's edge, and the first few boats were boarded without incident. The British soldiers helped the weakest and wounded into the boats as the Indian boatmen watched, fidgeting nervously. Some stared with a hatred that would never have been seen just a few weeks ago, and Lyman realized the pilots were quietly slipping over the side and wading toward dry ground.

Smoke and flames burst from the dry, thatch roofs of first one boat and then another where the fleeing boatmen had hidden smoldering red coals. Lyman leapt into the nearest boat and hurled the burning straw into the water, then waded from boat to boat putting out fires. Other tommies furiously pushed the blackened boats into the current, but they snagged on the shallow river bottom and the logjam worsened every second. He heard a roar, and looked up just as rifle fire from both banks raked the boats, killing dozens. Mothers with blazing hair and blazing clothes threw their children overboard, and then waded through the water, searching, screaming and wild eyed.

Through the smoke, Lyman spied Tatya Tope standing on the flat roof of the temple, his arm high above his head, grinning like a demon. Delighted with the suffering and carnage before him, he slashed his hand down with a flourish. Trumpets blasted, and another rifle volley ripped into the British wading through the water. Lyman froze, horrified, as hundreds of mounted sowars, veteran Indian cavalrymen, burst out of the trees and galloped into the water, their slashing swords taking the heads of those who moved too slow. Hundreds of shrieking sepoys splashed through the water behind them, finishing off the wounded with their bayonets. Death struggles raged between the boats, and under relentless fire from the banks and bridge the tommies strained to free the clogged boats. Lyman dove under the water and raised up just enough to peer over the floating debris in the red-tinged water. Pink geysers squirted into the air as whizzing bullets smacked the layer of trapped bodies that bobbed up around him.

Prema stood twenty feet away, waist deep in the river, helping a soldier lift her father into a boat. She turned to Lyman and gave a sad smile before the smoke covered her. The gray cloud shifted as a dozen rebels swarmed over the boat, clubbing and bayoneting the wounded before hurling them over the side. Lyman floundered toward her, but his boots filled with sand, and his legs, denied water for weeks, cramped with a fury that ripped a scream from his throat. As he crumpled, he saw a rifle butt coming at his head and everything went black.

Chapter Eight

Trading Post, Kansas

"Titus," Ruth yelled. The Kansas sun was burning hot when Titus dropped his hands from his sun-bleached plow handles and wiped a damp, gritty handkerchief across his brow. Patting his old mule on the rump, he stepped around her to see what his wife was fretting about as she shouted again. "Come on to the house. There's men coming. I don't like the looks of them."

"It's just Charles Hamilton," said Titus. "All puffed up and red-faced, as usual. It's nothing to be concerned about."

"Those men all seem to be carrying guns," she said. "Please, come on inside."

"It's all right, Ruth, don't worry about it," said Titus, with more calm than he felt. Hamilton had at least 30 men with him, and they were all looking sour. He was fifty yards from his homestead cabin, and the riders could easily cut him off if he made a dash for it. Hamilton was a loudmouth pro-slaver out here on the Kansas-Missouri border, but when his bluster expired, he was just another rednecked farmer fighting birds and varmints.

The group rode slowly forward, and Titus didn't recognize many of the men with Hamilton. They were young and mean-eyed, and carrying more weapons and bandoleers of ammunition than they would need in a hundred years of frontier farming. They had a string of pack mules with all manner of bounty strapped on their backs, and only when the riders were upon him did Titus realize that ten of his neighbors were walking along with them. They looked unhappy and frightened, and his father was among them.

"How are ya, Titus," Hamilton smirked. "Getting them clods all busted up?"

"Apparently not all of them," said Titus, his eyes flying between Hamilton and his father. "What do you want Charles?"

"We've just been visiting your neighbors," said Hamilton. "We're taking a little stroll down to the Marais des Cygnes to have a little pow-wow about the unpleasant animosity that's gripped our community of late."

"Run, Titus! Run, Ruth! Get away, they mean to kill us!" Titus's father shouted before a rifle butt crashed into his skull and he flopped to the ground. Titus spun. Ruth was in the doorway with the baby in one arm, his rifle in the other. He glanced down the road and a band of women, old men and young teens was storming down the road toward them, armed and shouting. Two of Hamilton's men fired at their feet and they slowed.

"You coming Titus, or do I need to grab that squalling brat to get you to come along?" said Hamilton. "Last chance. Just come along nice, like. Ain't nothing going to happen to you, nor that pretty little gal, if you do."

Cincinnati, Ohio
February 12th, 1861

"My dear, it is positively arctic out here," the man beside Ardent Donegan said, his fleshy face bright red in the chill.

"Yes, Uncle Finn, I'm right here beside you," she said, sliding her mittened hand inside his elbow. She pulled her wool scarves tight against the frigid winds cutting across the crowded Cincinnati rail platform, and only her eyes showed as she waited for President Lincoln's train. "But it's probably not much colder than when you last made note of it 15 minutes ago. And it will likely be roughly the same 15 minutes from now, at your next expected grumble. And the next."

"Lord give me strength. I don't recall your mother, my dear sister, being quite so insufferable," said Finn O'Flannery, with exaggerated exasperation. "Though she may well have been when I wasn't around. You had to have gotten it somewhere. And you look like a bandit with you face covered like that."

"I love you, and that should be all you need," she said, going on tip-toes to kiss Uncle Finn on the cheek. When he smiled hugely, but looked away, she said, "I see you, silly man. Quit pretending to be such a grump."

The crowd of largely German heritage anticipated Lincoln's arrival with excitement. Lincoln was a friend of the German, and they had returned the affection at the ballot box. His decision to give an address here had pleased a good number of people. In the festive atmosphere, vendors strolled through the crowd selling black bread and pungent cheese and bottles of thick dark beer. Every thirty minutes, the band ran through a short program of rousing patriotic anthems and old German standards in their native tongue. They chugged the beer, not minding the weather, and roared with delight when Lincoln's train pulled in at three in the afternoon.

Mayor Bishop, trailing his long entourage, marched out of the warm depot onto the exposed platform, where Lincoln greeted him with an overplayed handshake and beaming smile. After an hour of open-air knuckle wrenching and backslapping, the President's carriage was driven away, followed by a company of Washington Dragoons, along a waving, smiling, meandering route to the Burnet House. The elegant hotel was the overnight lodging of Mr. Lincoln, and the permanent home of Uncle Finn, whose big red barouche and matched set of Morgans rolled close behind the president.

"Ardent, this is weather for penguins and polar bears," said Uncle Finn, shaking his ample head. "The sacrifices I make."

"Aw, thanks Uncle. You know there is no old penguin as handsome and wonderful as you are," she said, kissing him on the cheek again.

"My dear niece, those Dragoons may protect us from secessionists, copperheads, and fire eaters, and any manmade hazards, but they can't stop this freezing cold. I am completely miserable."

"I am sorry, Uncle Finn, really, I am," said Ardent, as they finally pulled up in front of the hotel. "But this is all so exciting, and I had no idea this procession would take two hours to get here from the depot. Nor that it would be this cold. I'll make you some hot cocoa when we get to your suite."

Once inside, Uncle Finn drank the cocoa and promptly retired for the day, leaving his assistant to escort Ardent as she watched Lincoln deliver his speech from a stage bolted outside his Burnet House window. The speech itself wasn't much; A pep talk for German immigrants more than anything, with a few minutes devoted to the preservation of the Union. He boasted of the power of American industry, especially German-American industry, and finished with some subdued references to abolition and the looming, nation-destroying civil war. The whole address was peppered with the sly jokes for which the President was known. When he'd finished, the crowd surged forward, and Ardent surged with it, almost giddy at her chance to meet the President. Lincoln thrilled her when he told her he hoped she could vote, and not just campaign, in the next election.

Ardent was still glowing when she left her bedroom in Uncle Finn's suite early the next morning. Not seeing him in his parlor, she stepped inside his office, and was surprised to see several men quickly stand as she entered.

"Well, hello, Uncle. I'm sorry, I didn't know you had guests," she said. She thought she saw them all exchange glances. Even a flicker of something on Finn's face, irritation and annoyance. That wasn't like him.

"Oh. Well. Yes. Just conducting a little urgent business. These gentlemen are early risers as you see," Uncle Finn said, once again flashing his big smile. "This is Mr. Albert Pike, Colonel John O'Mahony of the 69th New York Militia, Mr. Bickley, and I believe you have met Mr. Devol, who worked with your Uncle Sean at Bhean Milis."

"Yes. Hello, gentlemen," she said, forcing an icy smile to match theirs.

"Col. O'Mahoney is a countryman, our boy from the sod, from Cork, just down the road from my family home," beamed Finn, whose pats on the shoulder did not warm the officer's cold glare. "He and my old friend Thomas Meagher are planning an Irish Brigade, in case this ridiculous bloody-shirt waving brings about a war."

Bickley and Col. O'Mahony, fierce as the Irishman's glare was, were average in appearance, and Uncle Finn was a round mound of red curls, freckles, and nervous energy. Devol was a large man, well over 6 feet and powerful. But Pike, with his long greasy black hair plastered to his temples and untamed gray side whiskers, was easily over 300 pounds, likely closer to four, and was one of the most repulsive people she'd ever seen. He towered over the others, even Devol, and his heavy, pallid jowls sagged like a hound's. His irritation was clear. Devol stared at her but said nothing. She retreated confounded. As she did, she glanced at Uncle Finn's gleaming mahogany desk which filled half the room. Behind his gold pen and clock set were several excellent charcoal drawings spread across the desk blotter. The drawings were of various angles of ferocious double-headed eagles, with their powerful wings spread and long sharp talons extended.

"Oh, my. These are exceptionally well done," she said, lifting a few. "Such eye-catching designs. Majestic."

"Just some doodling," said Pike, his turkey-wattle neck quivering when he spoke. "Just doodling."

"Well, they are certainly good enough for a gallery," she said, as she backed out the door, closing it quietly. She hurried down the hallway, her mind grappling with this scenario. Until now, she had no idea Uncle Finn maintained any business ties in the South, leaving all that to Uncle Sean. Why would that fiend Devol be in her Uncle Finn's office? Devol was a slave trader. For a moment, her fury at her uncle nearly erupted, but she knew it wasn't his fault. To avoid trouble, she hadn't told him, or her Uncle Sean, of the incident several summers ago, when Devol had grabbed her and ripped her dress when she refused his advances. That experience had shaken her, the instant transformation from man to raging beast, his face as fiercely red as Satan. She knew in that genteel plantation society it was frowned upon to make accusations against one of the pillars of south. Although slave traders were vital for the system to continue, the traders themselves, rough, vulgar, swinish men usually, were not welcome around the supper table. But Devol was different. His speech was refined, he was as handsome as a stage actor, and his manners were flawless. He'd fought and won several duels. Even the largest plantation owners treated him with deference. And she hadn't mistaken the murderous glares from Pike and Col. O'Mahony. Distracted by the behavior of the men in the room, Ardent didn't see the handsome man coming fast around the corner. They collided with such force it knocked her flat on her rear end. Papers, notebooks and journals fluttered across the floor.

"I'm so sorry," she stammered. "I'm not usually so clumsy."

The man was silent, snatching at the papers. An angry storm pulsed under a calm face, black eyes so fierce they made her pause. He coughed loudly several times, covering his face with a handkerchief when he lifted her smoothly to her feet with no apology. He was not large, but his powerful grip and strength were deceptive. And impressive. She looked up just as Uncle Finn stepped out his door.

"Who are you? What's going on here? Have you harmed my niece, you lout?" shouted Uncle Finn, his face suddenly pale and drawn. The man stared at Uncle Finn for a split second, then rushed away down the hall and ducked into the stairwell. His wavy black hair curled over his collar, and in the brief encounter, she'd noted his near feminine beauty and lean, athletic physique. He had the graceful stride of a ballet dancer.

"Ardent, are you all right? Have you been injured?" Finn said.

"No, I'm fine. That man just came around that corner so quickly," she said, stretching and rubbing her neck.

"Why don't you come back inside? These other gentlemen are just leaving."

"No, that's fine. I need to get downstairs for breakfast."

She slipped her journal and loose papers into her traveling case and headed to the ladies ordinary. As she sat under a Corinthian column eating French toast and strawberries, she sorted through her jumbled papers, surprised to see a thin sheaf of excellent leather. It looked almost exactly like hers, but she saw the name "Brutus" burned into the inside cover. There were several sheets of yellow paper that had been folded countless times, into the smallest square possible. There were codes. Some were in Gaelic, some were in ciphers. There were sketches, but clearly by a different hand than the sketches in Finn's office. The Burnet House sat at 3rd Street and Vine, and she recognized most of the drawings were of views of the Burnet House, either from 3rd Street or Vine. Interesting, she thought. There were rooftop views, sketches of balconies, and across alleyways. The artist was very talented, a master of architectural sketches such as these. She supposed they were done by the handsome man she bumped into, which only added to the mystery of why he had not returned for it.

"He must be staying in the hotel," Ardent said, when she showed the sketches to Uncle Finn after breakfast. "We need to find him."

"No, we don't," said Finn. "His behavior toward you was boorish, rude and inexcusable."

"What's that mean?" said Ardent. "I must give this back to him."

"No, dear, I don't think you should go near that man," said Finn, "I will leave the journal at the desk. They can determine who he is. We don't owe him more than that. I believe I have seen him in the company of ruffians."

Summer 1862, Athens, Ohio

Around 9:00am, Ty picked me up in his official "Athens County Sheriff" buckboard and we headed off to our favorite fishing hole for some bluegill fishing and crawdad hunting. His blonde-haired boys, Tadpole and Frog, three and five years old, sat in the back with cane poles across their legs. They were as frisky as baby goats.

"Catching some whales, today, boys?" I said, turning to look at them.

"Ain't no whales around here," Frog said. "Pa said."

"He's fibbing," I said. "He can't catch one, so, he's just jealous. He's not using the right bait."

"What's the right bait, Uncle Cage?" Tadpole asked.

"I've always found ornery little boys work best," I said. Usually, the boys liked me just fine, and loved it when I read them old tales of warriors, and battles, and other great adventures. Mostly they loved it when I told them the story of Samson and Delilah, and emphasized the ass, after "jawbone of an," when their parents weren't around. Now, they looked at each other like I was crazy, and went back to poking and pinching.

Tall and rangy, Ty, permanently tanned from a life of long days in the sun, had been our city's sheriff of three years, arriving in town when his youngest boy was only a few months old, with a recommendation from our retiring sheriff. He doted on his wife and boys and tolerated me. He frequently said being a sheriff in Athens was as exciting as watching sap drip, and if it wasn't, you were doing it wrong. On the rare occasions it wasn't, he suffered no fools. The local rowdies had learned this the hard way a few times, and a few times was all it took. He never talked much about his past. He'd been raised on the western prairies, and that was about as far as it went. I didn't think he'd been an outlaw of any sort, and even if he had been, it didn't matter to me. He was a good sheriff, a good husband, a great father and a reliable friend. Outlaws are a dime a dozen. Good friends are rare. Couldn't have been better if he was a loyal old blue-tick hound.

"Think the war will make its way here?" I said while the boys splashed in the creek. Ty and I were sprawled in the shade and, as usual, the talk turned to the war in late afternoon.

"It might already be here," he said quietly, and nodded toward the road. Three riders sat motionless in the shade of a big oak beside the road. They were staring at us hard. They offered no greeting, so I followed Ty's lead and stared back. They had rifles on their saddles that weren't meant for squirrels. Some days Ty wore a pistol, but today wasn't one of them. I wished it had been.

"Who's that?" I said.

"Don't know. Don't like it, though. Don't feel good at all. Boys, get to the wagon," Ty whispered, with an urgency I'd never heard him use. They got there in a hurry.

"Don't seem too friendly, "I said. "You think that's why they're here?"

"I don't know, but I plan to find out. There's been talk of border raiders lately, from across the Ohio River. I don't like armed strangers in my town, trying to intimidate good people," Ty said.

"What are you going to do?"

"I might just go whip the lot of them," he said, stone-faced serious. That still didn't sound like the best idea to me, either, but, again, I wasn't the lawman.

"I understand all you pacifist types, bohemians, but there comes a time when you have to stand up," Ty said. The riders slowly rode away when Ty started up the hill, with only the one in the back, the smallest one, glancing over his shoulder. He looked no happier than I felt. Ty pulled a full stringer of bluegill from the creek, and released the crawdads from their watery, mudhole prison.

The following day, I stopped by to see Henry at the Post Office, hoping for a letter from my fiancee, Ardent. Since the War had started, she spent most of her time in Cincinnati, Washington DC, or New York, working for the U.S. Sanitary Commission, a twenty-million-dollar charity for wounded soldiers and their families. Most of this trip had been to Cincinnati, helping raise funds for the Commission's two huge projects there, the Good Samaritan Hospital, which was already in operation, and the planned Soldier's Home. While there, she stayed in the Burnet House, with her wealthy uncle, who was a large stakeholder in several railroads, and whose shipbuilding companies were hard at work along the river producing massive war sloops and ironclads. He was one of the charity's biggest benefactors. I'd been to Cincinnati with her a few times, and the sight was awe-aspiring. No enemy country could survive the immense Navy being built by Finn and the other ship builders for long, and this was only a small percentage of the Northern might.

As if her Sanitary Commission projects didn't keep her away enough, sometimes Ardent still risked her neck venturing across the Ohio River to help those escaping bondage. Athens was only forty miles from the river, the boundary between slave state and free, and we had our own worries about the War. We'd had a good number of folks pass through on the Underground Railroad, and it seemed to me plenty of people were helping with that task, without her getting herself killed.

There was no mail, so I drove down to Herrold's Mill, the general store and grinding wheel where many of the local farmers did business. It was the place to hear the latest news. And opinion. And rumor. Mostly opinion and rumor, but the long-winded debates were nearly always entertaining. Most of the farmers in the area were abolitionists and Unionists, but, of course, there were a couple pro-slavers, and we had our fair share of contrarians, whose position changed depending on who was around to argue with. Such was the nature of our little town, and we were well-known for it. Jim even cleared a space for the amateur orators between the stacked haybales and pyramids of bagged grain. He called it the Wind Mill. I stayed for an hour or so, watching cold-blooded checkers and listening to the hot air, then headed back to town. It had been a good day with lively discussions about emancipation, the Anaconda Plan, and a good neck-stretching for the southern traitors, especially Jeff Davis and Clement Vallandigham.

"Hey Pete, how's everything going? Olivia, always good to see you," I said, greeting my neighbors, Pete Caballo and Olivia, as I walked out of the General Store. Pete was a veteran western frontiersman, a free black man the color of old saddle leather and twice as tough. Olivia was his very tall, almost regal daughter. She had a couple inches of height on her father, even with his bushy hair and long, shimmering braid. Pete said her ancestors were Amazonian queens. He was probably right. I didn't know anyone that didn't like Pete, and the whole county was so proud of Olivia that we nearly burst with it.

"Excellent. Olivia is just finishing preparations for school."

"Exciting times. I'm sure you'll make us all proud, Olivia," I said. My sister had been her teacher, tutor, and mentor for years. "Abby always says you are a brilliant student, maybe her best ever. She says she'll be lost without all your help."

"Thank you," said Olivia. "But I am a little nervous, a little frightened."

"I'm sure that won't stop you, it's never stopped your father," I said. "From the stories I've heard."

"It won't. I have some wonderful people helping me," she said. "Abby, of course. Everybody from home. Mary Jane Patterson has been such a help, and such an inspiration."

"She's the one with the degree last year, right?" I said.

"Yes, the first black woman in America to get a Bachelor's degree. And I have the gift of going to her alma mater. A dream come true, really," she said.

"When are you off to the big city?"

"I don't know that Oberlin is a big city," Olivia said. "But I'm thrilled anyway. I won't leave for a few weeks yet. I'm helping Ardent with a few things as soon as she gets back, but I just want to be ready."

"Well, you earned it. Too bad you couldn't stay here and go to Ohio University. Let's hope they'll follow Oberlin's example, and yours, and admit women soon. They're missing out."

As I continued down the street to Gamble's Saloon, a short, chubby man, my age, already balding, crossed the street waving a folded newspaper.

"Hey, hold up Cage," said Freddy. "Going to the saloon?"

"Thought I would," I said. "Just waiting around for Ab to put a shoe on for me. What are you up to?"

"I just had some tedious meetings at the college," he said. "Mind if I join you?"

"Certainly not, and I'll buy the first round," I said. Freddy was an odd duck, but a friend, and a professor of Botany at Ohio University where I taught Contemporary English Literature. Most people probably thought I was an odd duck, too, though odd ducks rarely know, I suppose. I was probably more of a dandy, while Freddy had pretty much discarded society's trappings. He always seemed to have a few crumbs of breakfast on his shirt, his rim of hair was like a weed patch, and he was happiest with bird watching and his plants, wildflowers especially. I wasn't prone to fainting spells, or wearing perfumed nosegays or French cuffs, but I'd be the first to admit that rugged was something I'd never been called.

We took seats at one end of the nearly empty bar, amid the gleaming wood and brass. From decades of salvaging railroad and ship wrecks, Enos had built a grand saloon, as fine as any in the state. He came down the bar toward us, wearing a spotless white butcher's smock and cleaning, probably for the tenth time that day, a beer mug. A handful of Union soldiers stood at the other end of the bar, talking loudly.

"Always the war," Freddy said, nodding toward them. "People still think it's a glorious thing."

"By the time the final tally is made, I can guarantee it won't be grand. Each battle is a little bigger than the last one. We already have 200,000 men, all Americans, no matter what anyone says, killing thousands of each other, on just one battle field. That's genocide, not battles. Savages is what we have become," said Enos, waving his hand at a couple thick volumes of Roman military history he was reading behind the bar. Enos received more newspapers, books, journals and magazines than the rest of the town combined, and never had less than three open books scattered behind the bar at any given time. His one exception to otherwise perfect order. He was the most voracious reader I'd ever known, and I was the literature professor.

"They keep promoting new generals. New generals like big battles, inept at them as they seem to be," said Freddy.

"These Yankees behind me have just been sharing Frank Leslie's accounts of the most recent battles. Malvern Hill, Shiloh, about the Seven Days, Lee and McClellan, any one they can pretend to have been in," Enos said, setting down two fresh, cold mugs. "15,000 casualties for us, 20,000 casualties for them. Good Lord, who could have imagined such a thing?"

"Can't you see, man, we've just got to go down there and wipe 'em all out. A damned lesson for any scum that survive," one of the soldiers shouted. He was answered with a chorus of hurrahs and calls for another round of drinks, paid for by some well-fed patriots just entering the bar. Enos delivered the drinks while the soldiers discussed strategy amongst themselves. Loud, but tolerable.

"Some folks don't truly appreciate irony," said Fred.

I finished my errands and was driving toward Ab's Livery and Blacksmith when Willie Wessels dashed past my buckboard, only to nearly be trampled by a speeding buggy coming the other way. Typical. Willie ran through town like a silverfish bug on a hot frying pan. His speech came out at a hundred miles an hour, and his feet seemed to rarely touch the ground. If he heard the curses and shouts from wagon drivers yanking their horses up short, he paid them no mind. Willie was a local success story. He had been raised in destitution, as miserably poor as a person could be, after his father died in a Sunday Creek coal mine, crushed to death by ten tons of kettle bottom. His mother soon fell into a black, seizure filled despair and, before he was ten, Willie was making deliveries and skipping school to do odd jobs for the family's survival. Now, not yet twenty, he had built a messenger service, a haul-and-freight service, and a new laundry service venture. He'd put together a team of rowdies that could destroy anything from a barn to a small forest in a day. He sold the proceeds for firewood or scrap. We all figured he was the best bet to be the town's first millionaire.

"Willie," I yelled, "Watch where you're going. I almost ran you over. What am I going to do with you?"

"Sorry, Mr. Carew," said Willie. "Have to get some papers to the courthouse."

"Well, you need to be careful," I said. "Didn't I see you driving a new wagon the other day?"

"Yes sir, I got my brother driving the old one now. He's thirteen. Past time for him to be earning his keep."

"Now, come on, Willie, don't you have enough money in the bank for your brother just to go to school?"

"Sure, I do, ten times over," Willie said. "But that's my money, not his money. If he wants money, he needs to earn it, school or no."

"You're not going to turn into one of those hunchbacked old churls that throws rocks at children, are you?"

"Mr. Carew, here's the thing. You really don't have the slimmest idea what being poor is. I do, and I won't be again. I will do whatever it takes, and I mean that. I'm not being rude, but you don't understand," Willie said. "I'm sure my little brother hates me right now, but it's for his benefit."

"No, I probably don't understand. Just be careful. You're going to get flattened."

After Willie darted off, I continued on to Ab's Blacksmith and Livery for some repaired harness and to get a troublesome shoe fixed on my old plug. When I pulled up, Abner Platt, proprietor, was banging and clanging away on his anvil, his forge blazing hot and his body pouring sweat. As usual he'd removed his shirt, and the sleeves of his tattered union suit had been ripped off long ago, baring his massive, burn-scarred arms and shoulders.

"How's business?" I asked as I stepped down from my buggy. "Someone make off with your Sunday shirt?"

"Been a long time since I wore a Sunday shirt," he said. "I expect that to continue."

"I'm not sure how you're going to get married without one," I said. I was to be Ab's best man. "The date approaches rapidly."

"Maybe we'll just get in the creek buck naked and draped with wild-flowers," Ab said. "Like them Oneidas do. That would suit me fine."

"I don't expect that would suit Nettie fine," I said.

"No, I expect not," said Ab. "She does have a taste for the finer things. And I'm happy to give them to her. Now, get unhitched and I'll re-wing Pegasus."

Devol

It didn't take long to find out who the three strangers were, and I shaded my eyes as their horses clip-clopped up my creek-stone lane. It was a pleasant sound in the cool morning, but the men didn't look pleasant. I watched curiously. Three fine looking horses. The powerfully built white man in front rode a pale one. The next man wore a turban. He was even larger, a giant the color of apple butter, and his thick-necked black horse was the size of a medieval war steed, heavily muscled and at least 20 hands high. The third man was several years older, smallish, and looked dumpy and uncomfortable in the saddle. He'd looked back.

"Good morning," said the man with the Van Dyke beard. There was a hint of menace in his deep, cotton-state voice. Dressed expensively in a burgundy brocade vest, bright white boiled shirt, and gleaming black riding boots, he sat tall in the saddle. He was muscular through the chest and shoulders, with eyes that were intelligent. And cruel. The men were from nowhere around here, that was clear. "Nice little place you have here. Lovely town. We're looking for Micajah Carew."

"That's me."

"Mind if my man here gets some water?"

"The pump's there. The water's free," I said, as wariness crept in. The huge, dark man dismounted and walked to the pump. He was nearly seven-feet-tall, and as sleek and graceful as a big cobra as he watched me coldly over the dipper.

"I didn't catch your name," I said to the white man. He was staring at me and played with a growing sneer.

"Francois Devol," he said, like it should mean something.

"Why are you here?" I asked.

"How refreshing. A man that comes to the point. We're chasing niggers," he said proudly. "Are you familiar with the Fugitive Slave law of 1850?"

"I have no need to be. This is a free state. We have many free Blacks up here. There are certainly no slaves. None of that is of my concern."

"Well, what is of your concern Mr. Carew? If I may be so bold as to ask," he smirked. "We are in search of absconders from legally established owners. From the great state of Kentucky. Your name has been given to us as someone who might harbor the swarthy travelers. So, have you noticed any darkies running free and easy around your idyllic hillsides?"

"What do you mean?" I looked down the road at Pete, who was running his dairy cattle out of the barn after their morning milking. He didn't appear troubled, but I saw him look at me more than once.

"The law says I am authorized to retrieve runaway slave property wherever I might find it. Got to take a look around the place here. Mr.

Carew, do you mind if Ashok goes in your house? We won't be a bother to you further."

"Yes, of course I mind. No, you cannot. This is private property. I don't know what you're trying to pull here, but you need to go. I think you're lost. This is Ohio," I said.

"Yes, exactly, and not many miles south is the Ohio River. And the blue gums pour over it like ants over an apple core. Don't try to tell me otherwise," said Devol in a growl. "Many niggers come through here, with your darkie town that way, and the niglets being schooled over that way, schooled by your sister, if I'm not mistaken. The Albany Manual Labor Academy? You Northerners are so trifling. Like feeding stuffed pheasant to a hog."

"What do you know about my sister? Why are you here?" I said.

"Never mind that. Now you are aware that hiding one of these so-called "fugitives from bondage" is a federal crime. There is no need to thank me."

"There are no runaways of any color here," I said.

"Time will tell. Time will tell," Devol motioned the others around, and they filed away. There had been plenty of other slave catchers pass through, too. They usually just talked loud and rough, huffed and puffed and threatened to blow our houses in. Sometimes they made some vague threats about illegal searches and conspirators going to prison, but never stayed around long. Like Ty said, these men felt completely different, and I didn't like it. But I didn't know what I could do about it. I had never been violent in my life. Nor wanted to be. My place was in a classroom, not arguing with rough men. My smoothbore musket was for ground hogs, possums and skunks, if I could even load it and if they were no more than five feet away.

Bob

I wasn't much of a farmer, but I had a few chickens in a coop behind the house, and I was still rubbing the sleep from my eyes as I stumbled out the door to gather my breakfast eggs. Pete was at the edge of his cornfield, and my brother-in-law, Jay, was riding a horse along the slight rise that separated our property. Both rose before the roosters, and had already been working for an hour.

I stepped off my porch and got slammed flat on my back. I must have screamed. Pete looked up in surprise. The dog howled, the chickens squawked like a bear was in the coop, and a fat raccoon darted from under my porch. Even a cow mooed. I rolled over and watched a young black boy, wearing muddy rags, speed away toward the tree-line fifty yards away. I jumped up and followed in breathless pursuit, but the ground was still muddy from yesterday's hard rain and we both slipped and fell several times. Pete sprinted after the boy, and Jay galloped down the hill and cut the boy off before he could reach the trees. Trapped, the boy turned one way and another, eyes bulging with fright.

"We won't hurt you, son," Pete spoke soothingly, moving slowly, like I'd seen him do with Jay's skittish foals. Those colts never looked as scared as this. Cautiously, Pete rested a hand on the boy's shoulder. The frightened newcomer looked at the three of us warily, then took a small canteen from Pete and drank.

"It's all right," Pete said. "You have crossed the River Jordan. You made it. There are no slave masters up here."

"Don't be so sure. We may be being watched," I whispered.

"Hurry, behind the trees," Pete said.

"Watched?" Jay asked.

"There are slave catchers from the south up here, must be looking for this boy," I said.

"Where are they?" Pete said. "How many?"

"Three. At least. I don't know where they came from, or where they are," I said. "They just showed up yesterday and accused me of harboring slaves. Said they were told I was. Then, today, there's a slave on my property."

"Where you from, boy?" Pete said. "What's your name?"

"Bob. Kentucky," the boy said. He looked 14 or 15 years old, thin, with thickly calloused hands. His old burlap clothes had been shredded by briars and tree branches, and ugly welts crossed his arms.

"Are you hungry, son?" Pete asked, after we were inside my house. It was clear he was, so I brought up some cold ham and biscuits and raspberry jam from my cellar.

"I'se not in the custom of spending too much time in white folks' houses," Bob said, uneasily, looking around.

"No, I suppose not," Pete said. "How did you get here?"

"They herded me up here, might as well say," the boy scratched his head. "Been tryin' to figger it out. This ain't nowhere's close to where I was trying to get."

"What do you mean?"

"Them folks at home that helped me, they said I could come this way if patty-rollers was looking for me at them other places. To Mr. Pete's place they said. I never made it to them other places. Nor Mr. Pete's place. Dey had it surrounded. Dey been on me since my first step off that plantation in Kentucky. Almost like they was waiting for me. Been behind and beside me ever step since, herding me, nearly. They coulda caught me anytime they wanted."

"O.K. get some rest," Pete said, as the boy shoveled the food into his mouth like he hadn't eaten in a month. His eyes drooped more with each mouthful. "We made you a bed over here."

"I will sleep, but I sho' miss my mama. I worry how she doing down there," he said. "I sure hope they didn't start whuppin' her."

"I'll bet," I said. His head hit the pillow and he was out.

The next morning Bob was devouring a second breakfast of bacon and pancakes when my sister Abigail came through the door with a canvas bag over her shoulder. She set the bag on the table, and began building a stack of books. Bob picked up the McGuffey's reader, then a Webster's Blue Back Speller, admiring them like they were Homer's rough drafts, coffee stains, splintered spine and all. Last night he had woken up just long enough to eat a huge supper and learned, with delight, that Abby was a teacher.

"You said last night you dearly wanted to read. Well, we like books in this family, about as much as air," she smiled. A worn chalkboard and broken color chalk sticks appeared on the table.

"No better start than now. We can distract ourselves from this un-pleasantry for a few days until things get sorted out," she said. He was eager, and for the rest of the day they read adventure stories and printed the alphabet. Abby was beaming, doing what she loved to do, and Bob's face lit up each time he recognized a new word.

"Miss Abigail, I have never heard such wonderful stories. I can see it in front of my face when you read them like that. I'll know how to read in no time flat."

"That's real fine, Bob. If you want to accomplish something, you can accomplish a whole lot more being able to read a book than using a gun, though many fools don't understand that."

"Yes, ma'am, I'se sure that's true," said Bob. "But ol' massa down there, we didn't stay put 'cause we was scairt he was gonna shoot us with no book. So, you understand…ma'am.''

"You make a valid point," she said, squeezing his arm. "Maybe we'll discuss it again. Either way, it is always a pleasure helping someone who really wants to learn."

"Yes, ma'am, I didn't mean nothing by that. My mama wanted me to learn how to read something fierce. Ol' Massa wouldn't have none of it. He is a mean sonofabitch. We wasn't the most whupped niggahs in that county, but we wasn't far from it."

For the next week, we stayed busy with chores and tending our gardens, looking as normal as we could. We kept watch while Abby stayed inside, furthering Bob's education. He had an astonishing appetite for learning, and for Abby's meals.

"See, someone that finally appreciates my cooking. These others are ungrateful Philistines," Abby said at dinner. "I'd retire my pots and pans and let them starve, but it would be a lot of trouble to bury them."

"I could help with that. I have a strong back, they say," said Bob.

"Oh, don't tempt me."

"Come on now," I said. "At least let us leave the room before you plot our murders."

"I am glad to meet a school teacher. I didn't think I ever would," said Bob.

"Now I'm sure you're knocked over in awe, too," she said.

"Yes, ma'am, I rightly am impressed," Bob said. "All this."

"You know, we have an academy down the road. In Albany actually. That's where I teach," she said. "Just for colored boys and girls. It's called the Albany Manual Labor Academy."

"Up here you go to school to labor?" asked Bob. "Down home, we picked it up right off."

"No, it's not that anymore, it's a common school now," Abby smiled. "We teach all the subjects the other schools teach. Have you heard of such a thing?"

"Nope, never heard of that. We didn't have no schools, at all, not for black folks," Bob said. "That sure sounds arrestin'."

"I know it's not safe for you right now, but after this war is over, and this despicable slavery issue is settled," she said, "You better come back. I would be thrilled to have you."

"Your friends stopped by yesterday," said Ty a few days later, sitting down in my porch rocker. "Dropped your name. Wanted to remind me that President Lincoln himself is calling for stringent enforcement of 1850 Slave Law, which explicitly states any officer of the law, that would be me, who did not arrest any desperado - that would be you, apparently, the desperado - harboring runaway slaves, will be fined $2,500. I don't suppose you'd mind telling what that's all about?"

I told him.

"Oh, boy," Ty said. "Where is Bob now?"

"Abby took him to her place, thought he might be safer," I said. "That's true about the fine?"

"Sure is," he said. "Which is why I keep my distance from any slave benevolent societies, real or rumored, in our fair city."

"I see. So, we're freeing slaves in the South, and returning them in the North?"

"Officially, we're not freeing slaves. We're preserving the Union. I don't make the laws, I just enforce them."

"You going to enforce this one?"

"Unlikely," he said.

Pete

"Show him your Spanish gold piece, Pete," said Abby, as we finished supper. She pointed at the Mexican gold piece Pete wore on a leather string around his neck. "Have you ever heard of Santa Ana? The Mexican general?"

"Like General Linkum?" Bob said.

"Not exactly," said Pete, and Abby told a wonderful rendition of the tale of Pete at the Battle of Cerro Gordo.

"So, Pete was scouting for Robert E. Lee when he discovered Santa Ana's chest full of gold and his gold-encrusted fake leg," she said when she finished the story.

"Is that true, Mister Pete?" Bob said, laughing like it was about the funniest thing he ever heard.

"Every word of it," Jay said.

"I know someone who was in a greater panic than Santa Ana, too," said Pete. "That was my little Creole friend, PGT Beauregard. I thought his brain would explode when he found out that Lee was brevetted to Major for that victory."

"Don't know what none of that means," said Bob.

"Means one got a whole lot better treatment that the other," said Pete. "Toutant was sure in a state, though. I've talked to him since, when I was in New Orleans. He believes Lee took all his credit for that dangerous night-time scouting, and built a legend for himself. There's a few that agrees with him. I don't, necessarily, but there's some that say it."

"How did you come to be friends with Confederate generals?" Bob asked Pete.

"All that started a very long time ago," said Pete. "During the Second Seminole War."

"What war was that? Why you folks always warrin' on somebody? Don't it get tiresome?" asked Bob.

"The Army declared War and invaded Florida to capture the Seminoles and move them out west to a reservation. Mostly because rich ranchers and plantation owners wanted the land, and to return thousands of escaped slaves that had joined them and were hiding in the swamp," I said. "In a nutshell."

"I've heard some awful scary stories about wild injuns," said Bob. "Worser than patty-rollers they say."

"Some were, no disputing that," said Jay. "But, usually, that was the only way they had to fight back against a huge army. And this Indian raid was as horrible as any I've ever seen, but what brought us together wasn't part of that war. Not what those raiders wanted us to believe, anyway."

"Yes, even after that war started, there were still plenty of Seminoles who traded at the post where our father sold his goods. That included hundreds of Maroons, the escaped slaves, Pete's people, that lived with the Seminole. I knew most of the local tribes, and the other people at the post did, too," Abby said. "The Indians that attacked us weren't Seminole. They were Creek, disguising themselves as Seminole. The Creeks had been enemies of the Seminole for years, and the army brought nearly a thousand Creeks in from Alabama who raided villages for the bounties on the Black Seminoles. I don't know if they thought no one would see through their disguises, or they didn't expect to see anyone that knew them, or they had intended to kill us all the whole time. But, all of a sudden, they realized they been recognized and started killing everyone."

"Oh, my lawd," said Bob.

"I was little, but I remember most of it. There was probably only about twenty of them, but it seemed like twenty thousand. Screaming and whooping. There were bloody, hacked-up dead people everywhere," I said. "Abby grabbed one of those twenty-pound cavalry pistols that were laying around, a box of bullets, a tin of biscuits, and me. We snuck out the back and into the swamp. I remember her just about pulling my arm out of my socket as she dragged me through the swamp. We hid out for two weeks."

"And you was only ten?" said Bob to Abby.

"A little older than that," she said. "My brother passed English, failed mathematics. Anyway, the Creeks came looking for us. We were the only witnesses to a massacre. The murder of our father. A mass murder, actually, treachery by our allies."

"That's horrible," Bob said.

"And it wasn't just the Creeks we had to hide from. The Seminole, since that's who we were supposedly at war with. And we had to worry about all manner of man-eaters, alligators and rattlesnakes, too," I said. "Abby had to whack a few alligators on the snout with an oar she found. The best one was that poor old black bear, though."

"You all had a scrap with a bear?"

"She did," I said. "The bear saw her with some fat honeycombs, and thought he'd help himself. We were about starved, and she wasn't having it. She grabbed that oar, and started smashing it over the bear's head like she was chopping wood. She didn't stop when he retreated, either. Broke the oar. Lucky for us no more bears came nosing around. Or gators."

"She's brave lady," said Bob.

"That's no lie," I said. "But while she was doing battle with the bear, we heard laughter in the brush. Once that shame-faced bear ran away, Abby grabbed the pistol and demanded whoever was out there to show themselves. A Black Seminole boy, no older than Abby, walked out of the trees, hands up, laughing so hard he could barely walk. It was Pete."

"You'se an Injun?" Bob said to Pete. "You'se pert near as black as me."

"My mother was a full Negro, the daughter of a slave that was brought here from Africa," Pete said. "My father was Spanish and Seminole mixed. He owned my mother, and my brother, John Horse, and me. He was a decent man, for that time and place. He never treated us like slaves, and he freed our mother. All the other people treated us like slaves, though, so we took off and joined the Seminoles. John was the best man in our village with a bow and arrow, or a rifle. He was a great hunter, and he was the smartest man I ever met. He spoke English, Spanish, Muscogee, Hitchiti and tried to teach me everything he knew. He started out as an interpreter for the Seminoles."

"How did ya'll get to be friends if you was at war?" Bob asked.

"Pete took pity on us, is what saved us," said Abby. "After he quit laughing, which took him much too long, by the way, he started to lead us out of the swamp. He knew of the Creek attack, too."

"But there was one other problem," said Pete, nodding at Jay. "When we found a patrol of soldiers to take the wanderers in, that one there wanted to shoot me."

"You was going to shoot your friend?" asked Bob.

"He wasn't exactly my friend at the time," said Jay. "He was an enemy warrior with a gun and what looked to be captives. And he had a bounty on his head."

"He wasn't exactly an enemy warrior, either," corrected Abby. "He was a boy that had just saved our lives."

"Anyway," said Jay. "All I know is that in the middle of that thick jungle swamp, a Seminole brave just popped up on the trail in front of me. A split-second before my men fired, Abby jumped in front of Pete, screaming for us to put down our guns. It was a real close call."

"It sure was," said Abby. "But it worked out quite nicely. I was able to convince Jay of the treachery of the Creeks, and he took it from there. He tracked down the Creek murderers and dealt with them the only way murderers of women and children should be dealt with. After that, he became an advocate for the Seminoles and Maroons, in general, and for Pete specifically, and got his name cleared."

"Cleared from what?" said Bob.

"A few months before that attack, Pete had helped his brother escape from an Army prison," said Abby. "He killed a Creek guard on the way out. The Army put a bounty on his head. Unofficially, of course.

"Why was your brother in prison?" Bob asked.

"John was acting as an interpreter for Osceola, and some other chiefs. They went into the fort, to negotiate with General Jesup under a flag of truce, of peace, trying to stop the fighting and bloodshed," said Pete. "But, Jesup, that worthless coward, had them arrested and thrown in prison. Knowing Jesup's treachery, we immediately feared for the lives of all our brothers. Because we were the smallest, Wildcat and I snuck inside the fort and broke them out. By that time, Chief Osceola had become very sick and could barely walk. A Creek warrior named King William caught him, and even though the Chief had surrendered, William was beating him to death. There was no time to think. I hit William in the head with my club and he died. Rather suddenly. That's when John and I went from interpreters to warriors."

"So, the Army put a bounty on Pete's head. Unofficially, of course," said Abby. "But after Jay went to his commanding general, and threatened to tell the newspapers about Andrew Jackson's hired Creeks murdering and terrorizing innocent white settlers, the Army suddenly decided the guy Pete killed wasn't that important after all."

"Yes, but my military career was killed in that battle, too. Rather suddenly," Jay laughed. "But, I'd pretty well soured on the military by that point, anyway. So, I resigned my commission soon after, and went to work as a liaison for Joshua Reed Giddings. He's a Congressman from Ohio. Was, I should say, until last year. He's what you call a firebrand."

"Don't know what that means," Bob said.

"Sword waving abolitionist and reformer, especially for the escaped slaves in Florida," said Jay. "He wrote a book about it that threw all of

Washington into a rage. He made an awful lot of enemies. His party, the party of Lincoln, didn't invite him back this last time."

"I think I can figger out most of what that means," said Bob. "But, what's a layzan?"

"Arranged meetings and such," I said, though it was a lot more than that. Jay was understating it when he said Giddings had a lot of enemies. They were legion and capable of anything, but he had persuaded the most unscrupulous of those enemies to focus their energies elsewhere.

"How did you end up working for the Army after what they done?" Bob asked Pete.

"It's real complicated. There was no way we could win. No way the Seminole could even survive a war. There were just too many Americans, so John surrendered in the spring of 1838. He'd been promised peace and a new, happy life for all his people west of the Mississippi," said Pete. "In the end, we marched half-way across the country with thousands of other conquered people. The Five Civilized Tribes. So many civilized Indians died, and the suffering was so great, that the exodus to Oklahoma became known as The Trail of Tears."

"Yes, and that's where Pete decided to become a dairy farmer," said Jay. Since Jay had left the army, he'd bred and trained Chickasaw horses, bloodlines from the same tough, little horses that Cortez and Hernando DeSoto had brought to the continent in the 16th century. "My family was cattle ranchers, and horse breeders. Pete went to the ranch and worked with them while we got things straightened about the Army trying to kill him. He's a real good hand with the horses. But, on that terrible march, those Indians got so hungry, they ended up eating half their herd."

"Never name something you might end up eatin'," said Pete, soberly. "Now we're partners, but he raises the horses, I tend the cows."

"Sounds reasonable," said Bob.

113

"Yes. And things didn't get much better once we got settled out west. Slave-catchers and the Creek bounty hunters, who didn't like going into those Florida swamps, swarmed the new Seminole reservations. Comanche attacks were terrible, and they took no mercy on us for our dark skin. They wanted their own slaves, or to sell them back to the Americans. So, anyway, my brother John formed a company that guarded our borders against slavers and rampaging Indians. Sometimes we worked for the Army as scouts and interpreters. The choices weren't great, and I already knew how the soldier and Indians story comes out. We lose. I joined young."

"I 'spose I can understand that," said Bob. "Why'd you come back here?"

"For my daughter. John did a good job. He established Wewoka, a town for escaped Florida slaves, and we even had our own school. Oak Ridge Mission. Abby was the first teacher. But, life on the prairie is no life for any young girl, no matter what color. The fighting never stopped. It was a struggle just to survive, and I didn't want her to go to a mission school. Abby moved back to Ohio to teach and raise a family, so, I brought her to the Academy."

"Your girl is lucky to have such a good pa, Mr. Pete," said Bob. After finishing off one of Abby's warm apple pies, we'd gone out on the dark, back-porch for some fresh air. "I sure wish you'd let me out there to work with one of you, on the farm. Now that I'se got some of Missus Abby's wonderful cooking in my belly, I'm ready to do my chores, too. Truth is, I ain't used to so much settin."

Eno's Rifle

"They were mean, dangerous looking men. Plenty of guns, for sure," I said, telling Enos about my visit from Devol when I stopped by Gamble's a day or two later.

114

"You need one?" Enos asked, low, so none of the soldiers in the place could hear him.

"You sell guns?"

"Combine a hillbilly, a saloon, and a railroad, and you can find about anything," Enos grinned. "I'll see what I have. Probably best left quiet, for now. And, for you, a special price."

"You say that to everybody."

"I've told you for five years you need a good rifle, and you wouldn't listen," said Enos.

"Right, because I'm just as likely to get myself killed, most likely by bleeding to death after I shoot my hand off."

"Well, should you ever decide you want to stop King Herod's gorillas from smashing in your door unhindered, I'd happily be your servant," he said. "These are not muzzle loaders. You'd have to try pretty hard to blow your hand off."

"Sometimes you're an asshole," I said. "What do you have?"

Ten minutes later Enos led me to his cellar, opened a large steamer trunk and extended a rifle with both hands.

"What's the furthest you ever shot anything with that old gun you have?" asked Enos.

"I don't know. Probably about halfway from my house to the road. What's that? Twenty-five yards? And that was a tree I wasn't aiming at."

"That's about right, I'd say," said Enos. "This is a Sharp's Breechloader. 52 Caliber. In good hands, this rifle can hit targets at three hundred yards. In expert hands, 700-800 or more."

"That sounds a little hard to believe."

"True. But that's the claim being made to the army. They outfitted a regiment of sharpshooters with them, and that's what they say. You'll have up to ten shots a minute."

"How much?"

"$60. Expensive, but this is what the army should be using for all their soldiers. They're going to be real hard to get soon," said Enos. "This war would have been over the day it started if our boys had these. Or their boys for that matter."

"Thanks," I said, turning the rifle in my hands.

"I'll include a couple boxes of bullets. You should use them. Here, take several. Have Jay and Pete show you how to shoot. They were marksmen in the Army, you know."

"No, I didn't know. I suppose I should," I said, "These slave catchers have me more than a little troubled."

Ardent

I smiled as Ardent stepped off the train and into the smoke and commotion of the busy train station. Her big strawberry curls fell over her shoulders, and her eyes, as bright and perfectly green as emeralds, swept the platform and jumped with delight when she saw me. Any thoughts of Devol disappeared as I grabbed her around the waist and kissed her.

"How was your trip?" I asked, waving away coal dust.

"Don't get me started. Long, tired, dirty. The noise. Sometimes dealing with these people is like walking through shit, er, pig pen," she said. "Ok, I can breathe now. I've been frustrated. Just get me home to a hot bath. Maybe for two. The faster the better."

"Fast was my plan. That's why I have two horses hitched. Water's on the stove," I said. "And you shouldn't cuss so much."

"You're the profanity police now?"

"Merely a concerned citizen."

"Thank goodness. I was afraid you were going to arrest me, and not have carnal knowledge of me. That would be a fix. The state I'm in."

"Home?"

"Don't dally," she said. I didn't, and when I entered the house after putting the horse away, she jumped me from behind the door and slipped a blindfold over my eyes.

"Stay put," she said, and I heard her walking into the bedroom. "Hear that?"

"No. What's that?"

"That was the sound of pantaloons hitting the floor," she said. "What's taking you so long?"

Abby

"How did your trip go?" Abby asked Ardent in the morning, as we sat at her breakfast table.

"Could have been better. Competition is fierce for donations, of course, but we did well in what we really wanted. That town is nothing but a bunch of cutthroat pirates, and new ones all the time. So much corruption that people are reluctant to give," Ardent said. "The shoddy tycoons are still there, too, even after Cameron was forced out six months ago. Companies open up under a different company name is all. Half of them were created by members of Congress, their kin, their mistresses, or any home state scoundrels not timid with a bribe. They have no shame, openly bragging about their boondoggles and swindles."

"It's completely despicable, what they do," said Abby. "Sending our men off in uniforms and shoes that fall apart in the first rain."

"Yes, and its worse than just shoes and pants. I was even introduced to a detective who is investigating fraud in the shipping contracts," said Ardent, beaming. "So, of course I couldn't wait to tell Uncle Finn about that one. I'm sure he can point out the crooks for them."

"Washington is a terrible place," Abby said. "Some of the men I met when Jay attended functions. No one had to point out the thieves. Easier to point out the ones that weren't. I'm sure it's even worse, now. So depressing and enraging. I hope all your trip wasn't like that."

"Oh, no, not at all. I spent a few evenings with Dorothea Dix. Mary Ann Bickerdyke was even there a few nights. Those girls are so silly, with all their cutting-up," she said. "Just a bunch of fun when they're all together."

"I'm jealous," said Abby. "Smart women."

"I know. Just one more reason this war must end. Women must have the vote," Ardent said. "Had the women in the North AND the South had the vote, we likely wouldn't be killing each other."

"Mm hmm, you've mentioned that once or twice," I said.

"How are things around here?" Ardent asked. "I've missed it. The quiet. Peaceful."

"I forgot to tell you this fellow Francois Devol showed up, claimed to be hunting for Bob," I said. "But showed up before Bob showed up. Rode right up to the porch and accused me of harboring slaves."

"Devol. Here? Why?" Ardent stammered. "Big man? Slave catch-er?"

"You know him?" I said.

"If it's the same man. Maybe it's not, but a few years ago, just as I prepared to return to Ohio from my uncle's estate in Georgia, a man named Devol pursued me aggressively. He's a business associate of my southern uncle, Sean, and apparently, my northern uncle as well. Uncle Sean has a large plantation, Bhean Milis," said Ardent. "I despise his ownership of slaves, completely, but I believe he is a fair man, in that regard. Uncle Sean is oblivious to the man's poor character, I'm certain. My cousins, Derry and Molly, are very sweet and insist their father is trying to sell the plantation, although not many people were buying with war looming."

"You met him in Georgia?" Abby said.

"Yes, but later they told me he sold slaves from Georgia to Texas. And for the right price, would track them all the way to Canada. He loves the hunt, they say. Most likely, illegally imported some, as well. He's nothing but a loathsome whorehouse pimp, and that's an insult to pimps," Ardent said. "They told horrible stories about him. With that absurd freak show giant that is always with him. He's likely a murderer, several times over. A sadist, certainly."

"And he's a friend of your uncles?" asked Abby.

"Not really a friend. I would hope not. He came through now and then. I don't know how to explain Uncle Sean," said Ardent. "Devol passes himself off as an aristocrat, honorable and cultured businessman. He sent his card to call. I refused to see him, and told him why."

"What do you mean? What happened?"

"He showed up anyway, and when I turned to walk away from him, he grabbed my arm and nearly pulled it off," said Ardent. "We'd walked away from the house. I believe he was trying to pull me inside the barn."

"Were you hurt?" asked Jay.

"Only a few bruises, but he ripped my dress half off, so I slapped him. His face turned demonic," Ardent said. "If my cousins had not run out right then, I'm sure it would have ended very badly. For me. I've never seen such fury."

"Why didn't you tell us?" asked Abby.

"He's the same man I told you about in Uncle Finn's office a year ago. I didn't know you when I had my dealings with him in Georgia three years ago," said Ardent. "I never expected I would cross paths with him again."

Gamble's After Brawl

"Get down to the saloon," laughed a gang of five or so boys the next time I went to town, swarming my buggy before I could tether my horse.

119

"What has happened?" I asked the boys. "What's got you all so fired up?"

"Last night, them big bad men from down south lit into it with some soldier fellas in Mr. Gamble's place. Scrapping something fierce," said a gangly teenager. "Don't know much other than that. Sure raised a ruckus though, from the way folks is acting today. Mr. Gamble said if we seen you, to hurry you down there."

"I heard there was trouble," I said when I entered the saloon, leaving the jabbering gang at the door.

"Yeah, I finally met that Devol fellow. He was running his mouth in here last night. He sure had some of the local n'er-do-wells entranced. Telling all the men if the North put down the Rebels, they'd be invaded by savages from the dark continent. He was buying plenty of whiskey. I was starting to get worried they'd go on a lynching party," Enos said. "Then some soldier boys came in and some harsh words were exchanged, and then everybody was fighting. But not for long. That brown behemoth threw those guys around like matchsticks. Devol did, too."

"How did you get them out?"

"I allowed them to wear themselves out. I've been in plenty of those, and I'm getting old enough that I know which ones to jump into, and which ones to leave be. I left it be," said Enos. "They sashayed out of here with some bloody knuckles, and barely a hair out of place. For the Yankee fellas, they were full of spunk, but it was a little rougher going. They all made it out the door though, and are probably laying up at Doc Sprague's about now, all bandaged up. Devol left two hundred Yankee dollars on the bar for damages. He was so damn smug, I almost refused it."

"And the third man?"

"Well, he crawled into the corner and stayed there. He may have pissed himself. Otherwise, near as I can tell, he's some kind of evangelist faith healer and backroom abortionist."

"By all means, let's shoot him first."

"That's what I'd do. Twice."

Abby

At midnight, Jay and Abby harnessed their team and drove east of town toward a secluded old shack that had long been rumored to be a stopover on the Underground Railroad. Pete lay under a canvas tarp in the back of the wagon, with a double barrel shotgun across his legs. They had not gone far when the silence was broken by the sound of horses approaching fast.

"Greetings good people," said Devol, emerging from the darkness. Beside him, Ashok and Bliss both held torches.

"What do you think you are doing?" challenged Jay.

"I should be asking you that," said Devol. "This northern obstinance is beginning to aggravate me. I am doing a perfectly legal service for owners that have lost valuable property. I am enforcing federal law. Your law."

"And your attempts at intimidation are getting tedious," said Jay. "I hear you're telling scary stories about roadside assassins and cannibalizing Indian liver. Whatever it is you're trying to do, you are not going to push us around."

"Well, certainly, that has not been my intent. I wasn't trying to scare anyone. Sometimes I forget my civility," Devol said. "Excuse Ashok as well. He means no harm. The warm winds of fortune have not often blown gently across his black heathen soul. Life's unfairness like that, well, sometimes it can make a man petulant. So, I try."

121

"How about you, have you blown gently across his black soul?" said Abby, sweetly.

"You bitch! I would kill a man for that remark, Mrs. Carter, and I should you," Devol snarled, veins throbbing down his forehead. "Do you teach white children with that mouth?"

"I do. White, black, red, brown," Abby said. "And not a single one has disappointed their mother as you have."

"You are trying to inflame me, Mrs. Carter," he said, and they stared at each other for a pause.

"This sure seems to be an awful long way, and awful long time, to spend on one slave," Jay said.

"Oh, yes, back to the matter at hand. Maybe he lays golden eggs. Frankly, I don't see where my business practices are your concern," Devol said. "But what is in that wagon is my concern. Go ahead and yank that canvas back."

"My wagon, my concern. Not yours," said Abby.

"Goddamn it, it is my concern. I'm hunting these runaways, and I will look in that wagon."

"Look, then, if you must," Abby said. Ashok lifted the canvas, but jumped back when Pete's shotgun barrel kissed his nose.

"Hey, neighbor," Pete said.

"Mister, you're no more chasing slaves than I am chasing unicorns," Abby said, pulling one of Jay's Colts from under the shawl spread across her lap. Jay already had the other pointed at Devol's face. Her voice and her hand were steady, while the fury returned to Devol's face. "I don't know who you are, or who you think you are, but nobody comes here and threatens my family. Or those poor little children at that school. I won't have it."

"This next one will amputate your leg," said Jay, pulling back his hammer after Abby shot Bliss's torch, sending a shower of sparks over the riders and spooking the horses.

"Which won't matter much if I blow your head off," said Pete, pleasure in his voice. Devol spun his horse and cast a last murderous look at Abby, then galloped away down the dark road. Ashok and Bliss were close behind.

"What time is it?" she asked when the torches disappeared.

"Almost two."

"Cage and Ardent should have Bob to the mill by now," Abby said, picking up the reins.

"A couple more miles," said Jay. "Let's keep him interested a while longer."

While Jay and Abby baited Devol to the east, Ardent and I hurried Bob toward the west side of town, where Jim waited in the dark at Herrold's Mill. By 2am, we were on a wooded hillside across from the mill, bruised and scraped from our unlit wilderness journey. The sliver of yellow light behind the window shade meant it was safe, so we sprinted across the road and slid down the grassy slope. We hugged the ground and listened for pursuers, but only heard the water rushing over the dam. Satisfied, Ardent tossed pebbles at a window until Jim came around the building with a pistol in his hand.

"No problems? Anybody see you?" he said.

"We didn't see anyone."

"Come on, get inside," Jim said, walking toward the road with his lantern. "I'll be in shortly. Just want to be safe."

For an hour, Jim and Ardent grilled Bob on his route. They studied the map, made sure he had enough food and water, and knew his stars if he got separated from his guide. Abby sent a couple books with him. When they were satisfied, Jim led us to a brush pile behind the mill, pulled away the bushes, and ushered Bob into the tunnel under the dam. I saw the glowing half-face of the next conductor behind a small candle, and as Bob scrambled toward his new life, we threw the brush back over the entrance and made our getaway.

Picnic

The sunny breeze in our faces was sweet with honeysuckle as our buggy trotted past the hillsides of cud-chewing cattle and farmers tending their crops. It was noon when we reached the secluded meadow where we often went to be alone in nature, and I took care of the horse while Ardent spread the blanket in a patch of red clover.

"I still wish you wouldn't go," I said, giving it one last try.

"Stop it," Ardent said. "Devol and his gang have been gone for two weeks. They are not loitering around to bother me. I'll be fine. I'm not scared of him. I won't allow myself to be scared. He's a bully and tries to intimidate the weak."

"Yes, and it worked," I said. "It seems like he has no problem backing it up."

"Devol threatened Ty with a federal lawsuit after Bob disappeared," Ardent said. "Ty said he was incensed, crazy with rage. Doesn't that prove he only came after Bob?"

"I know that. It could have been a ruse. Or his pride being injured, even if Bob wasn't his priority," I said. Devol had been an issue of contention between us lately. I thought she was too easily dismissing a dangerous threat, and she thought I was being over-protective. She stubbornly, and stupidly, in my opinion, refused to abandon her plans to take several wagons of medicines and supplies into the South and bring a couple highly sought slaves back.

"That's a little hard to believe," she said. "No more about Devol. Am I expected to never leave my house again? Devol is the last thing on my mind. We'll be perfectly safe. Olivia Caballo is coming with me, and we're meeting some others from Oberlin as soon as we cross the river. We'll be staying at homes for Christian ladies, which is neither fun nor appropriate, but it is what's available and safe."

After a nice lunch and short nap, we woke up to honey bees buzzing the picnic basket at our feet and a jangling cow-bell beyond the hill. We took a long barefoot walk along the creek, returned to the blanket and stretched out.

"I understand these blankets are for more than just keeping the ants away," I said, coyly.

"They are? Whatever else could they possibly be for?" she smiled, lying back.

"Well, to keep grass from tickling your private parts."

"How on earth could grass get in my private parts?" she asked.

"This way," I said, unbuttoning her dress.

We enjoyed our night under the stars, knowing it would be our last for a while. When we made it back to her house in the morning, a covered wagon, full of wood crates and brown paper boxes, sat out front. An old teamster sat patiently holding the harness reins, now and again jetting a rope of tobacco juice toward the road. Ardent hurried to join the others and shushed me when I tried to talk her out of going.

"I can be ready in ten minutes," I said. "I'd feel better if I could come along."

"Well, you can't come along," Ardent said. "Too many people traveling will only raise suspicion, especially men of military age. I'm just taking these documents and travel passes to the people that need them. All that anyone can see are crates of Sanitary Commission food and medicine destined to the prison camp. All quite legitimate."

"And how long will your ploy hold up?" I said.

"We will be fine."

Murder

I was on my knees pulling weeds and fighting sweat bees when Ty led a somber group of riders up my lane. Ardent had been gone four weeks, two weeks longer than expected. Olivia should have been back and off to college. When I'd seen the group ride to Pete's place earlier, I'd wanted to run into the woods and hide. The looks on their faces told me everything I didn't want to know. No one but Ty met my eyes.

"What's happened?" I asked.

"No easy way to say it. She's dead, Cage. We found her. Just this side of the river," he said, and I collapsed. Strong arms caught me and helped me to my porch, where I slumped against the post. "I need to see her."

"No. That would be a very bad idea. She's not her anymore. She's been in the elements a long time, the heat…animals got at her," said Ty. Lights exploded in my eyes and I vomited into the yard. When I finally stopped, Ty and Ab lifted me into the rocking chair.

"She had a dirty yellow scarf wrapped around her throat," Ty said, and everything spun. Hammers and horseshoes and Hell's own cymbals crashed and clashed inside my skull. "I assume that would be Devol's man. These clothes were nearby."

"Nearby?"

"Yes…it appears she had no clothes on. Neither of them did," Ty said.

"Appeared?" I said. "Neither of whom? What the hell did they do to her?'

"These are her clothes, aren't they?" asked Ab. I trembled as I looked through the pile. A locket and a bracelet I had given her. The washed-out gingham work dress with the berry stains on the cuffs. No question.

I fell asleep around dawn, slept until dark, and when I woke up, I found the nightmares were real. Abby and Jay were talking quietly in the front room, and Ty sat in a rocking chair beside my bed. He handed me a dipper of water and I slurped it down.

"Not telling you what to do, only that we are joining," he said, after I had another dipper and my head slightly cleared. "If you decide to, you're welcome to come with us."

"What do you mean?"

"The War. Several of us have been talking for a while. This is the last straw. They're planning a draft anyway," he said. "We might as well join up now, so we can all be in the same regiment."

"What about your wife, your babies?" I said.

"She understands. We believe in the cause. She supports my decision."

I nodded, but my head throbbed, and my hands were seized by tremors so bad Ty had to catch the dipper.

"We think this Col. Dan McCook sounds like a good man," he said. "He's been tearing up the roads, recruiting around here. Freddy and Teddy saw him up on a tree stump, giving one hell of a speech. Fiery, they said."

"McCook?"

"He's a lawyer. And an actor. The man can talk. I assume he can fight," said Freddy, stepping into the room. "There were 60-year-old women trying to grab a Springfield and a box of minie balls before he was half done."

"I just want to kill the animals that killed Ardent," I said. "I just want to kill those three. I don't care about anyone or anything else."

"The way I see it, the only way you can kill them is to get South. And the best way to get South is join the army," said Ty.

"I suppose you're right," I said.

127

"We'll have to hurry to catch McCook the way it is. It might be a while before there's another local regiment raised," said Ty. "Pickin's are getting slim around here, since the 18th left."

"Are you sure about this?" said Jay, after the others were gone. "Who all will be going?"

"Ty, Willie, Ab, Teddy, Viv, Freddy. Jake. Myself. Dell. Dovie, even. A couple others."

"Really think they all will go?" asked Abby.

"I wish none of them would go, but they will. These guys are plenty mad. They would go ten times if they could. We're going to Dayton. Col. Dan McCook's regiment. Ty's recommendation. Most of the regiment is from Jefferson and Belmont Counties," I said. "Do you know this McCook?"

"I know of him, of his family," Jay said. "Very prominent in politics in the state. And Dan Sr., is hoping for much more for his boys. Dan Jr's a good bit younger than me. He's been fighting out west. From everything I've heard, he is smart and fearless in a courtroom, or behind a blind pig, where he's been known to visit. His brother was killed quite recently, by Rebel guerillas, they say. Dan Jr. was in a law practice in Kansas with Bill Sherman."

"Gen. William Sherman?"

"The same. Of Shiloh fame. Crazy Bill. They were partners."

"That's interesting."

"I think the McCooks are good men, mostly good, better than most. There's a couple to watch out for, though. Dan's brother Alex is dumb as stump. Pete can tell you more on that. He had to rescue that fool more than once, lost and wandering in the Mexican desert, with a column of fighting mad troopers behind him. The troops finally got to the point they wouldn't leave the fort with him," said Jay. "There's a dozen or more McCooks in uniform, including the patriarch, who owns more

128

politicians than I own chickens. Big bugs. Future Presidents and congressmen and ambassadors and such."

"Brothers?"

"Mostly. And cousins. The Fighting McCooks. They're also called, or call themselves, the Tribe of Dan, who is quite vocal in his fervent belief that God has chosen him, and his boys, to lead the nation in these trying times," he said. "Be careful. These are good men, but are also seeking glory. For the old man, it's an even higher glory than man's on earth. Seeing as Alex is the idiot, I'll expect he'll be the politician."

"My mind is made up."

"I wasn't trying to change it, just letting you know what's up ahead," said Jay.

Mourning

I walked down to Pete's through the coming dusk, along his pasture filled with carts and buggies. White friends and black friends, and many people I had never seen before, spilled onto his porch and yard. Inside the house, the stopped clocks and black-draped mirrors, sorrowful hymns, sobs, and over-perfumed ladies drove me outside quickly. I found Pete soon after, sitting against a tree. He was alone, and I started to turn away and leave him to his solitude, but he saw me and called me over. I guess if there was anyone that knew how he was feeling right then, it was me. It took either of us a good while before speaking, and even then, we said little.

"I saw him, you know," Pete said. "Bumped into him at the mill."

"What was he doing at the mill?" I asked.

"Just getting grain for his horses, I think," said Pete. "Nothing sinister. Not until he saw me, anyway. We were on Jim's porch, where it's just wide enough for one man to pass. I knew who he was, and when I made him wait, I thought he was going for his gun."

"I'm surprised he didn't," I said.

"There were some axe handles lined up. I sure wish I'd grabbed one and beat him to death," Pete said, tears leaking down his face. "Oh, God, how I wish that."

"We all missed some opportunities, I think," I said. "Did he say anything?"

"Yes, but just what you'd imagine," said Pete. "Lynchings, beatings, whippings. Buying and selling. That sort of thing. You're joining the Army?"

"Yes," I said. "What are you going to do?"

"I've done plenty of scouting in my day. They'll put together some colored regiments soon," he said. "I'm going after him, too."

There wasn't much else to say, so we just sat there for about half an hour, until he said he had to go allow the others to grieve for him.

Inscription

The sky had turned dark and threatening as I hurried toward my buggy, with a box filled with my personal belongings from my classroom. I had stopped and said my goodbyes to Dr. Howard, president of Ohio University. He had done wonders with the school, doubling enrollment and the facilities in just a few short years. However, the fall term wasn't far away, and the University was suffering the effects of the growing war. The number of students had fallen drastically since the first hostilities a year ago. He'd been very kind, visiting me at home as soon as Abby had told him I was able, and he'd assured me my position would be waiting for me when I returned. I walked down the brick walkway and stopped at the Campus Gateway, reading the inscription for what I figured would be the last time.

"SO DEPART THAT DAILY THOU MAYEST BETTER SERVE THY FELLOWMEN THY COUNTRY AND THY GOD"

I figured I might be serving my country and my fellowmen in what I was about to do, but I didn't see how I would be serving any god. If I was, God was much more wrathful and bloodthirsty than even I had ever imagined.

Chapter Nine

Camp Dennison

We rode a train to Camp Dennison, a seven-hundred-acre garrison outside Cincinnati. The camp was a grid of dusty streets dividing one hundred and twenty whitewashed barracks, with each barracks holding one company of one hundred new recruits. The streets overflowed with 12,000 wide-eyed young Yankee soldiers, and we watched the long lines of shiny new soldiers josh each other at the horseshoe pits and compete in wrestling, backflips and footraces. A spirited crowd watched a base-ball game on the parade ground, and banjo and fiddle players provided entertainment in front of every barracks. Men marched everywhere, single men, columns of men, parades of men five across. Some had mastered it, most had not. I had never heard so much noise in my life.

Things became sobering when we walked past the massive camp hospital. It held two thousand patients, most of whom were still invalid-ed from the Battles of Shiloh and Malvern Hill in July. Back home I'd seen just a few wounded veterans return, missing an arm or a leg, or an eye, and I'd seen one or two young widows dab their tears beneath their black veil. Now, in such numbers I never could have envisioned, hundreds of wheelchairs held the sightless and disfigured, the amputees, and those whose minds hadn't left the battlefield. We were subdued as we headed back to our new home.

We ran into some men from the 18th Ohio, who were almost recu-perated from their wounds received in skirmishes in Alabama and were headed back to rejoin their regiment soon. The 18th was made up mostly of Athens County boys, and completed with men from Meigs and other localities. The regiment had marched out of Athens a year ago under Tim Stanley and Chuck Grosvenor.

Many local men had also joined regiments that had been formed in our state capitol of Columbus, where they had gone to work years before the war. Columbus was a rollicking town in those days, and it produced the type of men who made good soldiers. The rail industry was booming, and Columbus grew with it. Union Station, a terminal as big as any in the country, was built in 1851 and served numerous railroads and their passenger and freight customers. More businesses. More people. More industry. The population had tripled, from 6,000 in 1840, to 18,000 in 1860. Two new hospitals were built, and a "Blind Asylum," and a "Deaf and Dumb Asylum" were spurring growth in the city. Columbus was also home to the Ohio State Penitentiary, one of the largest in the country, with 1,500 inmates, and the largest Lunatic asylum in the world, with 1,300 beds. Progressive Columbus had also opened The Ohio Asylum for the Education of Imbecile Youth just a couple years earlier.

Jobs were plentiful, but they were rough, rugged jobs that required rough, rugged men. Ab and Teddy and many men from all over the state came to work in the yards and the cellhouses, and most wore scars from those jobs. The city overflowed with saloons to serve these young, healthy men. Quite a few men bore scars from those establishments as well. Teddy "Toughnut" Tucker had even tried his hand at prize-fighting. Both eventually found work in the foundries, worked hard, and saved money. Ab had learned blacksmithing, and came back to Athens with plans to settle down with Nettie and have a house full of kids. Teddy had come back to work at Herrold's Mill and tend to the mechanics of their big grinding wheel.

Lyman

"Who do you suppose that is?" Ab asked, pointing at an officer walking up the street toward us. The captain's build and bearing were exactly what I expected of a warrior. He had big, broad shoulders and the confident walk of Samson, but his tanned face was friendly as he crossed the street between the roaming bands of recruits.

"I have no idea. He's a big son of a bitch, that's for sure," said Ty.

"I'm looking for Company E, 52nd Ohio," said the Captain, with an accent that was definitely not from any part of Appalachia.

"Are you our company captain?" Teddy asked.

"If this is E Company, I am. Captain Dunnock," he announced.

"You're in the right spot," said several of the boys. "Can we ask where you hail from?"

"As an introduction, I am a professional soldier. I'm a native of Great Britain, though I've barely been there in 25 years. I've been posted mostly in Asia and India, but I've crossed big chunks of Africa, the sands of Arabia, and experienced the mysteries of the Orient. I even managed a few trips into Russia in that time. Can't tell anyone about that though," the brawny officer said as we crowded close around to hear him. "I am quite good at my craft. If I weren't, some dusky A-rab would be teaching you the arts of warfare right now."

"Why'd you come here?"

"Well, when I first got to Asia, I survived a massacre. And, in my last week in Asia, I survived a massacre, and there was one more in between. It finally sunk in that I wouldn't likely survive another," said Lyman. "So, I crossed the Atlantic. I need to eat, and can't dance or design railroads, so I signed on to help you young gents avoid a massacre. It was the absolute last thing I wanted, but here I am. Let's start with one basic rule. I will never needlessly put you in harm's way, but sometimes it will be necessary, and you cannot hesitate. We have to depend on each other, every moment, from here on out. Starting now."

Before anyone could ask another question, the Captain put his hand up for silence

"Tomorrow at dawn, we drill. Tomorrow afternoon, we drill. Every day we are in this camp, the 52nd Ohio E Company will drill. No one will out drill us, therefore no one will out fight us."

At dusk, our company was marched out to the parade grounds, and stood at attention with a thousand other men. A colonel, tall and thin, with sharp cheekbones and a neat goatee, faced us from a stage. A line of crisply uniformed officers stood behind him.

"Good evening Gentlemen," the Colonel said. "Welcome to the 52nd!"

"Yes, sir," several of us shouted, with not a clue if that was soldierly.

"I am honored and humbled. It's a pleasure to have you boys. I am Col. Dan McCook. You are my regiment. I will have the best fighting men in the army."

Not knowing what else to do, we cheered. The Colonel gave a brief but rousing speech about honor and duty, country and God. One by one, the officers standing behind McCook stepped to the podium and instructed us on this rule or that, getting this equipment or that. Once they were finished Col. McCook reminded us we would be up at sunrise, and in no time, we'd be formidable warriors. We cheered again.

McCook was true to his word. The sun was barely in the sky as we marched to the parade grounds, and even the early rising farmers in our group were still rubbing sleep from their eyes. Once there, we were issued new Springfield rifles, and spent the rest of the day running through the Manual of Arms.

"It is so damned hot," huffed Ab, rubbing his blistered feet, after our fourth hour in the sun on our third day of drill. "I ain't seen no pictures of this part of whipping the Rebs in Frank Leslie's newspaper. No mention of it, neither."

A few feet away, a strapping young soldier collapsed in the dust. I grabbed his feet, Ab grabbed his arms, and we carried him to the shade of a walnut tree and grabbed a few seconds of precious shade for ourselves. Several others were already there, more were under neighboring trees, and several more were on their way."

"No disrespect Captain, but how is it these other regiments come out here for a couple hours, and then back to town to pitch woo with them husband-huntin' Cincinnati girls?" asked Teddy.

"You have all your life to find a sweetheart. You only have a few days before other people will be trying to kill you," said Lyman. "So, whether it's fun or not, fair or not, these drills might save your life. And the man's next to you. It doesn't much matter how many true loves you have. If you get killed, it sure won't be you she'll be kissing under the stars. But she will be kissing someone, count on that. So, come on, lasses. You should have been with me in the Asian jungles and Arabian deserts. 130 degrees some days. My lads would've come here for the frosty breezes."

That was met with a chorus of groans, but after a few more men fainted, Captain Dunnock marched us into the woods to cool off. We had a brief rest, then were up, and for the 100th time that day, I grabbed my Springfield, tore the imaginary cartridge with my teeth and poured the imaginary powder. I rammed an imaginary ball down the barrel and primed the imaginary cap, all while the captain and his subordinates shouted in our ears that we were too slow. Another hundred repetitions later we marched back to their barracks.

"Excellent work, gentlemen, excellent work," crowed Lyman, "Tomorrow we'll push it a little harder."

Cincinnati Feast, August 25th, 1862

Four days after being mustered in, wearing scratchy blue uniforms and stiff new brogans, we departed Camp Dennison and marched seventeen torturous miles to the Cincinnati courthouse, where the Ladies

Auxiliary of Cincinnati had prepared a feast for us. Rows of tables were piled high with hams and fried chicken, biscuits and pies and cakes of every sort. We'd rubbed lard on our feet, but still raised blisters the size of baseballs. Thankfully, the pain went away when a cheering crowd greeted us at the courthouse, and as much as the flirtatious young maidens of Hamilton County fussed over us, we were convinced we'd already won the war.

After the food had largely disappeared, Col. McCook was called to the second-floor balcony of the courthouse, where the ladies presented him with a large silk National flag which was embroidered with "McCook's Avengers." He held the flag with arms outstretched above his head, and we cheered loud enough to be heard across the river when he vowed vengeance on Frank Gurley and his gang of bushwhackers.

"What's that all about?" asked a soldier standing nearby.

"Some Alabama rabble killed the Colonel's brother," said Ab, and told him the story. Robert McCook, who'd had a law practice in Cincinnati before the war, was a colonel at the Battle of Mill Springs in Kentucky where he was badly wounded. He was taken from the battlefield in an ambulance, in a wagon train which had to pass through territory where Confederate outlaw gangs ran free, terrorizing Northern sympathizers. McCook's wagons got separated from his column, and his small unit was attacked by Rebel guerrillas. Robert was killed, executed in cold-blood, as he lay defenseless in the wagon, according to Northern newspapers. The same papers accused notorious guerilla Captain Frank Gurley of being the cowardly murderer of Robert McCook, and bold headlines inflamed the public.

"And now we're going after them," I said. The 52nd was now "McCook's Avengers" and since I was seeking my own vengeance, I took that nom de guerre to heart. We slept at the fairgrounds wearing broad smiles, and in the morning, we marched to the Covington rail yards, blistered raw feet and all. It was a rough start, but soon enough spirits improved. We stomped down that road, bellowing marching songs and thinking the army was going to be mighty fine. However, when we got to the railroad depot, we found our accommodations would not be quite as swank as we thought. We'd be whisked off to Dixie in flat cars and cattle cars, and not the passenger cars we'd expected.

"You men stay here by the engine," said Captain Dunnock, placing sentries along the track. "Try not to let anyone steal it."

"How do we stop them? We have no bullets," said Ty.

"I doubt you'll need them, but we are in enemy territory," said the Captain. "Just keep your eyes open for anybody snooping around, and crack 'em in the head with your rifle if necessary. We'll sort it out later. Always a chance of a saboteur or spy."

At dusk the train whistle blew, and straggling Yankees came hurrying across the tracks, while behind them, a booming, oath-filled voice made everyone stop. A massive Yankee general goaded a stooped, gray haired man across the tracks with the point of his sword, bluing the air with a remarkable stream of curses. A handful of officers walked behind him, looking grim, staying close but not too close.

"Isn't that our corps commander?" I asked. "Not many others that size."

"Not any that size," said Ab. "He's considerable biggern me, especially right there on his front porch. I'll bet he could fit two hogs and a side of beef in there, without a need to loosen his belt."

"Oh, lord, Bull Nelson," said Ty, looking up. "Throwing one hell of a conniption fit. Smoke coming out of his nose."

Nelson's voice thundered above the noisy yard. He was a notorious and violent tyrant, and those on the yard fled out of his way. Like Ab, most of his mass was muscle, not fat, and the name "Bull" was well earned.

"What's he so mad about?" asked a soldier.

"Nelson's from Kentucky. He hates anybody from Indiana or Ohio," said Ty. "He's a jackass and considers us to be traitors or incompetents. No one really seems to know why."

"He sure loves to push his weight around," said Ab. "No matter who."

"Come on, get up here, he sounds like he wants to hurt somebody," said Ty, when Nelson turned in our direction. We scrambled toward the steps of the first car, but not quickly enough to avoid the charging Nelson, who moved surprisingly fast for a fat man.

"You men here," Nelson bellowed, pointing to the locomotive, his purple-veined face ready to burst. "For fucking sake, you idiots, don't look at each other. I'm the goddamn general! Now, get your worthless asses up in the cab."

We'd just made it when Nelson grunted and heaved himself into the cab, mashing us against the wall, and filling the space with sour body odor and cigar smoke. It nearly wilted us, but his bulk pinned us in place and we didn't fall. The hulking general yanked the engineer up the steps and onto the vestibule as easy as a child lifting a toy soldier. Barking out another string of curses, he shoved a bulbous finger into the man's face.

"Shoot this man!" Nelson barked. In the suffocating space, I twisted and raised my rifle over my head and angled it at the quivering engineer. Ab and Ty did the same. I wondered if Nelson knew that ammunition had not yet been issued.

"Not now, you fools. Shoot him if he tries to wreck this train. He's a traitorous, damned rebel and probably a spy, but we have no other engineer."

"But if we shoot him, won't the train wreck anyway?" asked Ab. "And we ain't got our bullets yet."

"You pie-eating son of a bitch, just do what the hell I say. If not, I'll shoot you personally." Nelson snarled, as he whirled and punched Ab hard in the chest. Nelson pulled a Colt Navy from his aide's gleaming holster and jammed it in my gut. "Use this if you need to. If you don't know how to shoot it, beat him to death with it. And then you better learn how to drive a fucking train."

Battle of Richmond, KY

Sunday morning church bells were ringing, and breakfast was over. Most of the regiment had gone into Lexington to fill pews and spark the local beauties. I sat in our tent playing cards with Ty and Ab, while bulging black clouds threatened overhead. Thunder rumbled, and the wind picked up speed, bringing the first fat drops of warm rain. Silver javelins of lightning ripped across the sky and landed with a crash, slicing open the clouds. The rain came down in buckets. Within five minutes, water rushed under our tent so fast we had to perch on our child-sized folding chairs, clutching everything we owned in our arms.

"There are a bunch of men headed this way in a hurry," said Ab, peeking out the tent.

"Are they ours?" Ty asked, grabbing his rifle.

"I can't really tell. I think so."

Dozens of rider-less cavalry horses galloped past, and a sea of reeling, horror-stricken Yankees poured through our camp in a free-for-all, getting tangled in our tents and ropes and churning the ground to brown soup. Cavalrymen flew wild-eyed down the road, flailing their horses and holding on for dear life. Ambulances and wagons appeared, slipping and sliding behind faltering mule teams that were muddy up to the collar and looked close to collapse.

"Where you running from?" Ty asked one man.

"Richmond. It's a mess," the drenched soldier said, walking toward our tent. "Just tore us straight to hell."

"What happened?"

"I don't know, except they whupped the daylights out of us. Half our boys will be in a cold grave, or Reb prison camp, by morning. Bull-and-Bluster Nelson panicked and crapped his pants, claims the whole Rebel army was out there," said the man. "Then the fat bastard took to sword-whippin' his men, and got himself shot in the ass. I'm fairly certain it was a Rebel ball what nailed him, but I won't wager it. He's gonna come to a bad end, just wait."

Bugles blew assembly. In town, the boys were pulled out of church, or from houses less holy, and double-quicked back to camp. Within an hour, the division was marching to Richmond, Kentucky, with a lot of nervous laughter passing through the column. The jokes stopped as we passed the first dead and wounded, lying trampled in the mud. Splintered and deserted ambulances and supply wagons and caissons lined the road. We reached the Richmond battlefield at midnight and walked soberly through the wrecked equipment and broken bodies.

"Ain't so funny now, is it, lad?" Lyman asked Teddy, whose endless supply of jokes had just ended.

"Not at all."

The Confederates were long gone, and blood covered surgeons labored in nearby barns and farmhouses. Late in the afternoon, we marched back to Lexington in a relentless downpour.

Galt Hotel Guard Duty
September 29th, 1862

We hopped off the wagon, and took our early morning Corporal of the Guard position at the Galt House. The opulent hotel quartered the Union generals, their staffs and guests, and was one of several guard posts the 52nd had been assigned around Louisville. Rumors of spies and seditionists were rampant, and new ones burned through Louisville hourly. In the overflowing border city, Southern civilians and military personnel crossed paths in unusual, and sometimes volatile, circumstances. Our post was at the entrance, but we spent most of our time watching the street. Lyman had shown us what to look for. Hard cases, cold-eyed pimps, pickpockets, muggers and grifters prowled at all hours, constantly looking for victims, committing crimes that Ty didn't even know there was a name for. A drunk private's savings, an entrepreneur's fat wallet or an officer's pocket watch would be a coup.

"These parade-hardened generals can order thousands of men into battle, but need watched over while they eat breakfast?" said Teddy.

"I wouldn't want killed at breakfast, not before a pot of coffee anyway. Likely I'd still be short tempered at the pearly gates," said Ab. I watched the lobby as bloated brokers and sellers mingled with officers with medal-swollen chests, lots of gold braids and bottomless government cheque-books. The room exuded commerce, not military planning.

"The only casualty in here will be me when I die of boredom," said Teddy. "They're wasting a good fighting man, leaving me with these paper shufflers."

"Now, you say that, and the next thing you know, one of them will get a paper cut and we'll have to carry him to the hospital on our shoulders," I said.

"If it ain't Nelson, I don't care," said Ab. "If it is Nelson, I'd sooner try to carry a horse."

"The Captain is right, I suppose. There could be saboteurs, certainly spies lurk amongst us. Even if those scrambled eggs in there are useless idiots, a bomb would kill a bunch of generals," said Ty, ever sensible.

"There are few fighting generals in this building," said Ab.

"Be that as it may, it would be bad press. I wouldn't want my name associated with it. The Europeans hate us anyway," said Ty. "They've been waiting for a sign the South can win. Dead generals, paper collar tea sippers or not, would make a splash."

The dining room and lobby stayed full dawn to midnight and always, above the din, Gen. Nelson's loud, profane voice drowned out all others. It echoed through the high-ceilinged lobby, and new guests to the hotel grimaced at his tirades. Most days, he cursed his officers for the disastrous Battle of Richmond. He cursed them all, but one more than the rest. The three-hundred-pound Nelson blamed and hated Gen. Jefferson Davis, the pocket-sized, hot-tempered general from Indiana. A few days previously, Nelson had ordered Davis out of the city, and, when he didn't go, had him arrested. The entire city knew that it was not finished.

We had just taken our position in the Galt when Gen. Davis, accompanied by the Governor of Indiana and his entourage, walked into the lobby. Glancing back, I saw Nelson coming from the opposite corner of the tight crowd. Splitting the cramped lobby like Moses parting the Red Sea, Nelson and Davis were headed toward a collision. Neither one looked up until they were an arm's length apart, and only a last second shout from a staffer avoided impact.

"Nelson will smash him like a bug. He's no more than a skeeter," said Ty, of Davis who weighed no more than 130 pounds. "Someone that ain't us should step in there and break that up."

"I don't know. He looks pretty scrappy to me," I said. The two generals were about twenty feet from me and I didn't want to be a part of whatever was about to happen.

"General Nelson, I want to know why you disgraced me by placing me under arrest," demanded Davis. They were nose-to-nose. Davis's jaw muscles rippled like a rough sea, and his eyes blazed with hate.

"Go away you damn puppy. I don't want anything to do with you," Nelson snapped. We could see and hear them plainly. Everybody could. Dropped silverware clinked and clattered on a dining-room full of breakfast dishes, and the entire room was slack-jawed in suspense as they watched the disaster building.

Davis leaned forward and flipped a calling card into Nelson's face. Nelson slapped Davis with a loud crack, and both staffs stood by, helpless and horrified. Davis threw a punch. Nelson blocked it easily and slapped Davis again, leaving a red handprint on his face and staggering him. Davis spun on his heel and stomped into the lounge, and Nelson headed up the staircase. When Davis reappeared and strutted across the lobby toward the stairs, I saw the pistol in his hand. Nelson headed back down when he saw Davis return, but I'm sure he never saw the pistol. I looked at Ty, the same as he was doing to me.

"You're the sheriff," I said.

"Not here I'm not, and I'm not trying to be."

"Not one step," Davis ordered, and raised the pistol. Nelson, for once, was silent. Davis fired. Blood gushed down Nelson's shirt, and he toppled backwards on the stairs. The lobby choked with gun smoke, and the well-bred ladies screamed and swooned spectacularly.

Officers, some from safety below their breakfast tables, bellowed a babel of orders as Nelson bled to death. The desk clerk rang his bell like he was smashing spiders, bawling at the bellboys to get water, towels, the police, Gen. Buell and a doctor. Newspaper writers and artists appeared magically in the lobby, pens and pencils flying. Gawkers tried to push their way inside, and pickpockets were already on the hunt. We kept the worst dregs away, while a hundred uniforms rushed through the door.

"Fetch a clergyman," Nelson moaned, sprawled on the bloody stairs, "I want to be baptized, I have been basely murdered."

Surgeons from the dining room were at Nelson's side, and dumb-founded adjutants tried to carry Nelson upstairs. They each grabbed a limb, but Nelson was dropped and bumped all the way up. While I watched that struggle, Davis marched up to me with the pistol still in his hand. He extended it, butt forward.

"I'll be in my quarters, should anyone wish to see me," Davis said. No one tried to stop him. He walked out with a jutting chin, and perfect-ly straight back.

"What was I supposed to do, arrest him?" I looked at Ty.

"Well, look at you," Ty said to me. "Ain't even fired a shot in anger and has generals surrendering to him. Our very own Bonaparte."

"Pin some medals on that banty rooster's chest and send him to Washington," Ab said. "That man's a problem solver."

Hot March to Perryville

The good thing about Davis killing Nelson was that we no longer had to fear Nelson's tyranny. The bad thing about Davis killing Nelson was now we had to fear the tyranny of Major General Charles Champion Gilbert, who was now III Corps commander. As far as we could tell, Gilbert had three qualifications for being a general. He was born in Zanesville, Ohio, about 40 miles from Gen. Buell, commander of the Army of the Cumberland. He had graduated from West Point in the famed Class of 1846 which included George B. McClellan, Stonewall Jackson, and George Pickett. And he was a wildly reactionary martinet. Unlike his many celebrated classmates, Gilbert had never been promoted above captain and resigned from the Army after the Mexican War. After the North-South hostilities began, Gilbert rejoined the service as a Captain. He was promoted to Inspector General, a bureaucratic position, and, from that rank, Buell promoted Gilbert to Major General, in com-mand of an entire Corps after the two ranking generals, Cruft and James

Jackson, refused to serve under Buell. He was now a bitter, vindictive captain ran amok. Even the fact that he was a graduate of my alma mater, Ohio University, and the first member of the Beta Theta Pi Fraternity there, endeared him to exactly no one.

Our column left Louisville on October 1st, marching toward Bardstown in the worst drought in Kentucky in decades. Temperatures stayed in the 90s, there was rarely a cloud in the sky, and eighty thousand men made a lot of dust which turned into gritty concrete in my mouth and nose. The only water we found was from shrinking farm ponds, coated with the slime of frogs and hogs, or lifeless creeks thickened to an unidentified warm sludge. We marched along at 90 paces a minute, common time, but most of us were still in the hay foot – straw foot stage, and some of the fellows were having problems with their first ever set of crooked shoes. Or shoes, period. Men staggered out of formation, overcome with heat and thirst. Some reached shade trees, others collapsed against fenceposts, and some fell on their face in the road. The withered brown grass beside the road was cluttered with blankets, frying pans and overcoats, even rifles, anything that could lighten the load.

"I come to fight," said Ab. "Not die from desiccation and ruined feet. Ain't we got trains to carry us?"

"Not enough for everybody," said Ty. "There's about a million of us. Everybody has feet as chewed up as yours."

"That's not as comforting as you might think," said Ab, who was not really fat, just the broadest back and hugest arms I'd ever seen. Still, that's a lot of flesh to get water to. We were all suffering, but Ab was down, pale and shaky.

"It's a character builder," Ty said. "Now, get up. We're moving."

"I ain't getting up," said Ab.

"You got to get up," said Ty.

"All them others ain't."

"All them others ain't us and you," said Ty, recently voted in as our platoon sergeant, "I won't have it."

"Well, damnit, I can't," said Ab.

"Ab, here comes the Captain," I said. Dunnock walked straight at us, and I thought we were about to get dressed down. Instead of a blistering, he handed us a knapsack full of fresh peaches.

"Private, I feel for a big man on a march, I really do. I've been right where you are. Didn't anyone tell you it was mandatory to have aching feet in the infantry? You can't break tradition," said Captain Dunnock, joining us in the shade of a big oak tree. We had already been marching for eight hours, each fifty minutes of marching with a ten-minute rest.

"He's suffering bad," said Ty. "It ain't even his usual shirking and belly-aching."

"These are emergency rations, so, don't be greedy. In the morning, we'll see what else we can forage," Captain Dunnock said, handing the sack to Ty. We each ate a peach, gave Ab two, and Ty held the rest back for any future distress. I felt a little better when we got back on the road, but knew if we didn't stop for the night soon, plenty besides Ab would have a rough time getting up. Fortified with peach juice, we returned to our march.

"Who's that up ahead?" Ab said, after we'd been back on the road for an hour.

"McCook with Gen. Sheridan beside him, at the crossroads up there," said Ty. "Look sharp."

"You're doing fine men. You're doing fine, 52nd Ohio. Keep working. We'll give 'em hell. Just remember for every callous you have on your feet, I have five on my ass," McCook said. "Do you want me to prove it?"

A laughing chorus of "no" rose from the men. Nobody was happier than me when neither Teddy nor Ab said something stupid.

"Unfortunately, the nays have it," said McCook, pouting. "Perhaps next month."

We finally stopped for the night and were able to give slight comfort to our feet and gulp down some coffee. It nearly killed the taste, smell, and bugs in the water. In the morning, the road was no softer than it had been yesterday, but the march was more pleasant. We passed neat, white houses and well-tended farms along Springfield Pike. Pink cheeked girls in their Sunday dresses, with sky blue ribbons in their hair, sold us lemonade and cookies and smiled sweetly as we marched past. Their brothers shouted, "Hurrah for the Union" and waved flags and whittled muskets. The homeowners smiled uncertainly behind white picket fences, but their daughters sold a lot of lemonade and cool water. I don't know where they got that wonderful water, but it was about the best I'd ever had.

"If those fields of Kentucky bluegrass weren't brown, and all those Kentucky thoroughbreds hadn't been conscripted by the Reb cavalry," said Ty. "I think I could enjoy myself around here."

Days passed, and the heat never let up, not even at 4 AM. The drought worsened. Men and animals were miserable and sick, too parched to move. Supply trains were woefully short, and when we could, we snuck off and prowled the countryside to survive. Unlike some others, we tried to pay the farmers market value for truck, but, to be honest, we didn't always spend that much time searching for a rightful owner. On this sweltering, steaming day, we were returning to camp down a forest trail, loaded with a bounty of fowl, eggs, carrots, turnips, and several clay jugs of fresh milk. We'd just stepped out of the trees when Ty hissed for us to stop.

Between us and the camp, fifty of our boys were bucked and gagged, tied upside down on wagon wheels, and dangling in pain from various other medieval torture devices. Another hundred of our men sat under guard in a pasture. Gilbert and Buell had a regiment of Indiana men aiming rifles at us, and were ordering them to fire if we didn't drop what we were carrying and surrender ourselves. Meanwhile, a hundred or so heat-maddened men from the 52nd aimed rifles back at Gilbert's henchmen as we tried to find grass to hide behind.

"Get to the woods, boys! And get out of sight!" McCook screamed as he and a howling platoon of riders blew past, close enough to touch. We got a face full of dust as the Colonel charged fearlessly straight into Buell's riflemen, and damn near into Buell's lap, earning our love and loyalty forever.

"Put those rifles down! What kind of idiots for Generals do we have in this army? Have you lost your goddamn senses?" McCook bawled at Gilbert and Buell loudly enough to be heard in Washington. McCook was instantly legend, and we watched from the trees as, in full fury, he berated his commanding generals for several minutes. More officers arrived, but we stayed hidden in the trees until order was restored, drinking that cool milk that sure was sweet in the shade of those big hickories. Around the fire after a fine dinner that night, we saluted McCook with generous swigs of sweet, purloined Kentucky applejack, knowing we had the best leader in the Army.

Even at our lowest, our plight was still better than many, and just north of Perryville, I got my first close look at slaves. Families of ragged Negroes sat in dry pastures, grazing their bony mules and gaunt dairy cows. Their battered wagons, full of their life's possessions, were precariously held together with rawhide and twine. They watched our column pass, not especially scared to see us, but not exactly overjoyed either.

"I wants to enlist me up," said an earnest young black man, jogging up to us. Another dozen young men trailed behind him.

"I don't know that you can, just yet, anyways," said Ty. "Not close by."

"So, we ain't free?"

"Well, you are, but, some things just won't be easy. Or fast," Ty said.

"Mister, I ain't knowed an easy day in my life," the man said. "I wouldn't know what to do with an easy day."

"I'm sure of that," said Ty. "All I know, they are putting some Negro regiments together in Washington. Just nothing around here. Keep going north. You'll find it."

Refugees continued to stream past, and we began to pass open pastures jammed with batteries of artillery, freight wagons, and row after row of ambulances. I didn't know we had that many cannons in the whole army, nor ambulances. We were all a little uneasy with all those empty ambulances. I know it was on my mind when I went to sleep that night.

3 a.m. to Perryville

"Hey Captain," I said, waking up to Captain Dunnock jostling my shoulder. "What's going on?"

"Just taking a small detail to the creek to fill canteens."

"At 3am? Won't it be there after breakfast?"

"Johnny Reb might be there after breakfast."

I sat up. Others were already pouring coffee pot dregs into the fire or shaking friends awake. Canteens lay in a pile near the fire, and we each looped a dozen over a shoulder and headed down the road. After a couple miles, the full moon revealed our destination, Doctor's Creek, which lay between two long, gradual hills. We left the road and followed the Captain to the creek, where sheer banks dropped to the bed six feet below. I slid down a log onto a sandbar, and felt like crying when I saw the dubious liquid between my feet. The stream was barely three feet wide, and nowhere more than a couple inches deep. The algae covered pools glowed green. We had a thousand men in the regiment, and this frog puddle wouldn't satisfy a hundred.

"Ugh, this water stinks," said Ab.

"Yes, it does, but I don't think it's poison," said the Captain. "Let's go now. Full canteens for your lads. Get to it. The Rebels want some of this too."

"They can have mine," said Ab, as we knelt in the creek bed and wrestled the canteens into the mud until water dribbled in.

"Get down!" The Captain hissed. He must have heard a blade of brown grass break at a hundred yards away, and we dove to our bellies as a group of riders came up the east side of the creek. I sprawled in a puddle with algae tickling my face, and froze in fear when the riders stopped and dismounted.

"Oh, shit, they got a dog," groaned Teddy. I opened one eye ever so slightly. The blockheaded dog peered down, sniffing and halfheartedly barking a few times. I expected at any second the Rebels would hear my heart pounding and shoot us all. The Captain had it under control, though, and silently made his way up the bank and tossed some scraps of salt pork in the grass. The dog wolfed down the treat with gusto, then stared at us with wet, sad eyes. When no one produced more food, he frowned and braced to howl. Half a dozen hands threw bacon and biscuits to him, then held our breath while the hound gobbled his unexpected reward.

In the moonlight fifty feet away, the rebels had plopped down under the trees and were passing whiskey bottles around. Their drunken laughter got louder, oblivious to any Yankees in the area, and soon a few of the Rebel cavalrymen staggered toward the creek bed. They opened their pants, and their urine streams splattered the backs of motionless

Yankees pressed into the mud. Even in the dark, I could see Ab's face flash from fury to terror to fury as Rebel urine arced perfectly into his ear. I kept his eyes on mine, found his hand, and squeezed it until my own ached.

The Captain, his back flush against the bank, was gripping an Alabama toothpick with a 12-inch blade and looking as serene as a Chinese goldfish pond. Above him, one of the riders made a slurred comment and his audience laughed loudly. None of us dared breathe as I listened to the snail cally-hooting up the mossy old log at my feet, sounding every bit as loud as a runaway freight train. Over that racket, I heard a fox barking somewhere in the trees. It seemed like hours had passed and I began to think the drunken cavalrymen would never dry up. At any second I expected the battle to start right there in the creek bed, but finally the last pissing Rebels staggered back to their chums. Immediately the dog came bouncing back, wanting yet a bigger bribe. We emptied our bread bags for the mutt, who then ungratefully followed the rebels over the hill.

"What do you think?" I asked Capt. Dunnock as they rode away.

"I don't know. Just out scouting, or sneaking out of camp to get drunk."

Then, no sooner than the Rebs had ridden away, the rest of our regiment began to drop into the creek bed. Several officers conferred with the Captain in hushed voices. He listened, nodded, pointed over my shoulder. Counted all the men he could see.

"OK, men, change of plans," he said quietly. "We're taking that hill up there. Silence until we're nose-to-nose. Don't fire a shot, don't even load your rifles. Wait until I tell you."

We quietly inched up the hill, but half-way up a dozen Rebel shots popped in the dark. I flattened myself in the cool grass behind a log and tried to load my rifle, but a loud patter of musket balls smacked the log and my shaking hands failed me.

"So much for no one waiting for us," I said.

"Ain't no glory laying here with my face in the dirt," Ab said, fuming at the Rebels for pissing in his ear. Eventually the firing stopped, and we finished our climb up the hill. At the crest, the slope in front of us was hayfield, but off in the moonlight, I could see the tall corn fields, and beyond them, a black forest I knew held thousands of Rebels.

"Bayonets!" whispered the Captain, his eyes bright and locked on ours.

"This is it," said Ty, as we snapped our bayonets into place and white-knuckled our rifles.

"Awaken iron, my thirsty little berserkers! Desperta Ferro! CHAAARGE!" Captain Dunnock screamed, and we raced down the slope. I was laughing like an idiot and struggled to hold my urine, absolutely terrified, yet giddy with an excitement I never knew existed. We smashed into the Confederate flank with fury. Curses and screams swirled all around me as minie balls found their targets. I fumbled two shots before the regiment surged into a narrow strip of woods, then I went to one knee, trying to slow my breathing when a tree branch snapped behind me. I spun, bringing up my Springfield as a Rebel soldier stepped into the clearing with his rifle pointed at the Captain's back. The man sensed me and whirled around, our eyes locking as I fired. My bullet hit him in the forehead and slammed him on his back. After a few seconds, I crawled over to him. The man lay in six inches of weeds, staring at the stars with a look of surprise. I pinched his eyes closed and knelt by the body for a moment, no longer giddy.

Dawn revealed dozens of dead men scattered on the front slope of Peters Hill, ours and theirs. I was still staring at them when a battery of cursing artillery limber drivers whipped their teams up the back slope, the 12-pound Napoleons sliding sideways in the morning dew.

"Take a look at the cornfield," Ty said, pointing about a quarter mile away. Two brigades of Confederates were stepping out of the trees, getting ready to march down the rows of towering corn. Quite a few Yankees, bragging that we had run the Rebels out of the state in our moonlight charge, had spent the predawn hours passing bottles of apple jack and not digging the rifle pits as the Captain had ordered. Now, it looked like our hillside had been invaded by an army of gophers and prairie dogs. There was more dirt flying backward over hurried shoulders than remained in the ground. We watched smugly. We'd started at 5am, and Ty hadn't let us quit digging until we reached the earth's core.

It was an odd feeling watching the Rebels. They seemed to be in no rush, no urgency, no fear that I could see. They looked confident, like they had done this a dozen times, and maybe they had. Everything about them looked bigger. Their rifles were bigger, their eyes meaner, their movements more soldierly. Even their little drummer boys looked like they could whip ours. A Rebel colonel grandly waved his brightly plumed Hardee hat over his head as he loped his horse up and back, cheering his men. They cheered him back even louder, then stepped off smartly, with the bright Stars and Bars catching the morning breeze and soaring above the golden stalks like a magnificent ship sail cutting the waves.

"On the word, men, on the word," an artillery man hollered. Our artillery crews leveled their Napoleons, full of deadly grapeshot, at the coming army. Just then, Rebel cannon, hidden in distant trees, started lobbing shots close enough to catch our attention. With a blood chilling yowl, the Rebels charged.

"Fire!"

The blast of six cannon convulsed the earth, and hundreds of shriek-ing metal marbles wreaked destruction through the exposed Rebels. Gaps formed in their battle-line and it staggered for an instant, like a fighter taking a good punch, then they shook it off and started back up the hill.

"Fire!"

The Napoleons blasted them twice and the Rebels froze. We sent several rifle volleys into them, and they fled. We gave chase, and pushed them back briskly but we'd outrun our ammunition and had to pull back. Cavalry joined us, and we advanced once again into the woods, faltered, and stalled. Two Rebel brigades reformed and attacked. The 52nd held, struck back hard, but couldn't hold the new line. There were 100,000 more men locked in combat in the line of hills, faring about like we were, going back and forth for the rest of the sweltering day, with the two sides rarely more than a couple-hundred yards apart. In our battles in the dense trees, we were barely ten yards apart, in deadly clenches, killing each other with limbs and rocks and bayonets. When the sun started to set, the Rebels retreated to the safety of the woods for the final time, leaving the ravaged hillside covered with dead lying elbow to elbow and wounded men crawling through them like bloody snails.

With the Rebels gone, I sat in the rifle pit wiping gun powder and sweat from my face and dreaming of cool water and waiting for the silt in my canteen to settle to the bottom. The dingy, gritty liquid in my canteen scraped my throat more than slaked my thirst. Miserable, with no chance of relief, I leaned back with my hat over my eyes and listened to the rumble of the cannons a few hills away. Some couldn't speak of what we'd just done, and others couldn't shut up. Our group, even Teddy and Ab, was subdued.

No sooner had I drifted off than a barrage of cannon balls blasted the hill and the air was filled with flying debris. I caught a rock under my eye, and concussion from the blasts threw me six feet across the pit. A shadow passed over me, then a ton of something dropped out of the sky and smashed me flat. It took a few seconds to clear my head and realize the weight was Ab, dead and gone, with blood pouring from a scalp wound. Just as my tears started flowing, the big man opened an eye.

"Am I hit? Am I dead?" he shouted, panic and blood all over his face. "Have they kilt me?"

"No, you got a new part in your hair is all," I said, after a quick inspection. The three-inch gash in his scalp was bleeding down his shirt, but was not fatal.

"What?" shouted Ab again, deafened by the explosion.

"No," I shouted, pain stabbing my ribs. I pulled a rag out of my knapsack and held it to Ab's wound. Eventually the bombardment stopped, and someone led Ab back to the hospital tent. I peered out of my hole at a regiment of Confederates at the edge of the woods, but they came no further.

I was dozing when the rattle of metal woke me. A blood moon hung in the sky as a line of ragged slaves shambled past, carrying picks and shovels on their shoulders and wearing eighteen inches of heavy chain around their ankles. Every 4th man carried an iron ball, and others carried lanterns. Mean-eyed men with shotguns walked beside them to the rows of bodies, blue and grey, laid out along the length of the field. The procession stopped, and the slaves started digging long trenches, working in an easy, familiar rhythm.

"Is it necessary to keep these men chained, sir?" I turned to see Col. McCook riding up to the man in charge.

"I wouldn't have these niggers long if I unchained them," said the man.

"I suppose so, but frankly, it offends my nature," said the Colonel.

"Frankly, the last damn thing I'm worried about is your nature. I would think leaving your young soldiers out to rot would offend you."

"You should remember I'm the one who'll be paying you."

"Colonel, you should remember I'm the one with the only bucks left in this county. I want your money, but don't need it," said the slave owner. "I reckon your soldiers is mighty tuckered out after all that retreating today. So, do you want some graves dug or not?"

Ty and I grabbed a lantern and walked the battlefield. Smoothbore muskets cluttered the field, discarded by Rebs in exchange for new rifled Springfields that dead Yankees no longer needed. Exhausted teams of litter bearers passed us in the dark, ready to collapse and bloody from neck to knees. We nearly walked over Col. McCook in the dark, his pistol pointed at Alva, a constantly grumbling rowdy from home, and one who we all wished would have stayed there. Willie was his only friend, and they often seemed to be up to no good. Alva was holding a boot, and a bootless dead Yankee was at his feet.

"You low-bred bastard," Dan McCook said coldly. "I should have you shot."

"I was wrong, But I don't have no shoes," said Alva. His words were contrite, but his voice wasn't.

"Why don't you have shoes?"

"I was robbed."

"Colonel," Lyman said, appearing out of the dark. "That man is from my unit. He lost his own boots gambling. I imagine he's preparing to lose those boots gambling."

"A lying grave robber that can't throw dice? A battlefield buzzard, picking our flesh?" asked McCook. "The choice is yours. You will fight me, and end this here, or I'll place you under arrest and you can take your chances at a court martial."

"I'll fight you, Colonel," Alva sneered. He was tough, good with his fists, and quick with his boots, when he wore any. "Whenever you're ready."

A circle formed. Wagers were made, and excited voices shouted over each other. Alva swung hard and missed, several times. McCook had trained as a boxer, while Alva's training had been beating up drunks. Alva was already winded when McCook stepped into him with a flurry of jabs, hooks, and crushing right hands. It could have been over right then, but I guess the Colonel really wanted to get his point across. He stepped back, let Alva catch his wind, then lit into him again. The big man swung wildly, and the slender McCook dipped inside and landed two hard jabs. Alva threw a tired overhand right and McCook bloodied his nose. Alva, eyes almost swollen shut, continued to curse and wheeze, connect with air, and get beat like a mule. A few minutes later, McCook stepped back and left Alva unconscious in the dirt.

"Let him keep the boots. He took a thorough beating for them. He may as well have them."

Stones River, Tennessee
December 31st, 1862

Shortly after the Battle of Perryville, our army made winter camp outside Nashville, which was also the Army's western supply depot. By the time the 52nd got there, Nashville was a garrison town under full Union Military occupation, protected by 55,000 soldiers. Four major railroads crossed the city, and there was open shipping on the Cumberland River.

Red-hot iron flowed through the city, and thousands of jobs opened in the furnaces and foundries, as well as depots, warehouses, hospitals and other support areas. Roughnecks, immigrants, and transients flooded the city. Prior to the war, the city had 17,000 residents, and that number had tripled, even with many loyal secessionists fleeing the city. City politicians and prominent society leaders, businessmen, and ministers were ordered to sign an Oath of Allegiance, and the Army took control of police and fire protection, hospitals and courts.

In late December, the Army of the Cumberland, as we were now called, left Nashville and headed southeast. There were still official inquiries into the questionable decisions all over the Perryville battlefield that hot, bloody day. The worst action was Gen. Buell's refusal to interrupt his meal and assume command of the battle, refusing to believe repeated reports from his officers that a battle was taking place. He had been dining with Gilbert for the first hours of the fight, and they'd found some crackpot scientist to say an "acoustic shadow," basically a hill, kept the sound of battle from reaching them. No one believed that, and even if that was the case, his officers had begged him to join the battle and he had ignored them. Either way, Buell and Gilbert had been relieved of command and others were facing the same inquiries. Reprimands and relief of command were still possible for Gen. Alex McCook, whose corps had shattered and fled the field in chaos.

I didn't really know what happened with Gen. McCook, but I had watched his Corps taking a beating only a few hundred yards away to our left. We could have marched there in less than ten minutes, and our cannons could have reached them without limbering. But, the truth was, it didn't look like they were doing much to save themselves. Correctly, or incorrectly, the consensus after the battle was that Alex and been lazy, late and sloppy in placing his force, and Buell's apathy nearly destroyed his own army. Some said there were personal rivalries and jealousies involved. Whatever the reason, I know Col. McCook was livid that he was not permitted to provide assistance to his brother. The Colonel, in an admirable demonstration of fidelity, had gone to Washington to defend his brother's battlefield decisions.

With the Colonel in Washington, the 52nd, and a few other new regiments, were to remain behind to protect the important city. Suffering from boredom, put off by the noise and stink of the city, and with the memory of Bull Nelson's murder fresh in our minds, a few of us decided we were done babysitting officers. Greusel's 36th Illinois was badly depleted by battle and illness, and we knew a few of their men, so it didn't take much for Captain Dunnock to get us temporarily attached as skirmishers for the Illinois men. We didn't expect any trouble when we went out. I don't think anyone really did, not those of us in the ranks anyway. The Rebels were close, but neither the terrain nor the weather favored battle.

Bands Before Battle

On December 30th, our division was camped two miles outside Murfreesboro, along the Stones River. Just a few farm fields away, the Rebel camp stretched across five miles of hills, with enough twinkling campfires to light up all of Tennessee.

"It's freezing," I said.

"I thought so," Ty said. "I see the snow."

"You're funny," I said.

"Did you really want to stay in Nashville and guard storerooms of fatback and beans?" he said. "Or watch another general get murdered?"

"No, but I wouldn't have minded guarding a soft bed and a warm stove," I said, but it wasn't that bad. It was a beautiful winter countryside, and a blanket of pure white covered everything. Big, sticky snowflakes slowly floated through the trees, and the drooping pine branches dropped tiny alabaster avalanches on our caps and shoulders. The grease of foraged geese and pigs sizzled and popped in the fire, and the mouthwatering aromas wafted through the camp along with the snow.

"Hey, would you listen to that?" I said.

"It's the Illinois boys," Ty said, "Over that way, putting on a symphony."

We walked toward the sound and found several regimental bands had assembled at the edge of camp and formed one big orchestra. As they finished a robust Yankee Doodle and started Hail Columbia, ten thousand voices joined in.

"That's real nice, but it's too cold for me," said Ty.

"Hold up," I said. "What's that, they're playing Dixie?"

"No, that's not us, I guess the Rebs were feeling left out," said Ty. The Rebel band, from 700 yards across the meadow, played "Dixie" and then "The Bonnie Blue Flag." For the next two cold, snowy hours, we cheered the Rebel band, and they cheered ours, back and forth, all the way to tattoo. For the finish, both bands played "Home Sweet Home." Blue and gray armies cheered raucously, and we all went to our tents with smiles, and not thinking so much about tomorrow.

At 1am, Ty and I dropped our heavy quilts, filled our canteens with boiling coffee, and slipped out of camp. The temperature had continued to drop, and a bitter wind whistled through our bones as we crept through the trees looking for sign of Confederates. We saw no Johnny Rebs, but the snow-heavy trees were filled with owls. Every few steps one would hoot, and I'd jump halfway out of my pants. I'd just got done jumping when another sound reached us. Ty heard it before I heard it, but together we crawled into dense brush and listened at the tromp-tromp-tromp of a large Rebel column growing closer.

"They are coming out right in front of Sheridan," Ty said.

"Two divisions," I said, when we got our first glimpses of the enemy. There were a lot of them.

"Yep, looks like that to me, too." Ty said. "Travelling light and moving fast. We're gonna get hit at dawn."

"Let's go!" we both said, and sprinted toward the Union line, hoping neither side would shoot us. We crashed and cursed through the snow-drifted, old-growth forest, tripping over briar patches and roots until we were within shouting distance of the Yankee pickets.

"To hell with Braxton Bragg. To hell with Jefferson Davis!" we shouted as we ran across an open field. "Don't shoot. We're friendly."

"Who's there?"

"52nd Ohio," said Ty, once we were facing the pickets. "We need to see the General."

"I thought we left you warm and cozy in Nashville. Something about your Colonel being a pain in the ass," said the sentry.

"You did, most of us. We are temporarily attached to the 36th Illinois," said Ty. "But never mind that. There's about 20,000 rebels not far behind us. If we don't get moving, the next person you talk to just might be Braxton Bragg, and then you can explain yourself to General Sheridan."

"You're sure about this?"

"Completely."

"Well, come on then," said the soldier. "You best not be trying anything funny."

We reached Col. Greusel's tent at 4:00am, which led to a frantic search for Sheridan. We finally located the General sleeping in a gum blanket outside his tent, rolled up against a log. I thought this was strange, but his staff didn't seem to. Whatever his sleeping habits, he sprang up shouting orders and his staff scrambled for horses, maps, lamps, coffee and surgeons.

"Get 'em up, get 'em up!" Sheridan shouted at his commanders, "Get 'em up now!"

The Slaughter Pen

After we gave our report, Ty and I hurried back to the rugged cedar forest at the center of Sheridan's frontline. In the dark, foggy morning, the long, cold slabs of rectangular limestone outcroppings, each big enough to hide half-a-dozen men, crossed the forest floor like rows of tombs. We hadn't been there long when the Confederate artillery erupted. Cannonballs exploded, soldiers screamed, and toppling pine-trees splintered. Jagged shards whirled through the blinding smoke and mist in the dense forest, striking men down like sweeping medieval swords.

We flattened ourselves between the big limestones and hugged the earth. After an eternity of destruction, the cannons stopped and the only sounds were the cries of the wounded and the timid peeps of a few shell-shocked birds. We crouched in dread, staring into the murky forest. Every birdcall became a bugle, every broken twig was a rifle shot and every squirrel was a long-bearded, bloodthirsty Rebel come to slit our throats.

It was almost a relief when lines of Rebels stepped from the shadows and started across the field. Now it was our artillery's turn, and the canister shot flew thick and furious. Our rifles shredded their line, but as one man fell, another stepped into the gap. They disappeared into a cloud, but at fifty yards, the Confederates burst out of the smoke, screaming like forest demons.

I was flat-footed when a yowling Rebel raced past me and sunk his bayonet between a Yankee's shoulder blades. I blasted him out of his floppy new Yankee brogans, but when I stepped toward my dying comrade, another Rebel charged from the dark. I parried his bayonet, but he was powerful, and I was soon whipped. He swatted me away easily, and bent me backwards over a slab of stone, his rifle crushing my throat. Even as I died, I smelled the man's sweet rotting teeth and saw the cold hate in his eyes. Then someone threw warm soup in my face. When I opened my eyes, the dead Reb had a bullet hole the size of an apple where his nose and eyes had been. The soup was his blood and brains, and I was dripping in it. He sagged onto me and I shoved his body away, checking myself for wounds but all the blood was his. After an eternity, the bugles called the Rebels back and I collapsed against a tree, gasping for breath and retching until Ty dragged me behind a rock, as limp as a dishrag. We watched them inch back, resentfully, silently, like a kicked tomcat, knowing they'd be back soon.

Before long, we heard them coming, but the murky gloom kept them hidden until it was too late. They came roaring back, many more of them, and wilder, and they were on us in a swarm. I fired at shapes and swung at shadows, until desperate hands dragged me down, clawing at my face. The ugliest man in the Confederate army gouged at my eyes and would have killed me if his ears weren't so big, but I grabbed one of those hairy, elephant flaps with one hand and drove my knife through his breast with the other. I won that one, but it wasn't long before I was dragged down again. And again. I got back up each time, bloodier, more desperate, desperate in a way I never knew existed, desperate to survive, desperate to inflict pain.

The Rebs pulled back for the last time, and I collapsed, too tired to even reach for my canteen. I woke up on top of Ty, between two blood-slicked limestone slabs. Two dead Yankees were an arm's length away, smashed like brittle strawmen and wedged tightly into the crevice by an unexploded cannon ball. Their toes pointed at the clouds, and their faces were in the dirt. Their ammunition boxes were still full, so we rolled the ball off them and pulled them out before they froze, straightening them for burial and pocketing their cartridges. Muddy, bloody and red eyed, we peered through the trees, too tired to talk, too tired to even look at each other until messengers from the rear returned with distressing news. The divisions on both sides of us had broken and ran early in the fight.

We were now the only division still fighting in that part of the battle-field, and we had been forced onto a narrow finger of land with Rebels on three sides.

"So, we're surrounded?"

"You could put it that way," said Ty. "I'd look at it as we can assault the enemy anywhere but back, and that oversight will likely be corrected."

"And alone?"

"You're painting an unattractive picture here. We have each other."

"That's cold comfort," I said.

"Those boys in the rear should be well rested, in case if they have to save us," said Ty. "So, there's that, too."

We dozed, and waited. Fear had been overcome by exhaustion. The sounds of battle had moved away and quieted when we heard a large force rushing through the trees behind us, but loud cheers quickly told us this was our Yankee reinforcements. Our boys who had fled early returned to the front to restore their reputation. Ty and I hurried toward the rear before anyone changed their mind, dropping into a bone-weary slumber in the mud with the remaining few who had defended that bloody circle of trees and survived.

After dark, we gathered some torches and walked onto the battlefield with the men from Illinois who were searching for their fallen friends. Our 5,000 men, attacked from three sides, had held off over 15,000 Southern veterans. The fields were covered with shattered bodies, and the forest floor was full of men who had lain there all day, bleeding and suffering. Many wouldn't be found for days, and some would never be found at all. The Illinois boys from the Chicago stockyards named that part of the woods the Slaughter Pen, because the blood-covered ground looked like a butchering floor at hog-killing time.

Sagging soldiers, covered in blood and black powder, stalked the woods, calling out, their voices lost in the smoke-hidden devil's chorus of cries of pain, cries for mother, cries for water. We hadn't been out long when we realized half of those on the field searching were Confederates looking for their own friends and brothers. Even in the middle of such death and destruction, the better part of human nature took over. Conversations between warring factions started, acquaintances were made, and the friendly bartering began. Small circles of men, who had been trying to kill each other a few hours before, sat around small fires, passing jugs. I was examining some goods when I almost tripped over a frail Confederate, a young boy, who sat in the field quaking with shivers and staring silently at something I couldn't see. He wore brogans that were more string than leather. I looked at Ty.

"Things have changed," Ty said with a shrug.

"Here," I said, pulling new ankle boots off a dead Yankee officer who had already lost his hat and coat, "It's cold. Put these on. He's done with them."

"All right, Yank, that was fair of you," a Rebel private said, holding the pair of binoculars I'd been admiring.

"How much?" I said.

"Them spy glasses will be dear," he said. "Is that a wad of newspapers stuck out of your bag?"

"Those are Yankee spyglasses. You just picked them up. And what do you boys need with a newspaper?" said Ty. "Don't know what you'd want with them papers. I reckon reading material for a Reb is as much good as a horseshoe on a goat."

"I been reading for a spell how us illiterate crackers is whoopin' you ballroom Yankees all over Dixie. I can read plenty well enough to make that out," said the man.

"Except not so much today," I said.

"You ain't looked around then," said the Rebel. "Looks to me like all them that's supposed to be beside you is well behint you, and us that's supposed to be in front of you, is all around beside you."

"Will you be coming back over in the morning?" asked Ty.

"Hellfire, I sure hope not. If we couldn't scrape you out of there today, we'll have no easier time of it tomorrow. Jokin' aside, you fellers is damn fine marksmen, and a good bit scrappier than for what you're credited," he said. "Even outnumbered as you are, the terrain favors you. Your position is strong. I believe we are about done in."

"Speaking for myself, I'd prefer you didn't," I said.

"Speaking for myself, I'd prefer to go home, and leave this damned place. Return this war to those that thought it up in the first place," said the bristle-faced man.

"Well, why don't you then?"

"I reckon I will. As soon as you do."

We took a rest, downed the last of our coffee, and rejoined the searchers in the cedar jungle, wading through the streams of cursing, overwhelmed litter bearers as they pulled wounded men from the rocky ravines and struggled through the trees with their maimed cargo.

"Over here," Ty said, standing over a groaning, bloody boy that had been shot through the neck. The boy's face was blue, and ice crystals glistened in his downy teenage beard. I summoned a worn-out contraband, and we loaded the boy into his empty wheelbarrow. I pressed a dead man's blouse to the boy's wound as we hurried toward the farmhouse hospital, but, at the door, a man stepped out and stopped us.

"Lay that man in the yard, you can't bring him in here," said the bald, bespectacled doctor in a blood smeared butcher's apron.

"We will not," I said. The slave turned to take the wounded man away, but we told him to stay put.

"Get on there, Daniel. We don't need your help at the moment. Go on now," snapped the surgeon.

"We ain't leaving," said Ty.

"I'm not trying to be callous about this," the doctor said. "But I'm told there are 30,000 wounded men on this bloody damned field. Many of those will be dead by morning. Your man there is no different than any other."

"Don't matter none," said Daniel. "Dis man stone daid anyhow."

"This is our reality. Not enough space. Not enough doctors. Not enough medicine. Hell, not even enough blankets," said the doctor. He motioned toward a hospital orderly holding a mirror to a bloody man's mouth. When the mirror didn't fog, he pulled off the dead man's blanket and went to the next. We returned to the field, where North and South had joined together to sing hymns and tend to the wounded around small fires.

"You hear that all three of Sheridan's brigade commanders were killed yesterday?" I asked Ty in the morning, after we finished an excellent breakfast courtesy of General Sheridan.

"I heard it. I'm sure glad Col. Dan was in Washington," said Ty. "Thank God for Braxton Bragg, though. Snatched defeat from the hands of victory once again."

"Sheridan's riding right this way!" shouted a young soldier as he sprinted past us, spreading the word, and we turned to see a beaming Sheridan waving his hat to the loud cheers of his men.

"Boys, if we'd had more bullets, we'd have chased them to Georgia. That won't happen again," said Sheridan, and gave a rousing speech to cheers and whistles. "I'll not take such a ferocious bunch off the line."

"You're the scouts from the 52nd Ohio?" Sheridan asked. He'd surprised us as we lounged around our meager campfire.

"Yes, sir," Ty said.

"I believe," said Sheridan, "You saved our asses. Without your warning, we would have been overrun, as most others were. Should your Col. McCook ever decide he wants to fight traitorous damned Rebels more than he wants to aggravate the generals in Washington, I'll inform him of your valorous actions. Either way, I am putting you in for commendations."

Union Army Camp

We lived in a cabin outside Nashville for the winter, and I didn't mind. Inside the city, the homes were too cramped, and the school buildings and warehouses too crowded and loud. We found a spot on a hillside where Teddy and Ab oversaw the construction of our sturdy cabin, with a floor, fireplace and chimney that was as good as mine at home. We bought a few extra boards from our traveling sawmill, and with some cotton from the Nashville wharves, we made some decent bunk beds and were quite comfortable the whole season.

Even in the worst weather, we amused ourselves. The morning after the first heavy snow, I joined my cabin-mates as they walked outside to use the latrine. Just when we were at our most vulnerable, twenty of our comrades from Illinois sprang out of the trees and pelted us with snowballs they had been packing hard all night. As we fled toward the cabin to regroup, a swarm of our friends in the 52nd charged from the woods and drove our attackers from the field. More men rushed to join in, and soon the rolling battle stretched to a mile of white fields and snow-covered fences. We flanked them, and they flanked us, but daring frontal assaults usually carried the day. The furious contest lasted until dark, and casualties were heavy. Bumps, bruises and twisted ankles were common, and someone certainly had an eye poked out. Nothing this thrilling, with so many reckless, wild boys running around, could ever occur without someone getting an eye poked out.

It was mid-March and drizzling the first-time Capt. Dunnock took the company out to the soggy meadow that served as the rifle range. We'd had few chances for target practice until now, and those had been with the entire company firing volleys at blankets draped from tree limbs and fence posts the height of a man and the width of a company front. Captain Dunnock said that shooting at those stationary walls was the way it had always been, so, this time we were surprised to see individual, man-sized targets pinned on hay bales a hundred yards away.

"What's this, Captain?" a few men asked.

"Be patient," he said. We relaxed on the hillside while the Captain talked quietly to a man leaning against a pine rail that ran nearly the length of the field. He was a slight man, with the tan leathered face of an outdoorsman, and silver curls trailed over the shoulders of his buckskin jacket. He held a Sharps breech-loading rifle, the same as mine at home, and eyed us coolly while he spoke to Captain Dunnock.

"These are my men, Sergeant Arnold," said the Captain, motioning toward us. "Yours for the day. These are good lads, smart and hard working. Ohioans."

"Ohio.... squirrel hunters, eh? Well, that's fine," said Arnold. "Thank you, Captain Dunnock, I'll have them back in time for supper. Most before that."

The Sergeant turned, and without a word, fired ten consecutive shots into the head of a man-sized target standing across the meadow. With each shot, we cheered a little louder, because all ten holes couldn't have been in more than a five-inch pattern. He finished and took a few steps toward us using a cane, and dragging a shrunken leg.

"I was one of the early students of Hiram Berdan. Who knows who he is?" the sergeant asked.

"The U.S. Snipers. The Tree Frogs," said a voice.

"That's right. And I was one of the best, but six months ago, I received this crippling wound. It was one of those hexagonal Whitworth .45 caliber rifles at 400 yards, hit twice within sixty seconds," said Arnold, and we sat silently as he continued. "Those mountains were full of South Carolina sharpshooters that day. Now they're full of dead Yankees with hexagonal bullet holes in them."

He walked up and down the line looking each man in the eye.

"Listen up, your enemy is a dangerous one. Back in Dixie, they spend their days on horseback with a gun, chasing baying hounds," Arnold said. "And their evenings they spend in a corn crib, with a back-clawing colored gal."

That got some belly laughs.

"Sundays, they spend fighting the pervasive temptations of incest. With mixed results," the Sergeant said. "But whatever they do, they can shoot. And they can get through the woods and mountains as quiet as a mountain cat. And just as deadly."

After the speech, Sgt. Arnold issued each of us a Sharps, and for the remainder of the day we lined up and shot likenesses of Rebel President Jefferson Davis, Robert E. Lee, and Braxton Bragg.

"I am awestruck with your marksmanship. You've never shot like this before," Ty said, and only about half of that was sarcasm. I'd practiced with Pete and Jay nearly every day after Devol had shown up at my house, and I was wrath on those targets.

"They said I was apt pupil. This is either very easy, or you guys are just really, really bad. Maybe I'm just a natural," I said, more surprised than Ty at how well I was doing, hitting almost every shot. The Captain had just stepped away, after a whistle of admiration at my work.

"Right. Sometimes my belly hurts all day from laughing at you," Ty said. After that, we drilled daily, as the Colonel had promised we would. Our officers were men of their word, but they also worked just as hard as we did and probably harder. I often saw Col. Dan in the lamplight working well into the morning, surrounded by charts, maps, and officers, all crowded under a low hanging tent.

Three months after the shared slaughter at Stones River, both sides were still licking their wounds. We jeered at each other, and occasionally sniped at each other from our picket lines, but that was pretty much the extent of it. The Union side stayed put in Murfreesboro and Nashville, and Bragg withdrew about fifty miles across the mountains to Tullahoma. In April, the camp came alive as the mountain flora greened brilliantly and the first rains of spring rushed down the slopes and washed away the stink and filth of 80,000 men. As the thaw softened the ground, the winter's dead were pulled from long-frozen creeks and snowbanks and buried in long graves at the edge of the trees. Wound tight as a clock by cabin fever, young soldiers rushed to make up for their winter of inaction with games and gambling of a hundred types, baseball, footraces, horse races, horse shoes, wrestling matches, the sun coming up and any act that involved moving or breathing parts.

At the same time, after many hours at the rifle range, a dozen of us exchanged our Springfield muzzleloaders for breechloading Sharps. We took our part in regimental exercises, but more often the Captain led our small group into the wilderness for separate training, sharpshooting and frontiersmanship, and fighting methods we'd never seen before.

I went every time I could, and the long days of practice were bearable, sometimes even pleasant, in the brisk air scuffing through the trees. My accuracy with the Sharps continued to improve, and my cabin mates soon found sport in standing me as a bully trap against actual backwoods marksmen from other regiments. They searched out braggarts and cocksure riflemen who saw me for the effete university dandy I was, and coaxed a challenge out of them. Being from Appalachia, I knew very well that many of these southern Ohio hill people were raised on panther milk and teethed on bear gristle. They were fine people, but like about anyone, they didn't care to be skinned. But even more than the shooters, their financial backers were never pleased when, after missing my early shots, wagers were tripled and I would hit my last ten or twenty. The fact I wanted no part of any chicanery discouraged my friends not at all.

We'd just taken sixty dollars from some Hoosiers the day before, and they'd tried to stir up the whole camp, claiming they'd been cheated. When they refused to shut up, Ab finally drove their spokesman's head into a honey bee hive in a hollow tree. Ab had been warned about roughing up our own men before, and I'd seen his victim earlier in the day. His face was swollen with bright red welts and he was mad enough to whip a bear.

That evening at our campfire, the disfigured man, with carbuncles seeping down his face like some mythological sea creature, burst out of the trees and charged. He was tackled before he killed me, but only calmed down after the Captain promised to hang him upside down on a wagon wheel for a day or two. Captain Dunnock's s long experience told him a military camp was no place for loud-mouth sore losers who'd made bad bets. With a good contingent of salty Indianans still skulking about, the Captain told us to gather our gear and get ready to march. When he returned 30 minutes later, he threw us some hardtack and bacon, pissed on the fire, and we were on our way.

Devol is Spotted

"Here comes Captain Dunnock," said Ab. It was a crisp, early spring day, and we were loitering outside our cabin, whittling, mending clothes and generally lying about anything that could be lied about.

"Some news, lad," Lyman said, after greeting us cheerfully and plopping down on an empty stump. "Some of Bragg's cavalry surrendered. Nathan Bedford Forrest's cavalry to be more specific. Your Mr. Devol is a colonel with Forrest's Cavalry."

"Are you certain?"

"Quite certain. These men are as disgusted and terrified of him as we are. It seems his crimes aren't confined to northern women. Or black women. But still the same crimes. Those are the rumors, anyway, according to the Johnnies," said Captain Dunnock. "They are not too far up ahead. The prisoners say Forrest's Corps is raising hell all through Tennessee and Georgia, raiding, bushwhacking, horse stealing, and the guerillas are riding in their wake, picking the bones."

"What can we do?"

"We'll get 'em, lad," said the Captain, "Just be patient. We'll get the black hearted bastards."

The Captain pushed us hard to use the mountains to our advantage, to fight the way he had in the jungles and deserts of Asia and Afghanistan. He pounded surprise, silence, and speed into us, and showed us how to use fear and uncertainty to our advantage. And he showed us how to build wicked looking traps with wooden spikes that he said came from the blackest-souled fiends outside of Abaddon.

If we were not building traps, or nearly blowing ourselves up making our own Ketchum grenades, the Captain had us practicing with every kind of knife that had ever been forged. I imagine he would have had us out sinking battleships if we'd not been landlocked. He showed us some throws and kicks he said came from sneaky Chinamen that could cripple you with one finger, using ancient fighting secrets older than the earth. He also felt that sometimes the best way to avoid a bullet was to get somewhere where the bullets were not, so, he came up with the depraved practice called running, and a lot of it. He said we'd be like the marathoners in ancient Athens. I guarantee no one in contemporary Athens was a marathoner. But, from then on, we could be found huffing and puffing across Tennessee. We weren't happy about it, and took a great deal of ribbing from other units, but he was the Captain, and he was the one that had survived three massacres. So, his argument seemed to have merit.

"Come on, now, lads, is it really as bad as all that?" the Captain asked, after an eight-mile run that brought us back to exactly where we had started. He sat on a shaded log, not even breathing hard and pointedly ignoring his canteen as the rest of us gulped and gasped and wheezed like tortured train engines. Any rebel in Tennessee could have heard us.

"Yes, it's as bad as all that," panted Ab, flopped face down on a bed of pine needles, but speaking for all of us. I was in agony, as painfully winded as I'd ever been, just like everybody but Ty, who looked as cool as peaches and cream. It was becoming annoying.

"Have we caught up with them yet, at least?" asked Ab, not noticing where we had stopped.

"We're not chasing anyone. We're practicing chasing someone," I said.

"Or being chased," Ty said thoughtfully.

"We ain't after nobody?" asked Ab. "That's what he said, but I sure didn't think that's what he meant."

"Don't worry," said the Captain. "These mountains hold plenty of Johnnies, and I'll walk you right up on 'em when you're ready. Right now, you're not ready."

At dawn a few mornings later, I slipped into the light fog and headed to the creek to relax and get away for a few minutes. I followed the sound of the gurgling water until I came upon Col. McCook, who sat on a smooth black rock with his pants rolled up to his knees.

"Good morning, Private Carew, an unexpected pleasure," he said. The mountain stream swirled around his calves, still bringing patches of ice down from the mountaintop. I followed his lead, but gasped when the cold water hit my feet.

"Wakes you up, doesn't it?" said McCook.

"It sure does," I said.

"I've been thinking about you, Carew. That was a fine job at Stones River," he said. "It looks like Capt. Dunnock's estimation of you was correct."

"It was a rough spot," I said. "For a while I wasn't sure we'd make it out of there."

"Yes, but you did. You and your partner, the sheriff," said McCook. "May have saved the day. Almost certainly saved the day. The Captain was proud. I'm proud. Sheridan is grateful. All the way to the top. That's always a good thing."

"I wouldn't want to disappoint any of you."

"The Captain tells me there's a certain colonel you want to find. What's that about?" McCook said.

"He didn't tell you?"

"He did, but I'd like to hear it from you."

"Devol is the colonel's name. He came to Ohio and raped and murdered my fiancee and another young lady. They were both exceptionally intelligent and beautiful and driven to making our world a better place," I said. "Devol and his men butchered them. He claimed he and his killers only came to Ohio chasing runaway slaves. He was gone before we found the bodies."

"And you don't believe that?"

"No. All that for a single slave makes no sense or money. She knew him, and had sharply given him the mitten a couple years prior. He took it poorly. But when he showed up, she was stubbornly certain it was coincidence, nothing more than an opportunity to frighten and bully us. I didn't think so," I said. "I don't think so."

"Because he was a slave catcher, you assumed he would eventually join the Rebel army, and you came here to get revenge?"

"Not assumed. I hoped I would find him, but I never assumed. But, yes, I came for revenge, and I will take it or die."

"And Captain Dunnock believes he's found him?"

"Yes. Devol is a colonel under Nathan Bedford Forrest."

"So I understand," said McCook. "I hear Gen. Forrest is an excellent strategist and tactician, a wonder with sword and saddle, but a vicious, remorseless, perhaps even cruel warrior."

"Yes, I've heard the same," I said. "It doesn't change anything."

"I would have been disappointed if it had. Captain Dunnock says he's had you out in the mountains, scouting and doing some sharpshooting, learning other skills," said McCook. "Did he tell you Frank Gurley also rode with Forrest? That there is a strong possibility that Devol was in the raid that killed my brother? What would you do if I told you to go after him?"

"After who?"

"Devol and any of his feral disciples. The bushwhackers and back-shooters. Until they're all dead."

"I'd do it."

Nashville

By late April the weather had warmed considerably, and we were now scouts for the 52nd. We were sure there weren't any Rebels anywhere within thirty miles of Nashville, but we still used every opportunity to get away from the noise and smells of camp. And to improve our skills. The Captain made the statement that Ty could track a flea over a flat rock, but the rest of us sounded like elephants dancing on a hill of coconuts, which I took to mean we needed to work on our stealth. After a couple weeks, we hadn't gotten anyone killed, and he grudgingly said we weren't all that bad.

One afternoon, in an on-and-off, drippy, dark day, we were relaxing in our cabin when the urgent rumbling of an agitated crowd brought us outside. A squad of cavalry rode somberly up the muddy street, leading two horses with a dead Yankee tied across each. Their arms swayed in stride and hangman's ropes bloated their purple faces. The horses stopped at a cabin close by ours, and a handful of rough looking men emerged. They were hard men, Ohioans from coal country. A barrel-chested, pock-marked man with flowing red-and-gray hair stepped out of the cabin, blinking in the sun. The others stood well back as the man walked to the horses, staring wet-eyed at the dead boys laying across the saddles. He walked around and gave each boy a kiss on the forehead then sobbed loudly and collapsed to his knees. His friends lifted him up and helped him inside the cabin. I knew exactly what he felt like. The anguished cries that came from the cabin were my own, and they carried through the pines.

The crowd parted, and went quiet as Col. McCook and his staff rode in, staring hard at the nooses. A soldier stepped forward and cut the hangman's ropes and gave them to the colonel, who waved them above his head to a roar of outrage. McCook's jaw clinched tight as he snapped orders, and grim volunteers with picks and shovels on their shoulders led the horses into the woods.

"It's Gurley done it," someone said. "And Charlie Wood."

The Valley

I was deep in the woods, watching a secluded trail about fifteen miles from Nashville which some runaway slaves claimed was heavily used by Confederate patrols and Tennessee outlaw gangs. Judging from the amount of horse sign, much of which was no more than a few hours old, they were telling the truth. More than a little uneasy, I crawled into a thicket near the top of the ridge and waited. I had about given up when a lone Confederate rode into the valley on a balky black mule, which, halfway across the meadow, stopped and would move no further. The rider dug with his spurs, but the mule responded with two strong kicks and some long, grating brays. The Rebel peeled off his shell jacket and slapped it across the mule's ears, but the mule only swished its tail and bellowed, defiantly lifting its chin and showing all those huge yellow teeth. The rider threw the jacket on the ground, and the grinning animal let loose some victory whoops. The soldier climbed back on and kicked some more, but the mule would not budge. I aimed carefully, dead center on the man's chest, but as I squeezed the trigger, something crashed through the thicket behind me. I spun around, expecting a company of Rebels but instead an 8-point buck leapt free of the brush and bounced away. The shot still clanged in my head, and across the field the mule was down. The Rebel's leg was pinned, and he kicked and punched and thrashed with his hat, cursing the lung shot mule as it wheezed and strangled, legs galloping in space as a red stain grew in the grass. My next shot hit the mule beside his earhole. As I crept toward the dying animal, the Rebel jumped up with a revolver in his hand, booming twice in my direction. I fired quick and missed. Another shot whizzed by an inch from my head. I fired again, hitting the rebel in the chest and throwing him backwards. I stepped closer and finished the suffering mule. When his heavy black head thudded to earth, I looked down at the rider, a little boy with freckles. He lay on his side, silently gasping like a hooked fish. His wide eyes stared across the open field, and I hoped desperately he would not turn and look at me. Every thirty minutes or so I'd leave my seat in the shade, and walk over to see if he still breathed. I didn't speak and neither did he. I didn't know if he could, I didn't know if he was aware at all, and I didn't want to find out. He didn't show any pain, just stared, and I didn't show any compassion. It took him three hours to die.

"Hey, who's there? Why are you down here in the dark?" asked the Captain, finding me in the trees. "What's wrong? You look sick."

"I am. I just killed a kid, a young boy," I said. "A child."

"How young is that?"

"12 at the oldest." I said, grinding my knuckles into my forehead.

"Are you sure that young?"

"He was years away from sixteen," I said.

"That's rough, but if he's carrying a gun, he's not a child."

"He was a kid."

"Was he a soldier?" asked Lyman. "Did he have on a uniform?"

"He did."

"I was not yet fourteen myself when I went to Addiscombe, and only fifteen when I arrived in Kabul," said Lyman. "Setting age limits for killing or getting killed is a fairly recent western philosophy. Where I've been, twelve is a seasoned veteran. And one who wouldn't hesitate to slit your throat. I don't expect these are any different."

"I know."

"Well, then, he is an enemy soldier and has to be treated as such."

"He never saw me."

"That's the only reason you're not the dead one," said Captain Dunnock.

"Well, this sure isn't what I thought a war would be."

"It never is first time out. After that I guess it's all what you make of it. No good ones, just some worse than others I guess."

"Cold comfort," I said.

"Yes. Don't expect it to get any warmer," said Lyman. When I didn't respond, he slapped me on the shoulder.

"Come on, lad," he said, pulling me up, "I'll show you some punji stick tricks. It'll cheer you up."

Lyman

"Mr. Carew, I promised to tell you my story one day. Today I feel like telling it. I suspect it's the liquor," said Captain Dunnock a few nights later. It was somewhere between midnight and dawn, and most of the others were asleep when he joined me by the fire. I could smell the gin in his flask and he was expansive.

"I'll certainly listen. But you don't need to tell me."

"But perhaps I do. There are few others around here that would understand."

"I'm not sure that's true."

"I'm chasing a man, too. I've suffered - still suffer - the way you suffer now. Every day I wake up, I suffer. I had my wife taken. Like you. Murdered by vile heathens, in India. Evil like the ones you're chasing," said Lyman. "By all accounts she was tortured horribly before she died. Very unlikely the guilty will ever be caught."

I just gave a slight dip of my head, not really knowing what to say.

"I was married for a good while. No children, thankfully," said Lyman. "These were rebels, too, although that's much too kind a word for them. Nana Sahib had turned them into monsters. I vowed to kill them, though simple killing is much too good for them, too. I'll do my best to help you get your revenge."

"I know you'll help," I said. "What happened to you?"

"I was stationed in Cawnpore. India. There was a rebellion and then a massacre by thousands of deserters, more than ten times our number. We tried to flee, but very few escaped. The black devils took 200 women and children hostage. When our army returned months later, we discovered the rebels had chopped the hostages to pieces, and thrown them

181

down an abandoned, dry well. My wife was among them. Several were still alive when they were thrown in, survived down there for days."

"What happened to the killers?"

"Hundreds were hung, or shot. Some were tied over the mouth of a cannon and blown to bits. All were forced to lick dried pork or beef blood, so they would be damned in their afterlife. A good many were tortured first, as you can imagine. Never let it be said the British take a second in torture, or depravity, to anyone," said the Captain. "But my wife, those murdered children, they never harmed anyone."

"And no one ever caught Nana Sahib?"

"No one. Its rumored he disappeared into the Ghat mountains with his top henchmen, but I don't know. Other rumors are that he made it to the U.S. and is a successful, secluded, business man. But there are many theories. I figure he's dead, but I'll keep looking. To what end I don't know."

"So, whatever became of those villains?" I asked, after the Captain told me about Kabul.

"Well, Akbar Khan was murdered. Poisoned. No one knows for sure who did it," said Lyman. "But most believe he was likely done in by his father, in a dispute over who exactly was boss. Not much kindness in this world. At least I always knew never to let my guard down around the lads of Castle Blackheart. We suffered no illusions of who we were, and who we weren't. That survival training at an early age has served me well over the years."

"Apparently so," I said.

"Loyalty is harder to come by than goldmines. But, there was always one, no matter how rough things got. Holly, of course, the best mate ever, and my old undefeatable chuckaboo Mowbray. Now there's a lad you would fancy. The fierceness of ten tomcats, and the loyalty of a bulldog," said Lyman.

"Mowbray survived Satichaura Ghat?" I asked.

"Oh, I'll say he did, that old lion-heart. When last I saw him, he was pushing a boat full of terror-struck ladies and nippers into the current, with a pack of crazed sowars bearing down on him. His flaming red beard was as wild as Samson's locks as he slew those little brown buggars, roaring like the stalwart Saxon warrior that he is," said Lyman. "But he somehow made it out, and was invalided home, heavily wounded. General Mowbray Thomson now. He's written a splendid book about it, and became quite the gad-about. Those were some rough spots. Awful rough."

"Amazing you survived," I said.

"Ain't it, though," Lyman said. "But, as far as face-to-face, hand-to-hand, cutting eye-gouging fighting, Cawnpore was not the worst. Nor Kabul. The worst would be the Battle for the Taku forts. Second Opium War. China. In '59."

"I don't even know what that war was about," I said. "I'm guessing opium?"

"Profits. They're all about profits. Always. Silk. Satin. Cinnamon. Force them to buy our opium, and lots of it. That sort of thing," Lyman said. "Eggrolls. Honestly, damned if I still don't really know."

"Worse than Afghanistan?"

"We were running away in Afghanistan. We were attacking at Taku, or thought we was, anyway."

"What happened?" A small crowd of young soldiers had formed, as it always did when Lyman decided to regale us with his stories of adventure.

"Taku is a big fort, with a half-mile-long wall of small forts connected to another big fort, strung out on the Pei-ho River. It was pure butchery. At high water, we could have landed our lads under their noses. Instead, after our gunboats cut loose on them, and the Generals didn't see nothing nor hear nothing from the forts, they ordered the land assault at low tide. Our landing boats couldn't get us to solid ground, so we had to wallow across 600 yards of mud and weeds. The ground was so soft, we sunk down nearly to our asses in that foul black gruel, and we were worn out just getting through it," said Lyman. "You've never seen mud until you've seen Pei-ho River mud, and the whole time we were slogging through the sucking goop, not a sound from the enemy. Not a chinee to be seen. It was in the middle of the night by then, mind you. We'd walked over half them and didn't even notice."

"You walked over them?"

"That mud bog was really a thousand mud-covered chinks that had lain there, like that, silent, not moving for two days, just waiting," said Lyman. "Waiting and waiting, doped on poppy paste opium, in their own shit."

"For two days?"

"At least two, probably more. Our scouts sure never saw them moving around. It was horrific," he continued. "Lads, I don't care if you're William Wallace himself. You will piss yourself when a horde of screaming Chinamen bust up at your feet, out of nowhere, chattering like demon monkey bats from the bowels of hell, swinging their Chinaman swords and throwing bamboo spears. Ten of them dragging an Englishman down and drowning him in the mud. Drowning themselves to do it. Ghastly-est thing I ever seen. Ghastly."

"Good Lord," I said.

"Those little yellow bastards can breathe mud, apparently," said Lyman. "Lord knows they eat enough of it without complaining."

"Eat dirt?'

"Yet another mystery of the orient."

"Good Lord," I said again.

"Right then, the fort opened up on us with hot grape," said Lyman. "The whole wall was rigged with cannons they had disguised. Grape, swivel guns and rockets that sparkled like fireworks. Arrows started coming down like rain. Fire Arrows! Our rifles were fouled with mud, and our ammunition soggy and worthless."

"They were firing into their own men? Intentionally?"

"Sure, they don't care," said Lyman. "The one thing China ain't shy on is Chinamen."

"Did anybody make it out of there alive? Englishmen?"

"We landed 1,200 men. Fewer than a third made it to the walls. We threw up the only siege ladder we had, and a hundred of those yellow bastards jumped up with muskets and shot us right off. We tried to pick up our wounded as we headed for the boats, but many of them had sunk, disappeared completely," said Lyman. "Not more than 150 of us made it back to the boats. I really hope them that didn't was dead before the celestials got to them."

"Let's hope," Ty said.

"And, if it makes you feel better, a lot of them weren't any older than ten," Lyman said. "Though it's hard to tell with a Chinaman."

Bliss's Last Sermon

A week later, our squad finally saw the Confederate camp we had been tracking. Enclosed by steep ridges on three sides, hundreds of dog tents were stretched out in rows of fifty. Clusters of Rebels sat around camp fires smoking their clay pipes and drinking coffee, playing chuck-a-luck or checkers, spectators gathered at busy horseshoe pits, and a baseball field was laid out behind a wagon park. Below us, two slave boys led a string of horses toward the stream. While I was straining to see Forrest or Devol, a man in a black frock coat and wide-brimmed black hat, clutching a Bible as big as a hat box, walked across the field to the rough benches in the shade of a big oak a hundred yards away. He sat his Bible down, and when he removed his hat and wiped his face a jolt went through me. Bliss crossed the stage a few times, beaming as the choir got seated and his flock filled the pews.

"Do you see who that is?" Ty said.

"I see him. Looks like he has done well for himself," I said. "I didn't expect to see him anywhere near a battlefield."

"Are you going to shoot him?" asked Ty, as a young soldier tickled the keys on a piano strapped in a freight wagon behind Bliss.

"I plan to. In just a minute."

"What of Devol?"

"Too far out of range, even if he is over there, somewhere," I said. "A bird in the hand, as they say."

The service got underway and the congregation sang the opening hymns. I shouldered my rifle and found Bliss in my sights. He wasn't the one I wanted most, but I had no problem taking him first. Give Devol something to think about.

"You got him?" asked Ty.

"I do. Get ready to run."

I exhaled and shot Bliss beneath his chin as he led the parishioners in "Nearer my God to Thee." He flipped dramatically and blood sprayed the first two rows of worshipers, sending the choir shrieking to the dirt.

"Amen," I whispered. "I'll bet he's surprised about now."

"Life is unpredictable," said Ty. "He can't get any nearer than that."

We made it out of there in a hurry and back to camp with no problems.

Mountaineer in Cabin
June 1863

Lyman now commanded three battered companies and lately had little time to work with us, but he trusted us so we were often on our own.

We had just spent a sweaty morning chopping trails through the man-eating thickets of the Highland Rim, when we stumbled upon a cabin down in a narrow hollow. Every cabin on this mountain was said to share blood and sentiment with Frank Gurley, who'd been captured and imprisoned for several murders, as had several other members of his clan. Charlie Wood now led the depleted gang and our orders were to bring Charlie in, alive if possible.

We spread out and crept toward the cabin until a pack of fierce-looking yard-dogs howled the alarm and loped toward us. We dove to the ground, but the dogs didn't seem inclined to attack. When no one left the cabin, we edged closer until the curs started to growl again.

"You in the house," Ty yelled. "Call your dogs."

"Who's there? You better show yourself," yelled a man's voice.

"You know who we are."

"We ain't got nothin' you want, we ain't done nothin' you claim, and we ain't giving up," an angry, old-before-her-time woman's voice rasped.

"Right now, I don't care if you do. But if you don't pen these dogs, I'll shoot the sons-a- bitches," Ty yelled. "I don't like shooting dogs. I'm less picky about secesh trash."

A few moments later a tiny woman with a face like a withered apple in a much-too-large, dingy calico dress came out and dragged the dogs into the house.

"What is it you want?" the woman shouted defiantly from her porch.

"Charlie Wood, and whoever else is shooting at our army."

"Ain't us," yelled the man from the doorway. "So, get your ass off my property."

"I got a better idea. You show yourself and any that is in there and we won't burn it."

"I wish to hell you would try to burn it, you damn tyrants. Charge the house any damn time you want. We'll be here."

"Well, just stay put then. I'll bring a Napoleon gun up here and drop a few cannon balls down your chimney," shouted Ty.

"I'm a civilian. I ain't done nothin'. That's criminal murder," the man yelled. "The world at large will frown on that."

"The world at large don't care for back-shooting bushwhackers any more than we do, especially a general's murderer," I said. "Keep flapping your yap, and you'll be counting match sticks in a minute."

"We ain't killed no general, no Yankee of no sort, as alluring as it presently sounds," the man yelled.

"Someone up here has been shooting at us. We're here to stop it," yelled Ty.

"Go to hell. If you wasn't up here, wouldn't be no one shooting 'atchee, now would they? Clearly, the man is a piss poor shot, for you to be up here peeving us at supper time. I'll need to speak to Braxton Bragg about this.''

"Go ahead," Ty said.

"Not about you, you ain't no more'n a vexatious bedbug. About our feller's undistinguished marksmanship."

"While I go get those cannonballs up to you."

"Who told you I run with bushwhackers?"

"Don't matter. If not one, then the next," Ty shouted. "The one thing I've noticed about you side-mountain bumpkins is you'd rather tattle than screw. And you all sure like to screw. By appearances."

"Charlie ain't blood. I want no part of this. What do you need to just leave me be?"

Mountaineer in Cabin

We'd been trudging uneventfully through the hot, sweltry mountains for two days when we came upon a lush green valley. It was divided by a misty, crystal-pure mountain stream fed by a waterfall about forty feet up. We knew this cool place between the hills would also be sought out by the Confederates, so we watched for an hour before leaving the safety of the trees and walking toward the stream. Ten steps from the water, a flurry of gunshots sent us diving for cover, with a bunch of hidden Rebels laughing as we knocked each other over on the narrow path.

"Anybody hit?" I shouted.

"Oh no! Oh no!" someone screamed off to the right.

"What is that? Who is that?"

"It's Toughnut, he's hit!" Ty shouted. "Toughnut, hold on, I'm coming over."

Poor Teddy, I thought, as Ty scurried behind the rocks toward him. More than any of us, Teddy had bragged about his soldiering exploits, his soldiering insights, and his tactical superiority to Buell, Rosecrans, Sheridan and any other damn general. He may have been right about the tactical superiority, but, the reality was, up until now, he'd had few exploits. Depending how this went, it could be his first time in a fight, after guarding the Nashville armory during the battle at Stones River. Before that he had been down and nearly dead with the alvine flux during Perryville. The dysentery had never quite left him.

"Never you mind!" shouted Toughnut. There was silence, then loud laughter, then curses. "I'm just fine, stay over there."

"What's going on over there?" I yelled.

"Toughnut just befouled his drawers," shouted Ty. "He'd rather lay in it than move back to the squad. I told him embarrassment ain't a luxury we have right now."

"I don't blame him. He has been a bit boastful, lately. I imagine they'd be a little rough on him," I answered.

"That's sure true," Ab whispered, having crawled behind the same rock as me. "It might be best if he doesn't mingle with the boys just right yet."

"It is a terrible mess," shouted Ty. "I had no idea one man could hold this much."

"They're gone," said Ty an hour later, after taking several men upstream and scouting the woods across the creek. "Teddy, get down to the creek and wash your ass. You can't be walking around like that."

"They'll shoot me."

"I'll shoot you if you don't!" said Ty. "They're gone. Now git."

Teddy peeked out of the ditch, grimaced, then duck-walked toward the creek, naked except for his soiled pants around his ankles.

"Hurry up," Ty yelled." If they wanted to shoot you, you'd have been shot by now. Get in and get scrubbed."

"It's freezing!" yelled Teddy, shivering and gasping and twitching in the icy pool beneath the waterfall.

"Then make it fast," Ty yelled. "Hurry up and wash your drawers out."

"What you doing, Yank?" yelled a deep southern drawl after a bullet pinged off a rock above Teddy's head. "That's mighty presumptuous, you think you can bathe buck naked in the middle of a dang battle. Were I prideful, that would sting."

"If you think this is a battle, I can see why you are losing the war!" I shouted.

"I was bein' figurative," the Rebel shouted again, somewhere in the trees beyond the creek.

"He shat himself," Ty yelled.

"He shot himself?" hollered the rebel, with devilish laughter behind him.

"No, shat himself when the bullets started flying."

190

"Hell's fire!" said Teddy, glaring at Ty. "Do you have to tell every damn body?"

"Yes, that will shame a feller. As well as cause a rash," the Rebel yelled. "But that's more an issue for a sawbones than us savage warriors entrenched in front of you."

"Well, can't you savage warriors give him the common decency of cleaning himself before you kill him?"

"I reckon, but ain't nobody told you taking a bath out here can get you killed?" the voice hollered. "All right, we won't shoot him. We've a few fellers here what probly needs a scrubbin' they own self."

Toughnut climbed out of the creek and struggled to pull on his dripping-wet, sand-scrubbed pants. Three shots clipped the weeds at his feet, so we were all treated to a few seconds of a naked Teddy performing a red Indian's war dance.

"You said you wouldn't shoot him, you traitorous sodomite!" Ty yelled.

"We didn't shoot him. I never said nothing about letting him get dressed. If he goes after those clothes again, we'll shoot him," the voice hollered. "And I ain't traitorous."

The Rebels put a couple shots in the mud and naked Teddy whooshed like a freight train toward our line with bullets nipping at his heels. With it clear we wouldn't be dislodging any bushwhackers today, we headed back to camp. The climb back was miserable for all of us, but especially for Teddy, his skin scraped and torn from sliding in gritty rock and hacking through prickly thickets. After a hard march, we stopped under an apple tree a mile or so from camp and had amassed a nice pile of cores when Col. McCook and his entourage came trotting down the road. The colonel started to say something, but the sight of Teddy, frog-squatting on a log, and wearing nothing but a cartridge box over his shoulder, flummoxed him. McCook stared, twice opened his mouth and started to speak, but nothing came out.

"Get to the quartermaster," his adjutant yelled over his shoulder as they rode away, McCook still shaking his head.

Smokey Row

We stayed in camp for the next few days, and with no pressing business, we set off for a day in Nashville to let off some steam. The business district of Nashville had been taken over by wartime industries and renamed Smokey Row. The war time industries were saloons, dance halls, creep joints and eight full city blocks of brothels. It was said, reliably, that Nashville had 1,500 prostitutes, the most of any city in the South. The lights never dimmed, and around the clock, news boys and barkers wound through the endless sea of soldiers, passing out coupons and handbills promising potent drink and the finest horizontal comforts.

"White, creole, octoroons! A plantation full of taboo princesses, black as sin! A sternwheeler full of single brow Texas debutantes and fallen French chanteuses by the bateau-load. All these lovely creatures embody this glorious city's free markets," bellowed an unevenly whiskered man in a tattered bowler and yellow-checkered jacket, pressing flyers into our hands as we walked past. "The most beautiful women in the world."

Maybe that was true, but at 10am on the moiling, muddy street, the inhabitants of Smokey Row looked pretty rough. Cracks showed in the painted faces of the wrung-out Cyprians sitting on whorehouse stoops, and their once unnaturally rosy cheeks were smeared and smudged over swirls of lipstick that had been blown away hours before. Black streaks ran from their eyes, and their toes poked out of run-down shoes straddling the growing brown puddles of tobacco juice. The morning sun exposed smashed bottles, broken chairs and pools of vomit defacing the grimy sidewalks. Dissipated tosspots were curled up in stairwells with their pants pockets pulled out, if they still had pants at all. The provost guard would be waking them up soon enough, and, undeterred, the majority of our group took off in search of carnal delight. As we walked down the middle of the street, a cadaverous man in a black suit stood with his arms flung wide, his Biblical twaddle a litany of thou's, thy's, and your-will-be-done's. As he beseeched the heavens to bring damnation to this modern Sodom and Gomorrah, a handful of queasy, pale, red-eyed young Yankees from the 52nd, half in and half out of a trash cluttered stairwell, watched him with equal parts fear and scorn.

"Let's pray for these young sinners, damned for having carnal knowledge of a Jezebel," shouted the long-winded zealot as one of the boys gagged on the curb. "The wicked shall not go unpunished, and these have turned their backs on the lord and turned their lips to whiskey jugs and harlots. Unworthy. The wages of sin are death."

"Think we should help those fellows home?" I asked.

"They do look a little green around the gills," said Ty, as a chain reaction of retching took hold of the boys. "I'll see if I can find a friendly wagon to throw them in and tote them home, if you're up to keeping an eye on the rest of ours. I guess that's our assignment for today, says the Captain. Our turn."

"Yes, go ahead and haul them back," I said. "I'll look after these others."

Behind me, the missionary went abruptly quiet. I turned to see Ab's huge, gnarled and scarred fist an inch from the man's bloodless face. I hadn't heard what Ab had said, but I heard what God's messenger said.

"Well, sir, no need for violence," he stammered. "If you're determined to refuse salvation, please present this card at any of the gilded palaces you might visit. I get ten cents for referrals."

Freddy

Everyone had gone their separate ways. Ty had taken the suffering young soldiers back to camp, and I'd gone into a few saloons but had been driven out by too much noise, too much smoke, and a few too many leering desperadoes waiting to cut my pocketbook. I found a small, hidden-away restaurant and had a surprisingly good meal, then, with little better to do, sat on a curb and watched the stupefying amount of debauchery with awe. By six o'clock, the show was old, and I went to retrieve Freddy, who had slipped off to Estelle's, purportedly the finest bawdy house in the city.

Freddy had never expressed much interest in girls, nor they in him. Many suspected, and a few had whispered, that he preferred the company of gentlemen, but I was pretty sure he was just awkward and unsure, and very naive. I did wish he'd stayed at home, though. He'd shown he was as fine a soldier as any man, but suspected these grifters that stalked soldiers like wolves would steal his money, or worse. Heedless of our warnings, he'd become a regular at Estelle's ostentatious house of hedonism.

Heavy rains had left the streets a deep black muck, and thunderclouds rumbled on the horizon. As I crossed the street towards Estelle's I saw Oscar, the blue-black piano player through the gauzy curtains, caressing lusty, musky notes from his 88 pieces of loin-stirring ivory. Earlier in the Yankee occupation, Estelle had protested the provost marshal's order for Oscar to tone it down, after she'd been warned that the pianist's notes were inciting unseemly and lustful demonstrations, even out on the street. The dispute made it all the way to a court hearing, in front of a judge who was a back-door regular at the establishment. He ruled in Estelle's favor. Oscar said that if his playing was the cause of so much temptation, he deserved a raise. He got his money. And back pay.

Occasionally, the Rebels moved their long-range artillery around to interrupt congress of all sorts in the occupied city. I heard the familiar deadly whistling and my foot stopped, hovering a few inches above Estelle's front porch one second before the 20-pound shell smashed through the roof and blasted half the front wall into the sky.

I woke up flat on my back in the middle of the street, making angel wings in a bed of mud and horse manure. I was completely deaf, but certain the naked people stampeding out the smoking walls of Estelle's were screaming. A dozen people stepped on my limbs, or tripped over me, as I struggled to my hands and knees, crawling out of the debris-strewn sludge. Men in sheets, towels, and tablecloths tried to look invisible. Most were soldiers. I recognized several high-ranking officers reduced to socks and garters and hats clamped over the groin. Two houses down, another cannonball blasted through a wall and terror-stricken patrons and shameless painted ladies poured into the street from every house on the block. Drunks dropped to their knees, slurring to the heavens with hands stretched skyward in supplication. A celebrated Brigadier General, nude but for a tasseled hat and stovepipe boots, leapt uninvited into a carriage loaded with the First Baptist Church of Nashville Ladies Salvation Society. The ladies were frantic that their campaign to expose wickedness had taken such a literal turn. The carriage driver slapped a cudgel across the general's head and he flopped into the dirt, his brash priapism aimed defiantly at the appalled pilgrims.

My hearing returned as spectators congregated around the damaged building and tended to the wounded, still scattered in the street. Before the smoldering stack of kindling, which moments before had been the flower of Nashville's whorehouses, a stout woman with a mass of unnaturally platinum hair stood in the yard, barking orders at a hulking bald man. Beyond them a young black woman pounded a jagged sign into the ground, warning, "Looters and Terpsassers Wood be kilt and percuscuted."

Freddy emerged from the ruins wearing a sheepish grin, one shirt-sleeve, one shoe and a thick coat of dust and black powder. As he crossed the street toward me, I could see plainly he had no major wounds, so I asked him to move his shirtsleeve to a more modest posi-tion. I'd had just about enough of seeing the fellows naked, and when his brain didn't appear too rattled, I ran off to buy him some clothes. When I got back, an attractive, rubenesque, blonde-haired woman held her arms, and a pillowcase, around him.

"Cage, allow me to introduce you to my fiancee," said Freddy, shak-ing black powder from his beard as he hopped around pulling his pants on. "Helga. She is from Vienna."

"Vienna?" I said.

"I'm Austrian," she said.

"Fiancée?" I said. "German?"

"Nein, Austrian," she said, with a bit of irritation in her eyes. I knew the difference, but it caught me off guard.

"She is coming home with me after the war," said Freddy. "Her job here pays for medical school."

"Medical school?" I said.

"Yah," she said.

"She's a Hapsburg," said Freddy proudly.

"At a whore house?" I said.

"Have you lost your hearing?" asked Freddy.

"No, it's not that," I said. "Just unexpected to find an Austrian Haps-burg in a Nashville whorehouse."

''I'll admit it's unusual,'' said Freddy. "For the less worldly."

"You met her here?"

"No, actually, we met watching birds. We're both amateur ornithologists."

"Oh," I said. "Like normal people."

The war hadn't changed Freddy like it had the rest of us. I hoped it never would. He loved his flowers and birds. For being a soft-handed academic, I wasn't too interested in sensitive, sensory things like flowers and paintings. I got my imagery from books, but, on occasion, when the crowding of the camps got to be too much, I would go into the forest with him. Somehow, in the middle of all this ugliness and inhumanity, when we reached some virgin forest the ambrosial sights and smells and sounds of nature became brighter and clearer than I had ever noticed.

"I wouldn't be the first Hapsburg to visit a whorehouse," she said.

"I suppose so," I said.

"Yah, and I ain't killed nobody, at least."

Rip van Winkle

Charlie Wood and his gang of cutthroats were still terrorizing the countryside, killing our soldiers every chance they got, and robbing sympathizers of both sides. We had just missed them several times over the past month. I had been promoted to Sergeant, and my squad had just about given up finding anything on this hunting expedition through the mountains when we came upon a bare-footed old man sleeping against a tree with an ancient smoothbore across his legs. He wore ragged clothes, and had a waist-length white beard full of leaf and bough.

"Look here, Rip van Winkle himself," I said, shaking the man awake. "Where are Wood and his gang?"

"Jumping Jehoshaphat," the man shouted. "You sure put a fright in a feller."

"We don't have a lot of time for cordialities," I said.

"Well, that sure ain't the friendliest way to meet a feller," the man said, squinting up at us. "'Specially since it seems like you're expecting something from me."

"It's about to get less friendlier," I said. "Just answer the question."

"Well, how would I know that? I only know where I seed'em last."

"Where did you see them last?"

"Well, lemme see. I'd like to say right there where you was hiding all day, making more ruckus than a herd of piney woods rooters that got into the sour mash. I woulda said something, but you all was so dang proud of yourself and your backwoodsmen skills that I didn't want to hurt your feelings none," the hairy old man drawled. "Some of you Yanks is sorely prideful about such matters, though the reason escapes me."

"Yeah, well, we captured you," said Ab.

"Or you has fell into my clever trap, General," the man said to Ab. "But, anyhoozit, that's where you was, and they ain't is. So, got to be some other place."

"Come on now," I said. "Are you trying for some knots on your head?"

"Ah was jes tryin' to rekamember when them rebel fellers went by. Memory's a turrible thing to lose. What was I saying?" said the old man. "Moughta been yesterdee. Moughta been a couple days before yesterdee. Cain't rightly recall."

"Would your memory improve for some coffee?"

"Cain't say. Could mighta. A feller sees so much up here, turrible busy, hard to keep it all straight. It's a whirlwind."

"Right. How about some white sugar and cans of fruit?"

"Things is becoming a smidge clearer," the mountain man said, tapping out his corncob pipe. "You shore want this feller orful bad don'tchee?"

I rolled my neck and looked at the sky in exasperation.

"You know," the man said, leaning against the tree, scraping a stick under the black mud packed into his toe nails. "I ain't never had on a pair of shoes. I always wanted to try me a pair of shoes."

We stared at the man's enormous feet. Then at Ab's.

"Are you kidding me?" Ab said, as he untied his brogans.

"Peel 'em off, big mouth,'' grinned the old-timer.

Charlie

We found Charlie Wood's cabin the next day by following a hog path the old-timer showed us. It cost Ab his shoes, and the rest of us some silver dollars, cans of fruit, Tabasco sauce and white sugar, but the old man finally gave us good directions. It wasn't far, and we surrounded the house and watched from the tree line, thirty yards of tromped-down weeds away. We had watched silently for half an hour when a rifle barrel crashed through the window and popped off a few rounds.

"Who all's in there with you, Charlie?" I yelled.

"Just me and my savior," said Charlie. "Something you godless, nigger-loving barbarians wouldn't understand."

"You're satisfied with that arrangement?"

"I am."

"You're timing's right. I admire a man with self-assurance."

"I'd rather you admire my gun work, looking up at six feet of dirt."

"Charlie? We're going to burn you out," I shouted, as Teddy started a small fire and a couple others built a stack of dry straw. Ab held a rotting bucket of lamp oil he found in Charlie's shed.

"Fuck you, and the leprous wench that birthed you," yelled Charlie.

"Here we come," I yelled, and Charlie fired again, hitting the tree two inches from my head. "Last chance."

"They're going to hang me anyways," yelled the bushwhacker.

"Probably so. Therefore, I'd recommend you use this time to get yourself right with your lord and savior Jesus Christ, whom you mentioned was inside."

"Enough of these bon mots. Come and get me you sons-a-bitches," Charlie yelled and emptied his rifle at us. We fired back with a fury.

"He's down in here," yelled a southern woman's voice.

"Is he hit?"

"Hit bad."

"Bring him out," I yelled.

"He's a big man," she yelled back. "I can't drag him."

"He can't help any?" I said.

"No. I think he's done for. I'm putting all the guns out," she yelled. She took two trips to lay a half-dozen assorted rifles on the porch. We made our way to the cabin door, peering in the shot-out windows as we went. Charlie was down, curled up in the corner, bleeding bad, but we entered the cabin with rifles at the ready.

"Ok, Charlie, let's have a look at you," I said, but Charlie whipped a blazing cavalry pistol from beneath the blanket and killed two young soldiers in the doorway. The others emptied their rifles in Charlie and the woman half-heartedly screamed a time or two.

"Who are you?" I asked, as the screams and smoke drifted away.

"The Widder Wood, apparently," she said, from her rocking chair.

"Didn't know he had one."

"He didn't, until you kilt him."

"I meant wife," I said. "We were told he didn't have one."

"Just one more thing you damned Yankees don't know beans about. Go the hell home."

"These mountain folk sure are a sentimental bunch," said Teddy, and he took some men to search the outbuildings while Charlie's body leaked in the corner. The Widder Wood put in a plug of tobacco, and hit her spittoon three out of three times.

"Don't hardly seem right letting him lay there and take his die that-a-way," the woman said. "Ain'tchee gone straighten him out at least?"

"You're his wife. We are the enemy, remember?"

"Yes, I know. But we ain't really got on lately."

"We ain't really got on either, you may have noticed."

"Out back there," a breathless young private stuck his head in the door. "There's more rifles in that shed out back. You know what else is back there? Fighting roosters."

"I'm taking these sons-a-bitches," said Ab, bounding out the door in his bare feet. I walked outside as the boys came out of the barn with crates of Union Army rifles and sacks and cages full of furious roosters. Charlie's aging horses were hooked up to his rickety wagon that was loaded with guns and chickens.

"Boots for birds," Ab said as he came out of a shed, giggling like a school girl as he held a burlap bag filled with some furious chickens. "It's a new army enlistment bonus. Some Illinois boys scared up some birds someway, and I aim to take their money."

Queen's Agility

"What was your closest brush with death?' one of the boys asked Lyman a few nights later. We'd gathered around the fire and a bottle or two of local white lightning was passed around the circle. The Captain's stories seemed to get a little more profane with each pull he took on the bottle, but I was pretty sure the details stayed true. He could sound like the coarsest high-seas pirate when he chose to, and the young ones, all of us, really, were spellbound by his tales. I figured I heard most of them, but Lyman never disappointed when it came time for ribald tales of adventure.

"The absolute narrowest escape? Well, I was very nearly run through with a dozen lances, right in the Queen's ballroom," Lyman said. "I had accompanied some pompous envoy or another to the Palace for a soiree, a celebration of preening jackasses."

"There was an attack in the Palace?"

"Of sorts," he said. "You're familiar with the queen?"

"Yes, I've seen pictures," I said.

"Agility wouldn't be the first describer to pop into your head, now would it be?"

"Unlikely."

"Yes, exactly," said Lyman. "Well, there I was at the bottom of the Buckingham Castle's curling stairs as some dignitaries came down. There was a sudden commotion, some shouting and squealing, and here comes the Queen, rolling down them stairs tits over teacups. Apparently, her handmaiden had forgotten to tether her drawers. She lands square on her crown, with her slippers pointed at the heavens, and, as I live and breathe, Mrs. Fubb's parlor squinting straight back at me."

"The Queen of England?"

"Aye. But she jumps up quick, gives a bow, and says, ""Did you see my agility just now, Captain? "And, I said, yes, I believe I caught a glimpse," Lyman said. "But I never heard it called by that name before. We calls it a cunny on the frontier."

"You did not."

"Next thing I know, the Royal Lancers have given me a necklace of their weapon points," he said. "And then they sent me to the other end of the world, with reduced rank. Which suited me fine, I might add."

"Really?" someone said.

"Well, why shouldn't it be?" said Lyman. "The best stories are ruined with that line of relentless inquisition. I can imagine you listening to some of Harry's tales of derring-do."

"Who is Harry?"

"My old chum Sir Harry Flashman, who other could it be?" said Lyman. "You Americans have no sense of history. Flashy was the grandest warrior that ever lived, and a Knighted Champion of the Crown. A true Corinthian. He has his detractors, those who say he is a scoundrel, a liar, a cheat, a thief, and a coward, and it's true enough that if medals were awarded for debauchery and fornication, Harry's chest would hold enough to sink the Queen's Navy. But, also indisputable, he was the finest swordsman in three continents, both horizontally and erect. Standing. Whatever. He dueled and bested the best warriors of the world, while bedding twice that number of the most beautiful princesses and maidens. But his end was gruesome."

"I've never heard of him," said Dovie, a gentle boy, and the others said the same.

"Well, it's shameful that you haven't. As daring as he was in battle, no one expected Harry to fall to an enemy," said Lyman. "We always expected he would be shot as he narrowly escaped out a boudoir window. He'd suffered more than one grisly injury in that manner. But, Harry's end came after he was crushed in the street by a temperance wagon as he escorted some nuns across the street."

"Oh, my," they said, as Lyman shook his head solemnly. "What a terrible way to go."

"Aye, but that's not what killed old Harry," said Lyman. "As a result of the accident, Flashy wasn't always able to perform his reckless boudoir acrobatics as before. The ardor was strong, but the flesh was unresponsive, if you understand my meaning. As the story goes, he heard of some rhino-horn magic cure to properly full-rig his man-o-war, so to speak. Full of hope, Sir Harry sped off to the deepest, darkest, most remote underbelly of Africa to find it."

He took a long swig of applejack, and looked around at his spell-bound audience.

"Well, poor old Flashy. He found the rhino horn, and he was fully rejuvenated. They say there was no female within a three-mile radius that Old Flashy didn't mount before the week was out. Then he disappeared into the bush for more," Lyman said. "It was the worst case of horn colic ever recorded in the history of armed service to the Crown, and horn colic ain't rare out on a campaign. When they found him several days later, he was torn and bloody, lying motionless on his back in an African savannah, with buzzards slowly circling overhead, sensing a meal. But, when our gents halloooed him, Old Harry points at those dirty old carrion birds with a lustful twinkle in his eye and says, "Shhhh. Ain't the lasses fetching in their feathered hats?"

Lyman took a drink and continued as his audience waited.

"Well, the lads were able to pull him away from such an un-natural and likely-impossible congress with the promise of a weekend spree at the nearest pleasure house, although that was a ruse. The lasses were only now barely walking from his last force majeure d'amore, and had made it abundantly clear they had no desire for a return romp. But on their way out of the undiscovered jungle, in typical Flashman style, he happens upon a virgin about to be sacrificed. Well, our hero had never left a damsel in distress in his entire life. Seizing upon an opportunity, especially in his current condition, Harry swashbuckled his way to the girl, grabbed a grapevine and swung away. He had an amazing talent for learning languages, and could learn a new one almost overnight. But, this mumbo-jumbo he didn't know, and had mistaken "virgin sacrifice" for "wife and murderer of chief's son." Poor Harry, they chopped his head off and ate him. They said they boiled him for two days and his bonnie Prince Charley never went down. That's my gallant old chum, Flashy. Every story is better, just by having Harry in it. He was many things, but never was he a dreadful bore."

Chapter Ten

Tullahoma

June 24 to July 3rd, 1863

Into the summer Murfreesboro remained Rosecrans's forward base and Bragg was still anchored in Tullahoma, about 30 mountainous miles to the south. Both armies had remained in place since the battle of Stones River, adding men and munitions for our summer offensive. According to the papers, Lincoln was growing increasingly impatient to get the Army of the Cumberland moving and was threatening to replace commanders, but Gen. Rosecrans held out, waiting for more supplies and reinforcements before breaking camp. We all liked Rosie. Perhaps he wasn't a dashing warrior, but he kept his men clothed, fed and protected from the elements, as best he could. Lyman said those generals often win battles that dashing warriors don't.

In late June, Rosecrans finally decided it was time to move against Bragg, whose entrenched Army of Tennessee held a seventy-mile defensive line in the Eastern Highland Rim Mountains, the hostile, saw-toothed ridges which rose about eleven miles from Murfreesboro and encircled the city. Four gaps, Liberty, Hoover, Guy and Bell Buckle cut through the Rim mountain range and their steep slopes, tangled with underbrush and briars, were guarded by pickets in strength. The narrow gaps held vital, but skeletal, railroads, and dirt roads just barely wide enough for two wagons to pass. Our objective was to drive the Confederates out of Chattanooga and seize the railroads that supplied the south. Rosecrans' plan was to send out four separate attack columns, each moving toward one of the gaps, with three of those columns as decoys. Rosecrans hadn't yet decided which column would carry the attack, nor which gap to attack. The terrain was too rugged for cavalry to explore, so the task fell to small units of infantry. Our squad left camp under a torrid cloudburst which never let up for two weeks, the hardest, longest rain on record for Tennessee.

Lyman

We were perched on a heavily wooded ridge overlooking Hoover's Gap, sitting on soggy leaves and moss as spoon-sized water drops fell on our shoulders with the beat of a funeral dirge. We were watching a section of track in the valley floor below us, but there wasn't much of a need to watch it. The hard rain had slowed to a drizzle, but the track was still flooded from the downpours and mountainside washouts, and the roads were little more than knee deep mud puddles that had dips that could swallow a wagon and eight mule team.

I had been scanning the opposite slope every few minutes. If there were Rebs over there, I couldn't see them through the dripping trees and dark shadows. But, once more, I lifted my Stones River battlefield binoculars to look around, and the moment I put them to my eyes, I caught a quick glimmer of metal, a shape that didn't belong. Something dangerous. Staring back at me was a hexagonal barrel, aimed by a bearded assassin in a battered hat that sluiced rainwater down his slicker. Peering down that telescopic sight he seemed huge, big enough to touch. I shouted a warning, but I was too late and the big Whitworth boomed. The whistling bullet passed an inch from my nose and hit the Captain dead center between the shoulder blades and blasted out his chest. His powerful body slammed face down, spraying his cheeks with black grit. We pulled him behind a log, and his face spasmed in agony but he never made a sound. I ripped up a shirt from my haversack and tried to staunch the blood pumping out his chest, but the sopping leaves filled with bright red pools. The rain returned, and I held the Captain's hand while Ab wiped the blood and mud from his face.

"Damn it," Lyman hissed over and over. "Not like this. Not shot in the back."

"Hush," I said, while Ty checked the wound. "Just hold on. We'll get you out of here in a minute."

"No, you won't. This is a mortal wound," Lyman grunted through clenched teeth. "I can't move my legs. Can't feel them."

"Just hold on, we'll get you out of here."

"My lungs are filling up," Lyman croaked, then was racked by a violent cough that sent ribbons of crimson saliva flying. "Just let me die. I'm done anyway, lads. Just go on and let me be."

Tears and rain rolled down our faces as Rebel bullets began to zip through the pine branches. Lyman was motionless but for his tortured wheezing.

"Can we get him down the hill?" asked Teddy.

"No, there's no way. Those Rebs would murder us out there in the open," said Ty. "Our only chance is up and over to that ledge we saw earlier. But, we need to move now."

"I wish to hell you would go on, nothing you can do for me," Lyman choked out a blood clot.

"Maybe so, but I'm not leaving," I said. We found some twine, tied together a poor litter and started up the slope but with every tug, Capt. Dunnock screamed and his limp body slid sideways in the mud.

"Stop, lads, stop!" Lyman whispered. "Just for a minute. Please. I must tell you something."

"What is it, Captain?" I asked, as we slid him up the wet grass. I held his hand and saw his fingers wagging, ever so slightly.

"You're a pip. I hope I wasn't never no ghastly bore to you," he winced, smiled, and suddenly his knife was out. He slit the twine and disappeared over the edge shouting, "Get off this goddamn mountain."

We were stunned into silence, frozen in place, as more bullets snipped the branches. We grabbed the Captain's gear and scurried over the ridge, and away from those deadly hexagonal barrels. Once we caught our breath, we went through the haversack. Freddy had grabbed the Captain's hat.

"What's this old magazine in his hat?" someone asked.

"See that rip," I said. "An Afghan took a swing at his head with a sword. Back then, he had it in his hat to keep warm. It saved his life. Since then, he's worn it for luck."

We found a lithograph of a beautiful dark-skinned woman in a satiny dress. Prema. Nothing else, anywhere, about family. A small leather purse and, inside it, something wrapped tightly in two women's silk handkerchiefs. Prema's. We opened a small box, and pulled back the velvet cloth carefully. Two small bronze cross pattées, with the crown of Saint Edward surmounted by a lion with the inscription "FOR VALOUR." Freddy identified them. Two Victoria's Crosses. Cawnpore and Second Battle of Taku Forts. Lyman had left the service as a major, not a captain as he claimed. He'd talked about the campaigns, but never this.

I was hit with such a wave of weeping and guilt for not knowing this man better, and that now, only this motley collection of drenched hillbillies even knew where he rested. And then only that his crumpled body was resting against a cold rock or soggy pine tree, somewhere down the mountain. I wandered off for a while and no one disturbed me. When I returned, they all showed me they had lined their caps with pages from Lyman's ancient Blackwood's Edinburgh magazine. I lined my hat, too, and kept it until the incident at Chickamauga.

Lightning Brgade

I never met Col. John Wilder, or knew his sense of humor, or sense of history, but his men, his Lightning Brigade, however they came about their name, were as fearsome a bunch to be found anywhere, in either army, in that war. Some men are born leaders, and the Captain and Wilder and Col. Dan were like that. I would, and did, follow McCook straight into death itself, but Wilder's wild, reckless charge, outgunned and outmanned into Hoover's Gap, was a truly awe-inspiring spectacle. It was every bit as stirring as Lord Cardigan's doomed Light Brigade charge into the maw of the murderous Cossack crossfire at Balaclava, and Tennyson's poem about that charge, which had captured the hearts and minds of every cavalryman, blue or gray, in that war.

Ol' Rosey chose wisely when he selected Wilder's brigade to lead the attack. Wilder, born in the Catskills, was most recently from Indiana but he had lived in Columbus, Ohio, before the War. Ab and Teddy knew him, both from Herrold's Mill, and from when they'd worked in Columbus. Together, they had cleared out a few of the city's rougher saloons, and it was during that time that our old sheriff had to ride up there in a hurry to save their bacon. Along with Wilder, in celebration of one thing or another, they had tossed a handful of rowdies, a couple constables, a coach, some mules, and a driver off the Broad Street Bridge into the Scioto River.

Wilder had arrived in Columbus in 1849, 19-years-old and dead broke. He found work as a draftsman, and then apprenticed as a millwright at a local foundry, and spent the next eight years in Columbus learning mechanical and hydraulic engineering. He moved on to Greensburg, Indiana in 1857 and built his own foundry. He was considered an expert, built several watermills in Indiana and Ohio, and patented some related machinery. He'd supplied Herrold's with expertise and equipment several times, and often stopped by when he was in southern Ohio.

He was not one to trifle with, and we tried to claim him for our own, but, even early in the game, just about everyone tried to claim him. The Hoosiers did, of course, but his Brigade was filled with men from Illinois who loved him. Even some New Yorkers tried to claim him. He was simply larger than life, one of those very few men of action in shoulder-straps, whose ranks were profuse with bloviating swaggerers.

Wilder had warrior blood. His grandfather and great-grandfather fought in the American Revolutionary War, and when the older man lost a leg in the Battle of Bunker Hill, Wilder's grandfather filled his place in line. When this war broke out, Wilder organized a light artillery company from the Greensburg area, and even cast his own six-pounder cannons at his foundry. The Union Army turned his company into infantry, Company A, 17th Indiana Volunteer Infantry, but Wilder kept the two guns. He was a driven, tenacious man who tackled all challenges in his way. As an infantry colonel, the two things that drove Wilder were the surrender of his brigade at Munfordville, and his frustration at fruitlessly pursuing fleet Rebel cavalry with plodding infantry.

Wilder had quickly earned a reputation as a gifted regimental commander, and in September 1862, he commanded the 4,000-man garrison guarding the Green River Railroad Bridge, an important military structure at Munfordville, Kentucky. Confederate Brigadier General James Chalmers decided to take the bridge, and surrounded the town with his 25,000-man column and demanded surrender. The brash Wilder answered the career military man with a curt "I think we'll fight for a while." Chalmers attacked, but Wilder, using his engineering background, had built a series of entrenchments and small forts around the city. Wilder's men turned back repeated charges, and by the end of the first day, the Yankees had inflicted nearly three hundred casualties, while losing only 37.

After two more frustrating, costly days, Gen. Chalmers issued another demand for surrender, "To avoid further bloodshed." Wilder's response was "To avoid further bloodshed, you should keep out of the way of my guns." They said Chalmers nearly had a stroke at this unmilitary impertinence. To our group, we knew his pugnacity was the influence of his formative years in central Ohio.

Wilder was stalling for time, wrongly assuming the rest of Buell's army was on the way. When no reinforcements arrived, and with ammunition running low and the civilians in the town suffering, Wilder made a counter-demand. He agreed to surrender if he could be taken behind the Rebel lines to count the attackers. Chalmers nearly had another stroke, but finally agreed. Wilder entered enemy lines under a flag of truce and saw the Confederate might, along with their fifty pieces of artillery, for himself. In the end, Wilder oversaw one of the largest mass surrenders of the war, although it was to a force five times larger. He spent the rest of the fall waiting for his parole to go through, and when it did, he immediately set about repaying the Rebels 10-fold for his humiliation.

Immediately after receiving his parole, Wilder returned to the command of his Infantry Brigade, now the 17th, 72nd and 75th Indiana, and 92nd and 98th Illinois, at the beginning of 1863. He was given the assignment of pursuing John Morgan's fast-hitting Confederate Cavalry Corps that was threatening to invade Ohio. It was an impossible task, but Wilder boiled with anger and refused to give up. He received permission from General Rosecrans to create a brigade of "Mounted Infantry," but instead of waiting for requisitioned Army horses, his men roamed the countryside, mounting themselves on Kentucky thoroughbreds, Tennessee Walkers, and swaybacked plow mules, anything "with a back flat enough for a saddle that didn't have horns."

When the farms didn't yield enough pure-bred riding stock, or plow mules, Wilder commandeered the mules pulling the supply wagons. That didn't make his men so happy, but provided an endless source of amusement to those of us who witnessed the unbroken mules pitch their riders off as soon as they sat down. Those introductions could be dangerous, but Wilder's men were tougher, and more stubborn, than those four-legged mules, and it always, eventually, got worked out.

As his soldiers were training recalcitrant riding stock, Wilder searched for better weaponry and was fascinated by the new repeating rifles. He was particularly drawn to Christopher Spencer's repeater, whose private demonstrations had awed Wilder. And President Lincoln. Under the best circumstances, the Springfield muzzle-loaders Wilder's men had could fire three shots a minute. The Spencer had a tubular magazine that held seven rimfire cartridges and could easily fire fourteen accurate shots in less than sixty seconds. The devastating weapons were also smaller and lighter, a necessity for his mounted troops.

Again by-passing the frustrating, and endless, Army red tape, Wilder asked his men to vote on purchasing the rifles, and they agreed unanimously. Using his own wealth as collateral, he then convinced his hometown bankers to accept his co-signed personal loans for each soldier, of $35 per rifle. It was a substantial amount for privates making $13 a month. When the newspapers revealed that Wilder's men agreed to have the money deducted from their pay, the Army was so badly embarrassed that they promptly paid Wilder for the weapons, $70,000 for 2,000 Spencers. The fact that the bankers had agonized through many sleepless nights before the loan was paid only made it that much more enjoyable.

For his finishing touch, Wilder, realizing how hopeless his men were with cavalry sabers, and since many of them had been Chicago stockyard butchers, issued them personal axes and meat cleavers. He reasoned his men were experienced with such weapons. Compared to that, I guess McCook's purchase of twenty or so Sharps for our unit wasn't that impressive, but I wasn't complaining. I liked my rifle and my Colonel just fine. I hadn't named the sturdy gun yet, but I was thinking on it.

Wilder's Charge

We were high on the spiny ridge above Hoover's Gap, holed up from the rain, watching as Wilder's Lightning Brigade entered the Gap three-and-a-half miles away. The valley floor was too narrow to let a larger force pass, but during our scouting, we had discovered that several of the Rebel batteries on the ridges above Hoover's Gap were actually Quaker-guns, sanded-down logs that had been painted black. That convinced Rosecrans to attack through Hoover's Gap, but even with diversions in the other gaps, there were still two regiments of veteran Confederate cavalry, and a row of real cannons, waiting at the end of the gap.

Below us, slumber-eyed Rebels went about their morning chores and the Confederate pickets, if there were any, were asleep at their posts. Wilder's men came slowly, deliberately, avoiding the deepest puddles, four thousand hooves slogging through the sucking mud. Wilder led the way, tall and straight in the saddle, almost smiling, looking as stoically confident as the best checker player at Herrold's Mill's hot stove championships. They toiled through the standing water and churned mud in the sodden valley floor until finally the Rebel pickets spotted them and the hue and cry went up. Col. Wilder roared the order, and the Lightning Brigade exploded into a charge.

The Confederates rushed to organize a defense, but Wilder's 1,500 men thundered around that last bend like a Mongol Horde, screaming some Pollack war cry as they crashed into the middle of the Rebels. Lord Cardigan's charge could not have held such daring and drama. Half the Rebels were captured before they could even saddle their horses, frozen in place by the sight of axes splitting the heads of the unfortunately slow-footed. Within three hours, the Lightning Brigade owned Hoovers

Gap and had sent Bragg's Army running south in full flight. Wilder's men only stopped because they ran low on bullets, and their supply wagons were stuck in the mud several miles behind them. The legend of the Lightning Brigade started that day, spreading fear across all the Rebel troops in Tennessee. Sometimes, they spread fear amongst us, too, but I was sure glad to have them.

With the gaps open and the Rebs on the run, our blue army lurched to life. In the camps around Murfreesboro, drums rattled, bugles blew, and sabers jangled. The sound became one unbroken rumble of clattering wagons, cursing, whip-cracking teamsters, braying mules and complaining horses. Orders shouted, orders repeated. The tromp, tromp, tromp of 100,000 feet, and the drip-drop-drip of a rain that slowed but never stopped. We'd inflicted many times the 560 casualties we had suffered, controlled the Tennessee River, threatened Chattanooga, and disrupted the railroads from Virginia to Memphis. In the west, we got plenty tired of reading about the Army of the Potomac and the Army of Northern Virginia, and this campaign enflamed those passions. With barely any notice from the press, and therefore nearly unnoticed by an ungrateful President, Gen. Rosecrans had won control of entire state with less than a thousand casualties. At the same time, Meade was credited with a debatable win at Gettysburg, with 23,000 casualties, and was being hailed as a new Caesar.

George and Jolene

We were crossing a rolling hayfield when a black man came running out of the trees toward us, bellowing like the entire Confederate army was chasing him.

"You gots ta come," huffed and puffed the grizzled negro, white whiskered and bushy headed. "Dey gon' kill her."

"What's going on?" I asked. "Who's killing anybody?"

"Yassuh, is you in charge here?" he asked.

"Close enough." Things had been very quiet, and Ty was back in Ohio. He had earned another promotion and a furlough home.

"Dey's men over yunder," the man said, pointing to a cabin on a distant hill. "Dey's killing and dern turrible stuff to the wimmins. They killed Miss Pamela. Now dey planning to kill Ms. Jolene. They tried to kill me, too."

"Whoa, all right, slow down."

"Evil, murdering, just no 'count trash, egg sucking Rebels," he said. "Just hurry. Please. Follow me."

"Rebels murdered someone? Sure it wasn't Yankees?"

"Yessuh. They murdered one woman and is fixin' to murder a second. They was all wearing Rebel uniforms. None of it makes much sense. We ain't bothered nobody, and nobody bothered us. Almost forgot a war's going on," said the man. "Can't I tell you 'bout it as we go?"

"Let's go." I said, motioning for the others.

"What's your name?"

"I'm George," he said. "Just George."

"Nice to meet you, George. Let's go."

"Me and Miss Pammy, the lady what owns me, well, last week I was in the barn. I heard some horses come in the yard. Bout ten of them. I seen it was Confederate soldiers, so I stayed hid," panted George, setting a rigorous pace. "Then, I heard crashes and yelling so I come running out. By that time, two or three of them was holding her down, and dat evil-looking officer was preparing to outrage her in de vilest fashion."

"Didn't you try to stop it?" I said.

"I went to, but somebody busted me upside my head. When I woke up, they had me tied all twisted and stretched upside down on de wagon wheel," said George. "It wasn't from no sense of compassion they didn't

215

kill me. No, they wanted me to watch dem have dey's way wid 'er. They wanted me to watch them kill her, then they wanted me to watch her rot."

"And they're trying to kill another woman, right now?" I asked.

"Yassuh, our neighbor lady. Our friend."

"Why are they doing this?" I asked. "Who are they? Bushwhackers? The home guard?"

"Nah, ain't no trash home guard around here no more. No bush-whackers lately, neither," George said. "It's just real quiet back in these hollers. The local folk got to where they didn't care nothin' about me and Miss Pamela, but then these barbarians just run over everybody."

"What do you mean?"

"We lived up in these mountains a long time. Alone up in heah, peo-ple can grow fond of each other no matter dey skin," he said. "Me and Miss Pamela had us a......'rangement. We was in love. Yassuh, she taught me to read, she taught me ciphers. A whole bunch of things. We fell in love like one a dem silly storybooks. That's how it was. I truly hope you ain't gonna try to whup me for that. I am about fed the fuck up with white men trying to whup up on me."

"No. Don't worry, nobody is going to bother you."

"We wasn't careful the night before them fiends showed up. I stayed there in the cabin with her overnight. They was riding by early monin', dat big, evil-eyed Colonel and about a dozen soldiers. They seen us. It wasn't no mistakin' what we done. They rode past, but come back to do their devilment. Today I seen 'em riding toward Miss Jolene's."

"That big Colonel?" I said. "What's he look like?"

"The Colonel?" he said. "Big man. Moustache and a chin beard. Goddamn but he's a mean, evil man, what he did."

"Yes, I may know him."

216

"Fire breathing about half breeds and race mixin' and lynching him some runaways."

"Yep," I said. "Sounds like him. Besides the soldiers, anyone with him, unusual?"

"The man that strangled her."

"A big dark-skinned man, with straight hair? Not a Negro?"

"Yessah, that's them, and a handful of young, hungry, dimwitted looking rascals. You know these men?"

"I do. They are evil men, as you said," I said. "Where's your people?"

"I ain't got no people. I ain't had no people for considerable time. Sold, died, what have you. Just me and Miss Pamela, and these white folks here. She put on like she own me. Not hardly no other colored folks 'round. No big plantation owners or patty rollers. Just us on these mountains, tryin' to farm a little somethin'. Truth is, about the only thing you can grow on this mountain here is more rocks."

"You didn't get the sheriff?"

"No good would come from it. No sheriff coulda stopped them men. Good folks or no, people round here still wouldn't want no black man runnin' round free, not around no white women. Dey's good, decent folks with nary an evil bone between them, but they gotta eat. Dere kids gotta eat. I'd end up getting sold way down in Louisiana or Mississippi, one of them plantations got 5,000 niggas and work you to death in de sugar fields or cotton. That's just how it is. Dead by 40. Or crippled bad and wishin' to be."

"How did you get free?" I asked.

"Some black folks was hurrying north and one of their boys come over the hill hunting squirrels. He hadn't expected to find an old goat like me hung upside down," George said.

"I expect not," I said. "Did he comment on it?"

"Not really," George said. "Just said, peculiar sights is getting a sight less peculiar."

George stopped us at the edge of a field. We went to a knee and watched from fifty yards away as Devol stood in the yard, looming over a young woman sprawled in the dirt. Four young Rebels kicked and mocked her as she struggled to crawl away. The woman's dress had been ripped away, and she sobbed and shook as Devol screamed, his face just inches from hers. Two more young soldiers drunk danced out of the cabin and threw a mattress into the yard, and the others put down their whiskey jug long enough to finish stripping her and tie her hands. Devol stared down at her as he unbuttoned his pants. I could only see Ardent there on the ground, trying desperately to get away from him in her last moments. I looked to both sides to make sure my men were ready. They were.

"Let's go!" I shouted, and we burst over the hill, screaming like banshees and firing as we ran. Two Rebels fell hard and stayed down. I kept my eyes on Devol, who was struggling with his pants buttons as he ran for his horse. Bullets zipped by, but we didn't slow, and two more Rebels flopped down beside the porch. We reached the cabin as Devol and his men lashed their horses into a gallop and disappeared down the road.

"Are you hurt?" I asked the trembling woman, as one of my young Yankees hurried out of the cabin. He wrapped a quilt around her and laid a skirt in her lap.

"I'll be all right, just a little shaken up."

"How did they end up here?" I asked.

"Other than just pure evilness, I don't know. They got away with rape and murder once," she said. "I'm sure many more times than once. I suppose they thought they would again."

"You better gather what you need and come with us. He won't stay gone. Not if there's something he wants."

"There's nothing about me worthy of a special trip."

"Evil doesn't need much reason. Devol certainly doesn't."

"Who?"

"Devol. That's that Colonel's name. I've had this conversation before," I said. "Come on, I'll help you inside so you can get dressed."

"No, just leave me be for the moment," she said, letting the blanket slide off her shoulders. "If your boys haven't seen a naked woman before, they probably should before they get killed in this battle you're in a hurry to get to."

"Yes, ma'am," I stammered. "Just, normally…"

"Oh pooh, we haven't seen normal around here for years," she said. "You want normal with two huge armies itchin' to kill thousands of each other in these mountains, maybe right here in my cow pasture. Now, that annoys me."

"There's no one other than George to look out for you?" I asked her.

"No one looks after me, Sergeant. Pammy was my dearest friend. A sister to me. George is my caretaker when we're gone," she said. "He's paid for that, and he checks on me, like a good neighbor."

"You don't have a husband about?"

"No. Not about. Just me here in peace. Normally," she said. "I just want to close my eyes for a while."

She closed her eyes and lifted her full face to the sun, a slight smile at one corner of her mouth. I draped the skirt back over her and didn't disturb her further. Her hair was long and yellow, and she had sun freckles. After an hour she woke up, blinking in the sun.

"You killed those men," she said, not quite a question, not quite a statement, not quite a thank you, not quite an accusation.

"Yes, I wanted to kill them all."

"How many men have you killed?"

"I don't know."

"It must be a lot then, if you can't count that high."

"I can count that high. I just haven't counted them. Why are you out here all alone?"

"After my husband and I got married, we bought this little place as a quiet hideaway. His folks are Nashville, a first family of Nashville," she said. "A bastion of the Southern aristocracy. He is quite rich, but we wanted a quiet, little place in the country, too. Away from noise and stink and such. Far from any city. This was before the war came, but we still wanted to get away. His family businesses were run extremely well and didn't require his constant presence. This time, I came out here when my husband left for the Army. You've seen what Nashville is for a woman alone."

"Yes, and he left you like that?"

"My husband was swept up in the entire Ivanhoe fairy tale. Valor. Gallantry. Chivalry," Jolene said. "Irresistible, I guess. The flamboyant cavalry officer, the Paladins of the South."

"Forrest's Cavalry?"

"No, Wheeler's," she said. "Does it matter?"

"No," I said.

"He is nowhere near. This was the most peaceful little valley you could ever imagine," she said. "And then that flaming lunatic John Brown decided he wanted some rifles. For God's sake, I don't understand how he was running loose up there. He should have been in an insane asylum."

"I won't argue," I said. "But his convictions were right."

"Everybody and their righteous convictions. It's because of that madman our own madmen responded and my husband is gone to war," she said. "I could have a hundred slaves if I wanted. I don't. My husband owns factories, not plantations."

"Perhaps he'll return unharmed."

"He's already returned. Quite harmed."

"I don't understand."

"He was wounded horribly. In the groin. That wound should have killed him, but it didn't. He's gone back to get a wound that will. He's a fool. He believes what he lost makes him less than a man," she said. "It doesn't, not really, not to me, but I don't think there is a man alive who doesn't think that way."

"No, I'm sure there's not," I said. "He came home and then went back?"

"Yes. He had to recuperate so he'd be healthy enough to get killed. My love for my husband didn't die when he was wounded, but he refused to believe that," she said. "Now he's determined to die. He says I shouldn't be saddled with less than a whole man. Honor, anger, martyrdom, bitterness, self-pity, whatever his reason, he went back. And now I have those same feelings."

"I see."

"Honestly, you probably don't," she said.

"Honestly, I probably do."

"Why are you here?" she said, after another long silence.

"I'm in the army."

"But the army isn't here. Maybe they're over there, but they're not here."

"Do all Tennesseans get so argumentative about where here, and there, is or isn't?"

"What do you mean?"

"Nothing. An old hillbilly skinned me for a years-worth of coffee and a new pair of shoes."

"You haven't answered me," she said. "What made you come this far from your column?"

"The War came right to my doorstep, too, and took the most precious thing in my life," I said, and told her my story. She nodded, closed her eyes, and was silent for a while.

"I think I'd like to walk down to the creek. Get his touch off me," said Jolene after a few more minutes of sun, wrapping the quilt around her. She led me down the gentle slope of her pasture, through twenty minutes of forest, to a gentle stream that was hidden by the trees along the high bank. The sun coming through the leaves left golden splotches on a quiet pool that was so clear I could count the pebbles on the bottom. A shale ledge protruded over the opposite bank of the pool and cast a wide shadow over half the pool. Jolene hurried ahead and slid down the bank, looking back at me as she walked across a bed of smooth gravel as the quilt began to slip off her shoulders.

"I'll turn my head," I said, as her quilt dropped.

"Ok, you can look now," she sang in amused laughter behind me. I turned, and she was standing, gloriously, breathtakingly, nude, bathed by the sun in a foot of water. Falling free, her yellow hair fell to her waist and her skin was bronze from head to toe.

"Oh," I said.

"If your face was any redder," said Jolene. "I'd fry an egg on your forehead."

"I wasn't really expecting…."

"Come on, get in," she said, taking a few steps into deeper water before diving in.

"I have no swimming clothes."

"Now, come on, do you honestly think that's going to bother me?" she said, water dripping off her body. "I didn't expect that you would. People that carry swimming clothes are bores."

222

"Well, I won't be no ghastly bore to you," I said, and shucked my clothes.

"Look at you," she said. "You didn't say you were in the artillery, soldier."

"It is only natural, you know."

"Oh, I know. But I was starting to wonder if you did."

"Just stay put, you're about to find out," I said, and stepped off the ledge.

We stayed at Jolene's for several days, and she treated us like kings. Ham and potatoes from her concealed cellar in the side of the hill, and fresh milk from the old Holstein dairy cow she kept hidden in the forest. The smell of freshly baked rolls and biscuits covered the hill like a warm blanket.

"Keep feeding us like this, ma'am," said Ab, on about the fifth day. "And I might not leave. Just keep tossing them fresh biscuits and redeye gravy at me. You'll see."

"I have plenty," she said. "You're welcome to stay as long as you please."

"I suppose I should go win this war first," he said. "I don't want to eat you out of house and home, not when the army gives me more than plenty for free. Plus, I can keep my weight manageable by chasing them rascal southrons over hills and cricks. But, I'll be back."

"You're always welcome," she said. "All of you."

That afternoon, she and I went down to the pool, as had become our habit. The other fellows got it in the morning, and we had afternoon rights. Other times they would go upstream or downstream, with cane-poles and fresh worms and come back with heavy stringers of crappy and bass which Jolene fried to perfection. She even kept some redeye gravy warm for Ab to dip his fish in, while he managed his weight there on the hill.

"We will have to be moving on soon," I said. "We don't have much choice."

"I know," she said. "I wish you could stay but I know you can't. I'm sick of this damn war taking people away from me."

"George will be around?"

"If he wants to be. The mountain folks usually pay him no mind, but times are rough for most people. They barely can afford owning a chicken, and the situation's desperate," she said. "If any serious slave catchers came around looking, I suppose they'd turn George in for a dollar."

"We can still try to keep an eye on you, send some men back from time to time," I said. "I can probably wrangle a horse to sneak back."

"I won't stop you, or pretend like I don't want you to. I can't imagine Devol is still around, but I suppose he could be," she said. "It will always be wonderful to see you. I won't hold George here. He'd like to get a few shots at the Rebels, too."

"I'd not put anything past Devol," I said. "And you know it's not just him. Plenty of bushwhackers crawling all over these hills."

"I know it can happen," she said. "I'll just try to be ready if it does."

By August, the sun had turned vicious. As we struggled up the parched mountain slopes, rivers of sweat drew every hornet, dragonfly, and sweat-bee in Dixie. We slapped and scratched more than we climbed, tempers flared, and we grew sloppy on the trails. The ridge we were climbing was bare, nothing but dust, some loose rocks, and a tuft or two of prickly weeds. We'd been without shade for hours, and our misery overshadowed any thought of lurking Rebels, or of caution. We just wanted to top the ridge and get under that lonesome stand of spruce trees that beckoned us from the peak. There weren't more than six of the scrawny things, and I was daydreaming of acres of tall, wide pines and wringing out my sweat-soaked hanky when a loud gasp froze me. Ten feet up Brice was leaning away from the mountain, clinging to a dusty, jutting rock. A fat rattlesnake stared at him, its sinister eyes burning into his, and those rattles were as loud as hot cannons. Nausea waved over me as the snake's tongue flicked and the ugly, doomsday head swayed in space. The snake launched, hitting Brice in the face like a boxer's punch. He screamed and teetered further off the trail, with the rattler hooked under his eye and blood spurting down his cheek. He flailed wildly at the monstrous serpent as he cartwheeled down the mountain, chilling screams echoing as his head slapped sickly against the rocks. We stared down the slope until Ty shouted for us to get moving. He'd found a stout stick of about five feet long, and smacked the rocks ahead of us as we went. We reached the top and sat under the trees for a few hours, watching the empty trails below. Nothing moved down there but the birds, and we went back down the mountain at dusk with Ty swinging the stick in front. We looked for Brice's body, but couldn't find it.

Marching across Tennessee, we passed an endless procession of Negro refugees heading north, men and women whose faces told tragic stories. They fled war and bondage in pieced-together, discarded, blackened army wagons, dilapidated farm wagons and two wheeled carts. All were pulled by beasts I didn't expect would last another mile, and perched on top of the wobbly leaning towers of household goods were gray-haired aunties and little wide-eyed pickaninnies in rags. Contraband camps mushroomed out behind our column, mobile versions of those at Nashville. The army provided food, shelter, and medical care, and employed the newly emancipated people as carpenters, teamsters, nurses, and laborers of all trades.

We'd been in camp for a few days when George showed up bearing gifts: A sack full of freshly killed rabbits. He walked me away from the others as Teddy fried the rabbits with bacon, potatoes and onions, smothered in a pepper gravy that gave me more comfort than a night of spooning.

"Why aren't you back there looking out for Jolene?" I asked.

"Wouldn't have been healthy to stay back there right now. Miss Jolene just fine as far as I know. She gone North to where she got some folks. Her husband succeeded in getting himself kilt. Lots of deserters has come back home, so of course, de home guard is back and running all through them hills," George said. "That rabble guard gets paid for taking boys back to get hung, and grabbing themselves an unowned black man would be a bonus."

"I guess you have a point," I said. "I'm glad she's away from all this. You, too."

"Yes, if they'd seen me, they woulda snatched me up and sold me off. Or just kilt me for pure devilment," said George. "So, I been stayin' close to the army, working with some of them pioneer soldiers choppin' down the forest and building your plank roads."

"Stayin' busy, and well fed, it looks like," I said.

"I'm faring just fine," he said. "But that ain't why I hurried up to find you. I was poking my nose around the other night, and I got some information I reckon you'll find troubling."

"Well, come on with it."

"Sometimes I kind of snoop around a little bit, and I been watching this one farm where folks said there was some bad dealings going on," said George. "I seen that big colonel you'se after, all cozy with some of your Yankee friends. I seen something worser than that, too."

"What else did you see?"

"They was unloading boxes of rifles from a Yankee wagon to a Rebel wagon."

"Which Yankees?" I choked.

"Only one I knowed was one of them that was at Miss Jolene's with you. That real skinny boy with the wide hat. Kind of limped. Him and a couple other Yankees, but I never seen them before I don't believe."

"What? Are you sure? Willie?"

"I don't know his name, but I knows his face," said George. "And I heard him say he was gonna be back there in a week from Saturday with more guns."

"George, are you working for the Pinkerton's?" I said after a long silence. Willie and Alva had found some new friends they spent more and more time with, and I'd never had a good feel for them.

"Some things is best kept secret," George said. "I just kind of keep my eye on things. Couple fellas I let know, if I see something might be of interest."

"You going to let them know about this?"

"No, I wasn't planning on it. Figgered this might be something you'd want to handle personal like."

"Thank you, George, for the information, and for bringing it straight to me. You need to be careful. Wrong folks see you sneaking around, you're gonna be swinging from a tree."

"I suppose that's real true if they'd a seen me last night," said George. "But, I ain't all that worried. My people have been invisible forever, only way to survive. You'd think someone black as me would stand out in the sunlight, but I don't, no more than the dog, no more notice than am old stump. But for my people, if you ain't invisible, most likely you're having a bad day."

"Just be real careful," I said.

After that, we took turns watching Willie. He spent an awful lot of time around the quartermaster and the arsenal, but we had no proof what he was doing, if he was doing anything at all. I wanted a shot at Devol more than anything, so we just sat back and waited. On Saturday, we followed George to a secluded farm as the sun went down.

"Right here," George said, pointing. "On that hill."

Soft yellow light glowed from a large farm house, and the lamps bobbing in the darkness provided glimpses of a barn, some sheds, and a few wagons. A dozen soldiers stood around a wagon full of rifle crates as we crept to within fifty yards. Willie and Devol were unmistakable in the lantern's glow, and the soldiers were both Rebel and Yankee. We stayed quiet, on our bellies, inching closer, watching the treachery transpire. Finally, they seemed to be wrapping up.

"How soon can you get some more?" asked Devol.

"Couple weeks," said Willie. "You just worry about making sure your money's good. That Rebel paper won't buy a pop gun."

"You just remember you ain't the only Yankee eager to take my money," said Devol.

I swallowed. Hatred seared through me. I whistled, and my young warriors burst out of the brush firing as we charged, screaming our own battle cry, shooting the closest Rebels from their wagon. Devol disappeared in the wheat, and Willie ran for cover as gunshots flashed in the dark. Half the conspirators fell, and the others ran toward the house. A lamp was knocked over and fire flashed across the dry hay beside the barn. I saw Willie get hit and go down. He crawled toward the horses, but I sprinted that way and cut him off.

"What are you doing here, Willie?" I demanded. He slumped against a water trough, a dark stain growing on his shirt. "What are you doing with these guns and these murderers?"

Willie stared at the ground, bleeding and heaving like a cat with a hairball.

"You'll face a firing squad," I said.

"Ironic, don't you think?" he grimaced.

"Devol gets his rifles from you?"

"He paid so much money. So much."

"How's that money feel now?"

"Insufficient," Willie said, fingering the red stain. I felt the heat as the first bullet whizzed past my nose, and the next two slapped the barn where my head had been. I dove for the ground and rolled. When I looked up, Willie was gone, along with the rest of the Rebels.

Deep Mourning

I smelled it first when I'd walked the muddy streets of Chattanooga, sad women preparing the widow's weeds, boiling walnuts for the black juice to dye their mourning clothes. Barely a day went by that we didn't smell it, from an isolated cabin or the main streets of villages. The large, cast-iron cauldrons filled the air with a foul, gagging odor that rankled the nose and puckered the mouth. It smelled like a stew of hot tar and scalded chicken feathers, seasoned with a mildewed horse blanket that the cat pissed on. Today I'd been smelling it for close to a mile, following the dusty trail into a small town. The crossroads wasn't much. A battered, broken-windowed country store, more paint peeled off than on, sat in the middle of four or five droopy houses. The porches sagged like a rope-bridge, and the doors were held up with twine. Any of the boys could have thrown a rock over the first drooping roof and cleared the last one by fifty feet. Two mangy hounds lay half under, half out of the porch, looking at us with the disdain of a drunkard eyeing a glass of spring water. Behind a split-rail fence were two half-dead horses that could barely hold their heads up, too decrepit even for the Rebel army to steal. Or eat.

On the slope behind the houses, outhouses tipped toward a lifeless creek. Closer to the creek, three women in black rags and shawls stirred the offending kettle over a fire. If it wasn't for the long stringy hair that looked like it hadn't been brushed since before the war, I wouldn't have been able to tell them from Negroes and it didn't look like their days had been any easier. Their faces and hands were black with the walnut dye, which set in the skin and stayed for months. These poor women had been making widows weeds for some time, and probably would be for some time longer. I'd seen my share of widow weeds at home, at Pete's place, other women in the cities. Nothing like this. Back home, if the black clothes were not store bought, the widow's caps and veils were sewn at home with unblemished new black bombazine and crepe. That was a world away from the reeking tatters and patches of these wrung-out women. If the South was going to rise again, this wouldn't be where it started, that much was certain. We found an old sack that we filled with bacon, biscuits, and beans, and tied it to the porch roof, in case the dogs weren't as lazy as they looked. Some days it was just hard to get real excited about killing Johnnies.

Reed's Bridge

On the 18th of September, our column stopped for the night two miles from the crossroads of Jay's Mill and Reed's Bridge Road. In the morning, we were to march east to Chickamauga Creek, on the Georgia-Tennessee border, where the Army of Tennessee almost certainly lay in wait for us. No sooner had I fallen asleep than I felt someone shaking my shoulder.

"What time is it? What's going on?" I said, blinking awake.

"It's about 2. Come on, get up, we have to get moving," said Ty.

"Where?"

"A bunch of Rebels have been crossing Reed's Bridge, just down the road," said Ty. "The bridge has to come down."

We double-quicked down the road and when we reached the bridge, I couldn't see why we needed to burn it. Someone had already tried to burn it once, but whether it was us or the Rebels, no one knew. The blackened structure was narrow and swayed, creaking and groaning in the moonlight. As we stood guard, a company of engineers went to work, sawing and ripping up the floor and rails, making the loudest racket I'd ever heard. On the slight chance every Reb in Georgia or Tennessee hadn't heard us, the engineers drenched the bridge in oil, threw a torch, and a huge orange fireball lit up the night.

We dug our rifle pits a few hundred yards up a cleared hill from the bridge, with our backs to a dense cedar thicket and a few acres of flat farmland directly in front of us. We stayed awake all night watching the flames slowly die and listening to Rebels out there prowling in the dark.

At dawn, the smoldering black bridge skeleton still stood, and Gen. Davidson's 1st Georgia of Forrest's Cavalry Corps waited nearby. Behind them, an infantry regiment was already hard at work on the neighboring farms, tearing down every board from the houses and barns and loading them onto a line of wagons headed toward the bridge.

"Look down there," said Ty, pointing down Jay's Mill Road at another column of Confederate cavalry trotting toward the indestructible bridge. The Rebs were rebuilding faster than I thought possible, and I watched a long parade of Rebel battle flags fluttering beyond the trees. "There's Pegram. Forrest should be here and there he is."

The infamous cavalry General casually trotted in our direction, barely looking up while the Illinois snipers landed dozens of minie balls all around him. His intense eyes burned, and his wavy black hair flowed from under his wide brimmed hat. With his straight back and chiseled jaw, he looked every bit the dashing Dixie Cavalier of legend. When he was done taunting us, Forrest flashed a wide grin, waved and rode away with a tip of his hat. A squad of cavalry loped up from the confederate rear, led by a huge shouldered officer wearing a Hardee hat with a blue cockade. After a brief conversation with Forrest, Devol turned and stared straight at me.

"Damn it. He couldn't know I'm here, could he?" I asked Ty.

"Scouts. Plenty of spies out there," Ty said. "Willie, if he's still alive, could still have friends among us, sad to say. Maybe others. I suppose he would know if he wanted to."

Smiling like the cat that caught the canary, Devol locked his eyes on mine as he led his column in a slow trot toward us, clattering over the bridge. At the bottom of the hill, the bugler blew charge and the Rebels thundered up the slope at a dead run, wailing like demons. Devol charged straight at me, his red-eyed horse flaring its nostrils like the flesh-eating mares of Diomedes. His pistol barrel was as big as a train tunnel. I had only enough time to get off one shot as Rebel bullets blinded me with pebbles and dirt. From nowhere, two mules kicked me in the chest and threw me across the trench.

Everything flashed red and black, red and black, and my screams came from somewhere inside the earth. The next thing I knew, a line of ants was crawling over my face, and a mantis sat on my chest, praying and staring, waiting for me to die. I waved a feeble hand at the bloated green blow flies swarming me, then decided to close my eyes, just for a minute, thinking that bastard killed us both.

But, I wasn't dead, and when I woke up, in more agony than I thought possible, I was face down in a red clay ditch, helpless and pleading. My tongue felt like a slab of salt cod, while above me, a hundred voices shouted over each other. I ignored them and lapped at a tiny pool of runny mud in the ditch. Then I heard Ty. I was happy he was there, but I was more concerned with that last teaspoon of orange water. It was the best water I'd ever had, and I wondered how such good water would come to be in a ditch. Clumsy, hurrying black hands rolled me onto to my back, and I saw an endless procession of shadow soldiers hurrying past. I'd never heard a bunch of soldiers this quiet.

"You idiots! You stupid sons-a-bitches. How could you drop him?"

"No, suh! No, massa! We didn't drop him. We had him fine on dat stretcher," I heard a panicked negro voice above me. "Dat big wagon up deh knocked us'ns over, laughing like dey in de corn liquor."

"The hell you say, you damn darkie!" A gravelly, northeastern voice slurred. The teamster jumped off the freighter and landed inches from my head. He cracked his mule-whip and cursed the negro litter bearers. "If'n you all can't get out of the way no fastern that, no wonder ya massa whip your black ass! Let's see if you can get out of the way of this."

"Mister, one more word and I will shoot you through the face," warned Ty.

"What kind of worthless coward are you, that you will allow these lazy bastards to drop that hurt man without a flogging?" the teamster growled.

"That hurt man is my friend, and here's the kind of worthless coward I am, right here in front of you," said Ty, menace in his voice, but still calm. "Quit wasting time. You have a fine wagon. Now, you start unloading that nice big bed until I can fit my friend in there real nice. After that you'll be taking us to a hospital in high style."

"I will not!"

"No? Well, then, I'll take your wagon, and leave you here with a bullet in your head," said Ty, cocking his revolver and jabbing it into the man's eye. I heard the fuming waggoneer climb into the wagon and start tossing out boxes.

I screamed and opened my eyes into a blazing orange sun that seemed less than an arm's length away. My mouth was so dry, I was sure my tongue had cracked in half and sawn through my lips. I tried to lift my head, but pain knocked me back on the thin bed of blood soaked straw. When I opened my eyes again, a smudged, black face peered down at me.

"Did I bleed that much?" I croaked.

"No offense sir, but dey all thought you was daid. Dyin' imnint, anyway, dat why you out year."

"What do you mean?"

"You dead ones, dem dead ones and doze ones bout to step into glory, just ain't no room for y'all under de covers," the orderly pointed to a cluster of hospital tents.

"You put us out here to die?"

"Weren't me that suggested it," said the man. "Don't be so tender skinned. I guess it was figgered your feelings wasn't going to get hurt no more worse than they already was. Now that you has distinguished yo'sef from the dead, I'll see if I can find you a cot. I'm sure a couple has become free since last I was in there."

They gave me a euphoric shot of laudanum while I waited for a place under the tent. Teams of litter bearers brought a steady flow of mangled men into the pasture, and an endless train of ambulances rolled away from the battlefield, rattling down the road surrounded by a mob of dazed and bewildered Union soldiers.

I craved water more than I had ever craved water in my life, dreaming of cups of fresh spring water, tin cups, porcelain cups, wooden cups, big and small cups. Sparkling mountain stream water, but the tepid, glowing green Perryville pond scum would have been just as heavenly. Contraband orderlies hurried past in all directions, and I shouted for water, but it came out as a dried-up croak. The entire field moaned, low, long moans that never ended, pierced by screams that sounded like a pit of burning witches. Finally, an attendant came by and held a canteen of fresh water to my lips. I had barely tasted it before he pulled it away. I would have killed him if I'd had the chance.

"Cain't," he said, "Cain't give you no mo'. Doctor say a bunch of water right now get you heavin' yur guts up. Tear all your tore parts more than they tore. They gonna commence cuttin' on you soon enough. If you'se alive after that, you can have more water than Jonah's whale."

"I need it now. Just a little," I said.

"No, suh, Mr. Billy Yank," said the orderly. "You just listen to them doctors up in theah. They'll fix you up."

In anguish, I watched the nearest tent, where four men held a thrashing patient on an operating table. The doctor slapped a chloroform soaked rag over the man's face, then attacked the ruined limb with a bloody bone saw. He counted strokes loud and fast, calling out, seven strokes, ten strokes, twelve, and the bone fell away. "Next" yelled the surgeon, and dropped the amputated arm onto the mound of ruined limbs already overflowing the washtub at his feet. A bucket of water was splashed across the table and a new man was lifted on. I squeezed my eyes closed, but the sounds and smells of such torment made me retch, water or no.

Chattanooga

I woke up in a hospital tent, wrapped up tighter than an Egyptian mummy. My entire torso was squeezed tight by thick layers of gauze, and my left arm was strapped tight to my body, immobile in a plaster cast. My right arm was in a sling, but I slipped my hand out and did some exploratory searching. All my courting tackle was still in place. All my toes and fingers wiggled, as painful as it was. I closed one eye, and then the other. Both worked just fine. I breathed a painful sigh of relief, took a slug of laudanum offered by a nurse, and went back to sleep.

When I opened my eyes again, I was still in the cot under the tent, and a woman in a dark green surgeon's uniform was meticulously cleaning my wounds. She had two Colt Navy revolvers strapped around her waist.

"What are you doing?" I said.

"Hopefully saving your life. Surprisingly, it doesn't appear your insides are as badly damaged as we assumed. Any of those bullets, an eighth-inch the other way, would have killed you, but it's nothing we couldn't stitch up or remove. Patched your head. Stitched up your lung," said the woman. "Took out several good size pieces of splintered rib. Several more are badly broken, but will heal fine, if you take it easy."

"Maybe a list of what wasn't broke would have been shorter," I said.

"Snipped a touch of your liver, and set your collarbone and straightened your arm fracture where a team of horses apparently trampled you," she said, pointedly ignoring me. "You get the idea."

"When did you do all that?"

"In between the serious cases," she said. "Quit being whiney. You're a lucky man."

"I'm not feeling so lucky at the moment," I said. "Who are you?"

"I'm Dr. Mary Walker. I'm aware of the fact that I'm a woman," she said, with somewhere between a tired sigh and snippish. "There's no need to point it out. Just as shocked as you are at seeing it, I tire of hearing it."

"Why are you wearing two pistols?"

"Because four are too heavy. I'm the least of your concern right now."

"Where am I?"

"Chattanooga."

"What's the date?"

"September 26th. You've been asleep for a few days. That's good, it helps you heal," she said as I blinked a few times, still trying to figure out what all this was.

The following day, I was surprised to see Col. McCook walk into the tent, and more surprised when he sat next to me. Every unit had been hit hard at Chickamauga, and he'd have a hundred wounded men from the 52nd to visit. Both armies had suffered 30% casualties, 16,000 for us, 18,000 for them. Two-thirds of the Union army had shattered and fled in shock, terror, and confusion. Rosecrans, Alex McCook, observer-Assistant Secretary of War Charles A. Dana, and most Union generals galloped with them, not slowing until they reached Chattanooga, twelve miles from the battlefield.

"How are you Dr. Walker?" the Colonel asked. "Thank you for taking such good care of my boys."

"I'm fine, Dan, thank you. They're good patients, for the most part," said Dr. Walker. "I'm sure they are fine soldiers as well."

"Sgt. Carew, how are you doing?" he said, patting my forearm. "I heard you got run over by a locomotive. I was nearby, thought I'd drop in. How's the pain?"

"It's better. Tolerable," I lied.

"That was a rough fight."

"Yes, sir, I understand it was, though I wasn't around for much of it."

"Here, I have something for you," McCook said, showing me two books. "The Woman in White, by Wilkie Collins, and the Confidence Man by Melville."

"That's excellent. Thank you," I said.

"Yes, well, one bookworm to another. Your sheriff friend mentioned you're a reader. I've been carrying these around for a while. I don't have the reading time I want, as you can imagine," he smiled. "Anyway. Mystery and Intrigue. New and exciting writing styles. Quite remarkable."

"I'm eager to read them," I said.

"Allow me," he said, pulling a stool close. He began reading aloud. I'd been drifting in and out for a few minutes when a nurse came by with more laudanum.

"I better be going," McCook said. "I see a deep slumber in your near future. Can I get you anything?"

"The food could be better," I said. Confederate General Bragg planned to starve us into surrender. Our ruined Army was already in chaos and out of supplies when we had arrived at Chattanooga with the 45,000-man Army of Tennessee hot on our heels. The Rebels dug in on the peaks of Missionary Ridge and Lookout Mountain, 1,100 feet above the city, locking us inside, ensnared between the Tennessee River and the two dominating elevations. Confederate snipers and cannons controlled movement in the city and on the Tennessee River, while Gen. Joe Wheeler's Rebel cavalry ran free along our only supply route, a 60-mile-stretch from Bridgeport, Alabama to Chattanooga. Just a few days past, they had captured a train of 800 wagons, which was too much loot for them to carry away so they burned hundreds of the wagons and shot a thousand mules.

"That one, I'm afraid, will be difficult. But, here, I forgot, take these," he smiled, and handed me six molasses cookies wrapped in paraffin paper. "I wasn't sure what you might prefer."

"Thank you, Colonel, I'm being well taken care of. As well as can be."

"Dr. Walker is treating you well?"

"Very good, sir. The best. Thank you."

"She practiced medicine in Columbus prior to the war, did you know that?" McCook said. "That's where we first met."

"No, I didn't," I said. "My fiancée, the woman that was murdered, would have been thrilled to meet her."

"Dr. Walker is a friend. Brilliant woman. Hotheaded, convinced of her own rightness. Few at the top ever wanted a woman. Some even wanted her arrested. I'm sure some still do," McCook said. "She's not shy about voicing her opinions and she has a low tolerance for fools, which plague armies like fleas as you've probably noticed. Strong. Very strong. Yes, sir. She could be the Surgeon General, but sometimes I think she's happier being a pain in the ass."

"Yes sir, no offense, but I've heard you described the same way." I said.

"You are not the first to make that comparison. I'm quite flattered by it, of course," McCook grinned.

"Bath time for this one here," Dr. Walker said, walking up behind me. "And my colleague has volunteered to assist."

"Yah," a woman laughed. "Mein diagnoziz iz he needs a gut schrub-bink."

I tilted my head back and saw Helga with a huge grin on her face.

"You are a real doctor?" I said, flabbergasted.

"She's been working with us since the day you arrived," said Dr. Walker, tilting her head at Col. McCook. "Apparently, you have influential allies. She knows what she's doing."

"You can't bathe me," I shouted.

"Oh, stop, you act like I ain't seen one or two peckers?" asked Helga. "You zink I ain't dosed about ten thousand of 'em at my last job? All you men think you're something special down there, but few of you are."

"No," I said. It was bad enough with both Col. McCook and Dr. Walker frowning down at me. When Freddy and Ty walked up, I tried pleading with them.

"Freddy. It's not right. Your fiancee can't bathe me."

"Do you want a proper cleaning, or do you want one of these order-lies to throw a basin of poison pink piss-water at you and call it a day?" asked Dr. Walker. "There's a reason you haven't gotten gangrene yet. We haven't been keeping all those germs out just so you can throw it all away in other men's filthy water."

"Yah, don't be a dumbkoff," said Helga.

"I don't even know what you're talking about," I said in despair.

"Do I need to give you orders?" asked Col. McCook.

"Fine, whatever you need to do," I said, dropping my head back down. I knew further protest was pointless with those three. "As long as she's not really using a wire brush on me."

"Nein, not me," said Helga, "Ve Austrians, ve don't like de rough schtuff."

After that, I got to know Helga fairly well, and I, clearly, had no secrets from her. When the Union Army had first entrenched in Nashville, the number of prostitutes jumped almost overnight to close to two thousand. The entire downtown business district, mansions, stately homes, booming saloons and back-alley hovels, all served the needs of the military men. The morality crusaders swarmed the city in numbers almost as large as the Army's, but Gen. Rosecrans was more concerned with the epidemic of venereal diseases threatening his command. He had tried everything to rid the city of the sisters of shame, but nothing worked. Desperate, he'd even once sent a riverboat full of them to Louisville and Cincinnati, but, not surprisingly, the women were not allowed to disembark.

The problem was overwhelming, and becoming worse every day, so Rosecrans sought out any assistance he could find. He met several times with Estelle, nee Pearl May, Franklin, who claimed her family had been providing patriotic comfort women to the American Army since that first chilly winter at Valley Forge. Estelle, who employed half the prostitutes in town, was, for that time and place, a fanatic about cleanliness and disease. She knew not only were syphilis, gonorrhea and the other diseases debilitating to the body, they were also debilitating to her profits. Helga was not a doctor, but she was next thing to one. She had been the only female student at the Medical Department of the University of Nashville before the war, and when war came, she volunteered but the Confederates rejected her outright.

Just when Helga thought all hope of practicing medicine was over, Estelle and Rosecrans requested her assistance with the problem. They came up with a plan where each healthy prostitute in the city registered for a $5 license, and Helga was given a position in Estelle's vast empire, paid with a generous stipend from the United States Government. From then on, Helga examined each prostitute weekly, and issued each healthy prostitute a certificate for a fifty-cent fee. With a guarantee of clean girls, Estelle's business quickly tripled, and the other brothels quickly followed suit.

Under the hospital tent, long rows of beds were filled with disfigured men staring at the ceiling, and nothing would ever compare to the hellish suffering and screams of those first days and nights. I was on my back, watching one-legged amputees struggle with crutches, and one-armed men break down in tears trying to dress themselves. Sanitary Commission nurses scrubbed, bandaged, and sedated their patients, and contrabands labored diligently under the direction of the surgeons. Orderlies led lines of young blind men in loops around the tent, each man's hand on the man in front's shoulder. They rarely made it more than a few steps before the chain broke and they all stood helpless and shamed. The worst were the men with their jaws shot off, and that horrid gasping, choking, gargling sound as they tried swallow. Their wild, white eyes flashed accusingly, desperately, all-day long, unable to even complain. Everyone was glad when they died.

241

Dr. Walker or Helga stopped by twice daily to sponge my mangled flesh with chlorinated lime and pack Boracic lint in my wounds. The pain was severe, but, at each dressing change, I frantically searched for the first pus of gangrene, and, when there was none, I wanted to kiss them.

At night, I watched a big man move amongst the pallets of Golgotha like an angel, speaking in a hushed, calming voice to the frightened young men as they suffered, some taking their last breaths. He was nearly the size of Ab, packed a worn Bible, but had no religious affiliation identifiers. Night after night, I watched him lean his bulk over the scared boys, caress slack arms or hold trembling hands, kiss a boy's head with the tenderness of an angel, or snip a small lock of curly hair and place it in a locket with a pretty girl's picture to send home. When his rounds were finished, I'd see him at the long table outside the tent toiling in candlelight until dawn, taking pen in one hand, a bottle of Irish whiskey and a vial of laudanum beside the other, and a stack of tear-stained stationary in front of him.

Snodgrass Hill

The Battle of Chickamauga had been lost when eight brigades of Gen. James Longstreet's rampaging Rebels smashed through a hole in the Union line at Brotherton Field. Our corps, Gen. George Thomas's 14th Corps, provided the rear guard during the wild retreat, and had prevented complete annihilation of the entire Union army. Gen. Thomas had earned the title "the Rock of Chickamauga," in staving off total disaster in the wild back and forth maelstrom, but it was Col. John Wilder's Lightning Brigade's heroic and ferocious defense of Snodgrass Hill that was decisive. Fierce, reckless charges and counter-charges raged throughout the day on that hill, and the lines constantly shifted. Some said there were 25 assaults, and others said it was one continuous slaughter. It didn't surprise me that my friends would end up in the middle of it, somehow.

"We were pretty much on our own stick by that point, just looking for whatever mischief we could find," Ty was saying. "So, when we see Wilder's bunch of crazy galoots galloping toward Snodgrass Hill, we emancipated some mules and followed along. We caught up with them right as they went down the hill and smashed into the Rebs like a horde of howling berserkers with their battle-axes."

"A grisly sight, but, goddamn, I'd pay good money to watch those rascals whoop bad guys," laughed Ab. "Five hundred crazy pollacks from the Chicago stockyards. Not a bullet between 'em, war-hooping, swinging their hatchets, splitting skulls with meat cleavers. Those boys is a whole 'nuther kind of fierce. The look on the Rebs' faces was a puuure deeeeelight to see.''

"Those Tennessee mad dogs almost got through us more than once," said Teddy. "Wilder's Spencer repeaters drove the Johnnies back a good mile, but they just wouldn't stay drove. The fightin' was desperate, and poor dead boys stacked up where they fell, blue over grey and back. As high as your waist in some spots, like nothing you've ever seen."

"The only water was that bloody pond. We had to push bodies out of the way to get to that water, sucking water out of hoof prints, the foulest you've ever seen. We left several boys from home beside that pond. Nothing we could do. There was more boys down than there was still upright to carry them," said Ty, of the Widow Glenn's small cattle pond. This part of Georgia had been without rain for the last month, and the many streams were bone dry. That pond had been taken and re-taken many times that day.

"We were digging through the poor dead fellas' bullet sacks, but there was not an unfired bullet to be found anywhere on that hill," said Ab. "We thought it was over for us, but right then, here comes Col.

McCook, galloping up like a pup with a stick in his teeth, so happy to get in the fight. The rest of the 52nd had been stuck in the rear with the Reserve Corps all day. And right behind them comes Gen. Granger's heavy ammo wagons flying down the road, driving like Jehu, rattling and bouncing over them tore up roads, damn near overturning when they hit a cannonball hole, pitching teamsters out on their heads. It was a whole train full of bullets, so, we grabbed a few boxes and lit into 'em again. Granger was something to see, right in the middle of it, every wagon he had, wheeling straight into the hottest of it, and kept 'em running until dark.''

"We held our own, coulda held that hill if we'd had enough ammo, but when the sun went down, they pulled us off," said Ab. "Wilder himself commandeered a wagon for us to ride back on. I've never been that tired. I've never been one tenth that tired. But, we hurried back here to check on our old chum."

"Yep, and there you was," said Teddy. "Sleeping, not a care in the world. Snoring soft as an infant, and drooling all over that purty pink cushion the church ladies give you."

"Is it true?" I asked. "Was Lytle killed?'

"Yes," said Freddy. "His men were completely cutoff and surrounded, so he led a bayonet charge, shouting, 'I will die as a gentleman. We can die but once. This is the time and place. Let us charge.' What else would you expect from him?"

"You saw it?"

"I caught some of it, down the ridge. I was a little busy, myself," said Ty. "All his men said about the same thing."

The news hurt almost as bad as losing a close friend. General William Lytle, our Poet-General was from Cincinnati, commanded a brigade in the fight, and his poem, Antony and Cleopatra, had won national and international acclaim. It was loved by Billy Yank and Johnny Reb, officers and footsore privates, and the women at home that loved them. It spoke to the ardor of a virile, young country determined to go to war with itself. Lytle's sense of tragedy throbbed through both armies.

Before the war Lytle had been to my Athens classroom several times, leaving no small impression on my students, and, on one visit, we ended the evening on the wrong side of the tracks, shooting some lively billiards at a seedy Athens pub. Some of the local toughs mistook Lytle for an effeminate fop, and proceeded to catcall his manicure, oiled curls, and precise diction. I was just as surprised as the guy on the floor when Lytle threw that jab that dropped him, but not nearly as shocked as the guy that lost a mouthful of teeth to Lytle's pool cue. The preening little dandy whipped those loudmouths up one side of that saloon and then the other, put his boot on the backside of both delinquents and pushed them out the door, then turned around and ran the table.

William Lytle was a splendid gentleman, now, like then, forced by circumstance to become a warrior. As sad as I was, I smiled when the boys told me that the Johnny Rebs recognized him and guarded his body, to make sure no trophy hunters got to him. Their generals sent a lock of hair to his family and promised to give him a proper warrior's burial. Freddy recited the first stanzas of Lytle's most famous poem, and we tried to mumble along. A couple other patients, a surgeon, some nurses, stopped and listened and quiet tears rolled down more than one cheek, including my own.

"I am dying, Egypt, dying!
Ebbs the crimson life-tide fast,
And the dark Plutonian shadows
Gather on the evening blast
I must perish like a Roman,
Die the great Triumvir still.

Let not Caesar's servile minions,
Mock the lion thus laid low."

Under Siege

There were few places on earth more dismal or dreary that Chattanooga that fall. The town of 2,500 citizens before the War was flooded
with 60,000 ragged, dirty, hungry soldiers, and thrice that many mules
and horses. The number of casualties was overwhelming. Most homes,
churches and schools in the city became hospitals, and heavy fall rains
deluged the city. With the Rebels controlling our every move from the
heights above, we were on near starvation rations. It was slightly better
inside the hospital but not much, weak broth and hardtack, sometimes a
porridge of some sort. Grits, I guess, being in the south, and all.

They said hungry men followed behind rolling supply wagons, picking up crumbs dropped in the mud, and stole feed from the horses. Some
even alleged dried horse dung was searched through. I was still in the
hospital for the worst of it, so I don't know if that's true, but I know the
life of an army mule is not a pleasant one, whether it be a two-footed or
four-footed animal. And, it is also true that during some of my wheelchair strolls around the city, I saw more than a few groups of soldiers
sitting on the street corner with knife and fork in hand, licking their
chops and waiting for some overburdened mule to collapse. Sometimes,
they had a Chicago stockyard meat-cutter or two with them, who twirled
cleavers as their hungry little minds slapped a butcher's diagram on a
struggling beast. That seemed to me to be a double indignity to the mule,
since it was the solder's robbery of his grain that contributed to the poor
four-legged-fella's weakened state in the first place.

After suffocating in the noxious hospital tent for weeks, I was delighted when Dr. Walker wheeled me outside toward the large, bald man
I had seen comforting the dying boys in the dark. He was puffing on a

clay pipe, and, his sack coat, made for a much smaller man, strained around massive shoulders. Behind his heavy, unruly eye brows and bad acne scars, a kind face smiled at me.

"Father, may this man sit with you awhile? He needs to get out in the air," said Dr. Walker.

"Certainly he may," said the big man.

"Father?" I said, crushed that my fresh air would come with a sermon.

"Was. A priest. No longer," the man said, in a deep, friendly voice. "My name is Columbus Pleasant."

"Not to be uncordial," I eyed the man warily, "But don't start in about my immortal soul. It's not your business."

"I wouldn't think of it. I have enough trouble worrying about my own."

"That's a refreshing change," I said.

"Not so much."

"I meant for me," I said. "I shot a preacher awhile back, him on the pulpit in front of a packed house. Somewhat packed, anyway. Right through the neck. So be careful on how the Lord moves you."

"Is that bragging or confessing?"

"Neither one. I had that little light. I thought I'd let it shine."

"I see. Well, it must have been a powerful sermon, but I guess you don't enjoy church so much."

"Just that once."

Lum was a sincere, friendly man. He was well read, which I expected, and quick witted, which I had not. Time passed easily, but the time for my dose of laudanum had come and gone. I grimaced and fidgeted in my chair, looking for Dr. Walker's orderlies to take me inside.

"Hurting?" asked Lum.

"Yes, something fierce," I said. "But I don't want to go back inside that pus bucket. It's miserable in there."

"This might help with your quandary. Laudanum. Same as you get in there, I just keep mine handy," Lum said, handing me a pint bottle, which I knew wasn't his first of the day. I took the nearly full bottle, eyeing the big man across from me. "Drink up, I have plenty. My pain's not so bad, today."

"You don't look wounded."

"Only in spirit. And that's a mortal wound."

"How so?"

"For another time. I wouldn't want you to get the wrong impression and shoot me."

"Thank you," I said, and took a gulp of laudanum. I shuddered at the stuff, bitter even with cinnamon and saffron, and the raw alcohol burned regardless. I handed it back.

"Relax. Have another," said Lum, waving away my return of the bottle. "Don't short yourself on it."

"So, what's to become of us, you think?" I said, as the buttery warmth spread through me. Before he could answer, I was asleep in my wheelchair with a puddle under my chin. Lum stayed with me, letting me breathe clean air.

Chapter Eleven

Eleven: Opening Cracker Line
October 29th, 1863

Gen. Grant relieved Rosecrans and took personal command of the Army in Chattanooga, and Sherman was already on hand. On October 29th, the Army finally opened the "Cracker Line", a well-defended, uninterrupted supply-line through the Confederate defenses. Food, medicine, bullets poured in, but even well supplied, we were still being victimized by both sniper and artillery fire from the mountain tops. Rebel cavalry still made off with a good share of Union supply wagons, and the riverboats operated under constant harassment. We were better fed, and well supplied, but that was often ruined by a cannonball landing in the soup pot.

The only way to end this harassment was to send the infantry up the steep slopes of Lookout Mountain and Missionary Ridge to dig the Rebels out. It took two months for our Army to gather the strength to attempt it, but, at last, on the morning of November 24, we heard Gen. Joe Hooker's division assaulting Lookout Mountain. Heavy fog concealed the Yankees, but we could hear them moving methodically up the slope under heavy fire. Sightless artillery blasted away, both sides as likely hitting their own men as not. In the afternoon, as the battle climbed higher, the clouds settled lower down, the warriors seemed to float and I expected to see Thor or Zeus at any moment. The fight continued until dark, and after the Confederates retreated over the mountain someone remarked that it was the Battle Above the Clouds, and that moniker seemed to stick.

The following day, I watched the action on Missionary Ridge through my field glasses while propped on church-donated pink pillows in my wheelchair. I saw Granger, Grant and Sherman watching the action from horseback, and since Granger was there, I knew my friends in the 52nd were somewhere in the mass of 20,000 blue uniforms preparing to charge up that sheer 600-foot ridge.

The grand assault began, and our boys quickly captured the first line of Rebel rifle pits, but it was costly. Most of the commanders in the field were casualties, and our men were pinned down and under heavy fire. Just when I thought the attack was doomed, the Yankees burst out of a belt of timber. In small clusters of blue specks they jitterbugged up that steep slope, in and out of patches of thickets and screaming "Chickamauga! Chickamauga!" as they charged. They moved too fast for Rebel artillery to adjust, and we cheered as they overpowered the batteries and bayonetted the rebel artillerymen at their posts. The Rebels stampeded the other way, and by the end of the day, Bragg retreated all the way to Dalton, Georgia, losing all the territory he'd paid so dearly for at Chickamauga. The Army of The Cumberland owned Tennessee once again.

Dovie's Wedding

In March, 1864, the regiment made camp at Lee & Gordon's Mills, near the edge of the disastrous Chickamauga Battlefield, where we stayed for seven weeks. Generally, our stay was pretty monotonous, with the most exciting thing in camp being pursuit of Molly Cotton-tail, the poor bunnies that wandered too close to a cooking fire. Sometimes a hundred whooping boys would be chasing the terrified creatures as they darted and dashed and zigged and zagged through the pasture field. Few bunnies ever ended up in gravy, though I'm sure the chases didn't do much for their already nervous dispositions.

The armies and mountains were full of healthy young people suffering from interrupted courtships and overflowing with hormones. Romance between our lonely boys in blue and those rambunctious healthy mountain girls was as likely to happen as the sun coming up tomorrow. Such affairs of the heart were strongly discouraged, and marriage was specifically forbidden, but that's a lot of young, homesick, excitable youngsters. I understood that part all right. There were times I was pretty excitable myself. Inevitably, one of our boys picked out a wife from among the country lasses. Dovie, the quiet, gentle, angel-faced balladeer couldn't wait for the war to end. It surprised us, but I suppose Dovie was exactly the type of boy a mountain girl might seek out in the middle of an apocalyptic war. His bride was a tiny little thing, and together they were as cute as a couple of speckled pups.

Even though it was supposed to be as secret as any military plans, close to fifty Yankees accepted the invitation and attended the wedding, along with twice that many family and friends of the bride. The ceremony was a joyous affair, and those mountain folks welcomed us warmly and just wished the war to be over. I don't know where they got enough food and liquor for all of us, but they were merrily free with everything they had. They had butchered a small herd of pigs, and shed-smoked them in vinegar, hot peppers and brown sugar for days.

Heaping platters of buttery, spicy pork, fried chicken, catfish, and frog-legs filled long tables, built just for the occasion. More tables sagged under an armada of crock tubs of butter beans, collard greens, sweet potatoes, mashed potatoes, and bacon-greasy Hoppin' John. Buckets of red-eye gravy, and cornbread stacked like pyramids, was available at half a dozen aid-stations around the yard. Everything was washed down with endless pitchers of sweet tea, and somehow, I was able to squeeze in some nibbles of a dozen different sweet pastries. Even Ab seemed satisfied with the amount of peppery red-flecked gravy that flowed through the mountains that day. Ab enjoyed himself some gravy, and I was growing fond of it. In the army, I had found that there's two things that almost immediately dampen a man's zeal for battle: A hot bowl of biscuits and gravy, or a rowdy session of marital congress. I was a staunch proponent of both.

The bride's folks had some sour-mash that made us Northern fellas jump up and wrassle a bear, as the sly, old masters of the copper kettles called it, watching with wide grins that hadn't held a tooth in ten years. The free-flowing Tennessee whiskey, applejack and peach brandy livened the step of many a blue-clad, ham-footed, clod-hopper on the dance floor that night, including my own. The mountain fiddle playing and banjo picking was about the liveliest I'd ever heard, and the fiddlers back home weren't exactly lumberjacks with the bow. After months of hospitalization and recuperation, I was finally getting my vigor back and I was right out in the thick of it, grinning like a lop-eared plow mule, crushing even the quickest of toes as I stomped through the squares and reels and promenades to "Turkey in the Straw" and "Lil' Liza Jane."

Just watching the sweaty-shiny happy faces of those mountain girls slinging nasty ankles as they cavorted to the Alabama Flat-rock was a refreshing pleasure for this old campaigner. Several opportunities to soothe my excitability arose, but I had some reservations. I wasn't accustomed to waiting for a gal to unpack the chew from her jaw and corkscrew a couple rinsing spits off the porch before commencing my love-making.

Before the night was over, I was feeling pretty bad for Dovie. Being from Ohio, the poor lad had no inkling of the peculiar, and downright cruel, mountain tradition of shivaree that had awaited him. I can see why it didn't catch on. Dovie's hazing was worse than most, because instead of a dozen or so friends and family, he had a full company of pent up soldier-energy blowing ox horns, ringing cow bells, banging on pots and pans, setting off firecrackers, and carrying him away from his marriage bed on a rail. Knowing they were unlikely to ever face a payback shivaree torture of their own, I believe only encouraged our boys to greater abuses.

There was, of course, no way the Colonel wasn't aware of the wedding, and being the good man that he was, he would probably have looked the other the way if he'd had the option. However, when morning assembly came through the trumpets, many of our boys still littered the bride's meadow, snoring like bears, with a jug not far away. A good many more were holed up with a pink-cheeked Georgia Peach, safely out of sight from her Pa when the sun cracked the horizon. I'll admit I was in that latter group, that last pull of applejack brushing aside my qualms about a union with a chewer of the Virginia weed. When the rooster crowed, I was looking into a pretty girl's sleepy, emerald eyes, golden hay in her golden hair, and just a dribble of ambeer backy-juice down the prettiest rosy cheek I had ever seen.

The Colonel was livid. Search parties were sent out, the wedding party was rounded up, and the majority of those who staggered back to camp throughout the day were still groaning and disgorging as they tried to form lines under McCook's icy glare.

I wasn't feeling so great myself. Better than most, I figure, thanks to that enthusiastic lass who'd fallen for my charms the night before. I'm sure our rigorous romp had sweated some of the alcohol out of me, but the only thing that saved me was that the Colonel had been so outraged at morning assembly that he ordered the search parties out without first identifying who his searchers were. Ty, leading one of the search parties, pulled me away from a group being escorted back to camp under guard. Those down-trodden souls I had just been marching off to the hoosegow with were not happy when they suddenly found themselves under my supervision, but they never spilled the beans.

The groom spent his honeymoon hanging upside down from a wagon wheel for marrying that little tow-headed girl with all the sun freckles.

He then joined his queasy groomsmen, and quite a number of his guests, in sweating out the next few weeks in the guardhouse under the sun's broiling glare. McCook eyed me suspiciously for the next few days, and I wondered when the miserable inmates would sell me out for some relief, but they were steadfast.

Chapter Twelve

Ft. Pillow
April 2nd, 1864

As he did every morning at dawn, Pete Caballo stood atop the western bluff above Ft. Pillow, looking for danger. The morning fog was still rolling in off the Mississippi as he swept the woods with his binoculars, but the dreary skies kept the tree-line in shadows. There was just enough light in the sky that Pete waited for the bouncing yellow warblers to start their morning chorus as they hopped and flexed through their courtship dance. The birds that lived in all the dead wood created by the fort's construction weren't the best singers by far, but neither was he, and their songs brightened the start of his days. It was too quiet, enough to be unsettling, but the murky shadows revealed nothing.

Pete was a Sergeant, the Chief of the Piece, in the 6th U.S. Regiment Colored Heavy Artillery, manning a battery of two 12-pound howitzers on the bluffs above Ft. Pillow. They'd arrived at the end of March, two weeks ago, and he was in a hurry to leave. It was the most un-military post he'd ever been in, going all the way back to his early days on the Texas frontier. The other unit at the fort was the 13th Tennessee Cavalry (U.S.), a regiment made up of "homemade Yankees," natives to the state, and who seemed to be more outlaws and raiders than soldiers.

The commander of the 13th, Major William Frederick "Bill" Bradford, was an attorney and wealthy land owner from Bedford County, Tennessee, the home county of Rebel General Nathan Bedford Forrest. Pete knew that before the war Bradford had led pro-Northern guerrillas in raids against Rebel sympathizers to grow his own wealth and punish political opponents. Bradford and his bandits were despised by the people of Tennessee, and stood accused of the most terrible transgressions against the wives and daughters of Southern soldiers. Escaped slaves and Rebel deserters also hid inside the walls, and there seemed to be little regulation on consumption of whiskey by the soldiers, on or off duty.

After two years of Union occupation, Confederate raids, counterraids, and midnight lynching parties from both sides, the entire area was ready to go up in flames. Everyday there was another, and more brutal, reprisal and now it had come full circle, with the hills filled with Confederate desperadoes waiting to ambush Union patrols. Pete's commanding officer, Major Lionel Booth, despised Bradford, and only with great effort had he kept his well-disciplined artillerymen from a fort-wide brawl. Pete was proud of the unit he commanded, his gunner and his cannoneers, and the chief of caisson and his drivers. Pete had some good boys here, all former slaves, and ready to earn their pay.

"Sgt. Major, Who's them men yonder?" asked one of the boys. "Why dey playing like that, pointing their rifles year?"

Pete turned, snapped his binoculars to his eyes and stared.

"Fire. Fire on them. They are Rebels," he screamed in disbelief, watching a company of Forrest's cavalry dismounting on a wooded knoll. The Rebels formed a line in the trees and leisurely unstrapped their rifles, sighting them on the battery, and laughing at the frantic behavior of the untried artillerymen. Instead of hearing his birds, the woods exploded with rifle fire.

Gen. Nathan Bedford Forrest
10:00 am

In a cold, misty mountain drizzle, Gen. Nathan Bedford Forrest's saddle cut into him like a rusty sword blade. Chilled, miserable and his back bent in agony, he and his staff were hidden in the soggy woods four hundred yards from Ft. Pillow, finalizing plans for the attack as his sharpshooting companies kept a steady fire into the fort. His men and stock were beat down and worn out, but his spies assured him the fort had ample fodder for his horses, plenty of fresh mounts, and a well-stocked armory. And Forrest planned to right some egregious wrongs.

Two-thousand men of his Cavalry Corps had been in position since before dawn, hiding in the dark forests in the hills surrounding the fort, an obscure post in West Tennessee. The stockade sat on a wide plateau overlooking the Mississippi River and was protected by three rings of earthen parapets 4 feet thick and 8 feet high, divided by trenches 12-foot-wide and six feet deep. The rear wall of the fort was a sheer cliff that dropped into the river, which was swollen with spring rains. Narrow, sudden ravines sliced through the fields of cut stumps outside the defenses.

"Yes, sir, all regiments are here. 2,000 eager warriors, dropped from the finest loins in the Confederacy, raring to go," said Devol. "Bedford, when I told these boys no prisoners, you would have thought I gave them a bottle of whiskey and a week's pass at Horny Helen's Whorehouse. There's a few of 'em that's never hung a coon before. I have no idea how that happened."

"Yes, and sadly it looks unlikely they'll be allowed to do so after the war. I cannot believe my own dear home state has fallen into this. Bradford, this vile, excretious traitor from my own county," snarled Forrest. "I won't give that base coward the chance to slink out the back like the chicken thief that he is. Him, and seeing as how Sambo has won his right to be kilt, let's assure them all they receive their full citizenship."

"At this point, Jeff Davis in God's own chariot couldn't convince our boys that those black savages ain't raping and killing their women," said Devol. "Me and my men have been finding those poor souls all over Tennessee."

"Yes, you sure seem to find a lot of them. You and that mute behemoth of yours. I fear no man. But him. And that's no piddling' amount," said Forrest. Forrest knew he overlooked some of Devol's methods when he probably shouldn't have, but they weren't from the southern aristocracy. Every day of their lives they'd had to fight, every step, dirty, no rules, or rules from the deadliest saloons and waterfront dives. Theirs had been lives of ridge feuds and dog fights and flashing knife blades and whipping posts and honor killings.

"Yes sir, Bedford, I'll admit, sometimes the big fellow gets a little carried away. But you got to remember his raisin'," said Devol. He knew it had been a mistake to send Ashok out to Albert Pike in Arkansas before the battle of Pea Ridge, and one that Forrest wouldn't let him soon forget. Pike had said he wanted to send a message, but giving three regiments of redskins all the fire water they could drink had turned them into bloodthirsty demons. When the news leaked out that the drunken Cherokee soldiers had taken the scalps of their vanquished foes, the Sovereign Grand Commander was very nearly locked up and hung.

"I'm quite familiar with it," said Forrest. "Just keep him on a short leash. A strong, short leash."

"General, don't you think you're too close? We are well within rifle range here," asked Forrest's newest burden, yet another dimwitted aide-de-camp of high birth, this one the scion of some Tennessee planting family, placed on Forrest by Jefferson Davis personally.

"I'm aware of that. Now, leave us grown-ups be," said Forrest, ignoring the errant bullets that zipped through the trees, just inches above them. "Was our estimate on enemy troop strength accurate?"

"Yes, sir," said Devol, lowering his binoculars to glance at Forrest. "Looks to be. Six-hundred soldiers, half white, half colored. Maybe a hundred-fifty civilian man who could fight, but likely won't."

"Hells blazes, I can't stomach the idea of a darkie pretending to be a soldier. They'll wish they'd reconsidered when I get done with their black hides," said Forrest. "Rising up against the hardest fighting men ever produced. Yes, we'll see."

"Yes, Colonel," said Devol. "If God saw the need to free the Ethiopians, I'm certain he would have done so by now. Clearly the Negro needs guidance from the white man's hand, even if we must be firm at times. Today, I foresee, the hand must be especially firm. And for the race traitor, fatal."

There was a slap, and Forrest's horse leapt upright. Front legs flailing, the animal teetered on two legs, shot through the lungs, pawing and squirting pink bubbles from the wound. With a furious, shuddering lurch, the horse toppled backwards, pinning Forrest underneath. As he screamed obscenities and fought the thrashing beast, every man on the hill rushed to aid him.

"General, are you all right?" asked the new aide.

"Fuck no, I'm not all right!" Forrest roared, bloody spray still hitting him. "What kind of goddamn idiot would ask if I'm all right with a bucking horse trying to kill me?"

"General, I protest your language. Must I remind you my father is a congressman?"

"I guess that answers my question. You congressional fucking idiot."

"How many horses have been killed beneath you?" Devol asked once they were remounted, Forrest on the Congressman's son's pedigreed Andalusian.

"Almost thirty now," Forrest said, "Them Yanks are the most pitiful marksmen I ever seen."

3:30 p.m.

"And you know he got it?" Forrest said. He knew Major Booth had been killed by a sniper's bullet, and his blood enemy Bradford was now in charge of the fort. Rifle and artillery fire had ceased when Forrest sent a note to Bradford demanding surrender.

"We wrote it down twice, and I read it to him just as you said it," said Devol, and read Forrest's note aloud. "The conduct of the officers and men garrisoning Fort Pillow has been such as to entitle them to being treated as prisoners of war. I demand the unconditional surrender of the entire garrison, promising that you shall be treated as prisoners of war. My men have just received a fresh supply of ammunition, and from their present position can easily assault and capture the fort. Should my demand be refused, I cannot be responsible for the fate of your command."

Forrest nodded, but said nothing.

"He won't surrender," said Devol. "He's challenging you, Bedford. Mocking, if you ask me."

"Bradford knows I plan to hang him," said Forrest, then spoke loudly to all his officers. "Gentlemen, another Yankee regiment is only a few miles up the Mississippi. We cannot wait. I informed the fort if there was no surrender in twenty minutes, maybe Jesus would have mercy on them, as we would not. The fact that Tennessee men would enjoin with niggers against the Confederacy wraths my blood like hell itself."

When the others spoke up in agreement, Forrest raised his hand for silence.

"Col. Devol, I cannot make the charge. The damned horse mashed me good," Forrest said, his face twisted in pain. "You will lead the attack. It must be your responsibility. Kill the traitors, and these negroes need to know fear again. And taught a lesson for thinking they are as good as white men."

"Yes, sir, General, I know what you mean," said Devol.

"Do what you do best," said Forrest. "Open up Hell for 'em.''

"You don't have to tell me twice, Bedford," said Devol, and Forrest's bugler sounded the charge.

On the bluffs, the Rebels had turned the Yankee cannons around and were firing into the fort. Rebel sharpshooters raked the outer walls, and dead Yankees fell off the barricades in scores. Confederate skirmishers had captured two rows of burning barracks and slave huts about 150 yards from the fort, and at the bugle, they leapt out of the ditches and fallen timber and dashed and darted through the smoke from three directions. The first wave charged across the culvert and knelt at the wall, while the second wave leapt onto their backs, and then onto the parapet roof where they blazed away at the cowering Federals. Not slowing, they tromped through the massacred Yankees in the ditches, using bayonets like walking sticks that pierced through the piled bodies at their feet.

Devol sat tall in the saddle amid the gunshots and screams in the swirling smoke. A long, terrible female scream came from a smoldering building and he saw a trembling black girl staring back at him. She whirled and ran, but she tripped, staggered and stumbled into the soot. Her dusty, tear streaked face and slight, heaving body ignited in him a white-hot lust as he closed on her. She fled through the haze, dodging fires and brawling soldiers. Devol chased her behind a building and she was trapped, sprawled in the dirt, sobbing and gasping, horror and despair on her face. Her dark chocolate skin was slick and shining with sweat and he stared at his prize for a few seconds, licking his lips, marveling at his luck. When she opened her eyes, Devol met her moist brown eyes and quivering, pleading smile with a grin of his own. Before he drove his fist into her face. He lashed her with a leather strap, and when she struggled to her feet, he backed her against a wall with the point of his sword, then slashed away her dress, revealing the slightest tuft of pubic hair and barely formed hips and breasts. A circle of Rebels paused to watch, and the nude girl ran pleading from soldier to soldier, but they laughed and pushed her to the ground as Devol doubled over in delight. He took his revolver and fired at her feet, and the sobbing girl clawed through the blackened dirt as Devol walked toward her, opening his pants.

The fort was filled with hundreds of shrieking Rebels, and cries of "Black flag" from the Confederates. Pete had known from the first volley that this was how the day would end. No prisoners. No surrender. Not for the escaped slaves who had raised their arms against their masters. Not for the treacherous Bradford and his band of rogues who had terrorized the countryside.

"Hey, you men, stop here," Pete shouted, jumping in front of a stream of black and white soldiers fleeing toward the river. "We have to fight."

"You fight, nigger, out of our way," shouted a burly, black soldier, pulling a bowie knife from his belt. "Unless you want to fight this."

"That's right, or this," said a scrawny Rebel deserter as another swung his rifle at Pete's head. Pete saw the desperation in their eyes and ducked as the gun stock shattered against the wall behind him. The men disappeared into the smoke of the burning buildings as waves of Rebel cavalry came vaulting out of it, ten Rebels for every Yankee. Union soldiers fled toward the River, but Pete knew it was a death trap. It was what the Plains Indian tribes called "pishkun," the buffalo jumps, or deep blood kettle, the huge hunts where they would stampede a herd of buffalo through a narrow alley and over a sharp cliff, causing hundreds of the massive beasts to plummet to their deaths hundreds of feet below. While the bison were still writhing, the Indians would start butchering amid the blood and thrashing beasts. Now, four companies of Rebel sharpshooters were doing the butchering, and the water's edge was a wide blanket of bodies bobbing in the pink tinged shallows.

"Look down there, look at that river, they got 500 riflemen firing straight down on there! Is that what you want? Is that how you want to die?" screamed Pete. His boys never had a chance. No amount of training could have slowed this madness, but, in ones and twos, young soldiers chose to make a stand. He rallied a handful of men to the battle flag, and they chopped their way into the armories. As they passed out rifles and ammunition, more soldiers joined them behind their bullet-riddled walls of barrels and wagon-beds. The rebels were massed fifty yards away, and he watched a big, swaggering Colonel roam through the smoke and flames, shooting the wounded Negro soldiers in the head. The Colonel turned, and Pete gasped at the face he'd seen on that dark road in Athens, and at Herrold's Mill, the face that had haunted him every night and day for two years. He screamed like a panther and was over the wall, with the others right beside him.

May 1864

We'd been tromping Indian-style through the miserably hot Georgia jungles for several days when we came over a small ridge and looked down upon a hidden spring. The slight breeze refreshed us with the scent of that pure, sparkling water and cooled us at a hundred feet away. We let out a yell and took off for that water at a rate somewhere between escaping a fire and rushing for the Thanksgiving gobbler. Leaving a trail of clothes and firearms as we went, we were ten feet from the water and mostly bare-butt naked when a familiar deep voice sent us diving for cover.

"You ain't suddenly bashful without your bloomers, are you?" drawled the big deep voice as we crawled through the bushes. "Ain't none of you girls bathing today? We ain't gonna shoot you, 'specially sugar-britches with the cute derriere what treated us to a dance number last time.''

"I'll break his neck," shouted Teddy as he jumped to his feet.

"No, you won't," I yelled, bursting naked from the brush and tackling Teddy around the ankles before he got us all shot.

"What is it you want, Reb?" yelled Ty, after we'd calmed Teddy down.

"Hot, ain't it, Billy Yank?"

"I'll grant that," said Ty. A few of us had taken to carrying sidearms, and now Ty retrieved his pistol belt and strapped it on. I bloodied myself scrambling through a razor-sharp briar patch and followed his example. Remembering the Rebel marksmanship when Teddy had reached for his clothes the time before, I took one look at the exposed trail and left my drawers lay.

"You've been waiting in hiding to inquire about the weather?" Ty continued.

"You've seen through the facade, you Yankees is quick," said the man, to some laughs behind him. "I was trying to judge how disputatious you was feeling today?"

"There's things to be said for a day without bloodshed," said Ty. "I'm an advocate, personally."

"Too hot to be harboring ill will, wouldn't you say?"

"It is," said Ty.

"That water is mighty inviting, and there's plenty of it, just as cold on both sides, what do you say?" the man said. "Some of the fellas is gettin' a mite ripe, and we savor a dip. We'll lay our weapons down and share."

"I'll agree to that. Let me check with the others. Teddy, your powder dry?" asked Ty. I guess the Rebels remembered Teddy's name, and they guffawed as loudly as we did. We joked, but the reality was, Teddy had nearly died from horrible dysentery, and its cures, more than once. Dysentery was killing many more young boys than bullets. Nearly everyone contracted it, but the amount of suffering varied and Teddy was constantly under treatment, and usually half-looped on laudanum. He had taken so many "blue mass" pills, a mix of chalk and mercury, that his skin was starting to shine. The doctors also tortured him with tea made from dogwood bark, variously adding strychnine, castor oil, turpentine, silver nitrate, and many more equally vile concoctions, but nothing they did seemed to slow it.

"This war sure would be a dreary place for you all, without old Teddy to pick on, wouldn't it be?" he said, but that was the last word spoken on it. We were all soon shed of the rest of our clothes, and that wonderfully chilled pool was full of Yankees and Rebs whooping and hollering like a bunch of drunk cattle drovers at the Lost Oasis of Zerzura.

"Howdy. Where are you from?" I said to the nearest Reb, after we had frolicked for a good stretch and found seats with water-lilies to our neck. He had a small, black cigar hanging from his lip.

"1st Tennessee, Company Aytche," he said, with a grin. "Sam Watkins, Maury County. And yourself?"

"Ohio," I told him, and we were soon swapping stories like old men.

"It's nice to have a decent conversation companion," said Sam, after a good hour of jawing. "These fellers get purty stale sometimes. When you're as hungry as they are, it tends to dominate your thoughts."

We stayed in that wonderful, revitalizing water the rest of the afternoon, and decided it just made sense to break bread together. Still, not a cross word had been spoken. Ab had been a solid citizen and started a nice fire and several pots of coffee. When that coffee smell hit the air, every Confederate there would have surrendered to me, so seductive was the aroma. We had to go in relays once Ab started hollering that it was ready.

"Have some coffee Billy Yank? I got some fine sweet chaw," said a gangly rebel, as the sun began to set.

"Sure, Johnny," Ty said. "Here's the beans, then. I don't want plug. Give me the smoking tobacco."

"Fine. Mighty fine," said the rebel, stirring the green coffee beans in his cap. I ain't had real coffee since President Davis was well liked."

"I didn't realize he wasn't."

"Well, he shore ain't by me," the man said, and they both laughed, slapped hands, and enjoined in commerce. That first night, Dovie hoofed it all the way back to camp to retrieve his guitar, and a Reb did he same. With no one saying much about it, we situated ourselves for a few days around the water.

Other than having a refreshing plunge only an arm's length away, we spent the next week doing much the same as we would have been doing in our own camps. Ty spent the first couple days writing long, loving letters to his wife as he lounged in the shade of a nearby oak. When a couple of our younger fellas said they wanted to go back, Ty said he would take them, saying he had some other business to attend to, and that he'd get word out to us if either side appeared likely to take up arms.

Men sang around campfires and shared tall-tales of monster trout, ten-point bucks, or romantic interludes from pre-Civil War lives, the same as any conversation around half-a-million other campfires. They speculated about enemy troop movements, the price of beans, and spoke with pride and longing about wives, sweethearts, and children back home while patching frayed pants or mending socks. The hunters in the group supplied us with plenty of venison for our stay, as well as an abundance of game, fish, and fowl of all sorts. Being less warlike seemed to agree with Teddy's troubled bowels, and his vigor and appetite returned. He even baked us some berry pies after we pooled all our odd bits of butter and sugar and flour, and they were as good as from any country kitchen.

Ab and the Confederate sergeant were both blacksmiths, and the two developed a quick rapport. Checkers or cards or dice games went on simultaneously, and almost around the clock. Not one of us took a shot at another, or even threatened to, and none of the squabbles over cards or checkers ended in takedowns by the ears. Even the devout ones, in the nightly prayer meetings and Bible verse reading, showed divine restraint and never started witnessing to the avowed sinners amongst us, or clobbering each other over an interpretation of peace and loving our fellow man. A couple of the rebel privates had been students at the University of Georgia before the War. They, and all the Rebels, were thrilled to hear my stories about William Lytle, and several of us, North and South, could recite his poetry. Sam sure could talk, and he was good at it. I didn't know whether to laugh or cry at his tales of privation in the Rebel army.

"I ain't no Biblical scholar," said Sam, when the conversation turned to slavery on our last night there. "But most folks didn't seem too troubled by involuntary servitude back in Bible days, unless they had the misfortune themselves of being in bondage. Then it seemed to be a whole new perspective."

"I'm not a believer, myself," I said. "But that doesn't make it less evil. There's just right and wrong."

"You're telling me that your moral code would make you leave your soft bed, filled with nubile concubines, and a full cabinet of good bourbon, and go pick cotton with your own dusky agricultural laborers?" asked Sam. "Day after goddamned day? Maybe they should write the Bible about you, because that' there is a step further than Jesus hisself took it."

"Now, that was uncalled for," I said. "Sam, why don't you just go on home?"

"Well, now, I ain't in no hurry to be a wage slave neither, cousin," said Sam. "I guess I'll take the devil I know, whatever that is, and let them legal and crusading moralizers figger out the rest."

"You can't believe owning slaves is right, Sam," I said.

"The kind that Jefferson and Washington they themselves had a plantation full of, while they was seceding from England? Ain't sure I see the difference."

"I can't explain that, Sam, it doesn't even matter. Whatever it is, you know it's not gonna stop. We're not gonna stop. You can't stop us," I said. "We're just too big."

"I know that. We ain't stupid. But I jest cain't bring myself to go home. I just cain't. I've got a reputation to worry about. It ain't much of one, but it's the only one I got."

"You can always surrender to me," I said. "Nobody needs to know. I can kick some dirt in your face if you want."

"Cain't."

"I'll be seeing you Sam," I said the next morning, as we all got ready to head back to our armies.

"I suppose you will old feller, I 'suppose you will," Sam said. "I'll try to get all worked up about killing you, but I don't expect I can. It really ain't in me."

"But you're gonna keep backing up to Atlanta?"

"I expect so," said Sam.

"And getting killed."

"Ain't no room around my fire for a quitter's blanket."

"Go home, Sam," I said. "It's a lost cause."

"Them's the best kind," he grinned.

Chapter Thirteen

Thirteen: Kennesaw Mountain
June 27th, 1864

Gen. William Tecumseh Sherman's 98,000 strong Army had marched into Georgia at the beginning of May, 1864. Our mission was to destroy, once and for all, new Confederate Commander Gen. Joe Johnston's 49,000-man rag-tag, underfed, and undersupplied army. Even Rebel president Jefferson Davis finally had enough of the dictatorial, half-mad, and utterly incompetent Gen. Braxton Bragg whose bumbling strategies were complete failures militarily, wasting many young lives on both sides as he retreated hopelessly across the South.

Sherman called this new campaign his "Big Indian War," and we'd been poking the Rebels with sharp sticks in small, fierce, fast-moving flanking movements all spring and summer, shedding blood at places named Rocky Face Ridge, Snake Creek Gap, Lost Mountain, Gilgal Church, Resaca, Dalton and 20 other creeks and bug-tussles. A decisive victory had eluded us as Sherman sent forth a regiment or two at a time, always giving himself the option to slip away and fight again another day. But Joe Johnston wasn't Bragg. He didn't take our bait, didn't panic, and now blocked our way, waiting for us to come to him, with no way around.

We were twenty miles northwest of Atlanta, and Johnston couldn't have picked a better place to make a stand. The Confederate Army had gradually shifted their lines eastward and had entrenched their artillery on the crest of Kennesaw Mountain. It was a strong position along the Western and Atlantic Railroad, and the Rebel cannons were blowing our supply trains to smithereens.

Big Kennesaw was the towering barbican that cast long dark shadows over the valleys below, but Little Kennesaw Mountain was just as heavily defended. Together, they were turrets at each end of the five-mile spiny ridge that looked like a cinder pile, but was one vast fortress, with miles of connected trenches that hid at least three divisions of hardened Rebels. Sherman felt a crushing victory here would split Johnston's army, open up the Chattahoochee River, and bring about the quick capture of Atlanta.

For two weeks, we'd watched the Rebels through binoculars, staring across at the mountain with the joy of condemned men watching their gallows being built. They got deadlier and stronger every day, adding to their fearsome medieval trenches on the summit. They now had four rings of jagged abatis and daunting, spiked chevaux de fries, the chest-high timbers shaved down to needle points that would pierce a man like a sharp spear. The obstacles overlapped in thick loops around the slope like spiked dog collars, and behind them another maze of rifle pits was dug deep into the hill. The bulge in the middle of the line overflowed with 2,000 rifles of the grizzled 1st/27th Tennesseans, Sam Watkins' unit.

We'd fought them in every big battle so far, walked in their footsteps across Tennessee, splashed with them in the spring, and now sat there in the mountains playing bluff. Even with their ragged clothes coated in trench-digging grime, and their cheeks sunken with hunger, they seemed to watch our movements in the valley below with bemusement. We'd already killed plenty of each other. They were as tough as wildcats, but, by that point, so were we. I knew Sam would be there, probably looking right back at me right now, and I thought I recognized his tattered hat a couple times. I fully expected him to do his duty. I planned to do mine.

At dawn, our brigade of five regiments, not quite 1,800 men, those that remained of the original 5,000, would form up in a peach orchard,

600 yards from the base of Big Kennesaw. We would charge 200 yards down a slight grade, and across a knee-deep, marshy creek. After clearing the water, we would jog another four hundred yards of flat ground, under fire, to the base of the mountain. If we still survived, we were going straight up the exposed 800-foot face, through knee-deep stumps and cut branches, and walled in by dense, twisted thickets as tall as a man and thick as a railroad car. Too tangled for even a rabbit trail, the walls of briars squeezed the field shut like a funnel, forcing our attack right into the center of their line and directly into the heavily fortified salient full of determined Tennessee Rebels.

Sometime after midnight, I was awake in the warm night and dreading the dawn. Some of the southern Ohio boys, from Carlin's and Mitchell's brigades, brought a jug over to visit for a spell. They sat around smoking, and after bit, when a loud poker game broke out, I went in search of solitude. I was sitting against a tree, staring up at the stars, when a glowing cigar bobbed toward me.

"Hello, Colonel, nice evening," I said.

"Indeed, it is," said Col. McCook. "May I have a seat?"

"Of course," I said.

He sat, and we remained silent for a few seconds, watching the Rebel signal lamps swinging on top their mountain.

"Watching the sky for signs?" Col. McCook said.

"Probably not, Colonel," I said. "Can't much see what good would come of it. It's probably best if I don't know."

"They say General Polk was over there on that mountain the other night, about where that lamp is," said McCook. "Praying for God to command the wrathful Confederate sword when one of our cannonballs cut him in two."

"I heard that," I said. "He's with his savior now."

"Half of him anyway," smiled the Colonel, but he seemed more troubled than I'd ever seen him. I waited for him to speak again, and he finally said, "We've spoken on this before. I know you're no stranger to the personal pain of this war."

"No, I'm not."

"Before I left home, I crowed to everyone that would listen, and those who wouldn't, that I would have glory or a soldier's grave," the Colonel said. "But it's been a long war, a terrible ordeal. My dear sweet wife has suffered, and we lost our infant child. My broken-hearted mother has buried two sons and a husband. She can't bury another son. It would be cruel for me to force her to do so, yet I cannot shirk from my duty, to the oath I took, and to you men."

"The Union is doing what's right. You do still believe that?"

"Yes, I believe in the abolition of the vile institution," said McCook. "I believe in the Union. But right now, I'm wandering at what price."

"Whatever it takes, I guess," I said. "That's not why I joined, and that's not what I believed when I joined up, but it's what I think now."

"You're right, certainly," said McCook. "But will the price we pay tomorrow be too high? Johnston is holed up in a citadel and we have barely a blade of grass for cover."

"Yes, sir, I've scouted it. It's going to be a hot one. It's going to be a deadly one," I said. "It's going to be a bare-knuckled, bloody one."

"You're familiar with the Lays of Rome, I'm sure?" said McCook, catching me off guard.

"Yes, sir, Certainly. Publius Horatius, Lartius and Herminus holding the Sublician bridge. In my opinion, a beautiful poem. Moving. Both the story and the language. Why do you ask?" I said.

"Just a thought."

"It's an interesting thought, given our situation," I said.

"I'm sure you already know we open the ball in the morning," said McCook. "Our brigade has the honor of being first up the mountain, the forlorn hope, straight up the big hill. We're the center ring. Our regiments will strike them like a battering ram. One after another. The Illinois regiments will go first and open a breach in their fortifications. The last regiment, the 52nd Ohio, will bust through the gap and deliver the death blow."

"Sounds like an ambitious plan," I said.

"Yes, doesn't it?" McCook said. "Would the boys feel better, you suppose, about charging that hill, if I led them with a poem?"

"Not if they knew how it ended, I imagine."

"Fair point. Well, I best start getting ready for the morning," McCook said.

"The men trust you Colonel, poem or not," I said. "Completely. Just know that when the time comes they will follow you. I will, too."

"Thank you, Carew. I pray I don't let them down. They're good men, all of them," said McCook. "I'm proud to have you. You've become a tenacious fighter. I wouldn't want to try to pry you off those mountains."

"Yes, sir. I wouldn't want you to try."

"Get some rest," McCook said, and walked away into the dark. Behind me, I could hear little Dovie playing his guitar as he sang Aura Lea so beautifully I had to wipe away a few tears.

> "Aura Lea, Aura Lea,
> Maid with golden hair;
> Sunshine came along with thee,
> And swallows in the air.
> Aura Lea, Aura Lea,
> Birds of crimson wing,

Never song have sung to me,
As in that sweet spring."

I knew he was thinking about his little Georgia bride, and I was thinking about Jolene. Nice thoughts. But, I remembered her question. I didn't count the dead men, they counted themselves, almost every night, peeking from behind the tree, waving from a balky mule, or appearing in a morning fog, counting off 1-2-3 until the last one said 32.

A few I didn't recognize. I'd just killed the last one two days ago, sharpshooting at Rebels in trenches, same as I had been for months. The last one always kept looking over his shoulder to see if there was a crush coming up behind him, and I couldn't tell if he was trying to be funny or not. Sometimes I saw my own face, and would jerk awake screaming. We all did that, at one time or another. The only time anybody got upset was in the winter, when we were all jammed inside a small cabin and some nights nightmares flew around the room like bats trapped in a cave.

The Peach Orchard

At sunup, we marched along the red-clay road, immersed in the sounds of impending combat. Bugles. Drummer boys tapping out the long roll. Shouted orders. Grumbling men. Complaining mules. Creaking wagon wheels, and jingly cavalry men trotting by. And the tromp-tromp-tromp of our reluctant boots amongst the thousands of boys in blue finding their place along the five-mile front. Ours was beside a peach orchard.

We were rough men and used to rough ways. I carried my Sharps rifle and a Colt 1861 Navy revolver low in a cross-draw holster, a Bowie knife with a 12-inch blade in a beaded sheath on my right hip and a dagger, given to me by the Captain, strapped around my thigh. It was a lot of weight, but I did a lot of killing.

"Well, hell, they must be planning on quite a show. They've even shined their cheese knives," Ab said, pointing as some officers strutted by in perfectly brushed and creased uniforms, their tunic buttons and swords gleaming brightly in the sun. The buttons had probably been shined a dozen times through the night, and it didn't look like the shoulder-straps had slept any better than we had. Most of the $300 down-payment-heroes had gone to the rear with the rest of the play-outs and wagon soldiers on the puny list, but not one man from our company was missing, even if some of us were shaking and pale as fog. Most of us in the ranks had taken to wearing identity disks around our necks, with our names and units and hometowns on them, and I watched nervous fingers fidget with them. I looked over at Dovie, and hoped the boy could get through this battle, this war, and start something nice out of this whole sordid mess.

The Great Awakening, the exuberant evangelical movement that had swept through both armies this past year, wasn't always viewed too favorably right before battle. We had watched the comings and goings in the over-night and early morning prayer-meeting tents, checking carefully for anyone that seemed especially moved by the Lord that morning. If possible, we avoided the newly "borned again," in combat, as they were prone to impetuous and irrational flights of heroism, especially without one full night of sleep to becalm the fervor of sanctification.

Filled with the spirit or not, many of the boys ditched anything that might doom their eternal soul, or mortify their mother. Across the orchard, poker cards flipped and fluttered, and specks of ivory revealed discarded dice. Actress cards skittered past in the grass, with come-hither doe-eyes, alabaster butt-cheeks or a dark, perky nipple beckoning from around a photographer's curtain. I really didn't have an answer for those Meigs County hard-cases blaspheming and praying to fill that inside straight all the way to dawn. Some seek prayer. Some seek sin.

Humans can be interesting creatures. There were always a few like that, with ice water in their veins, never going to sleep, looking for a winning streak to ride into battle. Rarely were markers or credit extended on these night-before-battle marathon debaucheries, but every once in a while, if the firing slowed, you could hear shouts of "Don't get yourself kilt, dumbass, you owe me money." Sometimes gallant life-saving wasn't always just about gallant life-saving, but extraordinary debt collecting.

"I wouldn't eat too many of those peaches. All that fresh fruit and bullets, you might have yourself another embarrassing accident," said Ty to Teddy. As we waited, our guts twisting and knotting, the smell of the ripe peach orchard was too tempting, and many men had snuck away to the trees and returned with their hats full.

"When them minie balls is zipping by, he has hisself an embarrassing accident anyway," said Ab. "Ain't nothing changed."

"Ain't you all got other things to contemplate?" said Teddy. "You sure like to pile on the agony, don't you? My bowels get discussed around here more than Sherman's strategy."

"What the hell are you doing here, Father?" I blurted when I looked over my shoulder and saw Lum three feet away. "Isn't this exactly the thing that has been tormenting your mind?"

"Yes, it is, absolutely," said Lum. "And I'm still greatly tormented. But I've decided I can't just sit in the rear while these boys are getting killed by the hundreds and thousands."

"And getting yourself killed will help this exactly how?" I said.

"Before I can ever minister to them again. I need to understand what they've been through. Experience what they have," he said. "The true toll on the mind and soul, not just body. I must do this."

"But, Father, you can't do this," said Teddy, the only religious one of our group. "What if you get yourself kilt?"

"If I get kilt, Teddy," Lum said, "I'll just meet you in heaven one day. But take your time about getting there. It'll be there for a good stretch yet. If I understand it correctly."

"You picked a bad spot to get experience," I said.

"I have my rod and my staff," he said. "They comfort me."

"They look an awful lot like a rifle and bayonet."

"You're not the first to remark on that, but we use the tools God gives us," Lum said. "The Lord came to me in a vision. He said bring a gun and some bullets, you idiot, if you insist on this foolishness."

"So, God himself thinks this is foolish? He must want you to stop."

"Well, you know, sometimes his answers aren't always easy to decipher right off. I am doing what is just," said Lum. "For he is the minister of God to thee for good. But if thou do that which is evil, be afraid; for he beareth not the sword in vain"

"Sounds like you've given it some thought," I said.

"An eternity," Lum said, and went to one knee.

"Praying for victory, Reverend?" Ab said.

"Right now, son," Lum said, "I'm just praying for a hole in that hill big enough to hide my fat ass, should I need to stop and change my knickers. Not my most noble of prayers, I suppose, but no reason to leave it out."

McCook 8:00 a.m.

Finally, at 8:00am, our artillery roared. The Confederate position disappeared under thick, white smoke, but within a minute, the Rebel cannon blasted back and when we dove to the ground, many lost their bounty of fresh fruit in the mass of scrambling bodies. With no time for coffee, some of the boys were mad enough to whip Ol' Scratch from the inside out, and forgot all about the Rebels shooting at us. However, they quickly reminded us of their ill intent, and we turned our attention back to our destiny.

The 125th Illinois was the first to assault the mountain and it began easy enough as they double-quicked through the creek, then across the open field and to the base of the mountain. We all held our breath as those brave boys started up the steep slope, but halfway up, Rebel batteries, up until now completely hidden in the walls of brush, erupted with a fury, and hot grape-shot cut them down like a scythe. When a thousand rifles appeared out of the trenches and sent a finishing volley of death into the Illinois men, our first regiment was blasted off the slope in ten minutes.

Col. McCook watched the action on the mountain stoically, his back and shoulders straight and square, then pivoted sharply on his heel and faced us. His jaw muscles rippled, and his eyes were sharp and shined like black sapphires as he stood with his back to the battle, giving it no more concern than a strong breeze. After the colors were brought up, including the Avengers battle-flag for its first time in action, McCook mounted a tree stump and held out his arms for quiet. Behind him, the third Illinois regiment was on the slope, crumbling before the Rebel fire. He shouted for silence and attention.

"Men, our cause is just, and we will prevail, even as soldiers die. Few men get the chance to be immortal, like Horatius, the brave Roman hero. If we fall today in this glorious undertaking, we will live forever," he shouted. He caught my eye, winked, and gave a fleeting smile. He cleared his throat and began.

"Then out spake brave Horatius,
The Captain of the Gate:
"To every man upon this earth
Death cometh soon or late."

And how can a man die better
Than facing fearful odds,
For the ashes of his fathers,
And the temples of his gods."

"Enough wobblin' jaw, Colonel," I heard Ty whisper beside me. "Let's get to it."

McCook saluted us, faced the mountain, raised his sword and charged. We cheered like idiots and ran down the slope, slogged through the marsh and grappled our way through the overgrown briars that strangled our charge. We loped the four hundred yards from the creek to the base of the mountain, hurrahing our men under the murderous fire on the slope to rise up and clear our way.

Barely up the mountain, the men beside me began to fall. Half-way to the first barricade, I dropped to a knee and tried to suck oxygen through the battle murk, watching shadows killing shadows. The cannons still roared right and left, filling the air with blazing shrapnel that tore through men and earth. Minie balls buzzed like a busted hornet's nest, but the noise couldn't cover the screams of the shattered men. I dove into a shallow ditch, and a dozen smoke-blackened faces stared back at me as bullets threw dirt in my face. Our crease was about thirty yards below the first row of Rebel trenches, and ran the width of the field. The fellow beside me raised up to look, and then thudded back to earth with a bloodless hole between his eyes. Dead lay around me like spokes on a wagon wheel. A dead boy in blue, shot in the temple, suddenly sat up and goddamned everybody by name as he pled for water. I pushed my canteen toward him and he clutched it, laid back down and died for good. I pulled my canteen back and drank, then wiped away grimy sweat as I was racked with smoke-filled coughs. I heard a commotion, and Lum plopped down beside me. He struggled for breath as we looked at each other, damned if we go, damned if we stay.

"Go with God!" Lum shouted, leaping to his feet without a need to change his knickers, and hurdling up the hill. We were up and out of the crease and hurdled right behind him. He roared like a lion and shot a Rebel in the heart, then clubbed another before disappearing into the smoke. I caught up with him, and we ran in short bursts up the slope, tripping over stumps and branches.

Frenzied men, caught up in bloodlust and desperation, rushed past me, pulling and pushing the overlapping spiked logs and falling in piles. I saw Col. McCook ahead of me, and my legs burned like fire as I ran toward him. A big-wild-eyed Reb charged out of the smoke, waving a pig sticker at the Colonel's back but I drove my bayonet through the man's chest and crawled higher. Suddenly, through the blinding smoke, McCook was beside me.

"Come on boys, the day is won!" he shouted, and with a nifty gambado, he pounced a-top the wall of spikes, whipping his sword grandly across the faces of the Rebels clutching at his feet. We cheered and surged with him, pushing the barriers apart just wide enough for the men behind us to squeeze through. I got a face full of splinters and rolled behind a tangle of bodies from the 86th, firing two quick shots at the Rebels in the closest trench. McCook still teetered above the jagged barbs, one foot on the main log, one foot on a spike, emptying his revolver and slashing his saber.

"Get down from there, Colonel. You'll get yourself killed," I yelled.

"Damn you, leave me alone," McCook shouted, and turned back to the enemy.

At that moment, a ghostly, hexagonal rifle barrel slowly materialized in the smoke, floating through the cloud like the bowsprit of a ship cutting through a thick New England fog. My world slowed to tree-sap as that deadly black barrel was pressed against the Colonel's chest. I screamed, and lunged to reach it but my wasted legs failed me. The shot resonated like ocean thunder as the Colonel stayed upright for a heartbeat, and then toppled backward into a dozen open arms.

"Stick it to them, boys," McCook croaked, blood soaking his shirt. The men locked arms under him and rushed him away from the fighting. In a rage, I screamed and charged ahead, my bayonet wet and shiny red.

Sam

I opened my eyes staring into the barrel of a .69 Enfield rifle. Sam Watkins' gentle, smoke-smudged grin was at the other end of it. His tattered blouse was smeared with dried blood, and a grimy, rusty colored rag was tied tightly around his head.

"Did you do this?" I said, rubbing the painful knot on my head.

"Nope. You brung that with you. I'll see if I can plump it up a bit for you if you're desirous."

I shot him a dirty look and examined my surroundings. I was in a trench about ten-foot-deep and ten-yards-long, on my shoulders, back and legs outstretched against the trench wall above me, and feet pointed skyward. I tried to move a few times but the pain in my head left me limp.

"Where's all your friends?" I asked Sam.

"Some's kilt. Some's getting mended up. Some's out stretching they legs, things of a personal nature," he drawled around a jaw chipmunked to its limit. "I told them I felt safe here, that you wasn't near as warlike as you put on. Especially in that deep slumber you was enjoying when you first arrived."

"May I upright myself?" I said, after closing my eyes for a few seconds.

"Certainly. I was beginning to think sitting on your shoulders was yet one more Yankee custom you brung to vex us simpleminded mountaineers," said Sam. "And growing despondent that we was losing the war to a race of men that sat on their heads."

"Shut up or shoot me," I said, and with great effort and pain, I rolled over and leaned against the trench wall. My head throbbed, and blinking lights floated in his eyes.

"Might as well get comfy. When life gives you lemons, make lemonade, they say," Sam said, extending a torn sack of sour candies. "I ain't got any of that, but these here lemon drops are sure hitting the spot. Trust me, the poor boy that had 'em ain't going to miss 'em.''

We were both silent for a minute while we chewed sweet, sour, sticky candy.

"You got anything else, a pistol or a knife?" Sam asked. My Sharps leaned against the wall behind him. I'd lost my revolver somewhere. "I trust you, brother, but someone might holler later."

"I think that covers it," I said, as I patted myself and showed him my knives.

"Ain't you a hellified gladiator? Keep the knives," Sam shrugged. "You might need 'em where you're going. But if you try to stab me, I'll find that a very unchristian thing to do. I don't suppose you'll give me your word?''

"I won't stab you."

"I'll accept that," said Sam, smiling. "This has been some doings, ain't it?"

"Where are the others? My friends?"

"There's some beyond them trees. It ain't a happy group, and you got the poorest excuses of soldiers back there guarding them. Too scared to square up and shoot at a Yankee, but all kinds of fierce when it comes to kicking around one that already been softened up for him," he said, motioning over his shoulder as he offered me a fresh canteen. "Here, you want a little of this?"

"Thank you," I said, taking several big gulps. "I appreciate you not shooting me.

"I'd a probably shot ya if I hadn't been so dang lonesome," said Sam. "Either these boys from home has got dumber as the war progresses, or I've just got more particular. I saw ya coming, and I was hoping you'd drop in."

I looked over at one of the poker playing hard-cases from last night, dangling upside down from a spiked barricade, his hair stiff with matted blood, one outstretched hand inches from mine.

"Friend of yourn?" asked Sam.

"I've seen him hanging around," I said, rubbing my scalp. "Does it matter?"

"Just if it was a friend of yours, I figured you might not want him staring at you all googly eyed," he said. "If not, I didn't figure you'd be particular."

"I'm not particular," I said.

"Everything OK down in there? Who's that Yankee ya got? Sherman, Grant, or Abe the Ape, the ugly ol' emancipator hisself?" yelled down a burly Rebel.

"Go on, now. He ain't bothering nobody. I know this man," said Sam, and the others walked away.

"Thanks, Sam," I said. "How long can you keep me out here?"

"Oh, until dusky dark I reckon," he said. "Unless your friends down the hill start growling and showing their teeth again. I sure hope they're not entertaining such grandiose idears. It wouldn't be well received."

The thunder and fury were over, but the dead air was poisonous with the excretions of men in death struggles and unbreathable from the stench of burning flesh. Horrifying screams came from wounded men who had dragged themselves toward the woods and had become trapped in the brushfires that raged on the parched hillside. Off to my right were the charred bodies of several soldiers, blue and gray, tangled in the blackened stubble where the fire had passed over. Down the hill, a thousand Yankees huddled in the crease, unable to charge, unwilling to retreat. Victor and vanquished, sinner and Christian, suffered the same on the mountain, sucked dry and disabled by sun-stroke. The pleas and cries for water from down the hill, and the screams of wounded trapped in the burning brush, never relented.

"We have to do something," I said.

"I agree, but your friends might misinterpret my intentions if I went to assist. I think they would shoot me if given the chance. They seem peevish," Sam said, and as the temperature shot over 100, we looked out on the battlefield. Yankees and Rebels stared at each other, done with killing but not sure what to do. Sam chose to eat more candy, and I joined him. In the shade of the trees, Rebels searched through pockets of dead Yankees for bullets and food, and traded candy, watches and actress cards. At least the poor, grieving mother of the dead Yankee wouldn't be further heartbroken by that detail. The afternoon passed without further aggression by either side, and Sam's comrades came and went, paying me little mind.

"You best gather your belongings. They're coming for you," Sam said, when the sun started to drop. I watched a group of Yankee prisoners coming out of the trees, their faces and clothes smoke-blackened. It was hard to tell captor from captive, and they all looked like they'd just climbed out of a burning building. My heart sank thinking of Andersonville Prison, but not much I could do about it.

"I figured," I said, and a patrol came along to round up all the other Yankees that had been visiting. I wasn't the only one.

"Maybe I can surrender to you on another day. Maybe some other mountain, but not today, old feller," Sam winked, as I was walked away. "Not today."

Andersonville

"Andersonville. That's where they are sending us. Would have been better to been killed on that hill," said a graybeard. "Gangrene, dysentery, cholera. They say 150 a day die there. Not a splinter of wood for shelter or fire. Not a clean drop of water."

"Hundreds of men a day starve to death, they say," said another.

"Maybe it ain't all that," said a young soldier. "Maybe they just say that in the papers."

"No, it's worse," said the vet. "Hell, the Rebs don't deny it."

"Boy, set your jaw. If I had a dime from every complainer airing their gripes, I could have paid my own train-fare to the place," Ty said, disgustedly. He was greatly agitated as we waited for the train to Andersonville, fretting about how to get a letter to his wife, to tell her he was as healthy and safe as the war would allow. He had lost his war bag, everything personal, including all the letters he had received, which was at least two a week since our first day in Camp Dennison twenty-four months ago. The loss had brought out the corn cob in him. She would be frantic, he said. We couldn't find a clergyman, so we bribed a guard to mail a letter home. Several of them in fact, but I still didn't like our chances.

Gaunt slaves brought baskets of fried fatback the size of a deck of playing cards and a generous share of moldy cornbread. We ate it without too much grumbling. There would not have been any point to it. An hour later, we were marched past a long row of wounded Confederates laid out along the train track. Threadbare cavalrymen rode past on bony horses, looking nothing at all like the dashing cavaliers of two years past.

"Son of a bitch," someone shouted as a young Yankee sprinted past. A dozen patty-rollers were not far behind, fighting the reins on a pack of frothing, glass-eyed Catahoula curs that were the size of ponies.

"Those dogs are huge!" said Lum, after the dogs vanished into the woods and the howls faded. "They'll eat that boy."

Unseen train whistles sounded and when the peeling black engine wheezed to a stop, the Rebels herded us into some weather-beaten cattle cars. Festering pig shit and straw covered the floor and walls, and the stench was made worse by the vomit of trapped, heat-sickened men. We hadn't been the first passengers that day. We sat locked inside, the train not moving, with no breeze and more men getting sick, for another hour. Finally, the train jerked, clattered and creaked, and when it picked up speed we kicked the side slats from our car. Hoping for some relief, we pressed our faces to the openings and tried to avoid the listing waste bucket.

The train rattled and strained and wheezed over the mountains until morning, when we climbed out of the car, achy and sick, stained and reeking and blinking in the sunlight. The stockade walls in front of us were spiked logs twenty-foot-tall, wedged so tight paper wouldn't slide between them. The guard force was pimply-faced boys, droopy bellied farmers and one-armed veterans. The enclosure was three hundred yards long, and about the same wide, and in that small space it was said thirty thousand sick, hungry men tried to survive.

"Prisoners, Attention!" shouted the guards as a scraggly-bearded captain trotted up on a white horse.

"Velcome du paradise. You vill be treated fairly if you do vhat you're told," he bellowed in a heavy German accent. "Und vot ever you are zinking, should leaf your mind. Vee have dogs, vee haf rifles, and ve haf zese mountains, in vich you vill be found dead zud you try to run away."

"Wirz," Ty said, nodding toward the man all the Northern newspapers were already reviling as a monster. The main gate was pulled open, and we stood dumbstruck as an indescribable thunderhead of stench rolled over us. We didn't move until the guards jabbed us with bayonets and forced us into the brown mass of shuffling, sunken-eyed skeletons. We were marched about a hundred feet in, and I stopped beside a battered freight wagon with a bed filled with dead men, mostly naked, stacked like firewood five feet high.

"What is this?" asked Ty.

"Get used to it blue-belly," the driver grinned. "That is the dead cart. The second of the day. Them that pass is piled up all day and the dead cart takes them out, once in the morning, once at night. This ain't the place for building lasting friendships."

As the gate closed behind us, a faintly familiar man squeezed out of the crowd and hobbled toward us. It took a few seconds to recognize the man from Company K in the 52nd Ohio. He was no older than me, but he was gray and sick, nothing but skin, bones and a thick layer of dust. The dozen men with him were no better.

"Sgt. Johnson, it's good to see you. I wondered what had become of you," I said.

"Got took at Chickamauga. Had a couple other stops before this one," he said. "They keep moving us south cause Uncle Billy is givin' 'em so much aggravation."

"If hell had an earthly face, this is it right here," said Lum, shaking his head slowly. "Lord have mercy on these souls."

"Well howdy, boyo's," bellowed an Irish accent. A strong hand clamped down on my shoulder and I turned to see a caveman brow and a leering simian jaw. An equally ugly gang of cold-eyed brutes backed him up.

"Back off, Collins, or I will drive this through your eye. He's one of mine," said Johnson, reaching inside his shirt. He pulled out a stout tree limb armed with a ten-penny nail, and each of his men brandished a similar weapon. The Irishman's crowd moved back slightly, but he flashed another ugly grin. Johnson waved his weapon in Collins' face, and Ty had squared up with another of the ruffians.

"Cool down," I said, grabbing Ty's arm when I saw a murderous look cross his face. I knew in the state he was in, he would kill any of these men with his bare-hands, but this wasn't the time and place.

"All right then, no need for that," said Collins, leaning into me. "Perhaps I'll see you again. In fact, I'm sure I will."

"What was that about?" I asked, as Collins and his men melted into the crowd.

"Stay away from those murderous thieves. Those two, Collins and Curtis, are the Jew Fagin and Bill Sykes to a pack of bubonic rats. Nothing happens without their say so. Even the slatterns that birthed them revile them," said Johnson. "They are thieves and murderers. They bribe the guards so they can commit their depravities at night without detection. At least the battlefield had some honor, or so some say. Here, its wild beasts and carrion-eaters, killing their own."

"Nothing can be done?" asked Ty. "Can't Wirz stop it?"

"We are trying to organize something. Wirz is difficult. Any suffering inflicted on Yankees, no matter the source, is great amusement for him."

"We need to go after them," said Ty.

"Yes, but so many of us are weak and sick, unable to fight, many even unable to defend themselves. The Raiders have networks of spies they pay well for word of any unrest, so we have to be discreet."

"How many are they?"

"Maybe ten ring leaders. Possibly two hundred that will do their bidding," said Johnson. "We hope if we chop off the head, the rest of the snake will slither away."

"Those are people living in caves in the ground?" I asked, as I surveyed my new home. Two grassless slopes made up the stockade landscape, and both were honeycombed with burrows and shelters made of tent halves or rags on sticks. A stagnant creek, the north end used for drinking, and the south end used for a prison latrine, split the slopes.

"Yes," said Johnson, "They're the lucky ones."

"How can anyone live like this?"

"Not for long. But many men have no shelter at all. Some get sick and die quickly, and others go mad," said Johnson. "The little bit of wood we can gather outside would barely build a cracker box, and has to be used for cook fires. Dig a hole and make a house out of whatever you got. Or pull out the deceased previous tenant, and move into something already furnished."

"This is not fit for a man," I said, when we got our first rations and I dragged my fingers through my small burlap sack of cornmeal. "This is barely fit for a mule."

"We have a cook house and a bakery, but dry corn meal is better, when we can scrape together a fire," Johnson said. "We can pick out some of the cobs and flies."

"I thought Sherman was sending rations here since there will be no exchanges," I said.

"Well, see, there's the irony. Sherman's doing a lot of this himself," said Johnson. "He's taking out Confederate supply trains meant for us. Then the Rebels are taking the trains Sherman meant for us. Hundreds of thousands of pounds of bacon and meal a week. We get to read about it in the paper sometimes, or the boys claim they can smell it burning fifty miles away, which is about as close as we get to tasting it."

"No one realizes that?"

"I don't think we're a priority," said Johnson. "Did you bring any money with you?"

"Yes, a few dollars."

"I'll take you up to robber's row later on," said Johnson, pointing to a row of sutler shacks. "And they are robbers. I thought our camp sutlers were bad."

"Anything else?" Ty asked.

"Just one more thing," Johnson said, pointing at the guards looking down from their guard towers perched every fifty feet along the top of the wall. "The Georgia Home Guard's finest. Don't loiter around the dead line. If you dare cross that line, they'll shoot at you. They couldn't hit a barn, so have consideration for your neighbor. We lose many more boys to missed shots than to well-aimed ones."

Dodd

Before dawn, Lum and I followed two of Johnson's men to the sinks. As Dodd reached the creek, a pack of men leapt from the dark and slammed him to the ground.

"Raiders! Raiders!" Dodd screamed. "Ohio! Ohio!"

Lum rushed toward the pile and yanked the attackers off Dodd like they were ticks on a dog. One raider sprang toward Lum with a knife, but I walloped him with a rock across his eyebrow and blood spurted ten inches. The raider howled that he'd been blinded, so I hit him a few more times just for lying. The attackers staggered off, and I checked on Lum, who was unhurt, but huffing and snorting like a mad bull when Johnson and his men reached us.

"They got me, goddamn them all," moaned Dodd, rubbing his scalp. "They took my damn pants."

"Why would they take your pants?"

"Because I had $160 in them and a gold watch," said Dodd, looking sick. "I'd like to know how they found out."

"More of Collins' spies. Don't worry, son, we'll get your money back," said Johnson, patting Dodd on the shoulder and smiling at Lum. "By damn, Reverend, you looked like a bait bear cuffing around a pack of hounds. How did it feel?"

"It felt fine, son, just fine," said Lum. "Kicking Satan in the ball sack is always refreshing."

The Hanging

"Why is this taking so long?" the other prisoners said. "We don't trust them."

The day after the Dodd attack, Wirz took Johnson and some other prisoners outside the walls to solve the Raider problem. When three hours had passed, the veteran inmates grew nervous. Wirz, they said, had a mercurial and violent temper, and it was a rare day that he didn't have a line of men flogged, bucked and gagged, or hung by their thumbs. A relieved murmur passed through those keeping vigil when the gate finally opened, and all the Yankees returned unharmed.

"We're deputized, I guess you could say," Johnson shouted, climbing onto the pronouncement- stump as a crowd gathered around. "Long enough to catch Collins and Curtis and the other animals. Wirz will hold them in the stockade outside until we have a trial. We can have lumber to build a courtroom and gallows. We'll have juries, and these murdering bastards will get a fair trial."

"Before we snap their necks," shouted several men at once.

"A courtroom?" I asked.

"Sure. We have a fair number of attorneys amongst us. We're to provide prosecutors and capable defense attorneys for the accused," said Johnson, then smiled. "Before we snap their necks."

"So, when does this begin?"

"Tomorrow. We have a list of those we'll put on trial. We're organizing teams," he said. "We'll go out just before sun-up. Likely those cutthroats will be in a drunken stupor by then, and won't know what hit them."

After three days, all the ranking generals of the Raiders had been captured, tried, and convicted in trials conducted through buckets of tears and pounds of regret. It was a thoroughly repugnant affair, with pleading defendants blaming the savage conditions, and their accusers demanding blood for sin. Six ringleaders were sentenced to hang, and about a hundred less serious brigands were sentenced to run a gauntlet of their peers.

The following morning the less egregious culprits were marched through the gates to a deliriously happy crowd. Hooting, foot-stomping, club swinging Yankees, flush with smuggled Georgia moonshine, formed a gauntlet that stretched across the width of the stockade. As the first man was dragged forward, he clawed, slobbered and bit until a club slammed his kidneys and he was flung head first down the human tunnel, where he curled on the ground as a dozen prisoners pummeled him. Finally, someone yanked him to his feet, and he was shoved and kicked until he lurched forward, arms crossed over his blood-smeared face as the clubs rained down. The rest were the same. The guards shoved the guilty into the tunnel faster and faster. Many went down, some stayed down, and stragglers were trampled by the desperate men coming right behind them. The screams, body blows, and tree limbs cracking skulls continued after the sun went down.

On the day of the hangings, a roar of drunken cheers greeted Wirz when he rode through the gate, resplendent on his white gelding and in a new white suit. The roar got louder when the Home Guards marched the condemned through the gate at the end of their shotguns. A four-gun battery of Napoleons was wheeled inside the gate, loaded with grape shot, and aimed at the spectators. Extra guards stared down from the pigeon roosts, nervously holding their double-hammered scatterguns as the condemned men passed. As a small band played the death march in a steady drizzle, vendors walked through the crowd hawking sassafras-and-cornmeal beer and cups of Georgia lightning. Curtis and Collins suddenly broke free, but they found no shelter amongst their old friends. Wild laughter and mockery met them as they were kicked and tripped through their tightly packed victims on the hillsides, closely pursued by cursing guards and hordes of inmates baying like coonhounds. The murderers weren't free for long. Or alive.

Surviving

Captured in the middle of long charge, few of us carried more than our canteens and empty haversacks. Many were even without hats to protect them from the blistering Georgia sun or jackets should the air turn chilly. There were fistfights over clothes from dead men, as prisoners, lurking like vultures, grabbed at garments or food before the dying man's last breath left his body. Our rations rarely surpassed starvation levels: a sack of foul cornmeal, and once a week or so, the Rebels scrounged up few tablespoons of beans or peas, and sometimes a piece of bacon as wide as a snuff tin and as thin as the Ace of Swords.

Andersonville was a battlefield that never ended, never emptied, no glory, no charges, not even the chance to fight back. It besieged us every day with disease, despair and death. As we'd been told, hundreds died every day. Measles, mumps, rubella took the young. Dropsy, dysentery, and even chicken pox took the rest. The ground was littered with teeth that had fallen loose with scurvy. Gangrene from scratches and bug bites in this mire and waste was just as lethal as a bullet, and the suffering was a hundred-times worse. I realized that Helga's and Dr. Walker's crusade against germs and bacteria had saved my life, and there was nothing in the world more heartbreaking than a healthy, happy young boy watching the black rot of gangrene eating his limbs a few inches a day.

Almost as deadly was the numbing, poisonous drudgery. We watched helplessly as prisoners became catatonic and wasted away, their spirits and minds atrophied, unable to go on. Suicides were frequent, often perpetrated by feigned escapes or taunting the guards to shoot. We tried to comfort the young soldiers as best we could, but many were simply too frightened or broken-hearted to eat and starved to death. Every now and again, some of the boys would light a shuck, but not often. They were already sick and weak, and those crippled-up cracker guards couldn't shoot or move fast, but they kept their dogs mean and hungry.

Despite the conditions, prisoners coped as best they could. There were a good number of talented musicians inside the walls who did their best to provide some entertainment for the others, and some sanity for themselves. String bands of fiddles, mandolins and banjos popped up overnight, and the collections of pickers, strummers, and fiddlers put some fun and energy into the air, smiles on drawn, hungry face, and brightened teary eyes.

Some proud bagpiping Scotsmen from the 12th Illinois, the "1st Scotch," had been captured at Nickajack Creek shortly after the disaster at Kennesaw. On the day the small band of Scotsmen arrived at Andersonville, we heard them coming long before they proudly marched through that stockade gate, blowing those goosenecked pipes with the sound of ten generations of MacCrimmons just come down from the misty mountain highlands on the Isle of Skye. They cut fine figures in their clan's tartan kilts and Tam o' Shanter bonnets with happily bobbing toories as they high-strutted through the gate, behind the drum-major who twirled and pumped that 20-pound mace like it was a mere sliver. Many of the Georgia Guard were mountaineers of Scottish ancestry, and on the drum-major's command, the entire contingent from the 12th Illinois bent at the waist with their bare rear-ends waggling at the guards on the wall, letting them know who the true Scotsmen were.

The Scotsmen added their talents to our musical endeavors and were generally jolly to listen to, but sometimes in the evenings we would sit on the hillside above the hospital, watching the twinkling fires in the stockade, while those pipers brought that high lonesome sound to the night breeze rustling through the towering mountain pines. We'd have a tipple or two of mountain dew, bartered from our hosts' deep holler moonshine stills, while Father Whelan, Lum and the bagpipers sang the ballads of their far away homelands. Lum and the Father had frittered away some talent when they had taken the vow. Their rich, sweet tenor and baritone could beguile a nun out of her knickers, or march the staunchest coward off to war. Few kept dry eyes as they sang of Danny Boy, The Trie Ravens, or The Drowned Lovers, Meggie and Willie, sleeping like sister and brither in the wondrous deep of Clyde's cold, black water. Even the hills of Georgia wept, as if they hadn't wept enough already.

Father Whelan

Upon entering Andersonville, Lum had immediately became fast friends with Father Whelan, the Confederate prison priest, and began working in the prison hospital. Father Whelan was the best chaplain any prisoner of war camp could have, since he had once been a prisoner himself. He had spent several months as an inmate in a Yankee prison after being captured in 1862 with a Rebel detachment at Ft. Pulaski. At any time, the Father could have gone with the officers and better conditions, or simply gone home, but he stayed with the enlisted men at Castle Williams, an old, crumbling, sandstone fort in the New York harbor where the conditions were little better than Andersonville. There was no sanitation, no heat, and no way to cook meals. Many prisoners died from disease, but Whelan remained, performing Mass and nursing the sick until the entire contingent was paroled. From their separate compound at Castle William, the Confederate officers, embarrassed at the sight of him in rags, gave him a brand-new suit, but they were shocked when, two days later, he was wearing his old rags again. Fearing he'd been robbed, they asked where the new clothes had gone, and he told them he'd given the clothes to a young soldier who'd been captured in his underwear. When asked why he hadn't given the soldier his old clothes, Father Whelan, in some pretty lofty company, replied, "When I give for Christ's sake, I give the best."

Most days at Andersonville, just as at Castle William, Whelan was as poorly wardrobed, ragged and gaunt as our own men. He was an oddly shaped fellow, with a melancholy grin on his sometimes-washed, sometimes not, sometimes shaved, sometimes not, always gentle face. It usually looked like he'd shaved the two sides of his face with two different razors on two different days, sometimes on two different weeks. His hair sprouted off as wild as thistle bush, his frayed and patched sleeves never reached his calloused hands, and his trousers were three-inches-short of his swollen, splotchy ankles. Some said he looked like a bum, but I figured he looked about exactly like Jesus. He and Lum were a matched team in that regard.

Ty and I were the only ones left from home, and we remained close allies with Johnson and his Ohio men in case of trouble. Near the end of July, we received word that Col. McCook had died on July 17th. The previous day, a messenger had brought him notice that he had been promoted to Brigadier General. He responded with: "The promotion is too late. Return my compliments, but I decline the honor." We were saddened at the expected news of his death, but tickled our courageous Colonel was a fighter to the end. It was the army's misfortune that they had not promoted him long ago, but his unflagging loyalty to his unde-servedly promoted brother Alex had hurt him.

Ty soon joined Lum working in the hospital, and I borrowed one of the tents to start a library, so we were allowed out of the stockade most of the time. Whelan lived in a tiny hut about a mile from the prison, which I had visited on a few occasions to help with deliveries of books, medicine or other supplies for the men. He rose each day at dawn, said his prayers, and walked down the hot, dusty road to the stockade, where he stayed until sundown. He was a good man, one of the finest I'd ever met, but the demands of this God-forsaken place were finally too much, and no amount of faith and devotion could keep his body and spirit from breaking down. He was removed by his superiors to save him from himself, but before he left, he raised $16,000 Confederate dollars and purchased 10,000 pounds of white flour. The heavenly loaves kept starvation at bay, at least for a little while.

General Sherman's troops captured Atlanta and its railroads and fac-tories on September 2, 1864. Although it would be a few months before he wrote his infamous telegram to Gen. Ulysses Grant, Gen. Sherman's massive army was already making Georgia howl. Well before the Battle of Kennesaw Mountain, Sherman had decided it was time for the civilian supporters of the Confederacy to feel the full burden and pain of the war, to teach the Georgians that "it isn't so sweet to secede." In addition to his soldiers, Sherman had to feed twice that many beasts of burden, and the tens-of-thousands of Negro contrabands who had attached them-selves to the column. Sherman didn't just make the state howl. He made it bleed and starve and weep in black rags as he burned cities and destroyed hundreds of thousands of acres of Georgia cotton fields and farmlands. His horde lived off the land that had little life left to give, and left their calling cards, "Sherman's Neckties," stretched across the state, miles of railroad track heated until it melted and was then twisted into knots.

The fear and terror caused by Sherman was just as powerful as the actual destruction, and the wives and mothers of Confederate soldiers begged their husbands to come home. Desertions were rampant, the cause hopeless, and the Rebel government impotent. Less than 50,000 Rebel soldiers remained in Georgia trying to stop Sherman's oncoming legions as they burned a wide swath through the state. It may have made for great press coverage from Northern newspapers, but, up until September, the strategy had won Sherman few friends among the desperately hungry Yankees in Andersonville. With Atlanta fallen, the Confederate command grew fearful of 30,000 angry Andersonville prisoners being unleashed upon their countryside and transferred almost all able-bodied prisoners, and most of the guards, to three other prisons. Lum, Ty and I continued working in the hospital for the 5,000 men that were too sick and weak to move. The food was more abundant, if no better, the water became cleaner, and much of the stench slowly drifted away.

It was during this time Freddy wrote to say that he was fine and had transferred to the provost office in Nashville, and Helga was a doctor in the hospital there. No one had heard from Ab, so we figured he was in a nameless mass grave somewhere on Kennesaw Mountain with a few hundred others. Freddy also told us Teddy had grown despondent after Ab went missing, and was taking more and more laudanum to ease both his mind and his bowels. Teddy had passed quietly in his sleep outside Jonesboro, the victim of too much of the powerful opiate, which was becoming a scourge to the Army as traumatized soldiers sought out comfort where they could.

Chapter Fourteen

Fall of Richmond
March, 1865

"What's next for you, Bedford?" asked Devol, as they grazed their horses in a secluded Virginia valley. Nathan Bedford Forrest knew surrender would come soon. His magnificent cavalry corps was no more, scattered in a thousand graves from Georgia to Texas

"I don't know. Just start over somehow and be-done with this destruction to our people. We can't win, and any man who favors further prosecution of this war is fit for a lunatic asylum," said Forrest. "And should be treated as a traitor to both sides, if you ask me. Hang 'em twice. Damn their hides.''

"I completely agree. I meant after you are back home, if it remains."

"It remains, at least for the moment. Though I can't go back to selling nigras, apparently. Tobacco will take a couple years to see a profit. Cotton, too, if we can even find hands to work it. But, I have my darling Mary, and I still have the land," Forrest said. "I'm sure I can sell some lumber, as long as the blue-bellies don't seize the acreage and try to hang me for violating the rules of war. Though I hate to wallow in the muck, perhaps I'll take a try at politics. Something that unseemly, I fear, would tarnish my legacy."

"Yes, Bedford, I guess we have a different rule book," Devol said, "Perhaps it's time to go west, or to Mexico. Join those going to Argentina, maybe, or Bolivia."

"Exactly. Rules is for Bridge, or social graces," said Forrest. "War is for hard men, and the only rules is get there first with the most men, and shoot them before they shoot you. I didn't dream it up on my own."

"Too bad Jeff Davis didn't remove Bragg two years ago, and let your old friend Bobby Lee run the show," laughed Devol, knowing full well Forrest's hatred of the gentlemanly Southern war leader.

"The only difference between Lee and Bragg is that Lee orders his men to their death with the serenity of a Sunday School teacher, and Bragg rants like a madman with slobbers and birdshit in his beard," Forrest snarled. "Anyway, should you be interested, speaking of old women, our President Davis is making a lot of noise about rebuilding the Confederacy."

"Not interested."

"No, not his vainglorious boast to create a second Confederacy. But that's not why I told you," said Forrest. "He has been quietly looking for a good cavalry officer who knows how to keep his mouth shut. Not for a rebellion, for a bank robbery."

"What do you mean?" asked Devol.

"Davis will soon be helping himself to the Confederate treasury. And more. There are several million dollars, in gold, stashed in the Virginia banks," said Forrest. "Some belongs to the Confederacy, some does not. Some people still have their life savings in those banks, their jewels, anything valuable. Davis plans to take all of it."

"Quite an audacious plan," said Devol. "That's worse than me. Almost."

"I knew you'd appreciate it. He doesn't have a right to that money. It was him that got so many of our boys killed. Grinding up our seed corn. For what? For nothing. Worse than nothing. The longer he keeps up this hopeless disaster, the worse it gets for every southerner, and all he's doing is running from a traitor's rope or a bullet in the back," said Forrest. "I'll never forgive any of them for allowing that fool Bragg to steal my corps. Gave them to Joe Wheeler so he could get all the glory. I should have killed him on the spot."

"Yes, you should have. I would have helped," said Devol. "If we ever cross paths, I will. You know, my man Ashok would be thrilled at the opportunity to work on Davis for you. No one would ever know."

"Damn tempting, but that would cause a lot more chaos than we need right now. Ridiculous martyrs," said Forrest. "Wouldn't you rather keep him alive until after he empties all those banks for you?"

"Good point," said Devol. "Robbing Davis after he robs the Confederacy. How delicious, as they say. When should I leave?"

"I'll telegram Davis, and remind him of your impressive abilities. You and your men should leave tonight. The Yankees are closing in."

Devol, April 2nd, 1865

Devol sat on the steps of St. Paul's church in Richmond while Confederate President Jefferson Davis attended morning services inside. Ashok and a small band of scrawny, young Rebels in tattered uniforms and scuffed cavalier boots were sprawled idly under shade trees nearby. A rider thundered down the lane, slid his lathered horse to a gravel-flinging stop, threw his reins at the hitching post and bounded up the church steps.

"What do you have, boy?' hollered Devol, springing up.

"Telegram. For President Davis," said the messenger boy. "Don't know no more than that."

"I suppose it is sealed?"

"Yes, sir," said the boy. "I can't open it."

"Listen to me close. Here's two silver dollars. Once you're inside, stick to Davis like a bear on honey. Except to come tell me what is in this telegram. I'll give you two more dollars, silver, not Confederate newsprint."

"That telegram was from General Lee," gushed the boy, back in a flash and shaking with excitement. "Yankees is down the road, and can't be slowed. Gen. Lee advised President Davis to flee, immediately."

Before the boy could say more, the church doors opened slowly and fearful faces peered out. When no Yankees greeted them, a few brave souls cautiously stepped onto the porch before the minister took several bold strides outside.

Suddenly, with a yelp and flash of white robes, the clergyman and two deacons flipped over the railing as Davis, long arms extended, burst through the church doors in fury of wild silver hair and red-faced rage. From the nearby field, the last of the loyal black coachmen had disappeared into the trees at the messenger boy's arrival, and now terrified parishioners rushed to their buggies to find them abandoned. The church yard was filled with a Babylon of blue oaths as five acres full of parked buggies crashed and collided, and frenzied drivers pulled pistols and cracked their whips at the family who'd been in the next pew five minutes earlier.

"Clear a way, Colonel, clear a way, damn you," screamed Davis at Devol, as cannons roared in Richmond and gunfire moved closer.

"Out of the way," Devol yelled at the cursing florid-faced man in the closest carriage.

"Go to Hell," yelled the man, but Devol leapt into the coach and slapped the driver's jowls until he cried like a toddler with two skinned knees. Devol shot the next carriage's horse, then yanked the driver from his seat and pistol whipped him unconscious. Ashok lifted another over his head and pitched him ten feet into the brush, while the bored troopers charged into action and gleefully forced the other carriages off the road at bayonet point.

Richmond in Flames

Devol charged into the mansion where Jefferson Davis had retreated with his cabinet. He ignored the guards in the hallway and burst into the room as the Confederate President, in front of his visibly shaken advisors, cursed and ranted at Gen. Richard Ewell, commander of the Richmond garrison.

"This man is disobeying my direct orders," screamed Jefferson Davis. "Burn everything. The factories, the warehouses, burn everything. Leave nothing for those murdering Yankees. But first, take this traitor out and shoot him."

"I can't, I won't," sobbed Ewell, a career military man of honor, and steadfast Virginian.

"I'll take care of it," said Devol, putting his hand on the man's shoulder. Devol had been expecting the orders to burn the city's armories and warehouses of tobacco, cotton, and food since first arriving in the city two weeks ago. During his days in the city, he'd grown oddly fond of Old Baldhead, who was nearly broken down by grief and despair. The odd little General was already eaten away with guilt, after Robert E. Lee dropped the blame for the Gettysburg tragedy at his feet then blithely rode away on his majestic steed, Traveller, with his dignity and whiskers perfectly intact.

"Gen. Ewell will take care of it. He will obey the order, not you. It is not your place to usurp my authority. I'll have you shot, too," raged Davis.

"Look, you miserable poltroon," said Devol, placing his hand on his pistol and glancing at the cabinet members in the office. None of the discomposed cowards spoke up in Davis's defense. "Be thankful I don't hand you straight over to the Yankees right now and stop all this as I should. Or hang you from the damned sour apple tree myself."

Devol watched Richmond burn from a hilltop, mounted next to the inconsolable Ewell. Richmond and Petersburg, the Capitol and armorers of the Confederacy, had been under siege for ten months. Hundreds of Yankee cannons had been bombarding the city, aimed at the Tredegar Iron Works and the factories that made nearly all cannons, bullets, and artillery-shells for the Confederacy. Shots landed wildly in the city, including those of "The Dictator," a huge, 17,000-pound, siege mortar whose 200-pound shells had flattened full city blocks.

Half the city was in flames or smoking rubble, and through thick, black smoke, the streets of Richmond streamed with throngs of maddened Richmond citizens, destitute and starving. They had discovered the warehouses where Davis's government and black-market speculators had hoarded hundreds of tons of bacon, cornmeal, sugar, and coffee. They swarmed into the burning buildings and emptied them as the upper floors collapsed in flames. Residents fled their ruined homes and businesses and walked the streets with bags and baskets of worthless Confederate currency, laughing as they drowned the piles in lamp oil and danced while it burned.

To prevent looting and violence the police had raided saloons and liquor warehouses, smashing barrels and bottles. They dragged kegs of whiskey and brandy from hotels and bars to dump into the street drains only to be attacked by surging mobs. The horde swilled what they could, or filled their arms and disappeared into the madness. The most desperate bent over the gutters that flowed with rivers of spilled booze, lapping it up like thirsty dogs. Some filled glasses and buckets, and others scooped it up in their hats and boots, guzzling it down and bailing up more, spitting out pieces of glass with each gulp. A strong breeze spread the fire, and flames from the burning warehouses shot hundreds of feet into the air. The free-flowing rivers of alcohol caught fire and ribbons of blue flame raced along the gutters of streets clogged with abandoned wagons and furniture. Mobs of drunken, plunder-laden marauders attacked trunks and boxes with giggles and axes while church bells gonged above them. Confederate deserters rampaged through the city, joined by thousands of freed slaves and Yankee prisoners liberated from the horrid conditions of the Libby prisoner-of-war camp. Hundreds of escaped convicts from the State Penitentiary, men so erratic and sadistic that the desperate South had armed its slaves before enlisting them, stripped off their stripes, donned new suits from abandoned mansions and joined the destruction. A chain of explosions came from the James River as Confederate Admiral Semmes exploded the arsenals in his fleet of heavy ironclads as he sunk them, their billowing blackened hulls protruding from the water. The Rebels fired the last bridge and the Tredegar Works and bullet factories exploded. The ground jerked, windows shattered, tombstones tilted, and rider-less horses leapt and bucked down the road. Grime-covered Christians dropped to their knees, beseeching the heavens as the tons of gunpowder, bullets and cannon-shells in the armaments factories blasted and the smokestacks collapsed.

"My God, what was that?" gasped Ewell.

"Lee's rectitude, by the sound of it," Devol said, watching as Lee's retreating army poured through town and disappeared into the west, marching toward Danville.

"General, Colonel," said a Captain, riding up with a small squad of cavalry. "We need to leave now, sirs. Union troops are only a few miles down the road. They appear to be racing each other to get here."

"What's so special about them?" snarled Devol. "There's a few things I'd like to do before I retire the field."

"It's the 5th Massachusetts, sir, the 22nd U.S., and the 36th, the 38th, too," said the Captain. "They're colored troops. It's about to get real ugly. Even uglier. Those streets will run with blood if we don't get out of here."

"Niggers?" said Devol. "I will not run from niggers, not a million of them. No, sir, I will not."

"Just think of the gold, Francois," whispered Ashok, leaning close. "That's why we're here. Nothing else."

"I guess that's the end, General. We should be going now," said Devol, quickly recomposed.

"Drunken fools, niggers and Yankee whores," said Ewell. "Destroying our capitol. Who would have thought it would come to this?"

"Well, General," said Devol. "Some would argue that's why we're in this fix."

Danville Bank

Jefferson Davis paced in and out of the Danville bank, shaking his great silver mane and cursing while he dictated a letter to the people of the Confederacy. Around him, straining men loaded heavy crates and bulging carpet bags of gold bars onto five heavy wagons. Varina Davis, the President's wife, barked orders at the laborers as they stacked her cherished furniture and heirlooms in the wagons to disguise the treasure. Confederate soldiers formed a perimeter around the wagons, bayonets at the ready, with orders to fire into the growing crowd, if necessary, as the people realized the bank was being robbed in broad daylight. By their President.

"You there, damn you, shoot them if they get closer," shouted Davis at Devol, for the 20th time in the afternoon.

"I'm not sure how this will work out, this fool trying to order me around," Devol said, chewing on an unlit Havana. "Acting like I didn't know he was stealing the Confederate treasury. Maybe I should just shoot the son of a bitch and be done with it."

"Too many witnesses," Ashok said, grinning, as he unrolled his rumaal. "But the woods are deep. They could wander off in the night, never come back."

"Not just yet. This could still work out just fine."

"Just keep calm, Francois," said Ashok.

Vicksburg

Doctors and nurses arrived at Andersonville within two days of Gen. Lee's April 9th surrender, with train cars filled with bushel baskets of fruit and vegetables and barrels of white flour close behind. Emptying Andersonville and transporting the 5,000 remaining inmates was a challenge, since many of our men were unable to walk more than a few feet. Hundreds of thousands of Yankees soldiers remained in the South, and the railroads were chaotic and overwhelmed.

We'd made it to the parole camp in Vicksburg, where a ticket on the steamboat Sultana waited for us, taking us up the Mississippi to Cairo, Illinois, and from Cairo, up the Ohio to Cincinnati. The main streets of Vicksburg were mobbed by revelers, just in from the field, hospitals and prison camps, bawling out one happy patriotic tune after another as we elbowed our way through the overflowing blocks of dubious cathouses and saloons serving the long-deprived soldiers

"The southern gentleman's worst nightmare. Drunk Yankees and free Negroes marauding through the street, proposing indecent acts to the maidens of this fair city," Ty said, motioning at the flocks of soiled doves beckoning from windows and stairwells. Captivating calves and an inch or two of milky fishnet thigh flashed from scandalously short ruffled skirts. Doorways and balconies and stairwells were filled with squealing, jiggling prisms of shiny silk and satin, creamy bosoms and bright feathers and lace garters. Vicksburg's sporting women were conducting a brisk business, trying to get one last big jackpot, but I was sure they didn't get the benefit of Helga's certificate of safe travel.

"Maidens. That's good," I said.

"Always so cynical. Let's see if we can find some food," said Ty, pulling me down the crowded street and then through the door of the closest saloon. A cloud of blinding smoke rushed out like it was pumped from a bellows.

"I'm going to tie a rope around our necks so we don't get separated in this smoke," said Ty. We had started to leave, but knew any place would be the same. "Whew, this is rough."

Inside, an army of blonde, buxom ladies of the evening overflowed their low-cut, satin gowns and the laps of the free-spending Yankees. The fallen sisters of Vicksburg were making money hand over fist, while their other parts took quite a pounding. Those cotton-clad pleasure frigates had been hit below the water-line by ten-thousand Yankee missiles, we sometimes said. There were some head-turners for sure, but there were plenty of stomach turners, too. A space at the bar opened between two hundred unwashed, drunk soldiers jammed into a space not big enough for fifty, sucking on soggy stogies and slapping the bar for more whiskey. Ty ordered, and the barman brought two chipped mugs of warm beer and a greasy green/gray lump of potted meat on rock-like brown bread.

"Are you sure?" I said. Ty looked a little green but recovered. "Maybe we're not the first fellas to chew this."

"Now, don't go getting biggity all of a sudden," Ty said. "We have to eat something, and we have a while to go yet. Bright side is, our systems are so used to foul dregs, it won't kill us."

It didn't kill us, and afterward, we headed back to the dock where we hopped up on a pair of large casks shoved against a warehouse wall. A few feet away, a man in a navy cap and peacoat slumped on a stack of pallets and tipped a pint at us. He took a big swallow as we waved a finger and eyed our vessel home. The Sultana was a Mississippi River side-wheel steamboat, about 300 feet long with four decks, and a 35-foot paddlewheel on each side. The deck was packed with very happy men, and the gang plank swayed under the weight of many more.

"Think we should get aboard?"

"Not just yet," I said.

"Look over there," said Ty, pointing as a huge wharf rat scurried down the wall and disappeared.

"Ugh, I can't even look at it," I said, thinking of the ten-pound flea-trampolines at Andersonville that grew fat on a diet of unthinkable nightmares, and the men that grew fat on the hideous rodents. "That was probably his kin we just ate.

"I don't know why you're acting squeamish. Wasn't too long ago when you thought a rat and a turnip and a sassafras beer was fine dining."

"That sure looks like a lot of people getting on that boat," I said.

"Yeah. I don't know. I don't know anything about boats, but it's a big boat. I reckon it can hold a lot of people," said Ty.

"You're being awfully trusting," I said.

"I'd paddle a leaky washtub up the Mississippi with a teaspoon if it got me home faster," Ty grinned. "I mean, this is still the Army. What could possibly go wrong?"

"Exactly why I'm worried," I said.

"You boys ain't going on the Sultana, are ye?" said the grizzled man on the pallets.

"Yes, sir," said Ty. "We have our tickets in hand."

"I'm going to tell you boys something," the man slurred drunkenly. "You might want to reconsider."

"Why is that? Is there a problem?" asked Ty.

309

"Problem is all you Yankees on it. Supposed to be 376. That's capacity. My reckoning right now is fifteen hundred of you boys, and more just keep coming."

"How can that be?"

"They ain't the first to run this game. Its damned profitable," said the man. "In this particular fleecing, the Army pays $5 for each one of you sailing to Cairo. And they will get what they paid for with their $5 for the first 376 of you. There is documentation on that. To send on to the shipping line, and the same list back to the army."

"I still don't follow."

"For the next 2,000 or however many of you they can squeeze onto that tub, the ship's captain still gets paid $5 for soldier, but it don't get logged in the books. They split it. He gives a piece back to the officer charged with getting you fellas home. Five dollars split 50/50, or whatever the cut, multiplied by 2,000. That is a hell of a lot of money for a trip upriver, and with so many soldiers coming and going from all over the South, the army will never notice. It's everywhere and everybody's palms are greased. They're going for one last jackpot. They're all in on it, damn near every man with a gold braid on in this town is filling his war-chest. To the top. You would be sick if you knew."

"I'm sick anyway," I said.

"How do you know all this?" Ty said.

"I've been on that tub since before the war. Because I was on the boat for the first eight hundred passengers of this trip. More than double capacity. Now look at it. I'm not risking a cracked boiler with all that weight on board."

"A cracked boiler?"

"Yep, two, truth be known. They just patched them, not replaced them, as they were ordered to do. If they took the time to replace them, they wouldn't have time to get a load and cash in. They were straining mightily to get us here," said the man. "It's damned scary, and I'm not generally inclined toward excitability."

"Now you're not on the boat?" Ty asked.

"No, sir, I am not. No longer. Not as of three hours ago. I suggest you find other transportation as well."

"Maybe we should find another boat," I said.

"With what? We don't have any money," said Ty. "I just want to get home to Rachel and the boys. Like he said, we have soldiers all over the south trying to get home by train, mule or pirate ship. Any boat will be crowded. If we knew it was only two days, but we don't know for sure. Besides, when's the last time you heard of a boat full of victorious warriors blowing up?"

"You're right, I guess. I doubt the Army will buy us a second passage," I said, looking at the jubilant mob on the boat.

"Ain't my funeral," says the old salt.

We squeezed our way up the gangplank and found some breathing room on the hurricane deck. Mobs of frolicking drunks wobbled around beneath us, singing, cheering, tussling, kissing each other, and kissing the deck. A few brave souls somersaulted and cartwheeled the length of the boat with such gusto I feared they would launch themselves into the mighty Mississippi. Grinning men struggled into flowery dresses and shimmering ball gowns, and a few twirled parasols liberated from the finest southern homes, looking like bright wildflowers in a dusty August field.

"I had not thought of that," said Ty. "Taking some plantation belle's gown home to the wife."

An ecstatic orchestra of fiddles, banjoes, and Jews harps had the men stepping high and lively across the deck. Those soldiers in ball-gowns paired up with those in uniform, suddenly as spry as those vigorous mountain youths at Dovie's wedding, flying across the deck to joyous calls of Allemande Lefts and Circle Rights, Do Sa Do's and Swings. Hooting spectators laughed and stomped and clapped, sporting the happiest smiles you ever saw, even if many had lost a few pearly whites to the ravages of war. If the Rebs were here, they'd probably be dancing, too, and I'm sure they would have been welcomed by most everyone. We were just that happy.

We rode that stinking boat for two days up the flooded river, stepping over snoring bodies in the stairwells and hallways, always looking for a decent spot to stretch out. Still, we were going home, and the inconveniences were trivial after nearly a year in Andersonville. Listening to the bands, and watching the boat easily conquer the powerful river, it was easy to forget the dire warnings of the sailor. Sometimes the boiler-room groaned and moaned like grandpa under harness, but with so many happy faces, the idea that something might be wrong with the boat seemed preposterous. At midnight, just a few miles north of Memphis, Ty and I stood at the railing, enjoying the cool river breeze. We heard the creak of metal twisting, and the boat seemed to sag and shudder. We had just enough time to exchange shocked looks before the boat exploded in a blazing orange ball that hurled us halfway across the river.

When I slammed face first into the frigid water, I thought I'd met a brick wall. I couldn't see, couldn't hear, and my nose gushed blood. I disgorged a gallon of Mississippi River water and screamed for Ty while around me hundreds of bobbing heads bellowed over each other. I fought to keep my head above water, kicked off those heavy brogans just before they dragged me down, and grabbed onto a cabin door that floated up to me.

"Sweet Jesus," I said, squeezing the door with white knuckles. "Sweet Jesus."

I rested my head for just a second, and in the light of the burning boat I saw Ty and paddled that way. He turned and saw me, grabbed the door and a relieved smile covered his face. With a roar, the twin smoke-stacks collapsed in flames, crushing hundreds as a shower of red-hot metal sizzled and hissed into the water. One final, massive explosion sent flaming shreds of the boat deck slicing across the water. I heard a whistle and watched helplessly as a whirling sheet of metal cut Ty in half.

Near Irwinsville, GA
May 10th, 1865

In a clearing deep in the white pine, wall tents lined the bank of the Ocmulgee River. After a month on the run, Davis's fugitive band had a routine. At night, wagons were pulled in tight and the men stood guard while the women tended the cooking fires. The Confederate President and his men rarely stepped away from the campfire. Devol smiled at their blissful oblivion, but still found it hard to believe that no one in the President's party had seen the two companies of Yankees lurking in the woods the last several days. He just hoped that court of dunces would not blunder them into a disastrous gunfight. This was not the time or place. The Yankee combat veterans outnumbered the Rebels ten-to-one, and a thousand more were camped not far away.

"Two companies?" said Ashok. "What are they waiting for?"

"I suppose to make sure no one will give them a fight," said Devol. "We're certainly not going to give them one."

"We won't?"

"Absolutely not. We'd help them if we could," said Devol.

"What are you talking about?"

"Those blue-bellies will be swooping Davis up soon. They'll be taking the gold somewhere. Further north, a big Yankee camp probably, with a railroad station. They certainly won't take it back to a Rebel bank to hold. So, they will be moving it by wagon."

"That's when we're going to steal it?" asked Ashok.

"That's my plan."

Just as breakfast fires were growing, a hundred Rebel-yelling Yankee cavalrymen galloped into the camp with pistols drawn. Hidden in the pines, Devol quaked with silent laughter as the panicked members of Davis's cabinet ran in circles, their buffoonery like something from a coon minstrel show. Cabinet members wriggled under the wagons, like that made them invisible, and acted shocked when the Yankee captain stuck his sword under the wagon and jabbed them. Secretary of State Judah Benjamin rolled and howled like he'd taken a minie ball to the groin. Two men sprinted toward the road, but were back quickly, shame-faced, at the point of Yankee sabers. Devol guffawed out loud when three women in wide sun bonnets jumped from the last wagon and dashed toward the river.

"Halt, or I'll shoot," shouted captain from the 4th Michigan, swinging his horse around to cut them off.

The despairing slave woman dropped to her knees, tears flooding down her cheeks while the very tall woman continued toward the river in long strides. She had a water bucket in her hand and cavalry boots and spurs under the house coat. Her bonnet was wrapped tightly to her head by a black lace shawl, but when the Yankee captain cocked his pistol, she squared up to fight.

"Do not move a further step, madam," the Yankee officer ordered.

"I said that was my mother!" snapped the other white woman. "Just leave us be, it's just my old mother."

"Remove the bonnet, ma'am, or I will fire," said the soldier.

"What's that?" said Ashok, watching Devol's amusement.

"Quiet," said Devol. "We are watching history. An unconquerable heart in a slave woman's bathrobe."

The smaller woman hissed like a wet cat as the tall woman ripped off the bonnet, revealing a thick mop of white hair. Every Yankee in the forest laughed hysterically. The time had come to mock the President of the Confederate States of America.

"Yes, that is President Jefferson Davis, and you will treat him accordingly. I warn you not to press him close, for your own sake," Varina Davis snarled. "He'll cut you, and bring destruction upon your head. He is ten times the man any of you raping savages are."

The Yankees rolled their eyes and repeated "raping savages" a few times. Then they hissed like a cat. The laughter was contagious, but didn't infect the Confederates.

"Many would say hang him, maybe hang the lot of you, from that tree right there," the captain smiled. "I'd most likely agree with them, so I'd suggest you be quiet and do as you are told. I'd be honored to supply the CSA with a martyr in your hour of darkness."

"You'll be held to answer for this," said Mrs. Davis, but her husband sat down weakly. She held his sagging head in her lap, and he fell asleep as she stroked his hair.

Chennault Plantation

"There's a plantation up ahead a couple miles," reported the latest scout. For a week after Davis had been taken away to Fort Monroe, Devol and his gang had covertly followed the treasure filled wagons down the Georgia back roads. "Was a nice place once, it looks like. Not so much anymore, but there's a decent old white man still living in the house."

"This is it, then," Devol announced with a grin. "This is the place. That's Rev. Chennault's Plantation up ahead. I'll bet that's where they stop. It's what I've been waiting for. If the Yanks stop here, we'll hit 'em tonight."

"Do you know it?" asked Ashok.

"Yes," said Devol, "We traded in slaves around here back when we could do the Lord's work. I chased a few niggers over this ground."

"Looks like we can finish the job without any prying eyes," said Ashok.

"Yes, most folks have cleared out," said Devol. "Any of these other poor, starving souls still left can't take time out from surviving to pay attention to us. I don't want to have to kill any more of them."

They watched from the trees as an ancient black man wearing a butler's uniform answered the door and he led the captain inside. The old slave then hobbled around the side of the house with a lantern and led the Yankees to the barn, where they unhitched the wagons and started cooking fires. The starless night was quiet but for the calls of the occasional owl or the swish of bats dipping low as Ashok and his students lay silently in a weeded-over cotton field. The young Rebels had been enthusiastic students of the Thuggee method, and always listened closely when Ashok told of his father's daring raids. They practiced with the rumaal nightly, on tree stumps and each other. Ashok regretted not having a Bangladeshi businessman they could tie to a log and use for practice.

"Reminds you of back home, doesn't it?" Devol said.

"It helps the loneliness, I'll admit," said Ashok. "Special occasions are always nice."

After the Yankee officer rejoined his men near the wagons, Ashok gave a night-bird whistle and his young assassins crept toward their targets. Ashok slipped behind the lone sentry and snapped the man's throat. He made another call and the Yankees were dead within thirty seconds, and the gold-filled wagons were on the road within thirty minutes.

"All right, gentlemen, get familiar with your Yankee friends," Devol said, as they tied the dead Yankees down in the wagons. "They're going to be your traveling partners for a while."

"How long we gonna carry them around?" said one soldier, "Killing 'em one thing, toten' thems another. I got to admit the idea gives me the jimjams."

"Just a few days. We're headed south, to the Okefenokee," said Devol. "Just until we get deep in gator country. Alligators are going to be our best friends, and we're going to show our appreciation with a fine meal of Yankee pot roast. And then they're going to guard our gold for us, deep in the swamp where nobody could find it in a thousand years."

Chapter Fifteen

Postwar Athens
May 1865

Tremors wracked my hands as the train flew over the southeastern Ohio hills taking me home. I'd wiped my palms a thousand times on my pantlegs, trying to dry the seeping sweat, without success. I knew that at least twice I had drifted off and jerked awake, shouting, my nightmares putting me right back at the Dead Angle on Kennesaw Mountain or the Slaughter Pen at Stones River. Now everyone on the train eyed me sideways.

"Excuse me, sir," said the rosy-cheeked man in the seat facing me. He looked down at my hands like they were the big, hairy, bird-eating kind of spiders. "Forgive me for intruding. I can't help but notice your hands. And nightmares. Is there anything I can do? Are you all right?"

"I'll be all right," I said.

"A touch of the soldier's heart," he said. "I guess that's what they call it."

"I guess," I said. "I'm fine."

Three years of army campaigns had left my delicate, slender artist's hands knotted, calloused and scarred. I clinched them in my lap and stole a glance at the man's soft, pudgy pink hands and manicured nails, sky-blue suit, and matching beaver top hat.

"You certainly gave me a fright," he said. I couldn't tell if he was concerned or annoyed. He seemed more annoyed.

"I apologize," I said, leaning against the window and pretending to close my eyes. "It will pass soon."

"Sadly, I didn't serve," he prattled. "I wanted to, you understand, but the family business, my father's and mine, was considered essential to the war effort."

"What business is that?" I said.

"Formaldehyde. Embalming tools. Things like that," he said. "My father was a student of Dr. Thomas Holmes."

"I see," I said. All soldiers knew of Dr. Thomas Holmes, and his new embalming methods. Innominata. He got at least 4,000 grieving mothers and wives to pay $100 each for his services. Some said he provided a valuable service. I thought he was a ghoul, he and his disciples prowling battlefields and mass graves for corpses to juice up and send home.

"Business has been good I take it."

"Oh, my yes. Booming," he said. "We couldn't keep up with demand."

"I suppose not," I said, wishing I could drive my bayonet through his throat.

"I know what you're thinking," said the man. "And think it if you want, but it was a service cherished by the families. If we can't promise these brave fellows a good Christian burial, what can we promise them?"

"For myself, I'd prefer the promise of not needing a burial, of any kind."

"I appreciate your sentiment and candor," he said. "We did well financially, but, well, that's just how it works. We sacrificed, too. Deadbeats. We took a loss on more than a few, you know, extending credit to some that didn't deserve it. But, I pray that now you all can return to great health and happiness."

"Some will, some won't."

"As for me, I'm to be married soon," he bragged, stone-deaf. "A wonderful girl. Absolutely beautiful. Monette Mapleton. From your home-town, actually. She is meeting me at the train station. I have to attend to a few business matters in Athens, and then we continue north to New York for our wedding ceremony and honeymoon."

"I don't know a Monette," I said, wondering which of my friends were his business matters. "But I congratulate you, sir, I'm sure she is as wonderful as you say."

"Indeed, she is."

We chugged into the Athens station mid-afternoon and I followed the embalming tycoon down the steps, where he was met by a young woman. Her bonnet shaded her face, except for a wide smile, but I recognized Netty, Ab's fiancée, and my hatred blazed for the man and this Monette.

"Monette, allow me to introduce my traveling companion," said the man. "Mr. Carew."

"Hello, Netty," I said. She looked up, her face gripped by panic and drained of all color. I stared in her eyes as she watched her gilded life disappear. "Our old friend's not doing so well, I understand."

"What did you say to her?" asked the man, a storm building on his face as Monette looked away quickly.

"Nothing, sorry," I said. "I thought we had met previously, but I see we have not."

"Yes, yes, darling," she pleaded. "Let's go into the restaurant. You must be famished. Nice meeting you Mr. Carew."

"Well, Mr. Carew, I think you are some sort of a lout!" he said. "I believe I want satisfaction."

I punched the man right in his mouth, and when he toppled backward his head hit the steps and bounced. His eyes were looking in opposite directions and blood dripped out the corner of his lips.

"Satisfied?" I asked as I stepped over him.

Rachel

"Hello," Rachel said, with a wide smile, but her eyes were red and swollen from crying. Ty's boys ran in and I rough-housed with them a little bit before she took them, kicking and screaming, to the neighbor's. I declined when she offered something stronger, just sweet water for both of us.

"It was good you got to see them, and the boys got to see you. I'm taking them home, where it's safe. Hopefully, it will be safe," she said. "I have a little money, and family outside Boston."

"When are you leaving?" I said.

"At week's end. I was hoping you'd stop by before we left. If you're ever in the area."

I told her I had no words for how guilty I felt for dragging Ty off to war, and getting him killed.

"It wasn't just loyalty to you that made him go," she said. "That was part of it, but don't flog yourself. Have you heard of the Marais des Cygnes massacre? The Kansas-Missouri wars?"

"I've heard of it, the name, nothing more, I think," I said. Everyone had heard the horror stories about Quantrill and Bloody Bill Anderson, the red legs and the bushwhackers. I couldn't imagine Ty being involved in all that terror and death.

"It was 1858. Ty was shot by a close neighbor. Charles Hamilton. One day, Charles and his murderers marched eleven of our men off their fields at gunpoint. He was a slaver, we knew, but never felt we had a reason to fear him. At first our men, Ty's father, who was an old man, the others, thought it was all a lark of some sort, but it wasn't," she said. "They were marched four miles to a ravine beside Marais des Cygnes River. The slavers meant to kill them all, but something scared them, and they fled before finishing the job. Ty's father was killed, like most of them. Ty was badly wounded."

I held her hand silently as she dabbed her eyes with a silk handkerchief.

"Our men were simple farmers and never harmed anyone. They had committed no violence except on the barren earth where they tried to grow crops," she said. "Ty had an old rifle he rarely took down from above the fireplace, not really that much different than you before the war."

"I wondered about his past some, but, he didn't seem eager to share," I said. "So, I didn't push."

"He healed, tracked a few down, did what he needed to do. I'd hated Kansas before, wanted our boys to go to decent schools, anything away from more killing," she said. "He changed."

"That'll do it," I said.

"He rode with the Jayhawkers when they raided Missouri. A couple times things got out of hand. He caught himself, but some bad things happened. To people that it probably shouldn't have happened to," she said. "So, we left. His uncle was the sheriff here. Titus Schwartz becomes Ty Blackmon, country bumpkin sheriff. Ruth becomes Rachel. You know the rest."

"I wouldn't think you'd want him to wear a gun, be sheriff, after that."

"I didn't. Not at all. But, I thought all that was past," she coughed, dried her eyes. "What possible trouble could come to sleepy, little Athens, Ohio?"

"The same kind that came to Trading Post, Kansas, I guess," I said, but whatever levity I was going for came out like rusty coalmine runoff. I left shortly after.

Ab

Ab had survived Kennesaw, but left everything below his hips in the burning brush on that deadly mountain. He'd been in Atlanta hospitals until war's end without telling anyone where he was. I avoided going to see him for a few days, but when I had no more excuses I rode to his stable. The strongest man in the county now sat leaning in his wheelchair with a cushion under his stumps, and his big, round, happy face was a bitter, sagging canvas of angry, purple spider-veins.

"Hi, Ab," I said, entering the livery, "How are you doing?"

"Well, I guess I don't need them damn shoes no more," said Ab, as tobacco juice dribbled down his stubbled chin. He managed a sad, whiskey and laudanum smile. "I guess that's one expenditure I no longer have to concern myself with."

"How are you doing?" I asked again. I smelled sweet horse feed and sweaty horses just back from a run. Two teenage boys were mucking stalls, and another brushed a horse. Ab stared, then looked at the stumps.

"What do you think? More horrible than anything you can imagine. I wish they had left me on that damn mountain with a bullet in my brain."

I had no response.

"I heard you saw Monette," he said.

"It's Monette now? I thought it was Netty," I said.

"No longer. She is class and sophistication. I don't blame her. Two of us don't need to live like this," Ab said. "You didn't have to hit that preening jackass on my account."

"I didn't. I punched him because he's a preening jackass. And because I couldn't punch her."

The Parade

The town was overflowing with folks from communities near and far pouring in for the July 4th Independence Day celebration. Old Glory hung from every store front, balcony and street post. Vendors walked through the spectators selling caramel corn and lemonade, and the lines never went down at booths offering crushed ice treats and confections.

A couple hundred of us in Union uniforms milled about, waiting for the parade to begin. Liquor bottles passed freely through our group as we swapped stories; happy ones, exciting ones, heroic ones, and tragic ones. We'd been home now for two months, and we all seemed to have plenty of each.

Elaborate red, white and blue floats lined the roads to carry the old-timers, a couple of septuagenarians from the War of 1812, several graybeards from the Mexican war, and another half dozen from various Indian wars. Another fleet carried the various holiday kings, queens, princesses, local potentates and blue-ribbon winners and there was a small fleet of decorated farm wagons just to carry the blind, the one legged, or those in wheelchairs. Ab was on one of them, though he desperately didn't want to be.

In the commotion before the parade I saw my old friend only briefly. He was red-faced drunk, weepy-drunk, and battlefield jittery, jerking in his chair at loud shouts and firecrackers behind him. I was pretty drunk myself, or I probably would have paid better attention before a pair of pretty, young nurses whisked him away in a cloud of giggles. The next time I saw him, he was strapped into his wheelchair, and his wheelchair was strapped onto the float. He looked so miserable, I should have stopped the show right then and taken him off. But, of course, I didn't. The group I was marching with was about ten floats behind Ab, and we stepped off quite merrily to the lively marching music, belting out the lyrics until the invalid floats passed the courthouse. Full of patriotic fervor, the city fathers fired the courthouse cannon with a tremendous blast that rattled the shop windows and sent half of us diving for cover.

Almost immediately, one of Ab's stable boys came racing down the street.

"Mr. Carew, we need your help," he shouted in a panic. "Mr. Platt's in a heap of trouble."

We sprinted to Ab's float, where he was sobbing and flailing at the straps holding his chair in place. I jumped onto the float, but Ab's eyes were huge and wet and terrified. He threw himself back one more time and upended the chair, escaping his bonds and crashing hard on the street. I leapt down, and something caught my eye as I lifted Ab's head. Monette was in the cluster of spectators ten feet away. Her pretty face trembled and tears ran down her cheeks, much to the fury of her new husband.

Early the next morning I was outside the general store with an armload of groceries as Ab's stable-boy ran past, shouting for the Sheriff. When the lawmen rushed out of the jail and hurried off toward Ab's livery, I knew what had happened. I fell in behind them, but there was no need to hurry. The curious were already gathered outside the barn when we got there. The sheriff motioned me inside, and the scene was tranquil as ever, with the smells of leathers and molasses and worn saddle-blankets and a dozen long-maned horses watching dispassionately over their stall gates. All except for Ab twisting slowly under the cross beam. The rope around his neck had nearly severed his head, and his grotesquely bloated face looked like a glass of red wine had been hurled into it. He'd used the big pulley for the hayloft to lift himself to the crossbeam and tie the rope around his neck. He had been determined. Ab had always been like that.

Two months after Ab died, I received a letter from Lum.

"Hello Dear Friend,

I trust all is well with you. As you can see, I am still in Georgia. I am working with the Sanitary Commission and Father Whelan, trying to get our new citizens a fresh start on life.

We are feeding them fairly well, and we have some medical help. We have started a couple schools, and only one has been burned to the ground so far. Things are rough, but better than most states, from what I hear. The race-haters are terrible, and these carpet-baggers are just as bad. They are soul-less vultures, a blight across the entire South. But we are surviving, in some cases thriving.

It is with a great deal of trepidation that I write you, but I have information you want. I stumbled across it quite by accident, and it is not information I want to give you. I think it will likely get you killed, but you deserve to know. Francois Devol has been seen. He was headed south to the Okefenokee Swamp, with a gang of armed brigands and a wagon full of mining equipment of some sort. They are all going to a small town called Big Swamp Point.

If you decide to come down here, you really must come by. I think you will be quite impressed.

Your friend, always,

Columbus Pleasant

PS: I also ran into Dovie. He said to tell you he'll be a father soon."

Finn

The carriage met me at the train station and hurried me to the Burnet House, where Uncle Finn greeted me warmly.

"I'm sure it's important for you to come all the way here. What brings you?" Finn said.

"I got a letter," I said. "Devol is in Georgia. A place called Big Swamp Point. He has armed men with him."

"Georgia? How did you learn that? What's he doing there?" asked Uncle Finn, sitting down quickly.

"I have no idea what he's doing, or why he is doing it," I said.

"Who told you this?" said Finn, regaining a little color.

"That's not important. I have a friend down there, is all. The important thing is I'm going there to kill him."

"Yes, of course," Finn said. "But, wouldn't it be better to wire the sheriff, or the army down there, and have him arrested?"

"No. On what charge?"

"The Pinkerton's don't necessarily need a charge. This is so dangerous," said Finn. "I can send a battalion of Pinkertons with you. He'd never be seen again."

"No, not yet. I want to look it over first. If I need help, I'll let you know."

"When are you going?"

"Today. The train leaves from here in two hours."

"Oh, damn," he said. "The timing couldn't be worse. Just prior to your arrival I found I had to go to England. Boat business. Leaving within a day or two. Probably for a good while. Let Jones, or any of my staff, know when and where you need Pinkertons. Or any help. Just keep them informed, they'll provide anything you'll need."

Seraphine

Seraphine Passibone was nervous and excited, as she always was when she visited the Voodooienne, Marie Laveau, the Queen of them all. But today, she felt it even more, much more, than any time in the past. That Marie had sent a breathless messenger to Seraphine's home yesterday, and requested a visit on such short notice, had her mind racing.

She slowed as she approached the humble cottage at 152 Rue St. Ann., breathing deeply, filling her lungs and spirit with the bouquet of New Orleans; the large, creamy flowers of the beautiful old magnolia trees, and the sensual scents and lovely blooms of the Voodoo Queen's garden which, even in a city known for the splendor of its flowers, was spectacular. Like the Voodooienne herself, the Belladonna, oleanders, Yellow Jessamine, and Angel's Trumpets were tempting, lovely and lethal. One of the old woman's fondest amusements was keeping the power-brokers of New Orleans from getting too comfortable, and she joked that her garden full of beautiful poisons said it best, keeping the powerful a little uneasy when they'd ride by and see her tending her flowers, fretting that some spells might soon be cast their way.

"Bonjour," Marie Laveau said, opening the door before Seraphine could lift the knocker. "Comment allez-vous?"

"Je vais très bien," Seraphine said. "Tout va bien."

Seraphine had been raised in Paris, and with her aunts, she often visited Molinard's and the other skilled parfumier and artisans who created the wonderful Parisian scents. Upon Seraphine's return to New Orleans as a young woman, Marie, her mother's old and dear friend, had introduced her to the seductive and coercive properties of perfumes and incenses. Marie's fragrances, like her elixirs, were said to lull the mind to sleep, arouse the body to great passions, or compel the lips to spill dark secrets. She was secretive about the formulas, and Seraphine knew they existed nowhere else in New Orleans, not in the city's largest, most expensive mansions, nor the most lavish and decadent whorehouses.

"Just lovely," Seraphine said, drawing it all in. "You've been to Doussan's? Or your own wonderful creation?"

"Doussan's," Marie said, of the French Quarter's pre-eminent parfumeur. "I just don't have the patience for the exactness anymore. But, I could spend hours in his shop. You, too, I'm sure?"

"Certainly," Seraphine said, watching Marie with admiration. At 70, Marie was still a striking woman, retaining her famous beauty and self-assured carriage. Mystery and intrigue had always swirled around the old woman. Seraphine looked into the large, hazel eyes that could make all of New Orleans snap to attention, the eyes that added to Marie's supernatural mystique. Few could hold her mesmerizing gaze for long. Today, she wore a bright silk tignon and a West African kaftan as she always did in her home. The royal scarlets, gypsy purples, and bright gold sunbursts cast her eyes in different hues with each new day, with pin-points of golden-rod, cinnamon, and turquoise that pulsed like fireworks.

As with every visit, the simple act of entering the remarkable little cottage was heady. Seraphine smiled as she crossed the floor and the tiny grains of brick crunched underfoot, testament to the Voodoo Queen's love of ritual and tradition. Marie's walls were filled with crucifixes, rosaries, paintings and beautifully carved figurines of Catholic saints amidst the shelves of voodoo amulets, candles, fetishes and mysterious pouches of gris-gris. There were many rumors, and Seraphine knew Marie spun many of those herself. With a white French father and freeborn Haitian mother, Marie came to the French Quarter as a small child before the turn of the century. She got her start in New Orleans' finest brothels, and using foresight, discretion and guile, she came into ownership of a few houses and her empire quickly flourished. She had made some formidable allies as a young woman, but many powerful enemies as well. In her early years, as a proprietor or as a courtesan, it was rumored her truncheon wielding cutthroats beat secrets out of the political and financial power brokers in the city. Others said it was simply blackmail, or the result of a drunk man's addlepated boasting. But many were convinced she used potions and black magic to uncover secrets and gain influence. She had become a legend, a mystic, a matriarch, greatly feared as a sorceress with sway in every social circle in New Orleans.

"Excellent coffee, is it not?" Marie asked, as the two women smiled comfortably and sipped chicory coffee and nibbled warm raspberry beignets in Marie's parlor.

"Wonderful, as always," Seraphine said. "And you look wonderful, as always. It appears you have survived the war mostly unscathed."

"I wouldn't say unscathed, but I didn't suffer like so many," said Marie. "I still think of poor Andre. Your husband was a marvelous man."

"Yes, thank you," said Seraphine. "I miss him, terribly."

"You are an extraordinarily lovely young woman," Marie said. "Your mother was one of the great beauties of this city. You favor her more each time I see you."

"Thank you," said Seraphine. "I'm glad you called for me. I have been meaning to call, it's just difficult."

"So much chaos. I understand, but, yes, I have something to discuss with you. A quest."

"I'm flattered. Why me?"

"To be frank, the item I have I do not trust in the hands of any man, north, south, white, or black, brown, blue, or made-out-of cheese," said Marie. "They would only use it to start another war. Or waste it on lustful urges."

"They sure do that," smiled Seraphine. "That still leaves a lot of people."

"Indeed, it does, but I've known you and your family for a very long time. I have eyes and ears all through the French Quarter. And you're the right person for this job."

"What job is it you have in mind?" asked Seraphine, taking a sip of coffee.

"Retrieving several million dollars."

"My," said Seraphine, coughing and patting her chest. "Choked."

"I'd like you to look at this. It's a treasure map," Marie said when Seraphine had caught her breath. She led her to another table, slid out a roll of paper and spread it out flat. It was a crudely drawn map of what appeared to be a vast swamp full of creeks, forests, lakes and islands. Seraphine thought perhaps Atchafalaya Basin.

"Like Captain Kidd and Blackbeard?" asked Seraphine.

"Not exactly," Marie said.

"What happened? It's not finished," Seraphine said as she traced her finger along the shaded route. The rough drawing stopped an inch from the bottom of the page.

"No, the man who drew this was killed before he could finish. As you can see, it's pretty sloppy. He was in a hurry."

"Yes, but how does it do us any good without pinpointing the location?"

"Because there is another map, and we know who has it."

"And the owner of the other map wants to share with us?"

"Not exactly. This map will get us very close. Close enough that when the other party begins digging, we need be ready. And when that party has pulled up the gold, we need to find a way to separate him from it."

"How do we do that?"

"That, my dear, is why I have asked you here. You have proven yourself to be quite creative and clever like your mother, and brave like your father. I'm sure you can find a way."

"I remain flattered," Seraphine said.

"There is one other reason I asked you," said Marie. "The map's in the possession of Francois Devol."

"Devol? Règle de démons?" Seraphine gasped. "Dit mon la verite'! Where?"

"He's in Georgia," Marie said, "But I'll give you all the help you need."

Okefenokee Swamp

I rode the train south shoe-horned into a car full of shifty-eyed carpet-baggers, unbathed scoundrels with greasy lips and grimy fingernails puffing on foul cigars. Most of them smelled worse than we did after a month of hard campaigning. I kept a tight grip on my own large heavy canvas kit and was relieved when the conductor finally tapped me on the shoulder.

I hopped down when the train pulled to a stop at the end of a one street town. There was the small, darkened railroad shack and livery stable about a hundred feet away. On the other side of the track was a cluster of houses, a couple saloons and a store. Some distant, dim lamplight and slow fiddle music came in patches through the towering pines, and a pair of baying hounds hunted somewhere in the night. Someone whistled from near the barn, and I saw a figure in the shadows. I hooked the bag holding my guns and gear over my shoulder and began walking. As I neared the barn, a silver-bearded, thickly muscled black man stepped into the light and watched me with a skeptical eye. A couple horses eyed me from over a board fence, then returned their noses to their feeding trough.

"Evenin'," the man said, with a battered axe-handle resting on his shoulder and an old shotgun leaning against the barn door. "Is there anything I can help you with?"

"I need a horse," I said, running my hand over a roan gelding's muzzle. "Rent or buy. Rent would probably be best for both of us."

"Mm Hmm," said the stableman. "Rent ain't ever hardly best for me, but maybe we can figger sumpin'. Which hoss you admirin'?"

"This one right here looks good. I don't think I'll be riding much, but I want a horse available if I need one. I'll pay generously, and he may never leave your stable," I said. "And, is there a hotel of any kind around here?"

"Mister, the only hotel we got is whatever bedroll you brought on your back. But, this heah a fine hoss," the blacksmith said. "A dollar a day hoss. You seem like a fine man. So, don't get my hoss shot. Or et by gators."

"Why would I get my horse shot? Or et by gators?"

"My hoss. You is the lessee. And in case they miss you. Or he just gets abandoned someway. Swamps can be mighty dangerous for a hoss. For any living creature. This swamp, particular."

"What are you talking about?"

"It would be healthiest for you to turn around and go back to Ohio."

"How do you know I'm from Ohio?"

"I didn't until now, just needed to make sure you're the right man," he said. "Seeing you is only about the third man in a year got off the train here, I was pretty sure it was you."

"Right man for what?"

"Ain't you follerin' someone?" he asked. "There's a bunch of crackers been in town a couple weeks, just kind of hanging around. Couple real big men running the show, and a slew of disreputable looking bandits wearing odd bits of Rebel cavalry uniforms. They sure did get excited a day or so back. They don't much like you, Mr. Carew, suh."

"How do you know my name? Where are they?"

"Don't worry yourself none about that right now," said the liveryman. "First thing we got to do is get you out of town before someone realizes you're here."

"So, I need to hide from Devol? He's waiting for me?"

"Bunch of them waiting for you. Like I said."

"I see."

"If you're determined to stay, just ride along, right down that road there," he said. "Couple of our men will keep an eye on you. You won't see them right away, but they will be there. Keep you from getting shot in the back. Miss Seraphine enlighten you when you meets her. Don't trust no white men you might meet on that road. None, hear me?"

I rode warily in the moonlight, feeling eyes peering through the six-foot walls of knotted brush lining the road. I jumped at the grunts and chirps and crackling twigs and owl hoots and chattering bat swooshes in the dark, but my trusty dollar-a-day hoss was unruffled. I heard a rustling in the brush ahead, and two barefoot, teenaged black boys stepped into the road. They wore ragged homespun barely past their knees, and were pointing repeating rifles at me.

"Hold up Mister. We'se your guides."

"You can put those guns down," I said, and showed empty hands.

"In a little bit," said one of the boys. "I'm Atlas. This here my brother Jupiter. You're Mr. Carew?"

"I am. Why didn't you just meet me in the stable?"

"We'se runaways from before the war. Our massa was mad as a shook jug of hornets when we run off, and made up a bunch of stories 'bout us, rapin' and robbin' de white women. We been in the swamps ever since. Wouldn't be good for the white folks to catch us," said Atlas. "Ever."

"Yes," I said. "I guess that war's not over."

"Nope, that one ain't never gonna end. When a rich white man say a nigger been rapin' white women's, that nigger gone get hung, war or no war. Emancipated or no," said Jupiter. "No matter what that bean pole Linkum say."

"I'm sure that's true."

"We had to make sure you weren't followed," said Atlas. "We got to be careful."

"Where are you taking me?"

"Deep into the land of the trembling earth," said Jupiter.

"What's that mean?"

"Nothing bad. The swamp, the old moss it on, tend to move around some. The Okefenokee ain't nothing to fret about. They ain't a frog puddle we don't know," said Atlas.

"Nary a one," said Jupiter, and we continued through the dark for an hour.

"Hold up, we got to stop here. Horses is no good where we going in the swamp. They sink in the soft ground, and the gators and snakes scare 'em awful. It ain't good to get throwed by your horse on top a hungry alligator."

"Yes, that's been pointed out to me," I said. "What's to keep me from turning around and riding off?"

"Sure not us, mister. Just the gators, the cotton-mouths, the rattlers, and the bears. And panthers," Jupiter laughed. He whistled softly, and two more boys appeared out of the bushes. "And all them gunmen I gather want to do you in. And common sense. Just that is all."

"Jes' let us go in first a little ways," said Atlas, as the newcomers led the horse away. Still grinning, Atlas and Jupiter shared a wink and we resumed walking. "Ain't too many gators this close to folks, but dey some. Keep your eyes out. Dey fierce hongry in the dark."

We continued for another hour, and when we reached a slow-running stream, Atlas pulled a small flatboat from beneath a brush pile. We paddled in silence down a tunnel of knobby-kneed cypress trees, looking like a gauntlet of disapproving Bible prophets with their heavy beards of Spanish moss in the hazy moonlight. Bullfrogs croaked a heavy jug-arum bass, and a sudden, deep roar from the nearby dark startled me and sent a flurry of creatures squealing through the tree tops.

"Bawz gator rat deh, bawz," said the boy, in feigned wonderment. They rocked with giggles as we pushed on. "Mornin' comes maybe we cotch him for you. Seventeen foots counted foots by foots. Dey's udders monstrous big, but he's de big balled obeseah in dis plantation."

We reached an island, and slipped through the trees into a large clearing where two campfires burned between three weather beaten cabins about fifty feet apart. In the flickering light of the campfire, a dozen black men, all armed, watched me silently from around the camp. Most looked very young, but there were two thick-chested solemn sorts that were holding rifles with a familiarity I knew. A young woman, not yet thirty, stepped out of the closest cabin and walked towards me.

"Good evening, Monsieur Carew," she said, handing me a cup of cool water. She had an abundance of full soft curls tucked into a cotton snood, and wore snug homespun pants. "My name is Seraphine Passibone. It's a pleasure to meet you. We weren't sure what to expect."

"Thank you, I'm Cage, but I guess you know that," I said. "Now, can someone tell me what's going on? Why do all of you know my name? And my business?"

"Go ahead and sit down, Cage. Eat this. We'll talk in a minute, about everything," she said. I sat on an old log, and one of the young men brought a steaming wooden bowl of rice, tomatoes and fish. It was wonderful, and the hot pepper opened my nose and set my tongue on fire.

"This is excellent, but I wish you'd start telling me what's going on. I don't like not knowing what's happening. Or any idea who you are," I said, as she handed me a full canteen and sat next to me. Her lively brown eyes sparkled with energy and intellect. And resolve.

"No, of course you wouldn't," she said, "I understand you and Monsieur Devol have some serious issues. Believe me, I understand completely. At the same time, he has something that we want very much. We have no objection to his being killed. In fact, we'll eagerly help. I'd love to do it myself. I'd prefer to torture him for a few days first. It's something I've dreamed for years. Just not too soon."

"Serious issues? You could say that. He killed my fiancée. And some of my friends. And tried to kill me. More than once."

"I didn't know the details. All we heard was you were a soldier, and there would likely be some shooting. Devol's men were blabbing it all over town. Both saloons and the general store."

"So, Devol knows I'm here?"

"There were many sets of eyes on you when you stepped off that train. If you'd walked toward town, I'm sure you'd be dead already."

"How did he know I was coming?"

"No one here can answer that. But Devol's men knew it. So, we knew it."

"So much for surprise," I said.

"I'm quite certain. And he has more than thirty men with him, as best we can tell. Assuredly, all veteran Rebels and sneaking cutthroat bastards," she said. "But to offset that, you now have twelve more, very eager, people than you did when you started. Most have military training. Some have provided services to my business partner before."

"Assuredly. But, actually, I started with an army of several hundred thousand soldiers, and he's still breathing."

"Point taken. We can get more if we need them, although it might take a few days for them to get here. And, now we have you. It sure put a start in those men when they heard you were coming. Are you some kind of gunfighter? Do you have a plan?"

"No, not a gunfighter. Just a soldier that knows how to survive," I said. "As for the rest, I don't know. I don't have a plan yet. I didn't know what to expect. Do you?"

"We're working on something," she smiled.

"If we want to even things up, we'll need to draw them out, catch them off guard, somehow," I said, thinking about Joe Johnston and the whipping he gave us at Kennesaw when he forced us to come to him, on terrain of his choosing, and us fighting and falling into his traps the whole way.

"Yes, that's the way we see it," Seraphine said. "Your arrival may do that. They'll certainly be by to see if this is where you ended up."

"So, why are you here?" I asked.

"We're here for what they have, what they are pulling out of the swamp. We're going to steal it."

"And what might that be?"

"$5 million," she said.

"What?" I blurted.

"Quite a surprise, isn't it? Maybe not that much. Maybe more. Maybe only a quarter that much, but either way, a fantastic amount of money," she said. "And I plan to kill him before that. Or during. Or after. But he's going to die."

First Morning in Camp

"Would you care for a cup of coffee?" Seraphine said, as I approached the breakfast fire.

"Yes, I'd like that very much," I said, in the crisp morning air. The sun had not yet burned off the thick mist of dawn, but the yellow warblers welcomed the coming light. She was silent while I took my first sips. "This is wonderful coffee."

"I brought it from home. Even in the rough, it's important to savor a few luxuries. Enjoy."

"You're alligator hunters?" I said. A dozen alligator skins hung on a thick rope stretched between the cabins.

"It's not a great ruse, but enough that it gives us a reason for being out here," Seraphine said. "Maybe enough to cast some doubt, at least for a while. Nobody has bothered us so far."

"I see," I said. "I'm ready for the rest of the story."

"It starts a very long time ago," said Seraphine, in a southern-slowed, honey-drenched, French accent. "I'm from New Orleans. I'm an octoroon. A free-born Creole of Color. In New Orleans we have an unusual social custom called placage. Concubinage, maybe some would call it. Lifelong affairs between rich, white men, usually already married, and free women of color. Usually, the women are not legally recognized as wives, although they prosper quite well from it, and are often left estates equally shared with the wives. Sometimes to the exclusion of wives. Have you ever heard of the Quadroon Society, the Quadroon Balls?"

"A little from newspapers and magazines," I said. "Not much. Quite scandalous."

"I'm sure it's not as lurid as the Northern newspapers want you to believe," said Seraphine. "I'm one-eighth black. My mother was a quadroon, one-fourth Black. My father was a Frenchmen, solid Parisian aristocratic stock. I had some ancestors that lost their heads in the French Revolution, so most of the others in the family came to America, with much of their fortune still intact. So, his whole family was incredibly rich, but also with a strong sense of Noblesse oblige, from my understanding. As you can imagine."

"Not sure this is what he would have had in mind, though," I said.

"No, certainly not," she smiled. "It's a terrible, tragic story, but we may be able to salvage something yet. I was raised in France, by my father's family, after his death. I was less than a year old when my mother was kidnapped by Devol and sold into slavery."

"What?"

"Start with the fact that my father didn't hide his relationship with my mother, and he kept her in a lavish lifestyle. Quadroon society is marvelously opulent, all part of this erotic fantasy," Seraphine said. "My mother and father were in love. His wife knew, of course, like they all do, but never acknowledged it publicly."

"And what of the wives?"

"Divorce associated with placage is nearly unheard of. That's simply the way it is. These are very wealthy men," she said. "And powerful men. Very few women want divorce. They'd lose everything. The courtesans have been raised in the system, and rarely expect marriage."

"I see. I guess."

"My father died suddenly, and just as suddenly, my father's vindictive wife had my mother snatched off the street, drugged and smuggled halfway across the country," said Seraphine. "They created an entire false identity and sold her all the way to Georgia, where no one knew her. And no one would believe the crazy story that she was a free woman. Or care."

"Sold her? How can that be? What happened to her?"

"She died, and hopefully found some peace. After the War, I tracked down some freed people who knew her in her captivity. Their stories broke my heart. Torn from her family. They didn't say it, but it sounded like she took her own life. She got worked hard in the rice fields, awful hard. She had never worked like that in her life," Seraphine said. "She was a kept woman, a pampered woman, a distinguished lady of the French Quarter and Quadroon society."

"How could anyone possibly get away with that?"

"My father's wife and the master and mistress of that original plantation were close. She tortured my mother. They beat her, whipped her. They broke her down. She got weaker and sicker," said Seraphine. "She couldn't work, so her owner built a little rape-shack. One where all the white trash would come over late at night and rape her. Degrade her in every way. I'm sure death was a relief."

"And the woman that had your mother kidnapped?"

"Tragic end."

"Quick and painless?"

"Not the way I heard it," she smiled.

"No?"

"There was this doctor. LaLaurie. Had to leave town in a bit of a rush," said Seraphine. "Left some tools and notes behind. Tragic."

"I see," I said. "Were you in the country during the War?"

"Yes. I was married to Captain Andre Cailloux, of the 1st Louisiana Native Guard. He was killed during the siege of Port Hudson," said Seraphine. "My husband was a remarkable man. He was born as slave, but had been freed, apprenticed as a cigar-maker, and sent to Paris for his education. His master saw early how special Andre was. He even received military training while in France. A brilliant man, a splendid horseman, boxer, and leader for the free-colored community in New Orleans."

I remembered reading about the exploits of Cailloux and the 1st Louisiana Native Regiment while I was on the warpath. Frank Leslie's paper, especially, wrote several in-depth articles about them. The 1st Louisiana Native Guard was one the Union's very first officially sanctioned colored regiments, drawn from escaped slaves and free men of color from New Orleans.

The unit's first combat came in an assault on Port Hudson, near Baton Rouge, in 1863. One thousand Native Guardsmen, led by Captain

Cailloux, charged the garrison of 7,000 in the heavily defended fortress, unaware that the attack by the rest of the 12,000-man assault force had fallen away in confusion and miscommunication. Wildly outnumbered as they were, they threw themselves against the fort's 20-foot parapets only to become stranded, trapped by steep embankments and swampy, flooded ditches down a narrow ravine. They were ripped to pieces by canister shot on three-sides, but Cailloux, wounded early, and badly, led six charges straight into the Rebel guns before falling, beside more than a third of his men.

"What happened to you after your husband was killed?" I asked.

"New Orleans was a very busy port in the Civil War, and filled with powerful people on both sides of the debate, loyalty oath or not," she said. "I'd like to think I did my part, making life a little more difficult for the slavers."

"Who are the twins?" I said, pointing at the two deeply muscled, ink-black men who were watching silently, and missing nothing. They looked tough and mean, layers of beef across their chest and shoulders like scarred hard cases from the docks. No strangers to violence.

"Marcel and Maurice fought beside my husband. They're from New Orleans. They know about Devol. They're very nice and polite, just quiet," Seraphine said. "If they weren't capable Marie would not have sent them."

"She couldn't have sent more than two? And Atlas and Jupiter? Do you really think your men, those two, these boys, can handle Devol's gang?" I asked.

"They have been handling evil, violent men since they were born," she said. "All are experienced with guns, and I guarantee they are enthusiastic and unafraid. And I can fight as well as any man."

"How big is this swamp?" I asked later, as I prowled my surroundings.

"Twenty miles this way, forty miles that way. About 700 square miles," said Tandy. "It takes a man around ten days to cross it. Experienced swampers like Atlas and Jupiter take half that. A person could stay hidden in this swamp about as long as they want to stay hidden. Or stay lost forever."

"There's more water than land, and sometimes the land ain't much firmer than the water. Don't you go off somewhere without one off us," Atlas said. "The water in the swamp is not deep, barely to your waist in most places, a few places a little deeper, and a very few that drop real sudden down to ten feet. Those gators will get down in there and dig underwater tunnels. They's lots of human bones in them gator holes, and they's well fed, you don't need to spoil them. They are always watching, and they can jump out of the water three or four feet and take your leg off."

"What happens if someone steals your boat?' I asked.

"Mister, if there's a man all the way out here that don't have his own boat, he's too bad of a man for us to scrap with," said Jupiter. "I'm surrendering right now. That's the plain truth."

"It's good to see you're relaxed enough to go fishing," I said over my coffee the next morning, when I saw some of the boys preparing to leave camp with fishing poles over their shoulders.

"I've discovered they're less likely to shoot a colored man that's got a cane-pole in is hands than one who ain't," said Atlas.

"Makes sense," I said, and I was soon seated in a small, flat boat where I spent most of the next two days. Atlas and Jupiter quietly paddled us up and down the maze of narrow, cypress-shrouded waterways as I tried to get familiar with this harsh environment. We had pickets out, and I stayed out of the few open spaces on land, or on open water, but the swamp was too immense to stop all prowling eyes. Still, I had to know where I was. There were a few big islands that were miles across, floating islands of soft, spongy black peat, millions of years old, covered by slash pine forest, and strewn with thick brush and random hedgerows of thick, snarled undergrowth. There were some big lakes, too, but mostly it was gator ponds the size of small farm-ponds, broken up by grassy marshes, some under a foot or so of water, and some just a few inches above it, all connected by hundreds of miles of tangled streams and winding waterways.

In the sunshine, cypress trees rose from watery shorelines and stream beds, towering over everything, with thick shrouds of faded, gray-brown Spanish Moss which draped the creeks and tickled our scalps as we paddled beneath them. The shores were defended by armies of knotty cypress knees, the long tree roots that protruded like stark, gray gar-goyles, or stretched out into the meandering streams, dipping in and out of the water like mythic sea-dragons. But the swamp was not dark and dreary as I assumed a swamp would be. There was still plenty of dark mystery under the dense canopy, but it was rich and vibrant and melodic and beautiful in its own way. In the sunshine, thick fringes of chest-high brown rushes and grasses lined the banks, and vast patinas of fragrant water-lilies with snowy white flowers that grew out from the lakeshores, covering the blackwater shallows and filling the air with sweetness. Patches of wild, purple orchids and grass pinks and blue irises bright-ened the landscape, while in the swamp's sodden prairies, fields of dazzling bright golden club spouted up and rainbows of carnivorous sundews and butterworts laid traps for unsuspecting flies.

The swamp was thick with rough, broken cypress logs that looked like alligators, and alligators that looked like cypress logs. Gangs of fat gators lounged at nearly every water's edge, and we couldn't go far without seeing a long, black snout cruising ominously through the black water. Every bare spot and bleached-out log had a snake or turtle or gator perched on it, sunning themselves, peering sideways, deciding who would eat and who would get eaten before that day was out. I pondered that as we made a rare cruise across open water. The only sounds were the songbirds and Atlas's muffled paddle, and the lake's water was so black and glossy and calm it mirrored every needle of the giant cypress trees that loomed above.

I was admiring my reflection in the glistening water when a crack like a hot summer lightning-bolt snapped my head up. Close enough to touch, gnarled black alligator jaws, as long as my arm, floated through the water, nonchalantly crushing the shell of a slowly flailing turtle. They barely made a ripple, and neither one seemed especially excited about their lot in life, but it sure gave me a start. A nice reminder that inches beneath us lurked monsters unchanged by evolution in a million years, mindless eating machines waiting for a careless finger or single pink toe to break water.

Later, I watched the long-legged wading birds in the shallows. Some walked slowly with their heads down among the water lilies and the cattails, probing the muddy surface for insects and crayfish. The bright white egrets stood perfectly still in a few inches of water, waiting for an unsuspecting meal of minnows or tadpoles, and striking with the speed of a cobra when one wandered into range. Flocks of little blue herons roosted high up in the trees, and white wood storks sat on dead cypress trees with patient black vultures perched nearby. Seraphine threw a stick at some long-necked Sandhill Cranes standing in the nearby shallows. The sky went dark as hundreds of the noisy, whooping birds exploded across the pink-ribboned evening sky, their powerful seven-foot wings churning the air in our boat.

"These are our early warning systems," she said. "More gifts from Marie."

"Marie? The Voodoo Queen?"

"Yes," she said. "She sent everything we'll need.

"Did she send me?"

"Can you prove she didn't?"

After sundown, Seraphine and I walked along the water's edge, in a slight breeze that carried the fragrance of the water-lilies and orchids, with bullfrogs and alligators' laying down a heavy bass behind the forest music. It was difficult to have less than carnal thoughts and Seraphine's delicate face and form-hugging pants had an irreversible effect on me. Under the full moon, I was unable to hide it, and her perfume of lavender and honey didn't help. She noticed and allowed her gaze to venture down my body. I was mortified and wanted to hurl myself into the nearest alligator hole.

"You've been away in the army quite a while I take it?" She gave me a small pitying smile.

"I was, yes, and haven't…socialized…since. I apologize for my condition."

"Don't apologize for being human," she said, her eyes twinkling, but she kept a straight face. "Be happy you have feelings at all after fighting a war, what you've been through. What we've all been through. But, fair warning. If you start following me around with that thing, I'll eventually get perturbed. But right now, no, that's not the thought I'm having."

"Thank you, I think I'll go sit down now."

"Yes, do that. I suggest staying in the shadows a bit until things relax," she said.

"I'm embarrassed," I said.

"Don't be. And don't do this," she laughed, running her hand up the inside of my leg. She gave a firm squeeze to the affected part and pranced away, light and graceful as a ballerina.

Knights of the Golden Circle

"Will you tell me about the uncle now?" asked Seraphine the following day.

"Not much to say, really," I said. "Obscenely wealthy. I saw them together several times, and he absolutely doted on Ardent."

"But you said she saw Devol and the others in Finn's suite," she said. "Albert Pike and George Bickley."

"Yes."

"I don't know this Finn. He must do a good job staying in the shadows." she said. "But, I don't see how it can be anything but the Knights of the Golden Circle. They can't survive without anonymous bankrollers like this uncle."

"So, who are these men?" I said. "What is this Golden Circle and what is all this subterfuge and talk of espionage?"

"They started as the Southern Rights Clubs in the 30s, then became the Knights of the Golden Circle in 1854, supposedly under the leadership of Bickley," said Seraphine. "But most people who keep an eye on such things believe Albert Pike was the genius behind it all. The Knights had a standing army before the war, and now have a couple hundred-thousand bitter Confederate veterans to recruit from."

"They're that powerful?"

"Maybe. They hope to be, so they have to be treated as if they are," she said. "They're powerful enough, or ambitious enough, anyway, to plan a Southern Empire with a capital at Havana, Cuba. They planned to take over Mexico, the Caribbean, and Central America, all paid for with cotton, sugar, tobacco, rice, coffee, and mining, worked by slave labor, of course."

"Of course."

"That could be what this sunken gold is for," she said. "More likely Devol's just a greedy bastard, but one never knows. Either way, I'm sure he'll take a healthy cut."

"What else?"

"The officer sounds like John O'Mahoney and his Irish Republican Brotherhood, the Fenians," she said.

"Uncle Finn has an entire movement named after him?" I said, wondering what the next unbelievable revelation would be.

"No, it's the Fianna Eireann," she said. "A 17th-century Gaelic warrior tribe. O'Mahony was a colonel in Meagher's Irish Brigade. Most of the soldiers in that brigade were from the Irish Brotherhood, and had come to the U.S. to escape the Gorta Mór, The Great Irish Famine. The Great Starvation would be more accurate, since a hundred ships a day still left Ireland, full of grain and farm produce, bound for merry old England. They say a million people died, and a million more emigrated from Ireland. It would appear England was purposely trying to starve them out of existence, so, I can't blame the Irish much for bearing a grudge."

"Yes, I knew a few Irishmen that came over," I said.

"There were many other Irish units. The consensus is that the main interest, for many on either side, was to get military training and experience," she said. "I think their energies are once again focused on saving their rightful homeland, but I'm sure they'd like some of that fortune."

"How do you know all this?"

"If you were colored perhaps you would know. Six-hundred-thousand people just died in a war fought over keeping us in chains," she said. "It's about self-preservation."

"I see."

"Whatever happened," Seraphine said, "The people in that room, the uncle, needed to make sure she could never tell what she saw, but couldn't dirty his hands."

"This makes no sense," I said. "Sorry, but it's preposterous to think Finn is involved in any of this."

"It's likely he had no choice. It was his niece that blundered onto the secret, and it was his job to fix it. Those type societies don't spend a lot of time on sentimentality," said Seraphine. "He needs a quick fix and lo and behold, finds a killer he already knows, one that already hates Ardent, right there in the office."

"You honestly believe Ardent saw something in that room she was not supposed to?"

"Yes, I do. Do you remember anything else she said?"

"Not much. She saw some sketches that belonged to a man in the hallway that day, that she thought seemed to really upset her uncle. She couldn't understand why," I said. "The journal was engraved inside with the name Brutus."

"Brutus? Are you certain?"

"Absolutely. Why?"

"Brutus was John Wilkes Booth's favorite role. In fact, Brutus is his father's middle name, and his brother's middle name. Sic semper tyrannous. That's what he shouted when he killed Lincoln. Brutus's line from Shakespeare's Julius Caesar."

"That's just not possible," I said.

"The uncle was entertaining both Bickley and Pike. And O'Mahoney. He's a very wealthy man, with a railroad, a fleet of ships, iron foundries for cannon. Who would have ever been better?" Seraphine asked. "So, think, how did Devol know you were coming here, and when?"

"I can't figure it out. Maybe I don't want to figure it out," I said. "The only thing I can think is someone in Uncle Finn's staff. Maybe somebody from home, but I don't see how. But, after what happened with Willie, who knows?"

"Knights of the Golden Circle is very persuasive," she said. "They assassinated a president."

"This is just too much to comprehend. It can't be," I said. "Finn's as enthusiastic a flag waving Unionist as any I've ever met. Proud of his contributions to the war effort. And he positively loved Ardent."

"Yes, I'm sure you've heard of patriotism and scoundrels?"

"Even if he was a scoundrel, he would never harm his niece. They genuinely loved each other."

"Think about it is all I'm saying," she said.

I guess I'd been quiet for a while, lost in thought, but she had another idea.

"I was thinking about the other night," she said, gently squeezing my hand.

"What were you thinking?"

"I was thinking about when you found yourself in a state," she smiled.

"I've thought about that several times myself," I said, truthfully.

"Several?"

"A few."

"More than once?"

"More than a few."

"I see. Well, these are uncertain times. What better way to get to know each other?"

"That's a good point."

"I have this boat," she said.

"Let's go," I said, and we walked toward the pier.

"I've heard New Orleans libertines have voodoo orgies," I said.

"None that leave witnesses alive," said Seraphine.

"I see. I don't think I need an orgy then."

"You won't," she said, and I didn't. Among many other discoveries over the course of the next couple hours, I found Seraphine had a .32

Caliber four-barrel pepperbox Derringer in a hidden fold in her waistband.

"Do you have anything else?" I asked Seraphine.

"Now, what would be the point of a lady having secret weapons, if she revealed her secrets?" she said.

Trumpets

"What kind of nails do you want?" asked Atlas, after I told them what I thought we could pull off, if we had all the needed supplies.

"Ten penny, all you can find, any size, but I really need a couple pounds of the long ones, five or six inches," I said. "Coal oil, straw, matches, shovels, rope. I'll write it all down. You're absolutely certain you can get gunpowder?"

"Yes, I know where there are barrels of gunpowder in that abandoned fort over that way," he said.

"How are you so sure?"

"Because I stole most of it and hid it there, myself," he laughed. "Plenty of powder. For their guns, and for blowing stumps, and such. It was a Rebel fort. Then Union. We worked for both. Took guns and powder from both of them, too. It's all still where I hid it. Plenty enough to shake up the world for those boys, if that's what you have in mind. That's where we got these spanking-new carbines."

"Excellent. We're gonna get creative," I said. Jupiter had drawn some nice maps and we'd put together a good plan for a perimeter defense. Figuring the swamp was pretty similar to an Asian jungle, I put some of the darker ideas Lyman had given me to use. "And any glass bottles to pack the oil and powder in. A bushel of rags. Anything that's there."

"Well, there was all kinds of things they just abandoned when the war ended, but poor people has got into most of it. Uniforms, coats, shoes, bacon, biscuits, bugles. I imagine most of the shoes and bugles is still there, is about it. They're really ain't no need for either of them in the swamp."

"Bugles?" I said. "Trumpets?"

"I guess so," Atlas said.

"Why in the world do you care about bugles?" asked Seraphine.

"Ever hear of the Battle of Jericho? In the Bible?" I asked. "It evened the odds, they say."

"You don't strike me as a man of the Scriptures," said Tandy. "You believe in the Good Book?"

"Nope, but I believe in fear," I said. "I just hope those Southern boys over there are all good church-goers. They must be, or they wouldn't have been fighting so hard doing the Lord's work, to keep the sons of Ham in bondage."

"A jungle full of horn-blowing Negroes? Running around in the dark with guns?" asked Seraphine with a smile. "Blowing stuff up?"

"Yep. Guns and bombs, I think," I said. "These bottle grenades. Guns and bombs and horns and snakes. That should about do it. Here is my plan."

"I like it," said Marcel, when I'd finished.

"I'm in," said Atlas.

"Me, too," said Tandy.

"Yes," said Seraphine.

Snakes

"Good luck, I see," I said, a few days later when Atlas and Jupiter emerged from dense brush, each carrying a heavy burlap bag at arm's length.

"Yes, sir," Jupiter said. "Four fine coral snakes in here. Pretty as can be, and as full of venom as any forty snakes in this swamp. Ain't no

Johnny Reb eager to tangle with these. But we could have brung you a hundred rattlesnakes in the time it took to get them. We can cut their rattles off, just like an ear of corn, so they stays quiet."

"The corals are hard to find, harder to catch. But we grabbed up a whole nest of baby cottonmouths. Must be a hundred of them. That sight right there is enough to give a man nightmares for life," said Atlas, reaching into his sack with a heavy, leather blacksmith's glove and pulling out a handful of writhing, tiny killers. "We can get plenty more rattlers. Plenty more cottonmouths, too."

"Good idea. Go ahead and grab some, we might need them," I said. "Scaring a man can be better than killing him. Nothing better than your partner screaming nonstop to shake a man's resolve. That's what I'm counting on. If they'll keep."

"They'll be fine for a few days. If we ain't ready to use them by that time I'll give them some water and some frogs, and they'll be just dandy," he said. "I'd imagine you'd want 'em pretty hungry."

"That's good. Keep them tied up tight. I don't want to find them slithering around my feet," I said, then saw Tandy walking toward us. "Looks like you're about ready."

"I been ready. What's all them spikes for?" Tandy said, holding a double barrel shotgun he'd cut down to about sixteen inches. Another cut-off scattergun hung from his shoulder.

"Tiger pits. Man steps in it, spikes go up through his foot. Put some spikes pointing down, a man can't get free without shredding his foot. Or cutting it off," I said, and demonstrated with a couple spiked boards and my wiggly fingers. I had a nice stack of 2x4s, tree branches whittled down to needle-points, and a large pile of nails. "We'll dig this hole down about four feet, layer the floor with spiked boards, cover the hole with leaves and branches and sit back and watch."

"Them stakes will kill him when falls in the pit?"

"Not fast. Just cripple him, keep him put while the snakes work on him," I said as Atlas raised his handful of snakes again. "He'll be stuck there a long time, screaming the whole while. Unless he decides to cut his own foot off."

"Lawd," said Tandy.

"I know," I said. "But get these men screaming about pits full of snakes, and even the bravest men will piss down his leg."

"So, what's this over here you trying to build?" said one of the twins.

"A spike board, just a little different. Springs up and drives the nails into a man's chest. Put that out there on the trail, at night, and one of them steps on it, the others will slow way down. There are a few others."

"Where did you learn all this?"

"My Captain. If I can do half as well as he did, we're going to be all right. I saw a man get struck by a rattler in a face once," I said. "Worst thing ever. The screams. I've seen many gun shots. Worse than gunshot screams. They go on and on and on. It'll work."

For the next few days we watched Devol's young bandits dredge a small lake from a floating platform. Devol sent rowboats out in different directions every morning, and Atlas said they couldn't seem to find much of what had been buried in the swamp. A few steamer trunks had been stacked near some tents on a wide island, and a squad of Devol's men lounged nearby, rifles at their sides. They were campaign toughened, no doubt about it, much more so than the men in my camp, but I started to like our chances, as long as we could keep the fight in our part of the swamp. The original owner of those cabins had thought it out, and picked a good spot to defend. With water nearly encircling it, and only one clear trail leading away, anyone trying to come across that wide expanse of water would be easy targets. If they came down the trail, we'd be waiting in a perfect crossfire.

Devol

"Some men coming, Miss Seraphine," said a skinny boy through the cabin doorway, chest heaving from a long run. "Dey almost across the water."

"How many?"

"Five or six. Pistols and rifles."

"Thanks, Joseph," she said, and we crawled to the window, peeking out until Devol and his men showed themselves.

"You're in charge here?" Devol challenged as Seraphine stepped out of the cabin. I stayed hidden, spying as Devol stood facing us with five men fanned out behind him.

"I can speak for the group," she said. "What is it I can do for you?"

"Oh, just being neighborly. Just thought we'd visit a spell," said Devol, eyeing her lewdly. "I heard tell there was a white man over here. Sounded like an old friend."

"I don't know where you heard that," Seraphine said. "There isn't one."

"Perhaps your memory is faulty," he said.

"I didn't see one," she said. "I'd remember if I had, because it would be an oddity. Those hides are why we're here. When we have enough, we'll be leaving. You needn't overly concern yourselves with us skinners."

"You're not from around here," he said. "Sounds like you and me share raisin'. New Orleans, yes?"

"Yes."

"And you're here for alligator skins?" he said. "That's why you're out here? Ain't there plenty over that way in the bayous?"

"These do tricks. That, and we're out here minding our own damned business," she smiled, sweetly.

"That's a good one, that's funny," he said. "Now that we're familiar, let's sit around the fire, just friendly like."

"I don't think my people really want to socialize," said Seraphine. "We mostly stay to ourselves. We don't bother anyone, nor do we allow ourselves to be bothered."

"I see. Well, I'll forgive your lack of manners this time," said Devol. "But we could have had a fine time. Found us a fiddler and kicked up our heels.

"Yes, I bought a new hat," said Ashok, smiling as he unfurled his yellow turban. "Just for the occasion."

"A swamp's an unusual place to go in search of entertainment," said Seraphine.

"I suppose it is," Devol said, looking her up and down. "You know, you don't really look much like no coonass hide hunter I ever knew. Those are some mighty nice riding boots for a slave, even for a house wench. Did you just have your nails done?"

"My boots become your concern right after I kick you in the balls with them," Seraphine smiled again. "My nails when I scratch out your eyes."

"Now, look," snarled Devol. "I have some important business in this swamp. You best hurry up and get out of here."

"I had no idea we could bring commerce to a stop like that. You go do whatever business you do, we'll jes' sit here and skin gators," Seraphine said. "Eat us up a heap of mudbugs, praising glory and waiting for Uncle Abraham and his gubmint's forty acres and a damned old mule."

"No need for that shuck," said Devol. "Just a little surprised to find you all here, and you a beautiful woman looking like you straight from the parlor."

"I'm flattered. I feel swoony," she said, laying the back of her hand against her forehead.

"One last time, why don't you just tell me why you are here?" he growled.

"Why don't you just tell me why you are here?" she said.

He glared.

"Where's Carew?"

"What's a Carew?" she said. Marcel and Maurice watched silently, wiping down their rifles. The others stared, too. "I don't even know what a Carew is."

"Sure a bunch of rifles in the camp. Good ones. Practically new it looks like," said Devol.

"It's good you noticed," said Tandy. "Now holler at them two out-laws sneaking around behind us, thinking they're wily. They're about to get a shock."

"What did you say?"

"I said, you'll be the first to get it if any shooting starts, which it's about to if them two in the trees don't show themselves," Tandy said. "Count of three, they bring their asses back over here where we can see them, or I'll just start shooting."

"Look here, boy," said Devol, "Thing's ain't changed that much. I'll shoot you for that talk, and there ain't a jury that would convict me."

"You won't be told again," said Seraphine.

"You uppity high-tone bitch!" snapped Devol.

"Look, cracker, the lady said move on, so move on, p'tit pute boug!" said Marcel, his rifle pointed directly at Devol's chest. "I ain't worried none about it. All they'll find of you is your peeving jawbone in the asshole of one of these gators."

"You goddamn niggers," Devol shouted. "All of ya!"

"No, we're just letting you know you won't come here like this again," Seraphine smiled. "We'll be right here, where the fishing is good, and the work is easy. Untroubled for as long as we want."

"If there weren't about five rifles aimed right at my back," snarled Devol, "You'd be singing a different tune."

"Is that right?" she said, her sweet smile returning. "Perhaps next time, you should bring that banjo after all."

Cherry Tree

In the morning, Seraphine took two of the boys to get supplies. I found a comfortable spot under a tree and was napping when the brush rattled and a tiny wizened man with dark copper skin stepped into the clearing. He wore a Union cavalryman's shell jacket and leather fringed breeches. He had a huge hooked nose, high cheek bones, and a thick, wild ledge of bushy eyebrows over dancing, energetic black eyes. Long white hair swept down his back from under his Confederate Hardee hat. The old Indian had a stout crutch wedged under his left arm, a well-used chamois pouch hung from his neck, and his empty left pant leg was pinned above the knee. A young Indian boy walked close behind him carrying a bulging carpet bag with a protruding bone-saw and other sharp instruments. A wave of nausea hit me at the sight of the saw.

"There is about to be a shootout down here?" the stranger said.

"It appears likely," I said. "Who are you?"

"An old friend asked me here to take care of any medical issues, should any arise," he said.

"Who would that be?" I asked.

"I'm sure you'll be told if you need to be told,' the Indian said.

"It's a secret?"

"Apparently it is. From you anyway."

"Where did you come from?" I said. "How did you know where to find us?"

"My friend who's in the same line of work. Same friend. She told me. By raven," he said.

"The bird?"

"Do you know of another kind?"

"No. So, this witch doctor sent a bird from?"

"Not a witch, and not a doctor. From New Orleans," he said. "I was in the neighborhood. You're asking an awful lot of questions. Maybe I should turn you into an Ibis."

"I don't think that will be necessary. I'm just curious and a little surprised. What should I call you?"

"The others call me Chief Cherry Tree. That's close enough not to bicker."

"You were in the war?" I asked the chief, nodding at the missing leg.

"You mean because of this leg? No, that's One-Eyed Walter. Huge old bull gator. One they'll call mythical one day. But he's None Eyed Walter now," he boasted. "After he chomped off my leg I cut out his good eye and throwed him in a gator pool. They're cannibals you know."

"You don't say," I said.

"You don't seem too startled," said the old Indian.

"No, sir," I said. "A friend once remarked that peculiar things is becoming less peculiar. I suppose one-legged old War Chiefs feeding alligators to each other would fit that category."

"Truthfully, I don't know if he got ate or not, at least not right away. I had to go get my leg tied off."

"Is that true?" I looked at him warily.

"Is it important?"

"I don't suppose it is," I said, remembering the Captain's words. "This voodoo stuff works?"

"Hoodoo. I've never had anyone complain," the Chief said. "Not the thankful live ones, and sure not the dead ones. Contrary to legend."

"Chief Cherry Tree, right?" I said.

"I prefer it to Alligator Bob."

"I can see why," I said.

Devol

Later in the dark, I was lying on a bed of straw next to Seraphine as she slept, listening to the hum and chatter of the swamp. Suddenly the night exploded with the ear-piercing whoops of startled Sandhill cranes flapping furiously into the night sky. Every creature for two miles screeched, honked or bellowed and I heard the cursing Rebels somewhere in the darkness as our group disappeared down our hidden rabbit paths.

As I had hoped, after the first few Rebels walked into the camp without incident, the others, even Devol and Ashok, carelessly gathered around the fire. They were self-congratulatory in their laughter that we were running scared, ten miles away. One of them picked up the leather satchel I'd leaned against an old stump. I'd thrown a handful of gold coins inside it, and scattered a couple more in the grass around it, and in this pack of thieves, this one wasn't sharing. He slyly pocketed the coins on the ground, then lightly shook the bag a few times, hearing more coins jingle as he glanced between the satchel and Devol, shielding it from view. Greed won out. With one last look at Devol, he pulled back the flap and peeked inside. He flipped backwards with a swinging coral snake hooked in his face, his screams sending the noisy cranes whooping and whooshing into the sky again. He shrieked as he yanked the snake free, his ripped face spurting blood as he tripped into the campfire. He rolled across the ground whimpering until Devol shot him in the head.

"Hurry up, check those cabins," screamed Devol, pointing at the trail of coins leading to the doors of the other two cabins. At the cabin doors, both men disappeared but their terrified screams carried for miles. The others ran to help, but froze when they looked into the pits. I knew what they saw. Their friends were impaled on eight-inch nails and punji spikes while a mass of enraged eastern diamondbacks and baby cottonmouths coiled around their legs, striking again and again. Ignoring them, Devol ordered more men into the cabins. They carefully stepped around the snake pits and into the cabins, where lamps burned in the windows.

"Sure you can you hit it?" Seraphine asked about the nearest lamp.

"I'll hit it."

"I'm ready."

"All right then, let's do it."

I shot the lamp in the closest window, spraying flaming oil across the floor. I fired twice more, shattering liquor jugs as a line of fire raced across the ground and the other cabins erupted in fire. The sacks of blasting powder we'd packed beneath the window exploded in an earth-quaking roar, and a ball of flame made the swamp glow as Marcel and Maurice's squad opened up from the east. Atlas and Jupiter led the others from the west, and Rebel bodies littered the campground.

"Back to the boats. We'll meet these savages when the sun's out," I heard Devol screaming, but it was too late, as another explosion rocked our little island from Devol's boat landing spot. Tandy's son and another boy were right on schedule, having chopped holes in the bottom of Devol's boats, then blown them to smithereens for effect. To send a message. There would be no escaping and coming back to fight again, unless they wanted to wade across three hundred yards of alligator infested lake on a night where the clouds hid the moon. I heard Tandy blast the first trumpet, and then the air was filled with a dozen more. Bottle-grenades exploded, and the hunters had become the hunted. I

361

allowed myself a small smile of satisfaction, knowing even Devol had to be feeling just the slightest bit of panic.

Running gun battles raged solidly for the next hour, at times at least a dozen weapons firing at once. I saw Jupiter drop out of the corner of my eye, and I saw two more of our boys down. Seraphine and I were creeping down the escape trail when a footstep cracked a twig and a hushed oath slipped out. I knocked Seraphine head-over-heels into the brush to the right, and rolled left as two repeaters blazed from the bushes. The boy with us was down, bleeding badly from a chest wound. I fired some quick shots in that general direction with my pistol. No one fell or cried out in the darkness, and footsteps hurried away. I waited silently, trying to hear Seraphine as I held the dying boy, but there was nothing.

Willie

Dawn found me alone, at the edge of a good-sized lake. The swamp had been filled with gunfire all night, ebbing and flowing, and sudden screams had told me when another raider had been speared by my traps. The morning mist was just lifting, and I was looking around a sunken prairie when a movement caught my eye. I waited and had about decided it was an otter when a floppy brown hat emerged from the sawgrass and cattails about a hundred yards away. Carrying a rifle carelessly, the raider stepped into the open and waded through the shallow water. I sensed some familiarity, a slight build, the hint of a limp. He kept his head down, but a breeze lifted his hat just enough for me to see his face. Willie walked straight at me and my rage burned through my chest. I wanted to stab my bayonet into his guts and twist. He'd been a friend. I'd tolerated him when he was a kid.

At fifty yards, I shot Willie in the right kneecap. He collapsed and thrashed in a blanket of water-lilies and six inches of bloody water. I shot him again. The thrashing stopped, but his screaming didn't. I walked toward him with my revolver cocked and ready.

"Can you swim, Willie?" I asked.

"No, of course I can't swim. You shot my knee out. You nearly shot my arm clean off," Willie sobbed.

"That was my intent, Willie," I said. "You expected something else?"

"What are you going to do?" Willie choked more sobs between curses.

"They killed Ardent. You knew that."

"That was before I ever met them. I had nothing to do with that."

"Maybe. Or maybe not. But you knew it, and the evil they did. I can't figure it. We all liked you. Almost family."

Willie screamed when I stepped on his shattered kneecap.

"I was just trying to make a little money is all, and, then, things just got out of hand. But I didn't hurt anyone. I'm not part of what they did," he blubbered. "Goddamnit, the war's over. You got to let this go."

"My war's not over, as I've been reminded," I said, as I ground my boot into his splintered elbow. "You set out to slaughter us last night. That creates some doubt as to whether the war is over or not."

"They forced me to come along. You can't just murder me."

"Is that right?"

"Yes, I swear it."

"You have one chance to live," I said. "Who is Devol's business partner? Why did Devol kill Ardent?"

"It's her Uncle Finn. He's bankrolling the operation."

"Why?"

"Knights of the Golden Circle. Them, and for his Irish friends. She saw very powerful men she wasn't supposed to see. She saw some papers. She even ran into John Wilkes Booth outside Finn's hotel room," Willie said.

"I'm disappointed Willie. Very, very disappointed."

"I can fix this, I can," Willie cried. "You've got to understand."

"I can't understand, Willie," I said, and shot him between his sad, pleading eyes.

I chopped my way through the thick jungle the best I could, following the smoke from the cabins. The smell of the burned cabins, and the men inside them, hung in the air like the fiery horror at Kennesaw Mountain. I walked out of the brush and a wide, shallow pond still separated me from the campsite. More than a dozen bodies, clearly dead, were strewn across ground, and Seraphine was lying near the water, curled on her side, with her arms crossed tightly across her chest. Blood had soaked through her shirt into the sand. Devol stood over her, triumphant as a gladiator, stomping her head and grinding her bleeding face into the mud. He sensed me, looked up, stared a burning hole at me, then yanked her behind a thick Cypress. I took a deep breath and charged into the water, watching for black snouts.

"Devol!" I screamed, reaching thigh deep water. He smirked around the trunk, kicked her in the head, raised his pistol and fired twice into the water beside me. My legs burned as I slogged through the water, ready to collapse. I fired another wild shot, but he only flashed another evil grin. Before I could get a good shot, he ducked behind the tree and I expected at any second to have my legs crushed by an alligator's jaws. He fired again, missed, but shifted his eyes away from Seraphine, crumpled in the dirt between his feet.

I screamed again, started to sink, and fired a wild shot. Devol laughed and calmly leveled his huge pistol straight at me. As he squinted, I saw Seraphine's little garter gun in her fist. She jabbed it into his groin and fired. He howled and rolled on the ground, yanking her by her hair and pummeling her with his pistol. She slumped beneath him, and he lifted himself to all fours, his gun unsteadily pointed in my direction. She clawed at his face, but when he slugged her again and rolled away, she fell limp and still. I screamed again, and he rose to his knees, steadying his gun with two hands. I flopped down in the water, splashing, the only move I could make. I watched him unsteadily move his gun, following me, as Seraphine struggled to her knees behind him. She slumped on top of him, straddling his back, and then I saw the little four-barrel pepper-box was in her hand again. She stuck it in his right ear and blew his brains out his left, emptying those last three barrels 1-2-3, stoic as a Roman. She looked at me, smiled, let his head drop with a dull slap in the black dirt, and collapsed in a bloody heap.

I staggered out of the water and knelt beside her. Her face was badly scraped, bruised and swollen, and I held her and picked sand and pebbles out of her hair as scattered gunshots came from the swamp. I raised her shirt and found a bullet wound under her right armpit. The bullet had gone straight through and the wound was clean. A second bullet had gone into her ribcage and hadn't come out. That was gonna hurt. I was just about to holler for help when two of our men hurried out of the trees, picked her up before I could say anything, and headed down the trail.

"Hurry," the oldest one yelled over his shoulder. "Cherry Tree is down this way."

Tandy

"We lost a few, but everyone's accounted for except my son. I found Virgil. He's dead. And a dead Rebel, but no sign of Ernie," Tandy said, when I met him at our rendezvous point near Devol's shattered boats.

"We'll find him," I said. "I would guess quite a few of Devol's men still came this way, hoping to find a board to float home on."

"Yes, I expect so," he said. "I told him not to stick around the water. He better have listened to me. It's not looking that way. How's Seraphine?"

"Beat up pretty bad," I said. "A couple bullet holes. I don't think any of them are life threatening though. Let's go, I'll follow you."

"That way," Tandy jabbed his finger, and charged away. I chased Tandy, zigzagging through dense thickets and splashing across creeks. We heard Ashok at the same time.

"This your boy, stable man?" Ashok screamed. He stood on a strip of land surrounded by acres of black water, with his left arm, with pistol in hand, crushing Ernie's throat while his right hand held a knife to the boy's chin. "You want him gelded up real nice?"

"Let him go," Tandy shouted. "Then you can go. Take as much money as you can carry."

"I don't think the professor shares your sentiment," Ashok said, shuffling in a backward circle, keeping the boy's body in front of his own.

"What do you think?" Tandy asked me.

"He will kill your son," I said. "No matter what we do. Stall him."

"If you try anything I'll gut this black bastard, and feed his entrails to the gators while daddy watches," the giant yelled. "Now, that would be something, wouldn't it?"

I knew he would do exactly that and I wasn't sure what to do. As long as he kept moving behind Ernie, I had no clean shot. A lot of water separated us, and two dozen alligators basked around the lagoon, pretending like they didn't see a feast preparing itself.

"I know a way around there," said Atlas, sneaking up behind us. "We have to go back up this stream a-ways to cross, but there's a trail that leads right to the sandbar. It'll take a little bit. Can you stall him five minutes?"

"I can try," I said.

Atlas was gone, and Tandy was right after him.

"I know you're out there, Carew," bellowed Ashok. "You best back away."

"All your people are dead. Devol is dead," I shouted, and saw two young Rebels a few yards to his right, aiming rifles at me from the high grass.

"Get me a boat, Carew, or I cut off his head. You know I will."

"Just let him go," I shouted. "Let him go and I'll get you a boat."

"You get me a boat and I'll let him go," shouted Ashok. "He comes with me until I'm clear of the swamp with a couple big sacks of gold. If I don't see sign of you then, I'll let him go. Otherwise its gonna get real ugly."

"Let the boy go and you can walk away," I lied. I kept my rifle on him, but he never stopped circling. "You can grab some gold on your way out. Devol was the one I wanted. He's dead. But you have to let the boy go."

"You think I'm stupid? You're gonna shoot me in the back."

"You have to trust me that I won't," I yelled. "Better trust me, too, when I say that if you harm a hair on that boy's head it will go rough on you. I can get creative with these spikes and vipers."

"Time's up, Carew," he shouted. "No more stalling."

"Just hold on. You'll need that boat, you know that," I said. "His father went to get a boat. You can't get out of here on foot. It will take a minute. It's got to get rowed over here. Just relax, don't do anything stupid."

He did seem to relax. The blade of his knife dropped a few inches away from Ernie's jaw. Ashok motioned at the two Rebs, and their rifle barrels dropped just a hair. We stayed that way, every few seconds one yelling at the other, making sure the deal was still in place. They had relaxed, but time was passing and Ashok was starting to tense up again. I could see it and hear it in his voice. I started to worry.

Ashok had lifted the knife blade when Tandy exploded out of the brush and raced across the sandbar, hatchet raised and screaming something savage and primal. Ashok shoved Ernie away and shot him in the head. As the boy fell backwards, a bright-red rooster-comb sprayed away from his skull. Tandy swung from the hip with his hatchet and knocked Ashok's pistol out of his hand with a crash and a clatter. He swung again, and Ashok ducked away from the axe and slashed at Tandy with the big knife. The two Rebels twisted toward Tandy, but they dropped into the tall saw grass. Just as I saw their barrels raise, Atlas burst out of the bush, emptying a revolver into them.

The Rebels fell dead, but shots from the trees sent Atlas diving into the rushes. Tandy and Ashok parried and circled and swung and stabbed but I couldn't get a shot. Tandy backed away, then charged Ashok with his knees pumping to his chest. He smashed his shoulder into Ashok's ribcage and they rolled down the sandbar, roaring and clubbing like two boar grizzlies brawling. I saw smoke and heard Atlas firing into the trees, turned back to the brawlers just as Ashok landed a crushing blow into Tandy's head, dropping him cold. When he raised up with his knife above his head, I shot him through the neck and he staggered into the lake, a fountain of blood spurting through his fingers. He collapsed face first into knee-deep water, but pulled himself up, searching for me as he sloshed blindly into deeper water. The gators smelled it and were already sliding into the water. I shot him again and he staggered, seemed to struggle briefly, then floated lifelessly facedown as his blood spilled out.

The shots from the woods had ended, and I looked back to shore, where Atlas stood, reloading his pistol. I heard a scream and spun around as an alligator with a head the size of a cannon-barrel erupted out of a wall of water. The horrifying jaws crashed down on Ashok's leg, crushing it with a series of sharp cracks. The gator log-rolled, flinging him around like a rag doll, the massive tail slapping up waves ten feet tall, then slowly submerged, taking the body underwater.

I turned back to the island. Tandy had come around, and Ernie was starting to. I was surprised to see the boy was alive. Blood covered him, but I ran my fingers over his head and found no bullet hole, just a bloody furrow that had replaced one eyebrow. I wrung out my shirt and twisted it tight around the wound.

"This ain't heaven, I reckon," said Tandy, sprawled on his back and still breathing raggedly.

"Most likely not, if I'm here," I said.

"How's my boy?"

"He's fine. One hellacious headache, I imagine. Other than that, no serious damage, nice conversation piece," I said. "He's right over there."

"We better get out of here," Tandy said, getting to his knees a little unsteadily.

"I want to make sure Ashok is dead," I said.

"You can't go in there. If that gator thinks you're trying to steal his dinner, you'll soon be part of it."

"We can wait for a minute, see if he floats to the top," I said.

"He ain't gonna be floating to the top anytime soon. But we need to go," Tandy said. "That much shooting is going to attract a lot of attention, even way out here. We can't be here when they find a swamp full of dead white men, and us black folks all shot up and armed to the teeth. There's only so many of these battles we gonna win."

"True," I said. "And the gold?"

"It's a good three miles over that way," he said. "Nobody's going to be all the way over there. We'll sink it again on our way out."

Seraphine

We'd lost Jupiter, Maurice, and five more young boys, and several more of them had fairly serious wounds. We prowled through the swamp for a while, making sure no more assassins waited for us, and found a couple of Devol's wounded men. It was just their bad luck that we had no way to take them as prisoners, and I was relieved when Marcel volunteered for that big job. It didn't take long for the bodies to disappear down the alligator holes.

In a small clearing, Chief Cherry Tree had erected two halves of a dog tent, and Seraphine lay inside on a piece of carpet. The chief sat just outside, with his good leg crossed over his stump, murmuring some incantations while his boy tended some dented cooking pots hanging from wire hooks over a small fire. A line of old stained bowls sat on an altar beside burning incense of sandalwood and musk, and three ancient, foreign coins were arrayed before him. Strips of dry snake skin and roots and colored glass figurines were scattered around the altar. He'd sniff a bowl, or taste a dipped finger, then add a pinch from the dozens of vials and tiny bottles his young assistant handed him. The Chief pronounced his gris-gris would fix her right up. I hoped so. He said she would fly with the hawk and run with the deer. I wasn't sure what that meant but I hoped so, too. Seraphine moaned and the boy brought a steaming kettle from the fire that smelled like fruit and ginger and sassafras and hot pepper sauce. Cherry Tree rubbed a green paste into her wounds. A couple of the boys came over, but the chief ran them off.

"You get away from here. This woman ain't covered proper, so you jes' git," Cherry Tree said. "That means you too, paleface."

"No need, Chief," Seraphine smiled groggily. "He's seen what I have to see. Can't you hurry up whatever voodoo you have cooking?"

"Hoodoo. Yes, I can hurry, but it won't be a healing poultice. It'll be pie filling," he said, as I knelt beside her and locked my fingers in hers.

"You sure this Voodoo mumbo-jumbo is going to cure you?"

"I'll be dancing naked under the moon by midnight," winced Seraphine.

"I'd like to see that," I smiled, squeezing her hand tightly.

"Come with me," she said, "It's cathartic."

About the Author

Roy V. Gaston is a native of Athens, Ohio and graduate of Ohio University. He now resides in Columbus, Ohio. He began writing after finishing his career as a unit supervisor in Ohio's Department of Rehabilitation and Correction.

Gaston writes historically based novels about 19th Century America, focusing on the American West and the American Civil War.

His novel *Beyond the Goodnight Trail* won the 2021 Western Fictioneers Peacemaker Award for Best First Novel and was the 2021 Spur Award finalist.

His favorite genres are historical fiction, noir, hard boiled, Southern Gothic, and Westerns. He is fan of Harry Turtledove, Clint, the Duke, Harry Flashman, Hitch and Cole, Gus and Woodrow, Hap and Leonard, Spenser and Hawk, Marty and Rusty, Gravedigger and Coffin Ed, Statler and Waldorf, Buck and Roy, Willie and Waylon, and Conspiracy Theories.

Now Available!
PEACEMAKER AWARD WINNER
ROY V. GASTON

For more information
visit: <u>www.SpeakingVolumes.us</u>

Now Available!

AWARD WINNING AUTHOR
MARK WARREN

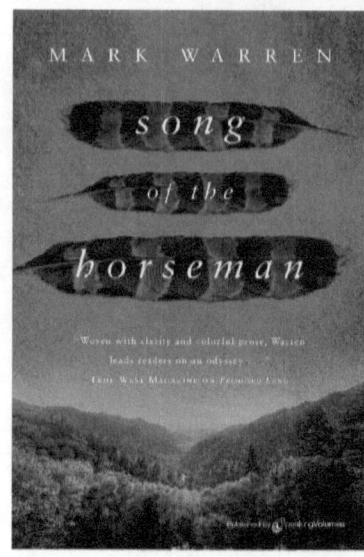

For more information
visit: www.SpeakingVolumes.us

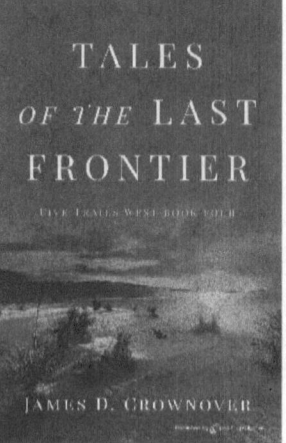

www.ingramcontent.com/pod-product-compliance
Lightning Source LLC
Chambersburg PA
CBHW030807260626
47169CB00001B/219